Praise f

"Morgan's debut n
Overall, the novel provides a compelling supernatural mystery
that will hold a reader's attention right up to the last page.
Recommend to fans of Kate Morton and Eve Chase."
—*Library Journal*

"Fans of ghost stories and gothic settings will love Shannon
Morgan's newest novel. Set in a haunted castle in Scotland, it
follows Edie and her daughter Neve as they work to unravel
the secrets of their family history—including the identity of
Edie's biological parents and the location of the famous,
cursed Maundrell red diamond. A dual narrative allows the
reader to get to know the ghosts as full characters as well. *In
the Lonely Hours* is a captivating mix of dark family tragedy,
haunting atmosphere, and very lively ghosts." —**Kelsey
James,** author of *The Woman in the Castello*

"Look for Gothic atmosphere and pleasantly creepy vibes in
Shannon Morgan's story of a middle-aged woman and her ex-
tremely haunted mansion." —**GoodReads,** Most Anticipated
Books of the Summer

"What an amazing story Shannon Morgan has delivered! With
a gothic twist, a beautifully haunting atmosphere, and a big
splash of family drama, this makes an incredible read for modern ghost story lovers!" —**Shanora Williams,** *New York
Times* bestselling author of *The Wife Before*

"Poetic prose and haunting heartbreak—a story that will stay
with the reader!" —**Lisa Childs,** *New York Times* bestselling
author of *The Missing*

GRIMDARK

Also by Shannon Morgan

Her Little Flowers

In the Lonely Hours

GRIMDARK

SHANNON MORGAN

KENSINGTON
PUBLISHING CORP.

kensingtonbooks.com

KENSINGTON BOOKS are published by

Kensington Publishing Corp.
900 Third Avenue
New York, NY 10022

All Kensington titles, imprints, and distributed lines are available at special quantity discounts for bulk purchases for sales promotion, premiums, fund-raising, educational, or institutional use.

Special book excerpts or customized printings can also be created to fit specific needs. For details, write or phone the office of the Kensington Sales Manager: Attn.: Sales Department. Kensington Publishing Corp., 900 Third Avenue, New York, NY 10022. Phone: 1-800-221-2647.

KENSINGTON and the K with book logo Reg. US Pat. & TM Off.

ISBN: 978-1-4967-5373-1 (ebook)
ISBN: 978-1-4967-5372-4

First Kensington Trade Edition: August 2025

10 9 8 7 6 5 4 3 2 1

Printed in the United States of America

The authorized representative in the EU for product safety and compliance
is eucomply OU, Parnu mnt 139b-14, Apt 123
Tallinn, Berlin 11317, hello@eucompliancepartner.com

For Mum: For the all the things I should've said and didn't, and for all the things I've said and shouldn't have.
And,
to all the headstrong women who would've been burnt as witches.
You know who you are.

PROLOGUE

❧

1641

The bells tolled midnight. Twelve deep knells . . . then a thirteenth.

It was said afterwards it was the Devil's doing . . . or perhaps the cunning women, whom everyone knew to be witches who danced with demons on the darkest of nights, when the moon was too afeared to show its mottled face. Who else but one in league with the Devil had the power to force God's bells to peal beyond the witching hour?

As the thirteenth toll vanished into the screeching wind, Euphemia Figgis stared up at the old church perched on the edge of the cliff, buffeted by spray from the spiteful sea raging below. She shivered and turned to Goodwife Kett standing in the doorway. She, too, stared at the church, holding herself clenched tight like a fist with fear. All sailors knew it was bad luck for a bell to ring unaided, and as a sailor's wife Effie knew this too. It didn't matter that the bell had rung on land; the village of Dar-

row End was in spitting distance of the sea and governed by its laws and superstitions.

"That's yar doin'!" Goodwife Kett hissed without making eye contact. Few could stand to look into Effie's odd-coloured eyes, one blue, one brown. "I wanted to git in the doctor, but Maggie said we were to call fer you."

"Duzzy pillock," muttered Effie, churlish in her trepidation, though whether she cursed the local doctor or Goodwife Kett was all to one. It earned a fierce glare from Goodwife Kett that dragged up and down Effie, taking in her worn, patched cloak, her clumping boots that had once belonged to her husband, where a dirty toe peeped out in accusation of its obvious need for repair.

"You and I together know the babe ent gorn to live the night, so she won't," said Goodwife Kett.

Effie did not disagree. She had known from the moment she had entered the birthing chamber yesterday morning to see Maggie, not yet sixteen and already into her second pregnancy, with her swollen belly roiling as though a trapped ferret thrashed within. Many hours later, her fears had risen when her hands, slick with the oil of white lilies and blood, had pulled out of Maggie's womb a sickly babe that gave a faint mewl with none of the power needed to work its lungs to full capacity. Her worst fears were confirmed as she had cut the navel-string not an hour ago. Her heart shrivelled with sadness; this labour would end in death, as Maggie's first had the year before.

She had worked under the piercing scrutiny of Goodwife Kett, the miller's wife, who had acted as Maggie's gossip and was unfortunately—for Maggie—her mother, too, in the sure knowledge it would be all around Darrow End tomorrow that Effie had bewitched Maggie to ensure her child would be born sickly.

Goodwife Kett leaned close until she was nose to nose with

Effie. "Yar a curse on us. Yar and that addled scold. Everyone knows she conjured up that storm to rid you o' yar good man and four others beside."

"Leave me mum be! That were ten year back, and she had nothin' to do with that storm. Though we be cunning, we've no truck with the Devil."

For a moment, Effie thought Goodwife Kett might spit in her face. Instead, she thrust a parcel into Effie's hands. "Take it and be gone. I'll not have yar sort in this house agin."

"Best to have the babe baptised as soon as possible," Effie muttered as the door was slammed in her face.

She lifted the parcel to her face. Smoked herring, and most welcome it was too. There was rarely payment in coin; the villagers gave what they could spare, which was little enough. But they all gave something, fearing a debt unpaid to the cunning folk far more than starvation.

Turning into the driving wind and rain that had battered the Norfolk coast for the past two days, Effie clutched the parcel to her chest and hurried down the narrow lane between slate-roofed fishermen's cottages from which not even two days of rain could wash away the stink of rotting herring and cat piss.

Darrow End had been clawed from the swampy fens that extended to the cliff edge, the land on loan to the humans, and then reluctantly, for the reeds crept back without vigilance and the channels flooded the alleys in heavy storms.

The very earth shook beneath Effie's feet with unnatural violence. From the bay came an echoing roar from the throats of the sea-gods raging against the gods of the storm. Thankful her pagan thoughts could not be read, she staggered to the end of the village where a single cottage stood in isolation, trembling on the edge of the cliff.

With a shiver of premonition, Effie worried for the tiny lights winking and blinking like fireflies with each wild heave and *toss of the vengeful waves. She prayed for the fishermen and cursed the Dutch and Turk pirates lurking along the Norfolk coast, then cursed them all for fools for sailing on a night such as this. Come what may, in the morn a ship would be wrecked on the jagged rocks in Darrow Bay below.*

But there was no time to dwell on what she could not change. Effie wrenched the cottage door open; the wind crashed it shut behind her.

"Git yar bible, Mum!" cried Effie, not bothering to take her cloak off. "I need to know if the child'll survive the night."

Germaine turned to her daughter. If ever a woman were to be named witch for her appearance, it was Germaine Figgis. Long wild hair frothed around her wrinkled, wart-encrusted face with a hooked pencil nose that almost met her chin. But it was her eyes most feared; milky with cataracts, blind, yet still able to see what most wished they could not.

A caustic retort hovered on Germaine's lips. She, unusually, bit her tongue, noting the desperation in Effie's tone, and nodded. She hobbled to the small table beside the bed in the corner of the single-roomed cottage where the lump of the youngest in the Figgis family murmured in disrupted sleep with Effie's entrance.

Placing the bible on the kitchen table, Germaine shooed the cat off the chair and sat down opposite Effie with a groan of tired bones. Without ceremony she swung the key by its thread above the bible like a slow pendulum.

"Ax it what you wish to know," said Germaine.

"Will the newly born Kett child survive the night?"

Effie watched the key, willing it to rotate a positive response. The key swung slowly from left to right.

She sighed and put her head in her hands.

"An ill wind blows through Darrow End," whispered Germaine in her fortune-telling gravel. "It blows from the south."

She gazed at her daughter blindly, and added in a murmuring hiss, "Catch him, Crow! Carry him, Kite! Take him away till the apples are ripe. When they are ripe and ready to fall, here comes baby, apples and all."

Effie's heart withered with dread. "None o' that, Mum," she whispered. "You and I together know what will come with the babe's death."

"Yis. But you and I together know that time ent yet."

ONE

Purple, Cló decided, smelt like the lavender cloaking the flat landscape of Norfolk in a knobbled skin, bloating the air that drifted in through the open car window with its sharp-sweet fragrance. Purple tasted like the wide skies and the distant lilac haze of the horizon. And if purple were to have form it would be as round and cushiony as the lavender bushes in their neat rows weathering the July sunshine with friendly stoicism.

"Cló . . . Cló? . . . Cló!"

Cló snapped to attention guiltily.

Jude shook his head with a fond smile. "You were well away with the fairies again."

"I *like* the fairies . . . what did I miss?"

"Nothing important. I was bitching about the state of the roads. I'd forgotten how narrow they are."

"It's a dreadful name, Grimdark Hall," said Cló, her face lifted to the sun, eyes half closed.

"It suits the place. You'll see soon enough." The warning in his tone echoed his fingers tapping nervously on the steering wheel as he navigated the twisting lane between flint walls.

"It can't be that bad. Look around us—it's gorgeous! All these crooked lanes and flint cottages. Then we're in glorious forest that would rival anything in Canada, and then it's wide and open and feels as if the edge of the world is just over there." Cló pointed out the window where the fens stretched flat and endless beyond the lavender fields.

Jude laughed, the fine lines around his blue eyes crinkling in the way Cló loved most. His laughter was what attracted her to him when they'd first met. He was not conventionally good-looking; his brown hair was too long, his cheekbones too sharp, his eyes too deep-set. He wasn't tall, shorter than Cló by a good inch, but he was attractive in an unsettling way.

"Now you're sounding like a tourist," he said. "Next you'll be calling it quaint and twee. You've been to England before; not sure why you're so enthralled by it all."

Cló pulled a face. "I was twenty-one and backpacking. It was a long time ago. And I love this because it's where you came from." The moment the words were out of her mouth she knew she had said the wrong thing.

Jude's face shuttered as it always did at the briefest mention of his childhood home, though they were hurtling along the lanes to get there. His past was a barrier Cló rarely managed to breach. Not a secret as such, more a distant land Jude wished never to return to, always skirting around a direct question, turning away with a haunted gloss in his eyes. At first, his reticence had felt like a test of strength of their relationship, but in time she'd come to realise it wasn't a test at all, but protection and a deep desire to prevent the wound in his soul from infecting their lives together.

Until a month ago, Cló had not pried or probed. Like a bargain made in a fairy tale to ensure their continued happiness, she had carved their marriage around the dark pit of Jude's past. She'd only broken their tacit bargain when Jude received the letter.

"There must be something you like about this place," said Cló, prodding the barrier gently.

Jude stopped his nervous tapping to grip the steering wheel until his knuckles whitened. "Don't look at me like that," he said, not taking his eyes off the road. "I get that you didn't have family and lived in foster homes, and I grew up in the Hall, but sometimes no family is better than one without love."

Cló swallowed the hurt Jude hadn't meant to inflict. "It can't have been that bad," she said in a small voice.

Jude's fingers went back to tapping the steering wheel, his nervousness edging towards irritability.

"Talk to me, Jude," said Cló quietly. "Don't let me walk into your family blind."

They drove a few miles before he sighed and said, "I can't remember a single time when my mother hugged me. Not once. She was a ghost, living in a fog of drugs. My father was never around to see my mum's decline until it was too late, too caught up in politics and his mistresses. And my sisters . . ." His lips tightened. "Constance was a bitch, and I doubt she's changed since I left. Ruth is . . . odd. There's no other way to put it. And she was sly, always watching me."

"They sound awful."

"They are," said Jude grimly. "Well, not Ruth so much, but she follows Constance in everything. If you can catch her alone, she's not so bad."

Cló's joy in the sunny day withered to fretful worry. His obvious loathing of his sisters gave a dark inkling to the shape of Jude's childhood and what lay ahead at Grimdark Hall. It reinforced that moment when he'd received the letter bearing the news of his parents' death in a car accident. His shock had been something she understood too well, for her parents had died in similar circumstances. She'd quickly realised her empathy had been misplaced when his shock hadn't deepened to grief but anger that the Honeybornes had managed to track him down after he'd broken off all contact years before. And that had been nothing to Jude's horror to discover he had inherited everything—the Hall, the lands and whatever money might be scrapping about—when he had been told he'd been struck from his father's will.

Sighing into the billowing silence, Cló admonished herself for giving in to worry and smiled with false brightness. "Tell me what I must or mustn't do to make this easier for you."

His eyes flicked her way in astonishment. "You are utterly perfect in every way and don't have to do or not do anything."

"You know what I mean, Jude."

His fingers drummed on the steering wheel once more. "Don't apologise . . . ever," he said finally. "Constance will see it as a sign of weakness."

"Then I'm screwed," said Cló, a perpetual apologiser.

"And try not to say too much about Canada; Constance still considers it a colony and will lord it over you, even though it's all bollocks. And she'll—" His expression knitted into a dark frown. "She will take issue with your physical appearance. She would find fault with the King, and she certainly won't keep her thoughts to herself."

"Then I'm doubly screwed." Cló looked down at her thighs spread across the seat, overflowing the edges like the underside of a mushroom, her stomach sagging below her enormous breasts. Her hand rose to her eyes, one blue, one brown, well used to the second looks she got. "I'm sorry," she whispered, her throat knotted with tears.

"I knew I shouldn't have said anything." Jude jerked the car across the road into a layby, switched off the ignition and turned to Cló. "You are the kindest, most compassionate, insanely imaginative, funniest woman I know," he said with soft intensity. "I can't tell you how proud I am of you, that you are my wife. You are perfect as you are and you have nothing to be ashamed of." He smiled and wiped a tear away from her cheek with a finger. "This is why I didn't want you to come. I know Constance will try to hurt you to hurt me. It's what she does, it's what she's always done . . . but I'm selfish, and I'm so glad you've come. I will need reinforcements."

Cló smiled weakly when Jude asked, "You okay?"

He kissed her hard and sweet before starting the ignition again, saying, "Just do what I do and avoid them as much as possible. God knows the Hall is big enough that we shouldn't cross paths too often . . . or at all," he added darkly. "And it's not forever. We'll get the formalities sorted out, then we'll leave. Nothing could make me stay there longer than we have to."

They drove on in silence for miles. Cló was aware of Jude darting worried glances her way. She was not helping herself with the image she was building of Constance as a human marabou stork, truly one of the ugliest birds. Yes, with a jowly chin like the marabou's gular sac that brought to mind an elongated scrotum. Oooh, and a beaky nose and small, beady eyes. She'd be disappointed if Constance turned out to be small and drab as a house sparrow.

"Who are you talking to?" said Jude, a smile in his voice.

Cló grimaced. "Myself?"

"Bollocks. You were having an intense conversation with someone in your head."

She bit her lip, not wanting to share what she'd been saying to Constance in the privacy of her mind.

"Come on. Be your best friend?"

"You *are* my best friend," she said by rote, coaxed into a reluctant smile, loving the intimacy of their corny inside joke. "I was thinking it's strange we both come from Norfolk," she lied.

Jude raised his eyebrows. "Your family *came* from Norfolk," he qualified. "But that was four hundred–odd years ago."

Orphaned at eight, the only thing Cló had inherited, apart from loving memories of her parents, was a family bible with the names of her ancestors written on the flyleaf. It stretched back to 1645, when two young people had taken the brave decision to sail to the New World from Ipswich. She was proud of her ancestry and hoped to do further research while they were in Norfolk.

"Wouldn't it be funny if we came from the same area?" she said.

"God, I hope not," said Jude fervently. He softened his harsh tone with, "I wouldn't wish Grimdark on any of your ancestors, and certainly not on you."

But all thoughts of ancestors vanished when they rounded a tight corner in the lane.

Like a spangled eiderdown, the North Sea spread out before them. An army of wind turbines stood to attention far out to sea, warily eyeing the Darrow Cliffs, colourfully layered in chalk and rust-red carrstone, wrapped around a horseshoe bay. Perched precariously on the knife edge of the cliffs, Grimdark Hall brooded in sullen defiance of the sun.

"You have windmills!" Enchanted, Cló's attention swung from the three black windmills with white sails behind the Hall. "And a cute little village . . . and an old ruin!"

"That's the Hermitage." Jude smiled, infected by Cló's enthusiasm. "It's one of the oldest parts of the Hall. It used to be a hermitage lighthouse—they're quite rare—and it's supposed to be haunted."

"Oooh! And ghosts!"

"And don't forget the witches and pirates."

"Pirates? In England?"

Jude laughed at her incredulity. "The Barbary corsairs were active along the English coast, and there were the Dutch privateers, of course. It got pretty bad here at one stage; that's why the walls were built along the cliff—to combat piracy." His eyes grew round with teasing wonder. "On dark and stormy nights lights are seen in the Hermitage, and a strange chanting has been heard that no one can understand. But everyone knows it's the ghost of a shipwrecked pirate." He grinned at Cló sideways. "There's enough here to keep your fertile imagination in serious overdrive."

Cló almost wrenched her neck as they flew past a modern building, quickly reading the modest sign for Grimdark Seabird Research Centre. "You didn't tell me there was a research centre here!"

"Didn't think there was any point, as we won't be staying long."

But she was already mentally planning a visit in the next couple of days. It would be sacrilege for an ornithologist not to pop in, perhaps see if there were work opportunities . . . She clamped down on the idea immediately. Jude was right, they wouldn't be here for long. There was no point looking for a job here when she had a perfectly good job back in Canada. And once the estate was tied up and sold they'd return to their lives, and Grimdark would be nothing more than a dreadful memory for Jude and a wistful what-if for Cló.

"Maybe a change of scenery will be a good thing for us," she put forward hesitantly.

Jude's eyes flicked to her with a frown.

"It might help us fall pregnant."

The word dropped between them like a pebble into a dark pond, sending out cruel ripples of haunting pain. Three miscarriages in the past three years had eroded Cló's dreams of a family into a pool of despair she was in constant danger of falling into.

"Please, no! Any child conceived in Grimdark will have an unhappy life . . . Christ, sorry, Cló," he added quickly, at her sharp indrawn breath of shock. "I didn't mean it like that. You know I want a child as much as you, but not here, not in this place."

She nodded and turned to the window to hide her grief. The

lane twisted along the edge of the cliffs, the boom of waves in the horseshoe bay loud on the warm air. A lone red kite fluttered gently on the thermals.

Like a dog unable to leave a bone alone, she said, "I spoke to Dr. Kilkenny before we left Toronto. He thinks I may not be able to carry boys, as the—the miscarriages were all boys."

"You didn't tell me about that. Is that even a thing?"

She shrugged. "Evidently some women can only carry one or other of the sexes to term. It might be my problem."

"*Our* problem." He took his left hand off the wheel and put it on Cló's thigh. She closed her hand over his. "But not here," he said, gently. "We'll try again when we get home."

Moments later, Cló was distracted from past hurts as they turned off the lane, passed through imposing gates and onto a long avenue of old beech trees. The forked branches laced overhead like woody fingers in an arched tunnel of light and shadow. Reed-throttled marshes flashed between the trunks, serenaded by the sharp rattle of a mistle thrush hidden in the verge.

Cló wanted to gush her wonder at the natural majesty sculpted by human endeavour, but Jude's dark expression as they neared his ancestral home forbade it.

As they broke from the avenue, an enormous gatehouse reared up before them with dark walls winging away on either side. It was taller than Grimdark Hall, taller than the ruined, spindly Hermitage to the right that crimped and shimmered in the heat, with every appearance of falling into the bay with the slightest suspicion of wind. They drove through the deep arch of the gatehouse into a cobbled courtyard.

Cló's first sight of Grimdark Hall took her breath away. It gloomed forbiddingly, commanding all it surveyed from the protection of high walls. Everything about it was dark. Its knapped-flint façade menaced under the glaring sun. A profusion of black turrets, towers and finials jostled for space amidst a legion of chimney stacks marching in decorative pairs across the roof's geography of valleys and peaks. Tall windows gave little warning of what lay within.

The Hall did not stand alone. A huge baroque fountain flounced up from the centre of the courtyard. A walled garden cosied up to a chapel, flourishing gargoyles from every surface. Old buildings, all dressed in knapped flint, huddled like dark-loving toadstools against the perimeter walls; stables, breweries and dairies from a time when Grimdark had housed hundreds.

"When you said you'd grown up in a country manor I was expecting something a lot humbler," said Cló, in rare reproach, too stunned by the sheer hugeness to process the wounded aggrievement colliding with her rapture of Grimdark untarnished by previous expectations.

Jude switched off the ignition and rested his forearms on the steering wheel to peer glumly at the two women standing on the terrace that swept around the Hall above a wide staircase.

"Sorry," he said, and puffed out a heartfelt sigh. "I never wanted you to be touched by Grimdark, not even in words." With reluctance he got out of the car and came around to help Cló out. He stood between her and the two women in an oddly protective way, shielding her from her first proper view of his sisters, or perhaps their view of Cló.

She took his hand and looked him in the eye, searching for shame that she was his wife, this fat, tall, odd-eyed foreigner. But she read nothing from his closed expression.

She gave his hand a quick squeeze of encouragement when he muttered, "Let's get this over with."

Stomach skittering with nerves, Cló pulled down her flowery dress that had seemed perfect for the sunny day this morning, but was now crumpled by the drive up from London. Aware she looked like a flowery blancmange, she wished she were thinner and shorter, that her hair wasn't a heavy dark cap on her head which she'd never managed to style properly, that her eyes weren't odd-coloured, that she was someone else altogether.

Cló straightened her shoulders, which she tended to stoop to make herself look smaller, and clung to Jude's hand as they walked across the ocean of cobblestones and up the vast staircase.

She put on her brightest smile to convey an impression of confidence she didn't feel. But as they drew nearer, her smile faltered. There were no responding smiles from Jude's sisters.

TWO

Hatred. It leached off the Honeyborne sisters, spinning towards Cló with spider silk stickiness.

"What on earth have you done to your hair?" demanded the sister with iron-grey hair fiercely permed into a helmet on her head. She glared at Jude's long hair tied up in a messy bun stuck through with two chopsticks. No greetings or hugs, not so much as a cold, "Hello."

"What I want to do with it," snapped Jude, bristling defensively.

His tension was a physical thing, coursing up Cló's arm from their clasped hands, setting her on edge even further. She raised an eyebrow at Jude to encourage introductions.

"This is Cló, my wife," he said, his face softened when he looked at her, then hardened again when he turned back to his sisters. "Cló, these are my sisters, Constance and Ruth."

"How—how nice to meet you finally," Cló stuttered.

Two pairs of round green eyes pinned her to the spot.

She cringed and turned to flee back to the car, but Jude's hand anchored her to his side and she stood frozen like a stunned rabbit.

The sisters were much older than Jude by a good twenty years, and they were day and night in every aspect. Constance, the eldest, was nothing like the marabou stork Cló had been imagining, but more like a belligerent shoebill; big boned, with the rounded shoulders of a rugby player and a ruddy, heavy face of someone who'd spent all hours outdoors in truculent disregard of the weather. Her eyes crawled up and down Cló's body, noting the crumpled dress, the rolls beneath straining against the fabric before returning to her face. Her sneer made it clear Cló was exactly the sort of pathetic wife she had imagined Jude would bring home.

Withering under Constance's obvious loathing, Cló smiled tentatively at Ruth Honeyborne . . . and stared in astonishment. As wispy as a newly fledged egret, fluffy hair floated around her neck like an apologetic cloud. Short and thin, Ruth had none of the green-eyed intensity of Constance, but a watery vagueness, her eyes magnified by bottle-bottom glasses. The faintest of birthmarks adorned one cheek in the shape of a cross, which she touched self-consciously when Cló's gaze passed over it. But it was Ruth's outlandish apparel that astonished Cló. Adorned in a bright red tailcoat with gold trim, and black trousers tucked into high black boots, she held a long whip that trailed on the floor behind her like a reptilian tail.

One of them was wearing a strong perfume. Cinnamon, apples and lilies. Sickly sweet, it made Cló think of death. It had to be from Ruth; Cló couldn't imagine someone as masculine as Constance wearing any perfume at all.

"An American," said Constance to Ruth as though Cló wasn't standing right in front of them. Ruth nodded and peered at Cló, head cocked to one side like a curious sparrow.

"Canadian," Cló said apologetically, very conscious of the sharpness of her accent. She felt a terrible urge to curtsey.

A dreadful silence welled up, pulled taut by resentment sparking between the Honeyborne siblings. Cló could understand the Honeyborne sisters' resentment. Here was the black sheep son returned to inherit everything they held dear, while they would receive only a small yearly annuity for the remainder of their lives and right of abode in the Hall. It must've been a bitter pill when the will was read out. Cló glanced guiltily at Jude, hoping he hadn't read her disloyal thoughts.

"We'll be in the Blue Suite," he said.

Constance's jaw locked pugnaciously. "We had thought you would be more comfortable in the Rose Suite, but"—she forced herself to shrug unconcernedly—"as you will."

Jude stalked past his sisters, dragging Cló with him.

"Dinner will be at eight in the Silver Dining Room," Constance called after them, then in a purposely loud whisper, she added, "Dear god, he's married an overfed mouse."

"She's rather large for a mouse," said Ruth, speaking for the first time, in the surprisingly high-pitched voice of a little girl. "And did you see her peculiar eyes? Quite gave me a turn."

"Yes . . . her eyes," said Constance thoughtfully.

Cló whipped around to see the sharp, knowing glance the sisters shared.

"Don't listen to them," said Jude through clenched teeth. He put his arm around Cló's shoulders protectively. "They want you to rise."

Cló swallowed the hurt tears tightening her throat and nodded, sensing two pairs of green eyes drilling holes into her back as she and Jude stepped through the huge double-leafed doors into Grimdark Hall.

Cló's jaw dropped.

"Vile, isn't it?" said Jude, scowling at the vast room.

"Vile? It's gloriously extravagant!" Cló cricked her neck to study the satyrs pursuing voluptuous women through swirls of colour on the ceiling. Golden cherubs beamed cheekily from huge columns. An ornamental fireplace took up much of one wall, and sculpted men, clad with a single fig leaf, peered down superciliously from their lofty plinths.

Jude shook his head, smiling. "You are such a tourist. I hate the baroque style—so overdone. A pissing contest in vulgarity."

"Stop being a snob," Cló said mildly. "Is the whole place like this?"

"No, just this and the ballroom."

"I thought this *was* the ballroom."

"No, this is the Great Hall, as opposed to the Little Hall that is only marginally smaller than this," Jude explained with little pride or care. "The whole place is a hodgepodge of styles. Each generation had to add something, and now it's a ghastly jumble of bad architecture."

"And now you're being a purist," Cló teased, beguiled by the hodgepodge. Happily, she couldn't tell one style from another if it had slapped her in the face.

She left Jude's side to wander into the middle of the hall, and turned slowly in a circle, cloaking herself in dust motes glittering like pollen on the sunrays streaming through the stained-glass windows.

She slowed her gentle spinning, her delight in the gaudiness fading. Perhaps it was the Honeyborne sisters watching her sullenly from the terrace, perhaps it was Jude's aversion colouring her vision, but the brightness and charm from a moment before dulled. The building tightened around her like a scowl, the cherubs no longer beamed but viewed her with suspicion, the blank-eyed stare of the statues followed her with hostility.

She caught Jude watching her with amusement. "You've already given the place a personality," he said.

"Just getting a feel for it." Cló believed all buildings had a personality. Some felt like a home the moment you walked in, some cold and snooty. Others merely gloomy and unloved. And then there were the houses shadowed with dreadful, bloody secrets that seeped from their very walls. Grimdark Hall fell into the latter category.

Shaking herself of silly fancies, Cló hurried after Jude as he opened one of the many doors facing onto the hall.

Grimdark was a labyrinth of rooms running into each other. The echo of their footsteps lingered in the long hallways. Feeling like Alice who'd fallen down the rabbit hole, and cursed with a similar curiosity, Cló opened every door they passed. Dust-shrouded bedrooms led to sitting rooms and bathrooms. Ornate staircases rose and fell. Surprising crannies led to nooks. Dour men and women frowned down from age-darkened paintings.

Skin prickling into goose bumps, Cló glanced over her shoulder, sensing she was being followed. No one was there, but she could imagine the sisters stalking them. They seemed the sort who listened at keyholes.

"Where is the Blue Suite?" Cló asked, almost walking on Jude's heels.

"Somewhere along here." They travelled down yet another hallway lined in green carpet, the gloomy portraits replaced by stuffed trophies, fur and feathers motheaten and rank with the sickly sweet odour of decay. Glassy eyes scrutinised Cló as though trying to decide what manner of creature she was. Their gaze was not friendly.

She shuddered at the thought of walking down the hallway under the weight of those gleaming eyes every day, wishing Jude had chosen a different room for them to stay in.

"Ah. Here it is." Jude opened a door that looked much like every other, then wheezed, "Christ!" as he dislodged a surge of dust on entering the room.

The Blue Suite was very blue. The cobalt canopy and drapes of the enormous four-poster bed matched the grimy curtains and aged carpet. Sapphire fabric lined the walls. A door led to a sitting room with spindly chairs upholstered in violet, which looked priceless to Cló's uneducated eye, not daring to test their strength by sitting on them. Another door led to a dressing room, and yet another to a dated bathroom finished in walnut and azure tiles.

Cobwebs had invaded the chandeliers; more had laid siege in every corner. The air was foul with mould and wood rot. The carpets crunched underfoot with mouse droppings and—Oh god! Mice skeletons.

"Maybe the Rose Suite would be better," said Cló when she'd finished her exploration. "It's been prepared for us and might have less dust."

"No!" he snapped, then hunched against Cló's shocked gasp. Jude rarely raised his voice and never snapped.

She watched Jude worriedly as he prowled about the room, noting the tautness bracketing his mouth that hadn't been there before, hostility bristling in the set of his shoulders.

"No," he said again, softer, almost an apology. "Constance will see it as a win."

"Does it matter?"

"Yes, it does. It's always about winning with Constance, and you won't know the rules of the game or that you're in a competition at all." He parted the drapes of the four-poster bed and sat down heavily, releasing a trapped cloud of decades-old dust.

"I knew you didn't get on, but I hadn't expected hatred." Cló sat down beside him, her heart clenching uneasily when he shifted to avoid touching her. She reached out to take his hand, then withdrew, not wanting to be rebuffed. "Constance hates you," *and me* she didn't add, but thought Constance's hatred of her, as Jude's wife, was a reflex, a rebound.

"And I hate her. I always have."

His hatred was a physical thing, a shimmering residue of the small boy he'd once been, who'd wandered these long, lonely halls. A revulsion not just for his sisters, but Grimdark too.

"Why does she hate you so much?" Her hand reached for Jude's again, withdrew again.

"Because I was born." Old bitterness clotted Jude's voice.

"Constance loves this place, and my birth scuppered any chance of her inheriting. She had thought that, without a male heir, our father might change tradition and allow her to inherit, as there were no male heirs except some distant cousin in Australia."

"It all seems rather archaic and pointless," Cló said, but she wasn't totally surprised. She'd felt like they'd stepped into a different time, a weird time loop, when they'd driven through the enormous gateway.

"It is . . . I suppose I can understand her resentment somewhat. She was twenty-five when I was born, and there hadn't been any other children after Ruth. My mother was forty-six when she fell pregnant with me, so it must've been an enormous shock." His face creased ruefully, and he took Cló's hand that had been creeping once again towards his. "It's not going to get any easier, I'm afraid. Constance is a class-A bitch, and don't underestimate Ruth. She doesn't say much, but she skulks about and reports back to Constance like the good little lapdog she's always been. And it won't matter what we do, it'll be wrong."

"Maybe if we try to be nice to them, they might be nicer to us."

"Constance will see niceness and kindness as weakness. The only way we're going to survive the next few weeks is avoid them or fight back."

"Oh dear," said Cló, a lifelong non-confrontationist. "I think I'm onto triply screwed now."

Jude forced a smile. "We don't want to give Constance any ammunition. She will use anything she sees as a weakness to make our time here a living hell."

Cló flinched at the unspoken *more* before ammunition. *She* was the more; the wife Jude must've known his sisters would never approve of and certainly never like. She squashed the niggle of doubt that he had married her purposely to spite his family.

"You could just give it all to your sisters."

Jude started, brow knitting in consternation, and shook his head. "I don't know if that's possible. My father's will was quite specific." He looked at his watch. "It's nearly eight. We'd best get downstairs for dinner."

"Before we go"—Cló looked around the room, oddly fearful the sisters might hear her, before leaning towards Jude to whisper—"what is up with Ruth? That outfit!"

Jude's lips twitched. "About the only thing I'd been looking forward to was your reaction to Ruth and her . . . eccentricities. Her ringmaster persona is mild. Wait until you see her in full Zulu regalia." To Cló's relief, he was grinning broadly now, more like her Jude. "That is not a sight for the faint-hearted."

"Is she—um—mentally unstable?"

Her relief was short-lived, his expression darkened again. "They're both unstable in their own ways . . . My parents took Ruth to loads of doctors when she was young. They couldn't find anything wrong with her mentally. She's just"—he shrugged—"bloody strange. Mother told me Ruth did it from the moment she could dress herself. Some of her costumes are amazing and her personas are pretty detailed; they all have names and history. I think she bases them on historical figures who've captured her fancy. I know some of them are based on real people."

"It's a little disturbing."

"Everything about my sisters is disturbing." Jude looked at his watch again, oddly nervous. "We'd best get down to dinner. Better not keep them waiting or we'll never hear the end of it."

The Silver Dining Room which, Cló soon learnt, was a few hallways down from the Gold Dining Room—only used for important guests, a category Jude and Cló did not fall into by inference—was certainly silver but dulled with tarnish. The Burmese teak table running the length of the room could have seated a hundred, but was laid for four, two on opposite ends. Cló didn't see any staff who might have prepared the meal and laid it out. She couldn't imagine the sisters doing so, not for her and Jude.

Dinner was silent, lengthy and ghastly, proceeding in six courses. Mostly average fare, given the spectacular if mouldering surroundings. Cló couldn't stop stealing glances at Ruth, now dressed in a striped navy uniform of a Victorian schoolboy, a little navy cap perched on her wispy hair and her thin white legs, criss-crossed with varicose veins, poking out of shorts.

Jude picked at his food and barely lifted his head. The sisters were silent throughout, but Cló felt their eyes on her, weighing her, judging her until she was quite literally squirming in her seat.

It was certainly one of the more peculiar dinners Cló had endured, though she couldn't fault the glorious apple pie with a mound of clotted cream so thick it scooped up like ice cream. She braved the disapproving looks of the sisters and went back to the sideboard for a second helping.

It was dark by the time Jude and Cló felt it wouldn't be impolite to get up from the table. Jude hesitated. He half-turned as though to walk down the length of the table to wish his sisters good night.

Constance and Ruth's eyes narrowed in unison at his indecision.

He took a step towards them, stopped and shook his head. He grabbed Cló's hand and hurried out of the dining room.

"Before you say it," said Jude, when they were well out of hearing range, "I know I should have spoken to them. I could feel you silently encouraging me to try, but it's too soon . . . or maybe it's too late." He smiled thinly at Cló. "Let's go to bed."

"Urgh!" she grumbled. "That dusty bed with the crunch of mice skeletons for variety."

"You won't sleep anyway. I expect you'll go roaming as you always do."

"I can't do that! I have no idea how to get outside, and I don't know the area at all. I could fall down the cliff or get lost in a marsh or something."

"Then roam about the Hall. God knows it's big enough for you never to visit the same room twice in a year of Sundays."

Cló flushed at the irritated edge to his tone. "This isn't our home," she said, keeping her own tone light though her heart ached. "And it's kind of creepy wandering about someone else's house. Like a weird stalker."

"Don't be ridiculous!" he snapped.

Cló gasped. "Jude! What is wrong with you?"

Instantly contrite, he shut his eyes briefly. "Shit. Sorry," he muttered. "It's this bloody place. I wish we'd never come." He bared his teeth, half grimace, half smile. "The Hall belongs to us. You can go wherever the hell you please and don't let my horrible sisters tell you otherwise."

"Yes," said Cló doubtfully. Insomnia was one of her many failings, and Jude was long used to her midnight meanders. But wandering around this big old pile was quite different to the quiet suburban streets around their little house in Toronto. Grimdark Hall felt too guarded, its heavy history leering at her from every nook and corner was repressive. She was not sure she was brave enough. Not yet.

THREE

In the dark, blue cave with the drapes drawn around the four-poster bed to keep Grimdark at bay, Jude's tension slipped away in a sigh. Cló revelled in the lulling intimacy of shared whispers, a hesitant discussion of the day, an exchange of thoughts unspoken but understood. Heads close together and face to face, they were just Jude and Cló, collaborators and conspirators, delighting in each other with assured caresses borne of long familiarity.

As the night deepened, their whispers quietened.

Cló stared up at the canopy with Jude's limbs tangled around her, trying not to sneeze in the dust that rose and fell with every breath she took. She listened to Jude's breathing, waiting for him to fall into dreaming. Their sleep patterns were off kilter; they always had been. Cló feared her dreams, and something in Jude's past prevented him from falling asleep unless she was beside him.

She had asked him about it once, in the early days of their relationship; it had led to their first fight. She had never asked again and he'd never told her. It hadn't hindered their marriage, which was a happy one. But here, as Grimdark settled heavily around them, stinking of generational pain and shame, Cló knew Jude's soul had been damaged within these walls. Something traumatic, a childhood wound barely scabbed over, that he couldn't speak of, even to her.

Cló's eyes drooped. They snapped open moments later with the sear of nightmare flames still hot on her skin. Every night death crowded her sleep with no rhyme or reason. Always her own, by flame or knife, hanging or drowning. Cló's was a forced insomnia.

Jude's breathing was steady and deep. Carefully, she lifted his arm draped across her stomach and clambered from the bed.

After a brief silent battle with the drapes, Cló grabbed her Kindle from her bag. She tried one of the spindly chairs in the sitting room. It creaked ominously under her weight, and she reared up in fright. Guilty thoughts of the double helping of apple pie at dinner, with the self-knowledge that she could happily have gone back for thirds, she determined to start another diet tomorrow. But Cló knew she would do no such thing. She loved food, she lived to eat, though every mouthful was laced with guilt, and she'd eat more to assuage it. It was her internal, eternal dilemma.

Unable to settle, Cló eyed a chaise longue that looked sturdier, until she noted the suspicious stain on the violet brocade and hoped no one had been murdered there. She could imagine any number of murders in Grimdark Hall.

Cló ended up on the toilet with the lid down and switched on her Kindle. She didn't take a word in, feeling silly sitting naked on the loo trying to read in the middle of the night in a vast stately home.

She stared doggedly at the screen. Her feet were cold on the azure-tiled floor. She wanted to be out walking. She stared at the screen.

With a sigh, she gave up and tiptoed back to the bedroom.

Dressing quietly, she put on a pair of sneakers. She winced when the door creaked as she opened it.

She froze at a rustle from the bed and Jude's sleepy, "Watch out for the ghosts."

"I thought you were asleep," she whispered and started back to the bed.

"I am. I'm fine . . . go and roam."

"Are you sure? I can stay."

"Don't. I'm fine." A pause. "Do you want me to come with you?"

Cló bit her lip, tempted. "No, go back to sleep."

"Take your binos if you decide to go outside. There used to be loads of owls about. There probably still are, especially around the chapel."

Ghosts, chapels and owls . . . The novelty of all three in one place was too appealing to resist. Cló grabbed her binoculars. A quick peek through the drapes. She smiled at Jude with his arm thrown over his eyes, then stepped out into the dark corridor.

She fumbled along the wall for a light switch, quite sure she caught a glint of glassy eyes as though a stuffed rhinoceros had blinked, or perhaps it was the impala with a startled expression.

It was a quirk of Cló's that while she was apprehensive of much in daylight—mostly the sometimes curious, sometimes nasty gazes of others at her appearance or her eyes—she had little fear of the dark, loving the quiet that night afforded. But she had no desire to roam this mausoleum of dead rodents and stuffed animals, and determined to find an exit to the darkness outside.

Her questing fingers found a switch. A single lamp flickered to geriatric life.

"Arghh!" Cló shrieked, face-to-face with a wildebeest glaring at her accusingly in the unaccustomed light.

Beneath the baleful gazes of long-dead African animals, she crept along the halls furred with thick dust. She randomly turned left, then right, up and down stairs, in and out of rooms shrouded in dustsheets. The starlit gardens she glimpsed through windows were frustratingly further away with every corner she turned, as though Grimdark Hall was being deliberately obtuse, changing its architecture to play a sly game of cat and mouse with her.

"Oh!" she breathed, as she stepped into a room that was all windows. Moonlight streamed in, turning night to monochromatic day. It had served as a conservatory once, with empty Grecian pots and rattan chairs grouped around low tables.

The conservatory led to a peculiar glass tunnel. Cabinets lining the clear walls captured Cló's attention. Feeling ever more like a trespasser and a thief, she scuttled from one cabinet to another, marvelling at jade figurines from China, sandalwood carvings from India, a collection of shrunken heads from Peru, and fans from Japan.

A wistful sigh of pure pleasure puffed up from her chest as she paused in front of a vast cabinet of glass birds sitting on a glass tree. Cló had never seen anything so exquisite, so fragile. Each little bird was given glowing life by the moonlight. A crimson sunbird shared space with a stately raven, a blue tit faced a violet-backed starling, a mandarin duck sailed serenely on a glass lake at the base of the tree with a whooper swan. Each bird, though not to scale, was perfect, a work of art in shape, colour and bill.

Some things needed to be touched to be real. Placing her binoculars on top of a nearby cabinet, Cló felt around until she found a small latch, and the wide glass doors split open. Carefully, she brought out a lilac-breasted roller and placed it in the palm of her hand. It was so delicate it appeared spun from spider's silk, as moonlight spilt through the wings and beak, creating a prism of colour on the floor.

"What are you doing?"

Cló shrieked. She whipped around, smashing into a cabinet

of Haitian dolls. The roller dropped from her fingers, shattering into tiny shards like fractured stars on the floor.

Constance glared at the carnage at Cló's feet. "You stupid cow! That was a priceless heirloom!"

"I'm so, so sorry!" Cló whispered, tears forming, her heart breaking for the loss of irreplaceable beauty. Cursing herself for a clumsy fat fool, she wanted to bolt back to the safety of Jude in their dusty blue cave. She forced herself to return Constance's terrible gaze. "I'm really so sorry," she said again.

"Sorry won't put the pieces back together again. Edmund Honeyborne brought those back over four hundred years ago from Venice, and not a single one has lost even a beak. You're here for two minutes and smash one to smithereens!"

"I'll pay for the repairs," Cló said, though no amount of glue in the world would repair the devastation at her feet. Fearful of the older woman's scorn, she dropped her gaze to Constance's boots, then up the workmen's clothes she had not been wearing at dinner.

"Are you going out?" she asked timidly. She forced her cheeks into a civil smile that was more a rictus of terror.

Constance's eyes narrowed, ruddy cheeks flushed with fury. Cló's politeness was wasted on this woman who obviously despised her, and whom she was trying not to loathe in return.

"None of your business," snapped Constance. "What are *you* doing out of your room at this time of night?"

Cló longed to snap back, "None of your business!" too, but her cowardly heart made her babble, "I couldn't sleep. I never can really, and at home I walk the streets to exhaust myself, except there's no streets here, so Jude said it would be fine if I . . ." She petered off to a blithering stop at Constance's eye-roll that spoke eloquently of her opinion of Cló and her sleeping habits, and how little she cared about either.

"Go back to bed. It's not wise to wander about Grimdark.

You never know what you might disturb . . . or break," she said with a pointed glance at the shattered roller.

Cló heard the underlying threat. Whether intentional or imagined, it sent a shiver of misgiving down her spine. "I'll clean this up first," she said miserably.

"Leave it! You may break something else in the process. Just go! I'm sure you'll manage to find your way back to your room."

"I really am so very sorry," Cló said yet again.

"Go!"

Cló fled. Down the glass tunnel and through the conservatory. Up stairs she didn't recognise and down others, through rooms that merged into a moonlit labyrinth. Breath hard in her chest, her footsteps echoed like mocking laughter, certain Grimdark was pulling her hither and thither, confusing her, scaring her.

She ran into a cavernous space. Quite by chance she'd found the Great Hall.

Panting desperately, she discarded any idea of finding her way back to Jude. With a quick glance over her shoulder to ensure Constance hadn't followed, Cló hurried to the doors leading outside.

A momentary fumble with the ancient locking mechanism, and Cló stepped out onto the terrace. Her hands on her knees, she puffed like a struggling steam train after her furious race through Grimdark. A barn owl's harsh screech reminded her she'd left her binoculars in the glass tunnel and would have to get Jude to help her find them again in the morning.

Still lightheaded, Cló straightened and made her cautious way down the wide stairs and across the courtyard, needing distance between herself and Grimdark Hall. Moonlight glinted darkly off the perimeter walls and the buildings huddled at their base. Beyond came the comforting suck and pull of waves.

Cló walked the length of the walls, searching for a stairwell to the top. The Hermitage reared up above her as she approached the corner. In its shadow, she turned to view Grimdark Hall.

Cló felt its sly gaze from blind windows, the ill-tempered slant to its roof; smelt its reek of human unkindness and suffering. And yet . . . from a comfortable distance, Cló wondered if she had mistaken slyness for apprehension. Her eyes roved the old building's walls, up its silhouetted skyline, and sensed a trembling withdrawal. The flinch of something wounded, like a dog that had been kicked repeatedly and snarled in defence, fearing another swing of a boot.

Sound carried loudly on the still air. The creak of a door opening, a furtive footstep on marble. Gooseflesh spiked across Cló's bare arms. Her heart clamouring with fright, she spotted a figure detach from the shadows of the Hall and edge across the lawn. Fearing what ghost of Grimdark she was seeing, Cló pressed her back against the wall, the knapped flint digging through her light shirt. Not daring to blink, she watched the apparition disappear into the walled garden only to reappear through an arch near a couple of garden sheds.

Then the apparition did something unghostly. It opened a shed door and slipped inside. Cló recognised the slouching hulk of Constance.

Infused with curiosity, she muttered, "What are you up to in the middle of the night?" Was Constance a night wanderer like herself? Night gardening maybe?

Constance reemerged from the shed carrying a shovel. So, night gardening. Cló rather liked the idea of gardening by moonlight; it made Constance a little more interesting than a grumpy old woman.

But instead of turning towards the walled garden, Constance, carrying the shovel over her shoulder like a pugnacious soldier on parade, stomped towards the chapel and disappeared inside.

"Now there's a thing you don't see every day." Cló hadn't taken Constance for the religious sort. Perhaps there was a gardening prayer that needed to be done at—she glanced at her wristwatch—at 1:47 a.m.

Biting her lip, curiosity ate at her common sense. Should she follow? In her mind she was already scurrying across the court-yard to open the chapel door. Her imagination unhelpfully supplied a creaking door and Constance whipping around as she knelt in front of an old stone altar. Cló's face flamed in imagined embarrassment, caught in Constance's round, green glare, with a "You again! Can I not be left alone in peace to pray?" The scene playing out in her head was so real she gave up any thought of following Constance. She was scary enough in Cló's mind without needing the reinforcement of reality.

Her curiosity suitably chastened by her cowardice, Cló turned back to the wall and soon found an old spiralling stair-case in the corner. Shoulders hunched, hips scraping the walls, she cursed the small stature of the humans who'd built it. The stairs opened onto a crenelated walkway along the top of the wall.

The North Sea spread out before her, gilded by a moon so big it bled a trail of white blood to the shore, trapping stars' re-flections in the restless water. Further out, clouds bunched up, lit up erratically by crackles of lightning within. A stiff breeze ran before the brewing storm, startling a tawny owl into flight with a trilling shiver of *ho-hoo-o-o-o*.

The thin beach of the horseshoe bay was lost beneath the tide dashing against the sheer candy-cane-striped cliffs, sending spray as high as the walls in a fairy mist. To Clo's left a few lights glowed in Grimdark village like Christmas lights strung along the cliff's edge. To the right, the Hermitage was black on black, a secret path snaking up to the stars.

Breathing in deeply the tang of salt and fish, Cló gave her imagination free rein, populating the restless horizon with old ships, galleons and cutters. Perhaps it was the mention of pi-rates on the journey from London, but one of the ships be-longed to pirates, running before an armada, spying the little bay, oblivious to the dangers lurking below the heaving waves.

The pirates would hear the church bells ringing the hour, as Cló did at—a glance at her wristwatch—at two a.m. exactly. They heard the solemn tolling. *One . . . two . . .*

The silhouette of the village church was forbidding against the night sky. She looked at her wristwatch again and frowned . . . *three . . . four . . .*

Her frown deepened with confusion as she counted under her breath, for the bells kept tolling . . . *seven . . . eight . . .*

. . . nine . . . ten . . .

The bells echoed like they were under water, each peal leaving an aftertaste of sound that penetrated deep into Cló's marrow. She felt it then, a fracture in time, an implausible memory that couldn't possibly be her own, changing the topography of the bay. Her vision blurred as the striped cliffs bulged further out to sea, a crop of houses huddled on its new length that hadn't been there moments before. A church clung to the precipice, smaller, squatter than the one further back in the village.

. . . eleven . . . twelve . . .

. . . thirteen . . .

As the thirteenth toll faded away, Cló wrapped her arms around herself to ward off the fearful chill. Something primeval stirred the air, a fearful superstition. A warning in the echoing chimes.

1645

Trepidation was a constant miasma over Darrow End. It was there in the faces of mothers worrying over their sons who had joined Cromwell's New Model Army, there in the smoke houses and mills standing empty with not enough hands to man them, there in the fishing boats languishing on the shore, useless in the pursuit of herring needed to feed the village. And as it was in any war, it fell to the womenfolk to push through the consequent famine and crippling taxes raised to fund the Great Rebellion.

Euphemia Figgis's problems were smaller and didn't stretch much beyond the borders of Darrow End as she made her way down the cliff path with her mother and daughter. Yesterday's sermon was playing on her mind. She attended church, as did the whole village of a Sunday morning—most of Norfolk was puritanical both in nature and religion—to hear the new priest say his piece. And say much he did. The new man's words had got under Effie's skin, distressing as broken glass. Worse than witches, he'd said of the cunning folk; a witch could harm the body, but the cunning folk harmed the soul, for many were more likely to seek magical aid from the cunning folk than put their faith in God.

It was all nonsense, of course, for Effie was a healer. Germaine, however, told fortunes, found lost items with a loaf of bread, and cursed and uncursed as the mood took her. None of it was real, but people still believed. Sitting at the back of the church, Effie had seen heads turning to regard the Figgis women with narrowed, suspicious eyes.

"That slummocking gret mawther be here," muttered Germaine, as she made her careful blind way down the cliff path, following the tap-tap of her walking cane that served more often as a weapon to enforce her point than a walking aid. "I can smell her stench a mile off."

"Nan!" cried Sophie, scandalised by her grandmother as only a sixteen-year-old could be. "Dunt let her embarrass me, Mum," she said to Effie.

"Dunt be cruel, Mum," said Effie vaguely, well used to Germaine's views of the villagers, which she rarely kept to herself.

"And our primmicky Lord be yonder. I can hear his squeak a mile off an'all," added Germaine, taking no notice of her daughter and granddaughter's sighs of resignation.

Darrow Bay, always wild and dramatic, was captivating in the late August sunshine, with long shadows pooling in unlikely places. A small curved bay enfolded by cliffs striped in rust and cream. From the Figgis women's high vantage point on the cliff path the sandbars and jagged rocks in the bay seemed deceptively small and harmless. There the deception ended; in the low tide a wrecked ship wallowed, surrounded by the bodies of unfortunate sailors who'd allowed their vessel to stray too near the coast during the previous night's storm.

A wrecked ship was a boon to the village, and everyone was down in the bay, scavenging for anything of value or use amidst the bloated, fish-nibbled corpses.

"*Goody Buskin said it's a pirate ship,*" said Sophie, her beautiful blue eyes alight with excitement.

"*Then I hope none survived, or they'll be fer Marshalsea,*" said Effie.

"*I hope some have,*" said Germaine with dark glee. "*We ent had a hanging fer many a month. Always enjoyed a good hanging.*"

The crescent of pebble-dashed beach and seaweed-cloaked rocks was aswarm with purposeful busyness. The Figgis women were late down to the bay and would have lean pickings. Fractured barrels and crates were disappearing with their new owners into the caves that honeycombed the cliffs and led to the village above through a warren of tunnels.

Germaine sniffed deeply, her milky eyes turned to the four men grouped near the hushing water. "*That snivelling shite o' a doctor's near,*" she muttered.

"*Yis,*" murmured Effie. Even she could smell the overwhelming odour of roses Dr. James Bulman slathered on a handkerchief to prevent him catching a whiff of poverty from the villagers.

Germaine lifted her long nose again and gave an almighty sniff. She spat to the side in disgust and cursed loudly about the rank stench of false sanctity.

Effie nodded to the four men with reluctant diffidence. It was not acknowledged or returned. She knew three of them: the long-faced Lord Honeyborne, lord of the Hall and all he surveyed, old Dr. Bulman with his apoplectic redness and mean eyes, and the new priest, Theophilus Braid, hunched like a raven in his black vestments unsuited to the mild weather. The fourth was unfamiliar, and handsome with the flush of youth.

"*The new blood has a fondness fer lavender water,*" said Germaine, not bothering to keep her voice down.

"*That'll be Bulman's new apprentice,*" muttered Effie.

"*He's lovely,*" whispered Sophie.

At that moment the doctor's apprentice turned and caught

*sight of Sophie. His dark eyes widened in surprise, and a de-
lighted smile quirked his lips.*

Sophie dimpled at him, then lowered her eyes demurely.

*Effie sighed, not at all surprised by the young man's response
to her daughter. Sophie had a beauty that could've graced any
king's court and so was especially astonishing to find in a small
village like Darrow End. The apprentice was not the only one
aware of Sophie. Lord Honeyborne's hooded eyes ran up and
down her length in a manner that made Effie's skin crawl. She
moved her daughter between herself and Germaine to shield
her from the calculating, lecherous gaze.*

*"His name be Benjamin Hobbis," whispered Sophie. "I
heard from Big Rueben that he studied in France. Old Bull ent
happy with him neither. Dunt like his new ways."*

*Effie nodded, staring proudly at Dr. Bulman as she passed
him. He returned her stare. There was a long-standing feud between them; Old Bull hated that the villagers turned to the cunning woman for their ailments before approaching him. But
times were changing, and though she still had a standing in the
village based on tradition, now it was based on fear. A fear created by the church in the form of Theophilus Braid and his cru-
sade to root out anything he perceived as witchcraft.*

*It was Old Bull who turned away first, for few could bear to
peer into Effie's odd-coloured eyes for long without a superstitious shiver.*

*The women kept walking, but Effie had heard some of the
men's murmuring discussion and the whisper of "witch . . .
witch . . . witch . . ." followed the Figgis women as they made
their way down to the water's edge.*

*"Won't be long afore Lady Honeyborne be fer the birthing
chamber, I sharnt wonder," said Germaine. She groaned slightly,
knees creaking, when Effie found her a rock to sit on.*

"Won't be naught to do with us," said Effie, a little sadly. While

she despised Lord Honeyborne, his wife was a decent woman and did good work in the village. "His Lordship'll be wantin' Old Bull to attend."

"More fool him," Germaine muttered. "You and I together know she'll be fer a difficult birthin', slip o' a girl that she be."

"That's a few weeks off by my reckoning . . . Now try not to menace anyone," said Effie, when Germaine had grumbled herself into a comfortable position on the rock.

"Mind yar tongue, Euphemia," snapped Germaine. "I'll say what I please to whom I please. Now you git on. Otherwise, we ent gorn home with naught but firewood."

None came near Effie and Sophie as they waded out to the wreck, leaving Germaine on her rock where she called out to all brave enough to walk past her. None of her comments were kind, and she had the uncanny knack of knowing each villager by the sound of their tread or breathing. It was enough to make everyone fear the old woman.

Little was left in the wreck. Sophie picked up a damaged crate and tipped out a gush of water. All the iron nails and ribbing were already gone. With a sigh, the two women set to hacking up the remaining wood in the damaged hull for firewood. They weren't the only scavengers; seagulls screeched their raucous disapproval of the Figgis women as they worked.

"Mum," said Sophie as twilight crept into the hull. "Nan's gone quiet."

Effie frowned at her daughter then peered out through a hole in the hull. Germaine had not moved from the rock where Effie had left her. A crowd of villagers stood near the base of the cliffs, staring at the wreck. Of Lord Honeyborne and the other three men, there was no sign.

"What's gorn on, Mum?" whispered Sophie as she joined Effie.

"Nan's listenin'."

Though Effie did not have Germaine's accentuated hearing

honed by years of blindness, she heard well enough the whispers that rose to a susurration of suspicion and rumour.

"Remember ole Nathaniel's cow?" said Elijah the blacksmith, with a knowing look. "Sickened and died when that ole scold demanded his debt be paid."

"And that black kittling what crept into Oliver's cottage when he were poorly. Died that night, he did. Bewitchment it were."

"And dunt forget our Maggie's wee babes. Not a one living in six years," said Goodwife Kett. "That Effie Figgis were in the birthing chamber each time."

Effie's eyes narrowed at Goodwife Kett who had conveniently forgotten it was she who had called for Effie though she'd said she wouldn't each time.

"I heard that ole scold nagged her good man into an early grave," said Goodman Hansill. "It were her that sent him to Marshalsea fer a stretch."

"And what o' that storm? Took Euphemia's man that night and four besides. And not hours arter we all heard her curse him to the Devil."

But it was Goodwife Kett's words that made Effie's blood run cold. "I heard tell His Lordship be paying to bring in the Witchfinder . . ."

"Dunt you have naught better to do than mardle?" Effie yelled, startling everyone on the beach. She leapt from the wreck into the water and waded ashore to stand by her mother. "What o' you, Goodwife Kett? Bread won't knead itself . . . And you, Elijah? No horses to shoe? And what o' you, Goodman Hansill? It weren't two nights back as you called me out to see to yar poorly mum."

"You duzzy mare!" said Germaine. "I were listening to them as were mardling!"

Effie ignored her. "So help me, if I sees you still here in two seconds I shall hex you all somethin' terrible. Fingers shall rot. Houses shall burn . . ."

"Mum!" cried Sophie. "What are you doin'? They hate us already. Dunt make it any worse."

But Effie was past caring. For months she had ignored the whispers and gone about her business, ministering to the very same who were now denouncing her for a witch.

Effie had the dull satisfaction of seeing everyone scarper until the darkened beach belonged only to the Figgis women. None took the cliff path, instead they took to their heels along the quicker route, through the cobweb of tunnels up to Darrow End.

"That were bloody stupid, Euphemia," snapped Germaine, poking Effie with unerring accuracy in the stomach. "What you go do that fer? That lot were . . ."

But Effie wasn't listening. She cocked her head instead to the hush and suck of the rising tide and the gulls above who waited for the humans to leave before they could feast on the drowned bodies not yet pulled from the water.

There it was again. A moaning.

"Sophie," she said without turning around. "Take Nan home. I'll be along shortly."

"Why?" said Sophie, watching her mother with a worried frown. "What you plannin'?"

"Nothin'. I'll go check the far end to see if anyone missed anythin'. But Nan needs to git home fer her dinner."

It took a bit of grumbling on Germaine's part and worried frowns on Sophie's before Effie had the beach to herself.

She lifted her heavy skirts and poked about the rocks on the furthest corner of the bay as twilight darkened to purple. Perhaps she had misheard. Perhaps it had been the moan of a dying man gasping his last breath.

It was almost completely dark and the tide but a few yards from the cliffs when she found him trapped between the cliff and a rock. Crabs and flies swarmed all over the open wound in his stomach. A couple of crows watched from a few rocks away, waiting for imminent death.

Effie hesitated, not daring to touch the man, a Turk by the cut of his dress, but European in every other manner from his white hair to the blue eyes barely open in a craggy, sunburnt face.

She poked him with her boot to see if he was still alive, then leapt back when the man jerked upright, eyes wide open and furious. He stared at Effie for a long, horrible moment. His face creased into a bewildered frown.

"Alstublieft!" he cried and flopped back into the rising water, his head glancing on a rock.

"Hush!" Effie whispered, glancing fearfully around the beach, and up at the walls surrounding Honeyborne Hall that melded with the cliff face.

She bit her lip, mind racing. If she brought him up to the village, he would be hanged for the pirate he obviously was. It would be a mercy to leave him here, let the sea take care of one of its own in its cruel way. But Effie was a healer, a cunning woman, who had spent her time saving life, not taking it.

She almost turned then, away from a dilemma not of her making. She stopped and looked up the towering cliffs to the thin tower that appeared small and squat from this angle.

There was another option.

FOUR

Bleary-eyed, Cló frowned into her cup of coffee. Her head felt fuzzy as though someone had shoved their fingers up her nose and tickled her brain. She prodded the flashes of dislocated images like an incomplete jigsaw, could still hear the bells chiming, taste the sea on her tongue, smell the stink of unwashed bodies, felt the splintered roughness of the shipwreck's hull. She knew it for what it was, imagination gripped by the romance of the starlit sea. Or had she dozed on top of the wall overlooking the bay and fallen to dreaming?

"Cló!"

Cló looked up. Jude stood beside the hob wearing an apron with an egg lifter in one hand.

"That's the third time I called you. Do you want eggs?"

"Three, please."

He turned back to the hob.

Jude loved to cook, and he especially loved breakfast, one of those people who were horribly chirpy the moment he woke up. Cló was not. She hated mornings. She wasn't grumpy; she merely struggled to fully engage until around eleven.

The kitchen had come as a surprise. More a series of inter-connecting rooms from opulent times, with larders, pastry rooms, steaming kitchen, butler's cupboard, cellars and a vast kitchen in the centre of it all like a fat spider surrounded by its web.

Cló and Jude were in one of the smaller rooms. Rows of bells attached to strings gave a clue to this being the servant's kitchen. Oddly, it was in here that Cló got a true sense of the powerful heritage Jude came from. The ghosts of servants scurried about them in a state of constant busyness to serve the whims of those abovestairs. Unlike the rest of the kitchens, there was evidence this one was still used regularly.

"How was your walk last night?" Jude threw over his shoulder.

"I met one of your sisters . . . Constance." Grimacing, she shut her eyes to admit, "And I broke a glass bird, a lilac-breasted roller." She didn't mention the peculiar dream, knowing Jude would have something to say about putting herself in danger by falling asleep on the wall.

"Ah." Jude wasn't surprised, he'd had years of firsthand experience of Cló's clumsiness. He considered it endearing, but that might change now a priceless family heirloom had been broken.

"One of the glass birds in the Hall of Curiosities?" he asked, facing her briefly.

Cló nodded miserably.

To her relief, he shrugged. "I wouldn't worry about it. There's hundreds of them. One won't be missed."

"Except by Constance," she said, and quickly related her midnight meeting with his sister.

"Sod her. It all belongs to us anyway. We can break every damn thing in this house if we choose to."

"She keeps odd hours," Cló grumped, happily forgetting she

kept odd hours too. "I saw her going into the chapel just before two in the morning."

"The chapel?" Jude turned to face her again, frowning. "Constance?"

"Yeah. With a shovel."

He opened his mouth, shut it, shook his head. "She's an idiot," he muttered, and returned to the sizzling hob.

"Why did we have to eat in the dining room last night when it looks like your sisters usually have their meals here?"

"Constance was trying to intimidate us."

"Why?"

"Everything is a battle of wills with Constance, and she almost always wins."

Now, *that* Cló could believe entirely. There was something about Jude's oldest sister that, frankly, freaked Cló out. While Ruth was eccentric and a little creepy, Constance leached life from everything around her to feed her sheer force of will. Cló had every intention of taking Jude's advice and avoiding Constance at all costs.

A draught swept into the kitchen and set the servants' bells ringing gently.

She stared at them, but she was hearing other, deeper chimes. "Your church bells ring at odd times here," she said. "I heard the church in the village toll thirteen at two a.m."

Jude froze, the egg-lift raised above the frying pan. "You heard the Bells?"

Cló heard the capitalisation. "Yeah, while I was up on the walls." She scowled. "Next you're going to tell me they're ghostly bells."

Jude grinned broadly. "They most certainly are."

"That is not funny, Jude! This place is already starting to creep me out."

"Bollocks! You're not scared of the dark, and you've been

wanting to see a ghost for as long as I've known you. You'll like this story; it has a witch's curse . . . Give me a minute." He found a couple of plates after banging through all the cupboards. After serving up their breakfast, he sat opposite Cló at the kitchen table.

"Well?" she demanded, when Jude tucked into his bacon and eggs without telling her what she knew he was dying to spill.

He grinned. "Once upon a time, in the seventeenth century," he began, then laughed when Cló threw a dishcloth at him. "Fine!" he conceded and shovelled in another mouthful before continuing with, "Norfolk has a rather dark history, especially in the seventeenth century. There was a bloke called Matthew Hopkins who went around as a self-styled 'witchfinder,' and for a few years he had hundreds of supposed witches put to death."

"Matthew Hopkins? That's a rather mundane name for a witchfinder. It should be dark and ominous like Damon Bloodbath or something."

"Except this really happened and isn't one of the horror movies you so love."

Cló pulled a face. "So, Matthew Hopkins . . ." she prompted.

"He came to Darrow End—which is what Grimdark was called then—when the local nobility paid for him to find a coven of witches causing all manner of horrible mayhem for the locals."

"By local nobility, we would be talking about the Honeybornes?" Cló said dryly.

"We *did* own the village then. Actually, we *still* own most of it. Now stop distracting me . . . So, Matthew Hopkins came riding in, and lo and behold he finds the suspected coven—"

"Hang on. How did he know they were a coven? Had he seen them dancing around a stone circle under a full moon or something?"

"Nothing quite so dramatic. More like souring a farmer's milk or a baby died or didn't die when expected. These were medieval times; people were superstitious, and the puritans were the worst of them. Most of the witches that were burnt were simply old ladies whom no one had liked, or someone had had an argument and accused the other of witchcraft."

"That's awful."

"Yes, it was . . . Now, can I carry on?"

Cló nodded. "Sorry," she added, grinning unrepentantly; it drove Jude mad when she picked his stories apart.

"So Matthew Hopkins finds the coven and interrogates them right here under Grimdark Hall, in the dungeons . . ."

"You have dungeons?" said Cló, astonished, and immediately curious to see said dungeons.

"Yeah. But they haven't been used in more than a hundred years. They are bolted shut," he added warningly. "No going down there in the dead of night. I mean it, Cló. They are dangerous, and god knows what dreadful diseases have been festering down there all this time."

Dammit, Cló wanted to see those dungeons. But she noted Jude's serious expression and nodded. "I won't, promise . . . Go on with the witches."

He eyed her suspiciously, well aware of Cló's penchant for the dark and grisly, then continued, "The women were cruelly tortured and confessed to everything. Then they were led up to Gibbet Hill—which doesn't exist anymore except as a street name—but as the flames consumed them, the witch known as Euphemia Figgis shrieked out a terrible curse." Jude's voice dropped to a dark, ghoulish tone as he leaned across the table. "She called on the old gods of the sea and told them to claim back what was rightfully theirs . . . and the cliff where Darrow End sat collapsed into the sea. And as the village sank beneath the waves the old church bells tolled thirteen times." He leaned back and grinned. "And ever since they say if anyone should hear the bells chiming thirteen times it's a portent of their looming death."

"Is this true?" Cló demanded.

Jude shrugged. "There really was a village called Darrow End, and the cliff really did collapse. You can still see the old church's spire on very low tides. So, some of it is true, though I doubt it was because of a witch's curse. But to a largely illiterate, superstitious people, I am sure a witch's curse was a way to explain, or perhaps justify, what was a terrible calamity. People always want something or someone to blame for a disaster, so why not the local witch?"

"That old story?" said Ruth as she came into the kitchen.

Jude and Cló shared a grimace. For a while they had managed to forget the Honeyborne sisters, and they were reluctant to leave the familiar intimacy they'd slipped into.

Cló prepared a bright smile, then blinked. Ruth was dressed as a monk in an off-white habit with the cowl pulled low over her face, her hands folded into the hanging sleeves.

Jude pressed his lips together to stop himself laughing at Cló's astonishment. When she looked at him with eyebrows raised, he mouthed, "The Cistercian monk." He winked at Cló, and said to Ruth, "Not every village has their own witch's curse."

"Have you told her about the Honeyborne curse?" said Ruth, gazing at Jude myopically.

She spoke of Cló as though she wasn't in the room. Jude's animation from a moment before vanished into a tight-lipped scowl. "I wasn't planning to."

"Oh, you should. It's a good one. Our Euphemia Figgis was rather good at cursing. People still come from miles around to hear about her." Ruth's watery green eyes slid Cló's way, then away, as though she couldn't bear the sight of her. "Foreigners do so like that sort of thing, don't they?"

Ignoring the jibe, Cló raised an eyebrow pointedly at Jude, who shovelled food into his mouth at a choking speed rather than engage in conversation with his sister. "This one I really do want to hear," she said.

"It's nonsense." He glared daggers at Ruth, as she pottered about the kitchen.

Ruth shook her head at Jude as though he were being a foolish little boy. She turned to Cló, her face a mere shadow within the cowl. In a voice with none of its high-pitched girlishness, she intoned, "*None born of the Honeyborne name shall live with honey, but grim and dark be their futures and their children's futures, that no heir shall suffer to live beyond a score years. And none shall a king's ransom claim until that same king's blood returns to these lands both grim and dark.*"

"It's bollocks," snapped Jude. "I'm a Honeyborne and the heir, and I'm thirty-four. It's nothing more than a bit of ridiculous folklore."

"Yet it bothers you," said Ruth with a puzzled cock of her head, like a robin spying a worm in the ground. "If it's not true, why are you taking on like this?"

"I'm not taking on!"

"It is somewhat true," said Ruth. "The Honeyborne future is looking rather grim and dark, isn't it?"

A muscle in Jude's jaw ticked.

"What are you planning to do with the Hall?" There was nothing vague about the look she gave her brother.

"I haven't decided yet," he muttered.

Cló clamped her lips shut at the blatant lie, but she had no intention of contradicting Jude in front of his sister.

"You may have inherited, Jude," said Ruth, "but this is also Con's and my home. I hope you're not thinking of doing something foolish."

He glared down at the congealing eggs on his plate, his hand tightening around the knife he held as though he would like to stab Ruth.

"Um . . ." said Cló when the silence grew taut and uncomfortable. It hurt when Jude stiffened and eyed her warily, as though expecting her to say something he would regret. "What does the curse mean about a king's ransom?"

Jude's shoulders relaxed. "No one knows," he said, latching onto the conversational lifeline Cló had thrown him. "Many kings have stayed at the Hall over the centuries. It could mean any or none of them."

"But some of Euphemia's curses did come true," said Ruth. "She cursed Matthew Hopkins that he would die when he was twenty-seven, and he *did* die when she said he would."

Jude rolled his eyes. "The Figgis women were renowned cunning folk. It wouldn't have taken a huge leap in conjecture that he wouldn't make old bones." He seemed to be reiterating a point from an old argument the two had had previously.

"Why not? And what are cunning folk?" Cló asked, out of her depth and envious of the history the English took for granted. It was seeped deep into the land, into the twist of every lane, every crooked house and crumbling tower.

"It's well known Matthew Hopkins was consumptive—tuberculosis," Jude added for Cló's benefit. "And the cunning folk were healers, and quite often midwives. Most people went to their local cunning woman before they went to a doctor. They were respected members of their communities. Not witches, as some like to portray them."

Before Ruth could respond, Jude stood abruptly, his chair grating along the old flagstones. "I need to get on."

"Get on?" said Cló, surprised. "I thought we'd—" The words died on her lips when Jude came round the table, bent to kiss her cheek and muttered, "Meeting with the solicitors. I'll see you later."

"But that's hours away, only at—" *eleven* died on her lips.

Jude was already out of the kitchen without sparing a glance at his sister.

Cló stared after him in dismay, then turned back to her cold breakfast. A prickle of disloyalty lodged in her throat that Jude was escaping his sisters and Grimdark, leaving her to fend for herself in a strange place with strangers.

"Well," said Ruth brightly into the hush of Jude's sudden departure. She didn't look directly at Cló, but at a point somewhere over her head rather than look into her odd-coloured eyes. A reaction Cló was used to. "I think her curses were real and she was a proper witch," she added as though her opinion had been asked on the matter.

"I'm sure you're right," said Cló meekly, wondering if she could leave soon without appearing impolite.

Ruth started searching through the cupboards again.

"Have you—er—lost something?" Cló asked. "Maybe I can help you look?"

Ruth turned and ran her round green eyes across the breadth of Cló. "I don't think so," she said. "You might break something."

Cló's indrawn hiss of shame was lost on her sister-in-law as she pulled open a drawer noisily. Cló revised her previous opinion that Ruth was the nice sister.

Putting her hands on the table, with every intention of getting the hell out of the kitchen regardless of whether it was polite or not, Cló stopped in midrise when Ruth said,

"How did you meet Jude?"

Startled, Cló said, "Um—he knocked me over . . . in a café," she clarified when Ruth frowned in consternation. "I wasn't looking where I was going, and he was reading while walking. I went flying, and he helped me up and was very apologetic as my coffee had gone all over me, then he asked me to dinner to make up for not watching where he was going."

"But you weren't watching where you were going either."

Cló's fond remembrance faltered at the accusatory tone. "No, I wasn't. I—um . . ." She bit her lip uncertainly under her sister-in-law's frown.

"And what do you actually do?"

"I'm an ornithologist. I was rather hoping to see some of your birdlife while I was here. I've heard your marshes—"

"Fens," Ruth corrected.

"Right—um—Sorry. Fens. I need to remember that one. Well, I've heard your birdlife is incredible, so . . ." She petered off again, before rallying with, "Perhaps you could recommend some places?"

"Oh, I have no interest in birds, I'm afraid. But maybe you could ask Constance. She knows far more about that sort of thing than I."

As she had absolutely no intention of asking Constance for anything, Cló discarded the suggestion immediately. "Um . . . I—er—think I'll be getting on."

"You do that," said Ruth.

She watched from the depths of her cowl as Cló stood up so fast her chair toppled with a crash and screeched horribly across the flagstones.

"Oh god. Sorry!" Cló muttered, quickly righting the chair before checking she hadn't broken anything.

Ruth tut-tutted and shook her head. She started humming under her breath.

"I'll see you later," said Cló, edging towards the door. She stopped on the threshold, her skin crawling. "What's that you're humming?" she asked.

Ruth was still staring at her. "*Catch him, Crow! Carry him, Kite,*" she murmured. "*Take him away till the apples are ripe. When they are ripe and ready to fall, here comes baby, apples and all.*"

A dark shiver rippled across Cló's skin. "That is horrible." She had always hated nursery rhymes—such dire warnings for children about everything that could go wrong in life, rather than concentrating on the good.

Ruth stared until Cló squirmed with embarrassment. "It's an old dandling rhyme. It's not known much nowadays except in these parts. But I rather like it. Constance and I created a whole game out of it when we were young."

"Right," said Cló. Quite sick with an unreasoning fright, she turned and fled.

FIVE

Grimdark village perched on the edge of the cliff with stoic tenacity. The little flint cottages eyed the horizon warily where the storm that started brewing in the early morning menaced the sea into a frenzied race to unleash hell on the mainland in a few hours.

Cló pushed through the stiff breeze, her heavy hair flopping about her face. The cottages huddled around her as she entered the village, close and tight, windows shuttered, doors bolted. Attempts to jolly up the façades with flower boxes of begonias and geraniums were a wasted effort. Little could liven up the dark alleys on even the brightest days, so dour was the atmosphere leaching up from the dank, cobbled lanes and flint walls.

Determined to be the tourist, Cló walked up one alley after another. Many of the cottages stood vacant with a sad air of decades-long abandonment. A couple of FOR SALE signs still valiantly declared their wares, and the village shop she stumbled across was shut.

Having expected to see a couple of tat shops and overpriced

art galleries at the least, Cló reached the far end of the village in a few minutes without seeing a soul but for a couple of bickering magpies. Looking back down the main street from a higher vantage point, she squinted hard, studying the village and the cliffs until her eyes swam. But try as she might, she could not fix the cliffs as she'd seen them last night with a deeper toehold into the bay. She could see only one church on the far side of the village. There was no squat church clinging to the precipice of the cliffs.

Her gaze rose to Grimdark Hall. It was far more picturesque from a distance, crouching at the head of Darrow Bay like a black toad contemplating its own mortality with the white-sailed windmills in the background.

A shiver goose-pimpled her bare skin. She knew it was her imagination but Grimdark Hall, dazzling yet sombre in a shimmering mirage, looked off-kilter, unfinished, with what appeared to be scaffolding running up its front façade. The image vanished between one blink and the next, and Grimdark stood steadfast and gloomy once more.

"Stop it, Cló!" she muttered, and continued up the cliff path to the promontory through a reed-strewn marsh—or *fen*, she corrected herself. Numerous channels oozed over black mud and stank of vegetative rot. The fen was a rhapsody played by the wind; the reeds aslither like a thousand violins, the sluggish water in the channels a soft percussion, and the deep booming croak of a hidden bittern setting the metred beat.

Her binoculars, which Jude found for Cló first thing that morning, remained unused around her neck. Birds weren't so foolish to be about in the rising wind, except for the secretive bittern. With a sigh, she turned to head back to the Hall, then stopped in surprise.

Cats. They were everywhere. Black cats sat on the cliff path, fur brushed spikily by the wind; more wove in and out of the reeds, and others sauntered out of the ruins of a cottage that had been mostly reclaimed by the fens. They came up to Cló from all directions with yellow-eyed suspicion.

Intrigued, she picked her way into the fen, her sneakers squelching into the black mud that was reluctant to let her pass without a fight for each step.

All that remained of the doorway was a buckled wooden frame. Cló stepped inside cautiously. The cottage hadn't been much; a single rectangular room and an earthen floor now riddled with pockmarks of a thousand storms endured. The roof was little more than a couple of rotting trusses and the wind hissed through the cracked flint walls like the discordant twang of harp strings. Black cats slipped through the gaps or sidled in behind Cló, curious to see what she was up to, while making it quite clear she was of no consequence either. It stank of cat piss.

But someone had been coming up here regularly; saucers of fresh milk and cat food lay about the place. Cló's feelings warmed slightly towards the village and whoever came up to this lonely spot to feed the feral cats.

For a brief moment, an overwhelming sense of familiarity swept over her, a strange sense of belonging, of coming home.

Startled at a flash of movement, she whipped around. Cló laughed at herself when another cat jumped through a hole in the wall with less feline grace than the creature would willingly admit. It ignored her and sat down, stuck a hind leg up in the air to lick its butt as though daring her to say anything about its momentary lapse in poise.

"It's haunted, you know."

With a screeched, "Haaah!" Cló spun to the entrance, a hand to her racing heart that threatened to leap right out of her chest.

A little girl stood framed in the doorway of the ruin, ethereal in the half-light of the storm rushing towards the mainland. She was the palest child Cló had ever seen. Hair so white it looked bleached, skin ashen, with the bluest eyes ringed by pale lashes. *Ghostlike* slunk into Cló's head.

"Hey, sweetie," she said, finding her voice. "Are you lost?" Her heart clenched as it always did when she saw a young girl. It was something she'd never told Jude, but as much as she longed for a child, her most secret, fervent hope had always been for a little girl.

"The witches lived here," the white-haired girl said solemnly.

"Did they?" said Cló faintly. She looked away with a shiver to avoid those old-soul eyes. "They can't have been very good witches if they lived here. It wouldn't have been much even before it was ruined."

"They were *good* witches."

"I'm sure they were," said Cló, because she couldn't think of anything else to say. While she longed for a child, she didn't actually know how to speak to children and hoped this wasn't an affliction but something she'd overcome once she had one of her own.

"You looked after people."

"*Me?*"

"Yes. When you lived here."

"Oh." Cló was out of her depth and quickly sinking. A sudden gust shook the shifting foundations of the ruin. "Shouldn't you be at—" *school* withered on her lips.

The doorway was empty. The little girl had vanished.

"That was weird," Cló told the cats, not entirely certain she hadn't been conversing with a ghost. Bewildered, she left the ruin and squelched back to the cliff path. There was no sign of the girl anywhere.

The storm chose that moment to upend the heavens onto the land.

Cló ran down the path. Her footsteps faltered, slowed, stopped. Turning fearfully, she cocked her head, straining to listen for the whisper she could've sworn she'd heard just as the storm erupted.

The wind shrieked, *Catch him, Crow!* . . . The reeds hissed, *Carry him, Kite!* . . . The watery channels sniggered, *Take him away till the apples are ripe* . . .

She half-ran, half-stumbled down the path, as fat raindrops splashed against her face.

When they are ripe and ready to fall . . . Here comes baby, apples and all . . .

Cló flew into the village and slammed into the first doorway with a protective porch. Shivering violently in the slither and chafe of the careering wind, she squinted up the cliff path, searching the storm's gloom for a figure, a silhouette, something human-shaped and skulking. Not the little girl. Someone else was up there, hiding in the reeds, listening to her weird conversation with the white-haired girl.

The Honeyborne sisters loomed large in her mind, especially Ruth after their conversation that morning . . . yes, that must be it. Of course, that's it! A vision of Ruth in her monk's habit drifting through the reeds flooded her mind and she kept her eyes fixed on the fens.

But all the while she sheltered under the porch, not a living soul ventured down the cliff path. By the time the storm abated enough to make a dash for Grimdark Hall, Cló had talked herself out of her fantasies. For why on earth would anyone be following her? Or had her imagination taken it a little too far and there hadn't been anyone there at all?

Cló saw little of Jude in the days that followed. As the storm battered the Norfolk coast he was up at first light for meetings with trustees of the estate, only returning late at night, long after dinner. She tried not to pry into his past, aware of the shadow it had cast over his life, and she understood his need to escape, to avoid his sisters and Grimdark. But it hurt that he wouldn't speak to her. She'd never known him this moody, this snappy, almost like he was slipping into a different persona or perhaps reverting back to the man he'd once been before leaving Grimdark.

With only his hated sisters if she wanted company, Cló haunted the Hall, drifting from room to room, unable to settle to anything. If ever a place should be filled with ghosts it was Grimdark. Draughts sent dust scurrying across the floor ahead of her with no obvious source she could find. Shadows piled up in corners like skulking creatures that fled when she turned the lights on. Her reflection caught in mirrors seemed to move a little too slowly as she passed.

But as she roamed the Hall, so, too, did Ruth and Constance. Cló wouldn't be in a room for more than two minutes when one of the sisters would appear and watch her just long enough for Cló to blush with embarrassment, unsure what she'd done wrong. It happened too often to be coincidence. Their constant vigilance was unsettling at first, but soon grew alarming. Feeling more and more like a trespasser, Cló found herself peeking into rooms before entering, tiptoeing down long corridors and eating at odd hours to avoid meeting the sisters by chance in the kitchens.

Though her mind was nomadic and far-reaching, taking everything one step further into the realms of *what if* and *if only*, nothing Cló imagined compared to the startling reality of Ruth Honeyborne. Her costumes ranged from a flamenco dancer to an ancient Roman in a toga that clung to her skinny chest, to full Venetian Carnivale regalia with an outrageous papier-mâché mask of blue ostrich feathers. And with each new persona, Ruth adapted her posture, mannerisms, patterns of speech—or spoke a different language. Cló was disappointed she'd not yet met the Zulu, her mind boggling at the idea of this white, wrinkled woman dressed in skins and little else. Dear god! Would she be bare-chested?

It was only at night, when Grimdark Hall was dressed in midnight, that Cló felt able to breathe freely. The dark was her disguise; it didn't judge like cruel daylight and held few terrors for her. But in those stolen hours, Cló and Grimdark came to an understanding. Though she still sensed its reticence, still a stranger to be viewed with caution, she gained a feel for the old building's foibles and quirks, and in return, it slowly revealed its secrets and treasures.

Just before 1:45 a.m. every night, Cló made a point of being in the Great Hall to watch Constance through the vast windows stomp across the courtyard to the shed, come out with a shovel and head into the family chapel. Cló's curiosity consumed her, but she had not yet built up the courage to follow her sister-in-law, fearing she might be confronted with her dark imaginings of Constance spending her nights burying the bodies of her victims.

It was four days before the weather let up. Jude had left early and Cló was left to her own devices once again. She ventured outside, desperate to escape the sisters' constant scrutiny, and was soon running pell-mell along the cliff path, glorying in the big, silent sky and the land so flat she could see the curvature of the earth. She delighted in the deceptive contradiction of the fens on one side, a death trap to the unwary, and the sea on the other, pushed back from the land, leaving rippled sandbanks stretching for miles; an uncertain, in-between place that was neither sea nor land.

Slowing to a walk with a sharp stitch in her side, her lungs heaving like bellows, Cló found a heathery spot on the cliff's edge and lay down. She wound the strap of her binoculars about her wrist and snuggled down into the damp earth.

The simple joy of birdwatching was that it could be done anywhere. The sea was as grey and wrinkled as an elephant's hide. Seabirds in their thousands exulted in the respite from the recent storm, screeching, whittling and cawing on the rockface, the stench of guano overpowering. On the sandbanks below, sandpipers scuttled and curlews nodded in a stately fashion as though their long curved bills were too heavy for their heads.

Binoculars glued to her eyes, Cló fell into a concentrated, hypnotic state, quickly identifying fulmars, and various gulls and terns, while aware of the staccato *pit-pit-pit-pit* of a shy Cetti's warbler like a tiny jackhammer in the fens behind her.

"Holy mother of fuck!"

"Oomph . . ." Cló moaned. Twisting onto her back she gaped as the woman who'd just trodden on her fell flat on her butt. She looked like a bedraggled scarecrow wearing a top hat, a sight so utterly incongruous on the edge of the cliff with the wide sky stretched out behind her.

"Sorry," said Cló automatically.

The scarecrow gave a sharp bark of laughter. "Sorry? I trod on you! I'm the one who should be apologising." She frowned at the binoculars still gripped tightly in Cló's hands, then startled Cló again by flopping onto her stomach in a jingle and clash of bracelets, rings and necklaces beside her.

"What were you looking at?" she asked.

"Um—birds?" said Cló lamely, and held out her binoculars as a defence and an excuse.

"Oh, a twitcher. Should've known, really. We're always getting your sort up and about on the cliffs. Plenty of birds about too." She waved both hands like she was conducting the birds' screeching cacophony.

Rolling back onto her stomach Cló tried not to stare too obviously at the scarecrow. "Are you on a walk?" she asked, unable to think of anything else to say and hoped she didn't gabble inanely as she usually did when confronted by strangers.

"God, no!" The scarecrow grimaced. "I've been looking for toads."

Cló blinked in confusion. "Toads? As in the ones that should be kissed to turn into a prince sort of toad?"

The scarecrow snorted. "Yeah, that sort." Another grimace. "Tricky buggers are toads, but fortune-telling doesn't pay as well as I'd like."

"Why on earth would you be out catching toads?" said Cló, storing the fortune-telling question for the next volley.

The scarecrow gave a grunting sort of laugh, rather like a hyena with more grunt than giggle. "There's a place down the way as needs toads for research. Some of them are endangered, but the scientists there are lazy buggers and pay good money for toads. That's if I can catch the little bastards; they're as slippery as all fuck and stink like a miner's armpit. But needs must, and all that good stuff." She stuck out a grimy hand. "Luna Destiny." She grinned at Cló's raised eyebrows. "Stage name, but Maud Figgis just doesn't have the same mystique."

Cló shook the proffered hand gingerly, the bracelets clashing madly. She resisted the urge to wipe her hand on the grass afterwards. "Cló Honeyborne. Pleased to meet you."

"A Honeyborne?"

"Through marriage," Cló was quick to add.

"Ah. You must be the wife. I'd heard down Grimdark way that the lord of the manor had returned." The sneer in her tone disappeared as quickly as it appeared. "My daughter said she'd seen you roaming about the Hall at night."

"Does she work there?" Cló hadn't seen any servants at the Hall, but there had to be some; she couldn't imagine the sisters cooking for themselves or cleaning their rooms.

"God, no! I'd kill her first. She goes up there sometimes at night and sneaks in. She likes looking at the treasures—not to steal them," she added hastily, mistaking Cló's horrified expression for suspicion. "She likes looking at pretty things, and the Hall has plenty and to spare that no one ever looks at."

Gripping her binoculars, a shiver of unease curled up Cló's spine. Apart from Constance, she'd not seen anyone on her nightly roaming. "And she's never been caught?"

"Not by the sisters, but they know she sneaks in. Not sure why they've never said anything. It's not usually their style. God knows they're always complaining about something and lording it over the village." She shrugged. "To be fair, they do own most of the village—" Her eyes narrowed speculatively at Cló. "Or perhaps they don't. Bet that's why you and your husband are back. Come to claim the inheritance, no doubt."

"Um . . ." said Cló, without any intention of telling this strange woman what Jude and her plans were for the Hall. She reddened under Luna's questioning stare.

"It's like that, is it?" said Luna with a knowing smirk. "You'd best watch out for those sisters. Evil bitches they are. And you seem a decent sort. Don't let them give you too much grief."

"Ruth's not so bad," said Cló, not because she felt any solidarity with the Honeyborne sisters, but her natural honesty demanded it. "A bit odd, that's all."

Luna snorted. "Very odd I call it, what with all those getups of hers. Saw her decked out in full Victorian crinoline once, mooching along the walls. Nearly scared the daylights out of me."

Cló raised an eyebrow at this, for Ruth was not the only one with strange costumes.

Luna pulled up a blade of grass to suck, her eyes narrowed on the sea. A breeze combed the reeds behind them, bringing with it a resurgence of little rustles of creatures making their way cautiously through the numerous channels after Luna's loud, jangling arrival.

"She's not so bad when she's by herself is Ruth," she said. "But never forget she's Constance's little soldier and does everything she says. That Ruth would kill as look at you if Constance gave the nod." She smiled brightly, a wild light in her eyes. "But as you're up and about at night, I'll be calling on you come the next full moon. Could always do with an extra pair of hands for picking."

"Picking?" said Cló faintly.

"Yeah. Got to be at the right time, mind, or my remedies won't work." She stared at Cló until she grew uncomfortable. "We've odd eyes in our family too," she said. "Rare that, is odd eyes. But at least you aren't squint like my Aunt Gertrude. Imagine odd eyes and a squint. She has a blue eye on the heavens and a brown eye on the devil. Scared the shit out of me as a kid, I don't mind telling you."

Cló had no response to this rather overwhelming statement but felt empathy for poor squinting Aunt Gertrude.

"Hah!" cried Luna. "Maybe we're related. Wouldn't that be a cackle? You and me meeting here at the arsehole end of the world and being second cousins ten times removed and not knowing. Fate and destiny are twin bitches, I don't mind telling you."

Cló's hand drifted up to her eyes. "Heterochromia. The—er—odd-coloured eyes is not hereditary as far as I know," she said hesitantly, not wanting to offend Luna.

"Isn't it? Well, that's a bit of a bugger to my theories."

The idea of being related to anyone in the area was not as unlikely as it sounded, but Cló decided not to mention her connection to Norfolk; Luna seemed the sort to take a little information and run with it until she'd have them as first cousins by marriage in a minute.

She leapt to her feet as suddenly as she dropped to her stomach, not able to stay in one place for long. "I'm off to find my toads. I'll be seeing you, *Lady* Cló Honeyborne." She sauntered off the cliff path and into the reeds where the fens started their soggy march inland.

Cló blinked owlishly; it had been a peculiar conversation, with possibly the most peculiar person she'd ever met. She scrapped that—Ruth still held that title. There were so many things she wished she'd asked: the fortune-telling, of course, but especially the name Figgis. The name of a witch who seemed like a character from a fairy tale when Jude told it. And if anyone were to be named witch it would be Luna Destiny, aka Maud Figgis.

She'll never catch a toad, thought Cló, as Luna jingled and crashed through the reeds. *They'll hear her a mile off.* She laughed out loud at the image of the strange, top-hatted scarecrow leaping about after toads in the numerous channels, her bangles and chains clashing, and the toads leaping away in fright from the jangling giant trying to capture them.

As Luna's top hat bobbed further into the distance, Cló smiled up at the brooding sky the colour of a week-old bruise. She had delighted in this chance meeting and hoped the mad scarecrow did come calling to take her picking.

SIX

Cló slipped through the old weather-stiffened door of the chapel as she came in from the cliffs. She hadn't meant to enter. If she was being honest with herself, which she wasn't often, she was rather terrified of the chapel; it had grown in her mind to represent Constance and her nastiness.

The chapel appeared bigger inside than it did from outside. It smelt old, the kind of old Cló had never experienced in Canada; built when the world was still believed to be flat, demons were as real as breathing, and Canada hadn't been more than a wistful dream of some seafaring European king.

Two rows of wooden pews ran the length of the vaulted nave creating a central aisle. Enormous piers, more suited to a cathedral, were interspersed by graceful arches that came to a rounded point at the plain apse.

Wandering between the columns, Cló soaked up the gentle silence, then stopped in the apse behind the stone altar.

"Oh!" she murmured in surprise.

Cló took out her phone and beamed its torch down the set of steps, the width of a coffin, carved into the chalk leading down beneath the chapel. Her toes curled with trepidation as curiosity tingled across her skin—if the chapel represented heaven on earth, surely what lay below must be hell. A quick glance over her shoulder; the chapel was as silent and empty as when she'd entered. No one knew where she was. It would be foolhardy to step down the path leading to hell.

Before she could talk herself out of it, her veins fluttering with nervous anticipation, her heart beating a little too fast, she crept down the worn stairs, feeling as intrepid as Carter entering Tutankhamun's tomb for the first time.

At the bottom was a closed door. It wasn't locked. She pushed it open; there was no creaking groan, though it was the sort of door that demanded a creak.

"Holy shit!" In the phone's meagre light, a groin-vaulted ceiling supported by a petrified forest of fragile pillars disappeared into midnight darkness. Between the pillars were tombs and statues, a sepulchral garden of death. It was dry and dusty with chalk dust, like the tombs she and Jude had visited in Egypt on their honeymoon. Yet Norfolk was a flat wet county, and she couldn't fathom how moisture hadn't seeped down here.

With no idea how far back the crypt went, Cló hesitated to move too far from the stairs. It was easy to envision getting lost amongst generations of dead Honeybornes to end up as the only skeleton without its own tomb.

Her breathing was the only sound, fragmenting as it left her mouth to curl around the pillars, returning with the faintest of echoes. Skin crawling, Cló twisted around, sensing another presence. No one was there. She was alone with the dead.

Chiding herself, she took her fear firmly in hand and crept closer to the nearest wall.

Cló recoiled in horror. Every inch was a relief of a macabre hell. Demons shovelled the damned into burning cauldrons. Sinners, with symbols of their heinous deeds tied around their necks, marched across one wall. The unrepentant were hounded by pitchforked devils and baying hounds. Cursed souls were eaten by horrible monsters.

No reliefs of heaven, no angels or a kindly-faced god for the virtuous. The Honeybornes were all doomed to hell. They hadn't needed a witch's curse, they had known they were doomed long before.

Cló backed away towards the stairs. Turning blindly, she barrelled into the arms of a statue.

Expecting more horror, she peered up into a face of sweet purity.

"Hello," she whispered to the beautiful woman, immortalised in white marble. The dry air took her uttered word and hustled it into the deepest, darkest recesses.

The tomb beside the statue was simple and elegant. It stood apart from the others, segregated in death, unsullied by later centuries. A beacon of innocence amidst the wretchedness of the lives that came before and after.

A plaque on the lid was in Latin, the only words Cló could make out was the name Isabella Matilda Honeyborne and, after screwing up her eyes to work out the Roman numerals, the dates 1200 to 1215.

"So young." Her fingers brushed across the epitaph, kept pristine in the silent darkness for eight hundred years. The love felt for this girl radiated from the distant past like a waiting sigh. Cló gazed up at Isabella Honeyborne's likeness, her frozen arms outstretched, a slight smile on her cold, pale face, hair covered by a veil. She would have been beautiful in the fashion of any century.

Cló wanted to share her discovery with someone, the one person she'd shared everything with. And Jude could read Latin, which had never been in any way useful before, but now seemed a positive boon. They might genuinely need a ball of twine, Cló decided, for she'd only explored one room, but she could sense spaces in the darkness, probably hundreds of them, and she had every intention of exploring them all.

She started towards the stairs, then stopped. Frowning, she hurried towards a tomb set back in a niche, more opulent and bigger than any of the others. Someone had gashed a hole in the side with little thought or care of what they might disturb.

Lips tight with anger, Cló directed the phone's light through the hole to the mouldering skeleton within that had lain undisturbed for centuries. She knew who that someone was. Constance Honeyborne.

And now she was looking for it, Cló noted the desecration of all the tombs along one wall of the deep room.

"So that's what you've been up to," Cló whispered, picturing her horrible sister-in-law creeping about the crypt in the middle of the night with her shovel. There had been no piety, no weird prayer she'd been doing before some midnight gardening—and that was some of Cló's gentler surmising.

But it raised a number of questions: Why? What was Constance searching for? What possible secrets could the skeletons of these dead Honeybornes be hiding after all this time?

"I met a woman I could see myself being friends with today," said Cló, snuggling deeper into Jude's side, revelling in his nearness that had been withheld from her for days. She hadn't been able to hide her joy when he walked into the Silver Dining Room halfway through yet another stilted, silent dinner with the sisters.

"That's great."

She heard the caution in his tone, felt the tension in his body, holding himself tight in her embrace. She ran her fingertips up and down his chest in long, soothing strokes, like she would a distressed cat.

"I know we're not going to be here forever, and we said no ties, but it was nice to speak to someone who has no connection to the Hall, and Luna was—" She grinned. "She's a little nuts, I think. But in a good way."

"And her name's Luna?"

"It gets better: Luna Destiny. A stage name for when she does fortune-telling."

Cló beamed when Jude burst out laughing. It seemed too long since she'd heard him laugh.

"Well, it's more mysterious than her real name, Maud Figgis, which is rather a dreadful name for a fortune-teller."

"Figgis? Then she'll be local. There's hundreds of Figgises in the area."

"I did wonder about that. The witch you told me about was also called Figgis."

"Don't read anything into it. I doubt your Luna Destiny is a descendant of Euphemia Figgis. From what I can remember of the story all the Figgis women were burnt at the stake, and there weren't any children. Your new friend is probably from a different branch."

"Pity. If anyone's witchy, it's Luna Destiny. I liked her. Oh!" Cló sat up, saying, "I haven't told you about that. I think I met a ghost in the village a few days ago." A prickle of guilt stabbed her chest, laced with sadness. She usually told Jude everything, but they'd had little chance recently and she hadn't wanted to bother him with how she passed her days.

Cló traced her fingers along the dark rings underneath Jude's shut eyes, and wiped away his heavy frown only for it to bounce back in deep ridges moments later.

"You're letting your imagination run away with you. There's no such thing as ghosts—except the Grey Lady—but every stately home in the country has a Grey Lady."

"Why am I only hearing about this now?" Cló demanded, shaking Jude's arm so he opened one eye, smiling slightly.

"I did wonder if you might meet her on one of your midnight meanders," he teased. "And there's supposedly a ghoul or something living in the dungeons. On very still nights you can hear his chains rattling." His jaw tightened, a muscle ticked under his skin. "My sisters took great delight in scaring the shit out of me when I was young about the ghostly rider who is only seen one night each year to let the family know some battle had been lost. Gave me nightmares for years."

"That's nasty!" Cló exclaimed, horrified and wondering if perhaps that wasn't the incident that stopped Jude from falling asleep by himself.

"They did far worse," he admitted and rolled over, away from Cló.

"Stop locking me out, Jude," she said softly, pulling him onto his back again. "Speak to me."

His Adam's apple shifted, and she thought he might confide his secrets in the sanctity of the blue cave where they were safe from his sisters, from Grimdark. But his barriers to his past were firmly up when he said, "Tell me about your ghost."

Sighing in defeat, Cló curled herself around him and spoke of her meeting with the little girl in the ruin.

"What made you go up there? It's right on the other side of the village."

"There wasn't much happening in the village, so I walked up a bit and sort of stumbled across the ruined cottage."

"And no one had told you that was the witches' cottage? The ones who were burnt?"

"No! Is that true?"

A shrug. "So everyone says. I doubt it. I'd say it probably went into the sea with the rest of the village when the cliff collapsed. Don't let your imagination run away with you, love. Not here. There's enough shite going on without working yourself up about ghosts and witches."

It wasn't meant unkindly; he knew her well enough to know she'd be fascinated by anything dark and creepy. It had always puzzled and intrigued Jude, this dark side of Cló's, that she was generally timid until in an old graveyard or an abandoned building and her imagination went into overdrive.

"How did it go with the executors today?" she asked when Jude's breathing didn't deepen with sleep.

"Not well. The village is a stumbling block . . . one of many," Jude amended. "It's taking a lot longer to tie everything up than I'd thought." He grimaced with his eyes closed. "I didn't have a clue what we, as a family, were responsible for. We own a lot of the houses, and I want to give them to the villagers, or anyone who'll take them, but the lawyers say I can't. There's some old legal precedent."

"I noticed a lot of the houses were empty or for sale."

"Mmmm . . ." said Jude drowsily. "No one wants to buy them. The cliff's not safe, and frankly most of the houses are on the verge of collapse. It truly will be a ghost town soon."

Cló pondered this, then opened her mouth to tell Jude about her discovery of the crypt that afternoon. She smiled. He'd fallen asleep in mid thought. Her discovery would have to keep until tomorrow.

With Jude's deepened breathing a quiet echo in their draped cave, Cló slipped out of bed.

Her nostrils twitched. There was an odour in the room. It didn't belong to Jude or Cló, or the mice she was certain they were cohabitating with. Yet it smelt familiar. Recently familiar. Unable to place it, she shrugged on her jeans and a sweater before stepping out quietly into the corridor.

Like all old buildings, Grimdark's noises that were lost during the energy of daytime came into their own at night. The ticks and creaks, and the occasional weird murmuring no longer made Cló dart for the camouflage of shadows or peer hard down long corridors. She ran her hands gently over its banisters and along its old walls as though gentling a frightened creature, and Grimdark responded with a deep purr that came up through its pipes, perhaps sensing she was a kindred spirit, another frightened creature finding comfort in the dark.

Traversing the Great Hall, she wondered whether to venture once more into the Hall of Curiosities, or perhaps explore a new area. Halfway across, she froze.

Voices were coming towards her.

Cló panicked. Eyes darting for a hiding place, she scuttled inside the unused hearth of the ornamental fireplace, big enough to hold five tall men standing straight. Heart beating like the clappers, she pressed against the cold tiles, as the disembodied voices grew stronger.

The gravel of Constance's deep voice became distinct as the sisters entered the Great Hall. "Are you sure it's her? You've been wrong before."

Then Ruth's little girl voice, "Of course I'm not sure."

"Mmmm . . . we'll need to keep an eye on her, see what she does. She could be the key."

They didn't switch any lights on but followed the powerful beam of a torch. Cló had never known such penny-pinching women. They lived in this great big house, and money was not tight according to Jude, who was privy to the accounts of the estate, yet the sisters lived frugally, as though they were a wasted penny away from poverty.

They were almost across the Great Hall, their features deformed in the unflattering torchlight, their shadows lengthening and twisting behind them like monstrous things, their voices loud and hollow.

"Well?" said Constance. "What are we going to do about the Fat Mouse?"

"Oh Con, you are so bad sometimes," giggled Ruth. It sounded wrong hearing a little girl giggle coming from a woman in her fifties. Constance snorted and Ruth said, "What do *you* think we should do?"

"God knows. And god knows why he had to bring her with him. An American! Of all the people to marry."

Cló's fragile self-esteem withered to a dried apple core, not knowing what hurt most, being called fat in such snide tones or a mouse.

Then they were gone, leaving the Great Hall in majestic, silent gloom and Cló in tears. She stepped out of the fireplace and wiped her cheeks, angry at herself for allowing their spite to bother her when the sisters weren't even aware their unkind words had hit their mark. *That's what comes from eavesdropping*, she chided herself. It was one of the few things she remembered her mom telling her: eavesdroppers never heard anything good about themselves.

The sisters' fading footsteps echoed back to Cló like a snake rustling across the Great Hall's dusty floor. Grimdark crouched over her in wary sympathy, trembling slightly as though fearful of being rebuffed with anger.

Cló reached up to pat the mantelpiece above her to soothe the old building. She sensed Grimdark didn't like the sisters any more than she did. They'd always taken it for granted: a possession, nothing more. They had no feel for the history that had shaped Grimdark, didn't care about its whims and traits. They didn't understand that Grimdark needed kindness to thrive.

With another comforting pat on the mantelpiece, Cló crept across the Great Hall, having lost her desire to explore the Hall of Curiosities. She opened the ancient locking mechanism with familiarity and breathed in deep lungfuls of cool night air to purge the taint of the Honeyborne sisters from every part of her.

Gathering her tattered courage, Cló's attention slid to the chapel. She could see herself hurrying across the courtyard to wait in the crypt until Constance came in with her shovel at 1:45 a.m. as she did every night. It wasn't far off that time now. Cló instantly discarded the idea as stupid. She didn't need to see with her own eyes to know it was Constance desecrating the tombs. Did Ruth know what her sister did in the middle of the night? Cló thought not. Constance's nightly activities spoke of a lonely furtiveness, knowledge meant for only one.

The decision was taken from her when she caught a movement on the walls out the corner of her eye.

On the breathless air came a high-pitched chanting, "*Catch him, Crow! Carry him, Kite* . . ."

Cló's stomach tensed with fascinated horror as a pale figure moved quickly along the walls, disappearing and reappearing between each crenelation.

"*Take him away till the apples are ripe* . . ."

"Hello?" Cló called, her voice thin, a warble of fear.

"*When they are ripe and ready to fall* . . ."

Taking to her feet, Cló raced after the apparition, keeping her eyes on it as she squeezed up the spiral staircase leading to the top of the walls.

"*Here comes baby, apples and all.*"

Emerging onto the high walkway, Cló was in time to see a flicker of paleness disappear into the ancient crookedness of the Hermitage.

Haring after it, she was forced to stop to search the rounded wall of the Hermitage for the entrance. She found it tucked away, a hidden portal only the foolish would enter. There was no door, merely a thin, unfussy opening in the stones.

The Hermitage rose above Cló like a kinked finger pointing out her fate in the stars; a short fate if she was to enter a desperately derelict old building on the edge of an unstable cliff in the middle of the night after something that was quite possibly a ghost.

Even so, Cló and her deadly curiosity entered.

It hit her the moment she passed through the walls, a visceral shudder of déjà vu. Without reason or memory, Cló knew she had been here before.

A stone staircase spiralled up the innards of the tower like a deformed spine, snapped off abruptly by a bricked-in door at the very top. There had once been floors above, the rotted trusses still poking from the walls with open doorways leading to rooms none could enter without a fearless leap from the staircase.

Without thinking, Cló stepped into the recess behind the skeletal stairs and frowned down at the floor layered with centuries of bat guano. Something should've been there, something was missing.

Shivering in the cool air oozing through the arrow slits, she breathed deeply to calm herself, determined not to take off on a flight of fancy that led nowhere.

There was a rational explanation. Of course there was. Perhaps it was something she'd read and retained like a loose memory. Or perhaps nothing so cerebral, but a scent, an odour remembered from somewhere else . . .

"I nearly died here."

Cló whipped around with a cry to the little white-haired girl watching her unblinkingly.

"You again! Who are you?" Cló demanded, her voice harsh with fright. "And how old are you? You should be in bed at this time of night."

The little girl smiled serenely and said nothing.

"Did you—did you die here?" Cló hazarded, on the off chance the proof of the supernatural was standing in front of her.

"No . . . I *nearly* died here. When I was a pirate."

"Oh," said Cló, nonplussed. "Well, that must've been nice . . . being a pirate, I mean." She shook her head at her lame response, but what did one say to a possible ghost girl?

"It wasn't. It was horrible. I was a slave first and got whipped all the time. I went to the desert, and that's where I became a pirate. Then I nearly died when my ship got shipwrecked down there." She pointed to the bay where the relentless waves seethed against the cliffs. "But you rescued me."

"Did I? . . . Of course, I did," Cló said when the girl eyed her expectantly.

"We were friends."

"Were we? I mean, of course we were."

The girl stared at Cló for a long uncomfortable moment. "You have her eyes," she said, and walked out of the Hermitage.

Cló ran after her along the walls. But the girl was gone.

Looking down at her trembling hands, Cló murmured, "It was just a ghost. Oh my god! What am I saying? It was *just* a ghost!"

A sharp pain burrowed into Cló's brain, sending her to her knees. She vomited, then staggered to her feet. Sobbing, she stumbled back into the Hermitage as someone else's memory imprinted on her retina with the crackliness of an old movie reel left to run.

1645

Effie hated the Hermitage. It straddled a corner of the wall guarding Honeyborne Hall like a gnarled thumb. Few entered the ancient tower, for there were stories of lights seen at night, though an anchorite had not acted as lighthouse keeper for many a century. And though the weather was mild, with barely a breath of wind to set the tower shuddering as she lugged the wounded pirate inside, her spine tingled with foreboding.

But for this very reason, it was the perfect place to hide an injured man, especially a pirate. For none would dare venture within these shivering, ghostly walls.

Effie set the pirate down next to the spiral staircase, out of sight of the doorway and the wind blowing in through the arrow-slit openings. She was almost too scared to touch the man though he was unconscious and hadn't woken as she had hauled him none too gently through the tunnels in the cliffs that led to Honeyborne Hall.

Cursing herself for a fool, she gingerly prodded him with a

*boot. He did not move, except a faint flutter of his white eye-
lashes. With a sigh and another inward curse, she knelt beside
him and took off his clothes, placing them in a neat pile beside
him. Once he was naked she felt around his body, feeling the
lumps of broken ribs in his chest, the terrible gash in his right
thigh, another at his waist and abrasions where the waves had
tossed the pirate repeatedly against the rocks, grating off his
skin. She turned him over and recoiled in horror. His back was
thick with a crisscross of scars from whippings over a long period.*

*"What happened to you, bor?" she whispered, running her
fingers lightly over the scars. "It ent been an easy life you've
had." She rolled him onto his back again. "You'll live if infection dunt set in," she murmured to her rescued patient, not liking the way her words susurrated around the shuddering tower
to come back to her with a sharp edge.*

*Head to one side, she regarded the sleeping man's face, the
thatch of ashen hair, the thin face more suited to a scholar than
a pirate. Her eyes narrowed. There was something about him,
something almost familiar. Perhaps the shape of his nose or the
droop of his eyes that reminded her of someone else.*

*Under her breath she muttered, "Catch him, Crow! Carry
him, Kite!" as she was wont to do in moments of stress. Germaine had said she'd come out the womb with the rhyme on her
lips, yet none knew where she had learnt it. For Germaine it had
been an omen, though whether for good or evil she was never
clear. She, too, had taken to chanting it whenever she felt a situation warranted a bit of shaking up.*

*"Hah!" she yelled and tried to pull away from the hand grip-
ping her wrist tightly.*

"Waar bin ik?" The pirate's words were slurred and heavy.

*"I dunt speak yar furrin lingo, bor," she said, speaking slowly,
as though she could make herself understood anyway.*

"Waar bin ik?" Urgent now, the grip on Effie's wrist increasing. Forcing her hand to lie limply in his grip, she swallowed. "Yar Dutch," she said, having heard Dutch sailors down in King's Lynn. "But yar dressed as a Turk. What are you then? A Dutch Turk?"

His grip loosened and fell away as he grimaced, arching against the floor with a spasm of pain.

"What's yar name, bor?" said Effie, keeping her voice and tone soft.

He stared at her blankly. He did not seem alarmed by her odd-coloured eyes.

Pointing to herself, she said, "I'm Euphemia Figgis. Effie most call me. You understandin' me? Effie."

A slight frown under his shock of bone-white hair. "Effie?" he hazarded.

"Yis. And who you be?" She pointed at his chest.

"Yusef an-Nur."

It was Effie's turn to stare at him blankly. "How's a body to pronounce that?"

Something in her tone sent the pirate's lips quirking into a small smile. "Misshien is Jozef Roggeveen beter," he said slowly.

"That ent much better," Effie grumbled. "Though I'm hearin' somethin' akin to Joseph, so we'll be callin' you Joseph. A fine name is Joseph. Can't be doing with the rest o' it. Why a body is in need o' two names is beyond me, and neither o' any sense."

The pirate said, "Joseph," to himself. He raised his pale eyebrows, shrugged, and patted the ground beside him. "Engeland?"

"You speak English?" said Effie, astonished.

A blank stare before the pirate scrunched up his face, as though dredging up a painful memory, and said, "Here . . . Engeland?"

"*Yis, yar in England, and much good it'll do you. You'll be fer the hangman if you dunt keep yar gob shut and lay low.*" The pirate stared at her blankly once more. Then his face creased with sudden panic, alarming Effie so she sprang to her feet, not sure if he was about to attack her or if he'd heard something outside that boded ill for them both.

To her astonishment, the pirate reared up like he'd been stung by a bee. He spied the pile of his clothes Effie had placed next to him. He ripped them apart, searching furiously through the pockets of his breeches, shirt and coat.

Effie took a step nearer, curious in spite of herself. "*What's the matter, bor?*" she asked softly.

He muttered something in his lingo, the only word she got was "*kiswa,*" and only because he kept repeating it. He shook his head at her blank look and searched once more through his clothing.

His panic receded when he pulled out a small scrap of tapestried material. He kissed it, then collapsed onto the floor once more as his spurt of strength vanished, and held the scrap of material to his chest.

"*What's that then?*" asked Effie, baffled by the man's panic over a small bit of material.

He babbled once more in a mash of two languages, some words guttural like those she'd heard the Dutch sailors speak, others lilting, flowing into each other like a spoken song.

Gazing at Effie's blank face, he sighed and held up the bit of tapestried cloth. "*Kiswa! Kiswa!*" He pointed to the ceiling, and mimed what looked like a dome, before snipping his fingers like a pair of shears. "*Geluk!*"

"*I have no idea what yar saying, bor, but I'm thinking that there bit o' rag be important to you. A talisman?*" She reached out a tentative hand to touch the cloth, then withdrew it when the pirate pulled it out of reach. "*Well, yar welcome to yar bit o'* rag . . . *Now listen here, Joseph, yar to keep yarself quiet whiles I go git what I'll be needin' to tend yar wounds. You understandin' me?"*

After a pantomime to get her point across, the pirate nodded, before closing his eyes.

With a shiver of apprehension, Effie scanned the bare, ruined tower, unable to shake the off-kilter feeling she was forgetting something. Shaking her head, she covered the pirate with the jacket she'd taken off him, and headed out into the night.

Few lights still burnt in Darrow End when Effie emerged from the honeycomb of tunnels into the village. She didn't pass anyone on the way, though her being abroad at night would not have raised undue comment, for the cunning folk were the ones who were always called out at odd hours to tend those in need.

The narrow, crooked alleys between the fishermen's cottages were quiet but for the plaintive mewling of a cat.

Effie ignored the distressed cry. She could not be distracted, having already made enough trouble for herself with the pirate.

The mewling grew louder as she neared the last cottage. Effie's footsteps slowed, her heart sinking with the knowledge of the cat's suffering. She stopped altogether, now hearing the desperate scrabble of claws with the mewling.

Effie touched the cottage wall and ran her hands along it until her fingers came away damp with newly buttered mortar around a couple of bricks. Taking out a small knife from a pocket, she levered out the bricks and sighed at the black kittling that had been boarded up in the wall to ward off witches. It was a common practice, but one she despised.

She picked up the kittling and huddled it to her chest until its little heart pounded in tandem with her own. She spied a little stone bottle hidden with the kittling.

"Pillocks," Effie muttered and snatched up the bottle. She quickly put the bricks back and patted the damp mortar into *place before hurrying along the short path to the Figgis cottage on the edge of the cliff.*

Once inside, she put the kittling onto the floor. It was immediately surrounded by the black cats Effie and Germaine had rescued over the years from a similar fate. A saucer of milk, and the kittling was purring.

Effie glanced at the single bed in the cottage where Germaine and Sophie slept. A bowl of porridge covered by a cloth waited for her on the table, but she didn't have time to eat. She hurried over to the sideboard, hid the witch bottle at the back of a drawer with the others she'd found in similar circumstances, then rattled quietly amongst the pots and bowls on the counter. She was out of what she needed for the pirate.

Cursing herself for a fool, not for the first time that night, Effie headed out again and across the wide fens. Guided by what little light the gibbous moon provided she made her way to Dunge Marsh, a mottled patch overlooking the Wash. A sharp, gusting wind rose from the Wash, that great tidal estuary that flooded the fens every day.

Effie set to digging by the light of the moon for what she needed, before moving into Tangled Wood that was no wood at all but a large copse of trees not far from Dunge. To the sleepy murmur of bees, she grunted her way up a tree and shoved her hand into the hive hidden in a hollow halfway up. While the bees buzzed halfheartedly around her, none stung her. They were clever creatures and knew it was Effie who left sugared water in a nearby fork of their tree in payment for the honey she took, but never too much to destroy the hive.

It was too beautiful a night to hurry home, though Effie knew she must. But she took a rare moment for herself and stepped up to the edge of the cliff overlooking the Wash. Its black mud and scurrying waters were transformed by the night into a place both lovely and eerie, of shadows and moonlight.

There was a gilded freedom in stolen moments like these. She could be someone else, living someone else's life, forget the dank and gloom of her own. And perhaps the moonlight infected and addled Effie's mind, for her vision swam and took on the view of another, not far from where she stood, down in the Wash but in a time different to her own, into the past. She fell to her knees and, through odd-coloured eyes so like her own, viewed the beauty before her replaced by stinking death.

SEVEN

❧

Grimdark Hall hunched over Cló like a black heron wrapping its wings around her in a canopy of false security as she waited in the Blue Suite for Jude to return. Queasy yet starving, she couldn't face the Silver Dining Room and the sisters by herself tonight.

Her world had tilted a degree. As much as she tried to put last night down to imagination, Cló couldn't stop feeling something else altogether had happened in the Hermitage. She'd always been sensitive to atmosphere, able to weave the fantastical around the mundane. And if ever a place screamed atmosphere, it was the Hermitage; the ancient tower on the verge of toppling into the wild sea below coupled with a ghostly child sprouting nonsense about pirates.

Logical explanations were in short supply. A hallucination brought on by a tricky stomach and exhaustion was her most rational answer, but she kept prodding at the edges of impossibility. A waking dream? A vision? A delusion? The manifestation of some sort of undiagnosed latent psychosis?

All of those options would be feasible if it had been the first time, if it hadn't felt so real. Even now she could recall the stench of blood and body odour of the man, Joseph, the fur of the kitten against her chin, the lazy buzz of the bees in the tree like a faded memory . . . Someone else's memory. Her snort of derision was loud in the Blue Suite. A memory from someone not of this century? Even for Cló that was a stretch. A portal? Except she hadn't stepped through anything—unless the Hermitage itself was a portal.

"Jesus," Cló muttered. "What am I thinking? I'm not twelve!" That had not been a cupboard leading to Narnia or stepping through a wall to platform nine and three quarters. It had been dark and smelly, and quiet and dangerous in a way her twenty-first-century perceptions could not understand.

She tried to concentrate on the screen of the laptop as she had been all day. But a moment later she was staring out a window obscured by the heavy fog that had rolled in from the sea during the early hours of morning. It clung to Grimdark like a cold sweat, obliterating shape and form, sliding clammy fingers across the glass.

Growling at herself and the ancestry website she'd registered with that morning, Cló opened her family bible, breathing in the odour of old cracked leather and slightly rank suet. It was precious to her, her one heirloom that reinforced the differences between herself and Jude, who had heirlooms aplenty and cared for none of them.

The only information she had to go on was the list of names written on the flyleaf in a neat, old-fashioned hand, with Benjamin, Reginald Hobbis, and his wife Sophronia at the top.

It wasn't the first ancestry website Cló had registered with; she'd tried to trace her origins some time ago. The information she'd gleaned then was the same as what she was staring at now; one Benjamin Reginald Hobbis, and his wife, Sophronia, boarded the *Dilligence* on the 30th of September, 1645, in Ipswich and arrived in Jamestown, Virginia, on the 3rd of December, 1645.

Cló thought Sophronia must've been pregnant before they left England, for the next entry in the bible was for a boy, not three months after the *Dilligence* arrived in Jamestown.

The dry words told her little, but her imagination happily filled in the blanks of the stinking harbour of Ipswich, the dreadful voyage across the Atlantic, throwing in a few storms and icebergs for good measure, and their arrival in Jamestown, little more than a famine-stricken, disease-ridden settlement.

Cló's sigh of relief fluttered around the Blue Suite when footsteps sounded in the hallway beyond. Jude was coming. She watched the door expectantly when the footsteps stopped. The handle turned slightly, very slowly, with a faint, drawn-out creak.

Frowning uneasily, Cló stood up. It wasn't Jude. The footsteps were all wrong. His had a heavier tread. What she had heard was lighter, quicker.

The handle stayed lowered, a hand resting on it, hesitant to enter. Perhaps whoever had been cleaning their room each day. Shaking herself, Cló moved to the door. Of course, it was the cleaner!

"Hello?" Cló called. "It's okay, you can come in."

The handle released with a sharp click, followed by a rustle of clothes and footsteps fleeing down the hall.

Opening the door, Cló peered out in time to see a flash of hurrying motion turn the corner. "What the—?" she murmured, her nose wrinkling at the faint, lingering perfume. She recognised the scent; she'd smelt it in the Blue Suite before. Cinnamon, apples and lilies. She was fairly certain it was the perfume Ruth wore.

Why would Ruth try enter their room without knocking? Cló was horribly used to the sisters dogging her movements elsewhere, but it left Cló in a sour mood if they'd taken to snooping in her room. She struggled to see Ruth as a snooper; she was too vague to be truly interested in what Jude and Cló did. Constance even less so; the woman was too insular to be a snoop, with too much self-interest to be a gossip. Unless Constance had *told* Ruth to snoop. But why snoop at all? Jude didn't keep any information about the estate here; it was all with the lawyers and accountants and such.

Oh god! Had Ruth been cleaning their room? A wave of guilt swept through Cló, even as a giggle tickled her throat at the image of Ruth in Victorian crinoline dusting the bathroom.

Seven o'clock came and went and still Jude wasn't back. By the time Cló had showered and dressed into something smarter than sweatpants and a T-shirt, it was ten to eight. It would take at least ten minutes to get to the Silver Dining Room.

And still Cló dithered and faffed, delaying the inevitable, wishing she was the sort of person who could forgo dinner altogether. But her stomach rumbled, and she was naturally punctual, though she loathed the formal dinner arrangements with her sisters-in-law.

Cló waited another five minutes, then ten, then left the Blue Suite and thundered through the corridors, arriving at the Silver Dining Room out of breath and red in the face.

"You're here!" she cried indignantly. She hesitated in the doorway when Jude and his sisters, standing a little away from him, turned at her noisy entrance. Jude's expression was stony, annoyed furrows stitching his lips together. The prickly energy of an unresolved argument coursed between the siblings.

"Sorry I'm late," she said, and moved to hug Jude.

His arms tightened around her as though he hadn't seen her in months. "I thought you would be down already," he muttered into her neck, accusation in his tone.

"I was waiting for you upstairs," she muttered back, eyeing the sisters over Jude's shoulder. They were both staring, uncomfortable by the display of affection.

"Who is Ruth supposed to be tonight?" Cló whispered. Ruth was dressed like a man in some sort of medieval garb with a long, sweeping black cloak and a tall black hat. She looked like a neat crow.

"A lawyer from the seventeenth century."

Cló scowled at the sisters, wanting to wipe the supercilious expressions from their faces. Rebellion stirred with the imp of an idea. She grinned and did something she would never normally do in company. She kissed Jude long and hard, surprising them both.

"What was that for?" Jude whispered when she pulled away. "Not that I'm complaining, but you get weird if we hold hands in public."

Cló shrugged, unable to explain her need to shock her patronising sisters-in-law. "A promise?" she muttered, reddening.

"A promise I'll keep you to."

After serving themselves from the sideboard, Cló and Jude sat at their end of the vast table. Cló hadn't quite got over her streak of rebellion and considered shouting down the length of the table to ask the sisters to pass the salt. She stifled her giggle, earning a raised eyebrow from Jude.

"Tell me about your day," he said. "Anything to take my mind off the shitty day I've had."

"You first."

"Not here," said Jude, with a swift glance at his sisters.

"Anything interesting?" Cló dropped her voice to a whisper.

"No, but I'm still not discussing anything here."

Cló nodded and opened her mouth to tell him about last night, but as the words formed in her head, she heard how crazy it sounded, so instead she said, "Not much. Some ancestry research. I didn't find anything new."

"I sense a *but* coming," said Jude as he wolfed his food down now he was on a promise.

"Last night—"

"You saw the Grey Lady?" Jude grinned. "I knew you'd start seeing them if I told you about the Hall's resident ghosts."

Cló pulled a face. "I didn't see the Grey Lady, but I keep seeing this little girl," she said, coming at her explanation obliquely.

"The one you saw in the village?"

Conscious the sisters' silence had deepened to listening, cursing the acoustics of ridiculously large rooms, she told Jude in barely a whisper of the little girl and their odd conversation.

She didn't have a chance to describe her weird experience in the Hermitage when Constance boomed down the length of the table, "It's only Gwenn."

"And there goes our private conversation." Jude looked at Constance reluctantly. "And who is Gwenn? Another of the ghosts you used to plague me with?"

Constance smirked. Ruth tittered. Not with fond familial remembrance judging by Jude's darkening expression.

"She's the local nutter's child," said Constance. "She's always creeping about the place."

Their gaze swivelled to Cló. She quailed under their scrutiny, feeling like the fat mouse they'd called her, pinned by the two cats' lamplight glare.

"Then speak to her mother," said Jude, looking faintly alarmed. "A young child should be under supervision."

"The mother's as odd as the child," said Constance. "One of those new-age sorts."

"Gwenn doesn't do any harm, Connie." Ruth's glasses shone like moons in the chandelier light as she placed a placatory hand on her sister's arm. "She's a thieving little magpie, but to be fair to the mother, she always brings back what was stolen."

Constance smiled fondly. "That would be your kind heart, but the girl needs a damn good thrashing."

Jude pushed his plate away. "There will be no thrashing," he snapped. "I had enough of that as a child. I wouldn't wish it on another."

"Didn't do us any harm . . . What?" Constance demanded at Cló's indrawn breath of horror.

Cló ignored her. "You were thrashed?" she said to Jude. "By your parents?"

"No." Jude's eyes narrowed at Constance tellingly.

"You thrashed your own brother?" Cló demanded, forgetting who she was yelling at.

"Cló," Jude warned.

She saw the panic in his eyes. Her lips tightened, determined not to back away from an uncomfortable conversation. "Tell me," she said.

His gaze flicked to his watching sisters, then away. "My parents weren't around much, and as my sisters were that much older than me they took it upon themselves to discipline me any way they saw fit."

"Oh, I think you're exaggerating just a teeny bit," said Ruth. She giggled. It grated on Cló's nerves. "You were terribly naughty, and Nanny never could control you. If it hadn't been for Constance, you would quite likely have killed yourself in one of your silly escapades . . . He was always trying to escape, you know," she added earnestly to Cló.

"Escape . . ." Cló murmured, her heart swelling in sympathy for the boy Jude had once been, living in this huge, mouldering building with two horrible, much older sisters as his only company. Unable to wrap herself around him as she wanted to and protect him from the hateful focus of his sisters, she put a hand on his arm.

"I've lost my appetite," Jude muttered. He stood up and stormed out of the dining room.

Hurrying after him, Cló tried to keep up with his furious strides as he stalked up and down stairs and along hallways.

He stopped abruptly on reaching the hall the Blue Suite opened onto. He turned to Cló, his face working with emotions he couldn't articulate.

"Take your time," Cló said, and hugged him tight, a deep-pressure hug to ease some of his tension.

He stood stiff and uncertain in her arms like a wooden doll. Cló pulled away, unable to keep the hurt from her face.

"Did I do something wrong?" she asked. "I know I shouldn't have yelled at your sisters. I'm sorry. I'll apologise to them to-morrow."

Jude gave a bark of harsh laughter. "You did nothing wrong. You're probably the first person who's stood up to them. I know I never did . . . Thanks," he said with a strained smile.

"Tell me what they did to you," Cló said, keeping her voice low and encouraging.

Jude opened his mouth, shut it and shrugged. "It was no bet-ter or worse than what siblings everywhere do to each other."

"You're lying." Cló held up a hand to stop Jude's retort. "I *know* something happened to you here, and I'm convinced it's something that horrible Constance did. I've never pushed you to tell me; it was in your past and I wanted you to tell me when you were ready—"

"It's nothing," he muttered, not looking her in the eye.

"Nonsense," she said with more force than she would nor-mally. "Since our first night together you haven't been able to fall asleep unless I'm there, and you've never spoken about your family. Not in ten years, Jude!"

"Nor do you!" Jude snapped back.

"I don't have any family!" she cried, hurt curdling in her chest. "You are my entire family!"

Jude shut his eyes briefly. "God, I'm sorry, Cló. That was uncalled for."

"This place is changing you," she said softly. "I knew it wasn't going to be easy, but you're—you've lost something here, some part of you. I think we should leave. Just give it all away. You don't want it, and we were doing fine in Canada. We were happy there. *You* were happy there. Give it to the National

Trust or something. I've seen their signs everywhere; they'll be thrilled to have it all, and then we can go home and—"

Jude nodded, but he was shuttering down again. "I don't want to talk about it." He rubbed a hand over his face. He looked truly exhausted, drained. He tried to smile and said, "Why don't you go out early."

"And how will you fall asleep?" she asked. It was a cruel jibe, popping out her mouth before she could stop it.

"I'll manage." Jude turned on his heel, with Cló's "I'm sorry" racing after him. He didn't turn to acknowledge her apology.

Cló watched him walk away, knowing she'd only make it worse if she went after him. A cloying, sickly shame pressed down on her chest.

EIGHT

Fog hugged the glass tunnel, creating mirrors all around Cló and the glass birds trapped in their cold fragile cage, reflecting their frozen flight into infinity. The echo of her sobs died in the midnight quiet of the Hall of Curiosities, her tears dried on her cheeks.

Her dark thoughts drifted through the gloomy passages of Grimdark to Jude in the Blue Suite, alone, knowing he'd be as sleepless as she was. The acrid aftertaste of their fight was still thick on her tongue. It's not that they never argued. All marriages needed the occasional venting of words to clear a buildup of nerve-hitting niggles. She hated fighting with Jude.

But this felt worse, different. She'd been ambushed by Jude's tainted past the moment they'd set foot in Grimdark. She felt it now as the old building hunkered over her, the air slippery with dark secrets and the aftermath of their argument; felt it in Jude's withdrawal from her, his inability to speak to her of what had happened within these walls that had scarred him so deeply. She worried the pain of his past was breaking something between them. A crack had formed, eggshell fine, but there all the same. All that was good and honest about their marriage might not be able to survive Grimdark and the Honeyborne sisters.

Gusting out a tremulous sigh, Cló longed to be outside, but the dense fog crowding against Grimdark Hall deadened all sound and sight. The world beyond its flint walls was a changing landscape of unstable cliffs and deceptive fens, an unforgiving death trap for someone as fumble-footed as Cló.

She walked up the Hall of Curiosities, shining her phone's light into each cabinet. The Honeybornes had been ardent collectors of the beautiful and the macabre, a passion that went back centuries. Cló gloomily contemplated the shrunken heads, incongruously placed beside pinned butterflies that certainly hadn't lived or died in the British Isles. Crystals fetched up against the skeleton of a baby monkey. Something swimming in green liquid that looked suspiciously like a human hand waved at lumps of brain coral, bleached with age. A whole cabinet of odd little earthenware bottles stumped Cló; she turned to Google to discover she was looking at a collection of rare witch bottles.

At the end of the glass tunnel, a vast iron-studded oak door blocked her way. She had never ventured this far and pushed at the round ring that served as a handle. The door creaked loudly, as though it hadn't been opened in a thousand years.

The room beyond was filled only with dust and mildew. Extreme old age seeped from the flint-black walls. Cló couldn't hazard a guess at its function. Three doors led off from it, two to rooms as bare as the first, the third was locked. The third door was so old it appeared to grow organically from the surrounding flint, pitted with metal studs and wrought-iron hinges.

She gave the ring handle a good rattle to make sure it was locked, then turned to leave. She shivered, and stopped again, a sense of familiarity tickling her skin. It was gone as quickly as it arrived. Shrugging, she closed the huge iron-studded door behind her and walked slowly down the Hall of Curiosities. Everything inside her demanded she go upstairs and speak to Jude, clear the air, push the issue, and—

"Arghhh!" Cló shrieked in terror at the stark white face staring at her from outside.

Then the face did something ridiculous: it opened its mouth wide and blew against the glass like a fish.

"Luna?" Cló hazarded, a hand to her chest, her heart rate galloping at a rapid-fire tempo.

"Hurry up!" Luna yelled through the glass. "Time's ticking and the moon doesn't wait for anyone."

"Now? It's the middle of the night."

"And that's rather the time the moon is up and busy. Now *you* get busy and hustle outside. We have picking to do."

Her white face disappeared into the mist.

A grin spread slowly across Cló's face, surprised and delighted Luna had come around so soon after their brief, bizarre meeting the day before.

Cló hared through the conservatory and along the halls with a confidence gained from her nightly explorations. She crossed the Great Hall and slipped outside onto the terrace. The mist was so thick she couldn't see the stone balustrade a few metres away.

"You've been skulking about the Hermitage," said Luna, as she loomed out of the mist. She was gloriously extravagant in purple from head to foot, crowned by a ridiculous hat festooned with sprigs of lavender like a messy haystack.

"How did you know that?" Cló demanded.

Luna grinned wickedly and tapped the side of her nose. "Trade secret that . . . Come on." She took off and was quickly swallowed by the mist.

Wishing she'd thought to wear sturdier shoes than sneakers, Cló hurried after her.

"I met a little girl in the Hermitage," she said when she caught up to Luna. "It's actually the second time I've met her. I thought she was a ghost at first. I'm still not entirely sure she isn't one."

"A thin kid with white hair and blue eyes?"

Cló nodded, then frowned when Luna burst out laughing.

"That's only Gwenn," she chortled.

"Yes, that's what Constance said. She evidently comes into the Hall when she's not supposed to." Cló decided not to air Constance's brutal views on child-rearing. "I can't tell you how glad I am she's not a ghost."

"Of course, she's not!" Luna snorted. "Gwenn is my daughter. She's a bloody menace I don't mind telling you, and the imagination on that girl . . . I don't doubt she put the wind up you about pirates and witches and such."

Cló's eyebrows shot up in astonishment. "Yes, she did."

"She's always down in the tunnels too. I've told that girl a million times to stay away from them, they aren't safe, but I've a gnat's chance of telling her what to do. Bloody menace," she added fondly. Then she stopped abruptly and pulled Cló close to the perimeter wall.

"Speaking of menaces," she muttered, her eyes narrowed into the mist.

Cló followed her gaze, expecting to see a little white-haired figure sneaking into the Hall. But as her eyes adjusted to the gloomy whiteness, it was the clumping, masculine figure of Constance she made out instead.

Luna and Cló stood dead still, as Constance disappeared into the chapel not three metres from them. The door shut behind her with a small thump, deadened by the mist.

"Now what the hell is she up to in the middle of night skulking about," said Luna, staring at the chapel door, "And with— Was that a shovel?"

"Yes. I've seen her go into the chapel every night. I know what she's up to."

Luna turned her bright curiosity on Cló. "Do you really?"

"She goes down into the crypt and digs up the old tombs. I think she's searching for something." A stab of guilt pierced Cló for telling a virtual stranger about her discovery when she hadn't yet told Jude.

"Mmmm . . ." Luna grinned, eyes dancing with laughter, which rather confused Cló. She thought it was a terrible thing to dig up the dead. "Silly old mare. Bet she's digging for Bad King John's treasure."

"Treasure?" said Cló, hurrying after Luna again when she took off without warning, the mist shredding around her into pirouetting shapes that seemed almost human.

"You're not much of a tourist, are you?" said Luna, as she slipped through a small doorway in the wall. "Everyone knows about King John's treasure that got lost in the Wash. I learnt about it in school, and it's in every bit of drivel that's dished out to tourists."

"I haven't found any tourist drivel. I've not left Grimdark much." She hadn't been anywhere but Grimdark since they'd arrived a week ago. "And I don't know who King John is. You've had hundreds of kings."

"He was Richard the Lionheart's brother . . . You *have* heard of Richard the Lionheart?"

"Um . . ." said Cló meekly.

Luna shrugged at her ignorance. She strode through the mist as though it wasn't there and she owned the world, saying, "There's rather a lot of mystery around it all, but the long and the short of it is, eight hundred years ago King John's entire baggage train, with all his jewels and bits and bobs, ended up in the Wash—"

"The Wash?" asked Cló, bewildered.

An airy wave of Luna's bangled arm. "It's a vast coastal estuary a mile or so from here as the crow flies. You'd like it, plenty of birds . . . And it's not just old Bad King John's treasure that's a mystery," she continued without breaking stride. "For not a few days later, he died under mysterious circumstances. Truth be told, that was no great loss." She stopped when they reached the cliff path that led down to the village. Though it was shrouded in mist, like a primordial itch of warning, a yawning abyss opened on their right to Darrow Bay, felt but unseen.

"You've heard of the Magna Carta? Rise of the Barons? Battle of Runneymede?"

At each Cló shook her head, feeling stupid.

"Well, it's to be expected, I suppose. I know bugger all about Canada, except it's sodding cold and has mountains." She patted Cló's arm consolingly and strode off again, talking as she went. "So a little background ... Bad King John was a right bastard, heavy taxes and such, wars on all fronts, didn't listen to the nobles, which pissed them off and led to the barons revolting all over the shop, which led to the Battle of Runnymede where King John got his arse kicked and was forced to sign the Magna Carta—"

"And that is?" Cló interjected, following in Luna's footsteps. She couldn't see a thing except the purple figure striding ahead of her with arms waving about as she talked.

"It was sort of like a peace treaty with a bunch of laws that the barons forced on King John. And that of course pissed him off, so not long after he gave the barons the finger with an 'Up yours, I'll go my own way, thank you very much.' And that set off another bunch of wars with the barons trying to give the crown to the French, and the Scots coming down from the north while all hell was breaking loose down south ... With me so far?"

Cló nodded, not sure she was, but was rather fascinated by the way Luna talked so fast and energetically. Luna talking was a whole-body experience.

"So King John's running around England, putting out fires and starting new ones, and he comes up to King's Lynn, which was Bishop's Lynn then—bit of useless information for you there—and this is where the mystery starts. The king travelled with this insane retinue, bringing everything with him—all his gold, even the crown jewels, and tapestries and bedding and such, and cooks and tasters, and the whatnots that make a king's life comfy on the road. And this baggage train stretched for miles. Can you imagine?"

It was the wrong question to ask Cló. She could imagine it quite clearly; the hustle and bustle, the horses and the creaking carts. But all she did was nod when Luna whipped her head around to peer over her shoulder.

Satisfied with Cló's nod, she continued, "So old John pops into Bishop's Lynn; he's in a hurry because the Scots are coming down from the north and the barons are causing shit in the south while waiting for the French bloke to pitch up and take the crown, but he's caught like a piggy in the middle here. And he needs to get up to Lincoln because he has a big strong castle . . . anyway, to cut yet another long story short, John's in a hurry, but it's still a fair way to Lincoln from Lynn. So he gets some local to guide his baggage train through the Wash while he goes around it. And that's where things go totally tits up for John, because his baggage disappears into the Wash, never to be seen again. And there's old John up in Swinehead, getting pissed with the monks at the abbey, when he gets the news. And not a week later, the bloke is dead . . . So Constance is looking in the wrong place because the treasure is still stuck in the Wash somewhere."

"Unless she knows something you don't."

"Huh! Me and every other bugger who has a theory about its location."

They entered the village. By tacit agreement, neither spoke. There was something puritanical about Grimdark that forbade frivolous chatter after sundown. But perhaps it was the mist that dampened the villagers' desire for frivolity, threading through the alleys in clammy tendrils, creeping up to windows, listening to the whispers within.

Cló thought they were the only ones about at this hour, until a figure loomed from a side alley. She squawked in alarm.

"Well, well," murmured Luna.

"Miss Destiny," said the man, startled and not a little terrified at the sight of two women appearing out of the mist when he had probably assumed no one in their right mind would be about so late at night.

Then Luna did a curious thing. Instead of returning his greeting, she scratched her upper thigh in a suggestive manner and chortled throatily. She turned away dismissively, meant to wound, as the man averted his eyes and scurried back the way he'd come, hunched and cowed.

"What was that about?" Cló asked, as Luna kept walking up the street.

She smirked. "Just reminding the cheating sod that I know what I know and I won't forget. Keeping him in his place." She sighed at Cló's blank expression. "He had an STD."

"So what?"

"What you should be asking is where he got it from and how it affected his wife—ex-wife now," she added with satisfaction. "It pays to know what goes on in the village. All those ferrety secrets."

"Ah." Cló looked at Luna with new respect. "And good for fortune-telling."

Luna paused, mouth open to retort; then she grinned. "Aren't you the sharp one?" She shrugged unashamedly. "It pays to know what's going on, keep up with the gossip . . . and people are idiots, mostly. They tell you something about someone, and after that it's not hard to guess which way the wind will blow, and I'm very good at guessing its direction. But these buggers don't know it, and they'll come up my way all sly and shy, wanting to know what their future brings. And all those little bits and bobs of knowledge are grist for my mill."

"Yes," said Cló slowly. "I'm not so sure that's ethical."

Luna stopped in her tracks to stare at Cló with genuine surprise. "What's ethics got to do with it? Money's money, and gossip makes me mine. Got to feed my daughter, after all. Her bloody father does nowt to help, so . . ." She took off again, out of the village and along the cliff path beyond, past the old, ruined cottage Cló had discovered a few days ago.

"Where is your daughter?" Cló asked. She had been assuming there was a husband in the picture and was the person looking after Luna's daughter.

"Right there." Luna nodded at a pinprick of light haloed like a will o' the wisp.

Cló sensed space all around her, yet she had no directional pull. When she turned, thinking the village was behind her, she couldn't see a single light through the mist. She worried that she was standing in a marsh, for the earth beneath her feet was soft and squelchy, and stank of vegetative rot.

"You live there?" Cló asked.

Luna nodded. "That's our caravan. The farmer who owns Dunge Marsh was that grateful when I detected the early stages of cancer in his wife a few years back, he's let us stay here ever since the divorce. His wife is the one watching Gwenn now . . . Don't you go listening to those in Grimdark that think Gwenn is allowed to run free all night." She grimaced, faintly ashamed. "Though to be fair, the little menace does take to wandering when she shouldn't. More so the last few weeks. She seems a bit unsettled." Luna grabbed Cló's hand, giving it a squeeze and said, "Come on, this way."

Reeds brushed against Cló's arms as she was dragged along a squelchy path she couldn't see, surrounded by a fen she could only sense, following a woman she didn't know but couldn't help liking, and rather enjoying what was turning into a mini adventure.

"I'll bring you up here in the day sometime," said Luna. She stopped and put out a hand to stop Cló walking further. "Careful, we're on the edge of the cliff."

The mist was patchier here, allowing a few valiant stars to peer down at the flat blackness stretching out in front of them, like they were standing on the edge of the universe.

"The Wash used to be much bigger than it is now," said Luna.

"Most of it's reclaimed land these days, but once it ran for miles inland. My idiot of an ex-husband was always in the Wash searching for King John's treasure, when he wasn't pissed as a lord. He knew every theory . . . God knows I've heard him sprout them all. But he wasn't the only one. The scent of lost treasure turns all men into fools. Even now, there's a new excavation going on."

As Cló stood on the edge of the cliff, with the desolate emptiness of the Wash before her, a shiver rippled up her back until she was trembling with an edgy certainty that she was losing her mind when she whispered, "It's not there."

Luna glanced at her askance. "For someone who'd never heard of King John until a few minutes ago, you seem awfully certain."

"Yes, I . . . was." Cló shook her head, confused by her utter conviction that the king's treasure was nowhere near the Wash.

Luna nodded to herself. "So that's the way of it, is it? Gwenn was right; you've remembered."

"Remembered what?" said Cló, staring at the purple-clad woman.

"Who you once were."

10 October 1216

In the smokiness from a thousand torches, figures bustled and weaved with steady purpose, casting long shadows against the imposing façade of Gaywood Palace. The huge, sprawling complex was proud to declare to all that power and wealth lay within, even in these uncertain times of civil war.

"Fortitude," whispered Walter Hulot as he and Ralph Honeyborne hurried through the small mobile city that accompanied King John wherever he roamed across his kingdom, to tend to his every need. "Do not falter or all will be lost."

Ralph Honeyborne licked his lips uneasily, unable to look his half-brother in the eye. "Perhaps . . ." he murmured.

"He deserves no leniency," Walter hissed. "Remember all we have lost because of him."

"And what we have gained."

"At the expense of our loss . . . The king is no fool; he's summoned us for his own means that will not bode well for us. We must use this opportunity, for it cannot reflect back to us if all comes to pass as we plan." It was the last Walter could advise as

the two men pushed through the bottleneck of servants hurrying in and out of Gaywood Palace.

From the two hearths along one wall issued more smoke that hung from the vaulted rafters of the Great Hall like a suffocating shroud. The chamber was packed with knights, mercenaries, servants scurrying back and forth with trays of food and ale, shouts and laughter echoing up to the clouded ceiling, a veritable roar of noise.

Walter grabbed a passing servant's arm, forcing him to stop, and yelled, "Where be the king?"

The servant nodded to the far end of the hall, shook off Walter's restraining hand and hurried back into the crush.

Another query, and they were directed towards a closed door off the hall. The two guarding knights stepped aside to allow them entry, and the brothers pushed the door open.

It was not often the king had to wait for his subjects to appear once summoned, and King John did not look at all pleased when he looked up from a goblet of wine to glare at the brothers as they shut the door behind them, muting the cacophony without.

Being richly dressed, in a ruby-red robe lined with green, did not detract from the king's athletic, compact frame that belied his forty-nine years. Not so his grey hair worn to his shoulders, and the grey beard disguising a small mouth. Exhaustion etched deep, lined shadows under his dark eyes—not surprising, as the king pursued a relentless trail of vengeance on his rebellious barons across the kingdom . . . and perhaps—dare Walter hope it?—the flush of fever, for his eyes were too bright.

"Your Grace," murmured Ralph, sweeping into a low bow. Walter bowed too, though he gave no formal salutation.

With an angry flick of his head, the king indicated a chair on the other side of the table.

Ralph sat down, tense and wary. Walter stood behind him,

scanning the room, richly adorned with tapestries, for hidden danger, or a sign that he and Ralph had walked into a trap. The only other occupant was the king's scribe, taking up little space in one corner and posing no threat. When satisfied all was well, he turned his attention to the king, unable to veil his intense loathing for the spiteful ruler.

"There appears to be one missing from your party," said the king. He licked his lips. "The lovely Isabella. We expressly requested her presence."

It was a cruel opening, one intended to wound deeply, no doubt in retaliation for their late arrival; the king's network of spies was well known. They reported any changes to the landed gentry and nobility in his kingdom, both friend and foe—and of foe there were many. For never had a king of England been more hated than King John—especially by those families with women whom the king lusted after, as he had after Ralph's daughter.

Ralph's hands, hidden under the table, clenched into fists. Before he spoke, his throat convulsed visibly. "Isabella died not one year ago."

"Ah." The king's eyes flickered to Walter, then away, for not even kings liked to look into the odd-coloured eyes of the steward of Honeyborne Hall. "And it has come to our ears that you have finally fathered an heir."

"Aye." An unwitting smile from Ralph. "Richard. He's a strapping lad."

"So, comfort for you. As one child dies, another is born."

Walter's shocked intake of breath at the king's callousness was audible in the small chamber.

The king raised an eyebrow at the steward. "You do not agree?"

"The loss of one child can never be replaced by the birth of another," he growled, mind whirling. Was it possible the king's

spies had discovered the truth? No, impossible. There were only four people who knew, three whom Walter trusted implicitly, the fourth paid well for his silence.

The king shrugged and met Walter's odd-coloured gaze without flinching this time, before sliding back to Ralph. "You do the Honeybornes a great honour by bestowing on your heir our brother's name." The king's lips twisted into a sneer, besmirching his words—all knew that his jealousy of his brother had not diminished with King Richard's death.

"Of course," murmured Ralph. His shoulders visibly relaxed when the king's attention returned to Walter Hulot.

"De Grey informs us that you are brothers."

Walter frowned, aware Ralph had tensed once more. It was no secret he and Ralph shared the same father, with Walter born on the wrong side of the marital blanket, though they were as day was to night. Ralph Honeyborne looked the part of the current Lord of Honeyborne Hall: tall, thin, stately, though stooping now as he entered his fifty-second year. His defining feature was a shock of bone-white hair he'd had from birth. But his pale blue eyes were gentle, and he often wore a faint smile as though bewildered by life. Not so Walter, who peered at the world with suspicion of everyone and everything. He was tall and well-built, as would be expected of a man hardened by years of battle. What was left of his face was a patchwork of old scars and a nose broken many times, topped by a totally bald head.

"You fought for our brother, Richard," said the king, when neither Ralph nor Walter denied their shared blood.

Walter nodded, trying to second guess what was on the king's mind. "For many years in the Holy Land."

"And now you act as steward to the Honeyborne estates. A remarkable achievement for a bastard."

Eyes narrowed, Walter nodded, not trusting himself to speak.

"Which, it has come to our attention, is doing exceedingly well."

"Aye," said Walter cautiously. Had the king summoned them to demand another loan? One that would never be paid back, as indeed, the last two had not been. War was expensive, and the king was fighting on three fronts: Many barons had revolted against the king after he reneged on the Magna Carta, signed not a year ago at Runneymede. The barons had invited the Dauphin of France to take the crown, an almost bloodless invasion by invitation, while the Scots had taken the opportunity to attack from the north. The Honeyborne estates were financially sound only due to the severe austerity imposed on all who lived there. A necessary demand and sacrifice when the Honeybornes had chosen to side with the barons secretly, sending funds towards their war against the king. It was a precarious situation for the Honeybornes.

But there was another way out, a devilish, fiendish possibility, which, if it worked, was for the good of not only the Honeybornes but of all England. It was imperative the possibility succeed, for a further loan to the king would cripple the Honeybornes.

King John's attention turned to Ralph. *"It would do you well to support our cause, as surety of your continued loyalty to us."*

Ralph opened his mouth, then shut it again when Walter poked him in the back.

"Of course, Your Grace," said Walter smoothly. And though he seethed within, his anger stiffened his resolve, for loyalty bought through fear was no loyalty at all. Walter's loyalty lay with the Honeybornes, who had, even as a child, treated him with far more kindness than most bastards received. And that loyalty now demanded retribution.

"De Grey has told us you acted as guide when we passed through last. We shall require your services once more. We must push on to Lincoln with all haste."

Walter's sigh of relief was inaudible. "*Of course, Your Grace. When does Your Grace wish to depart?*"

"*Two days hence.*"

"*Luck is with you, Your Grace, for the tides are at their lowest at this time of the year.*"

NINE

⌒❧⌒

"So much for picking tonight," said Luna, eyeing Cló's ashen face. "We need to talk." Without waiting for a response, she took Cló's arm and led her to the caravan.

It was a glorious thing: its bow top sparkled green and a metal chimney, wearing a conical hat, puffed out smoke that mingled instantly with the mist. The short wooden walls were painted red, with intricate gold curlicues carved into the corners. Four brightly painted yellow wheels sunk halfway into the black mud, and a little stairway led up to a tiny porch and a green door with golden hand-carved birds in flight.

Beside the caravan stood a large cream-coloured yurt, from which hung dreamcatchers and windchimes that tinkled occasionally. The biggest horse Cló had ever seen stood not far away, its head hung low in sleep.

"Are you—um—Romani?" Cló asked once Luna had said goodnight to the matronly farmer's wife who had been watching over Gwenn.

"I wish," she said. "But this is a genuine vardo. I found it in the farmer's yard, just left to moulder, so I had it off him, got it fixed up in the traditional manner." She smiled at the caravan fondly. "I would've loved to have lived with the Romani. Never tied to anyone or anything except family. Moving about as I choose, with none to tell me what I can and can't do. Maybe I was once, in a different life . . . Do you want to see inside?" she asked, when Cló tried to peek through the door left ajar.

The interior was a tiny palace on wheels with liberal splashings of gold paint. A cast-iron stove hunkered between ornate glass-fronted shelves holding little bottles with handwritten labels. On a high bed at the back, Gwenn's ash-white hair spread across the pillow, the rest of her was hidden under a nest of colourful blankets. A row of willow-pattern plates beamed down fondly at the sleeping girl from the shelf above.

Extravagant opulence bulged in the tight space. Charming yet terrifying for Cló, who worried she'd knock something over merely by turning around.

"I love the vardo," said Luna, when Cló squeezed back out, "but it's a bit of a crush, so we spend most of our time in there." She nodded at the yurt and stomped across to it without waiting to see if Cló followed.

The yurt had Luna stamped all over it. A balustraded deck out front led into an open-plan space. The latticed framework of bamboo, like a many-fingered star, met at a glass skylight in the centre of the roof. Strings of beads hung here and there, rippling with a pleasing rustle. Framed tarot cards covered the canvas walls, and scarves hung in strange places. The whole place was mismatched, yet felt exactly as it should be.

Half the circular space was partitioned by a swathe of black curtain with a dark sparkle in its folds. Cló assumed Luna did her mysterious readings there, and pictured a glowing crystal ball on a round, star-spangled table, with maybe a skull perched on a pedestal to keep an eye-socket on the proceedings.

"Gwenn scared the crap out of me when she first started

speaking," said Luna as she led the way to a couple of comfortable chairs, then pottered about in the small kitchen. She handed Cló a glass smelling strongly of juniper before plonking down on the chair opposite. "In her first years she spoke a language I didn't understand, like she was speaking in tongues. I took her to doctors and such, and they thought she might be on the spectrum. Then she and I were in Blakeney one day, and there were Dutch tourists about. It was them as figured out my Gwenn was speaking Dutch—and not any Dutch either. She was speaking Old Dutch, which hasn't been spoken in hundreds of years. Imagine that?" She leaned forward to stare at Cló intently. "My daughter, who'd never met a Dutch person, and certainly never been to the Netherlands, speaking Dutch as her first language!" She leaned back as though she'd made her point and was happy with it. "She was four before she finally learnt to speak English, and that's when the pirate stories started coming out, and then I knew . . ."

Goose bumps shivered up Cló's arms. "Knew what?" she whispered, caught up in Luna's story, told in the light of the single hurricane lamp as the muggy mist stole into the yurt.

"That my Gwenn had been here before, in a different life."

"Mmmm," said Cló doubtfully.

"You may well scoff, but Gwenn says she knows you—from before, in a different life. Well, different lives. Your fates are entwined."

"Reincarnation?" Cló snorted. She was a perfunctory Christian, but she'd always consigned reincarnation to something oddballs and new-age people believed.

Luna shrugged off Cló's disbelief. "Do you get strange dreams? Ones that repeat themselves?"

"Not dreams as such," said Cló warily. She took a sip of the strong gin and tonic to dull the panic building in her chest. "More like nightmares . . . of burning alive and being stabbed." She took another sip, then a few big gulps.

"I think you'll need quite a few of those before the night is out." Luna refilled Cló's empty glass. "Tell me about these nightmares."

Biting her lip, Cló sighed and went for the truth. "It's nothing sequential," she began. "More intrusions into dreams. It doesn't matter what the dream is about; they always end the same way, with my death. It can start as something happy or comforting—something simple or routine—but as the dream progresses, it grows darker, and no matter how I try to change the dream, I know what is going to come, and every dream still ends the same way." She smiled weakly. "I'm sure it's just my subconscious working out some weird fear I have—I'm not even sure what the fear is. I don't fear death, at least not abnormally so. I think I fear the manner of my death more."

"Or they're memories intruding into your subconscious."

"I know what you're trying to say, but I don't believe in reincarnation."

"And yet you die in a horrible manner in every dream." said Luna. "Look at you, here at"—she squinted at a plastic wall clock shaped like a witch in the kitchen—"nearly three a.m. and still bright-eyed and bushy-tailed . . . Do you get déjà vu a lot?"

Cló hesitated before saying, "No, and frankly I think that's a lot of nonsense too."

"Just because *you* think that doesn't mean it's not real." Luna's eyes narrowed. "But you've been feeling it here, haven't you? Since you arrived in Grimdark."

Her eyes bored into Cló's, who thought Luna must make a good living out of fortune-telling. She didn't need to say much, merely ask a few well-placed questions, then stare at her customers until they told their own fortunes and paid Luna for the privilege. Cló was just as susceptible to that stare.

"Yes," she said in a small voice. "Up on the cliff, and in the—"

"Figgis cottage."

"I was going to say the old ruined cottage."

"Same thing . . . Tell me about the Hermitage."

Caught off guard, Cló said, "What about it?"

"Something happened in there. Gwenn said you came over all queer."

"It was nothing," Cló muttered. "I've always had an overactive imagination, and it went a little too far. I can make myself cry at will just by imagining something sad, or make myself vomit by imagining something gross. That's all it was."

"Bollocks," said Luna without heat. "Tell me what you 'imagined'—if it makes you feel better to think of it as such."

So Cló did. She told her of the wreck in the bay, the three women, one young, one middle-aged, one old. She spoke of the villagers, the man hidden amidst the rocks with old scars crisscrossing his back, and the terrible fear of discovery.

"It was strange," she concluded. "It didn't seem like anything exceptional . . . Okay, a shipwreck is exceptional, but it didn't seem that uncommon in this"—she waved a hand about to capture the right word—"imagining. That shipwrecks had happened before, but something felt—I can't explain it. Just something was important, and I have no idea what it was because it all happened so quickly and was over before I could quite grasp whatever that something was. And it all felt so incredibly real, as though I were seeing it through my eyes, with my thoughts. I could smell it, feel the clothes against my skin . . ." She cleared her throat, aware she was gabbling. "It scared the crap out of me. It felt psychotic. I couldn't tell what was real and what wasn't."

Luna was quiet for a long time, peering into the silvery sheen of her gin and tonic as though it would provide her with answers. "He was a real person, you know. The pirate," she added when Cló looked baffled. "I checked after Gwenn started saying these impossible things about a man she couldn't have known about. I thought she would grow out of it with time, but it got worse as she got older."

"How old is Gwenn?"

"Nine." Luna grinned. "Everyone thinks she's younger. She's small for her age, and she acts strangely. A lot of people think she's simple or autistic, but she's not. She's just different." There was fierce motherly pride in her tone, and Cló wondered what harsh words had been cast at Gwenn and the fight Luna had taken up on her daughter's behalf, for it was there, an undercurrent in Luna's voice that spoke of battles won at great social cost.

"And you think Gwenn is the—er—reincarnation of this pirate."

"I don't think it, I know it. Gwenn knows details about him that no one could know unless they were him or had known him intimately . . . He was an interesting man. There's quite a lot about him; he was famous in an infamous way."

"Joseph," said Cló, her thoughts far away. "His name was Joseph." She put her head in her hands. "Oh god! What am I saying? This is all so crazy."

"Jozef, according to Gwenn," said Luna, not unkindly, "started off as Jozef Roggeveen in Rotterdam. He was a sailor until he was captured by Barbary corsairs when he wasn't more than fourteen or so. Ended up as a galley slave, poor bugger. But he turned Turk, as they said then, converted to Islam and styled himself as Yusef an-Nur. It's quite a pretty name, means Joseph the Light, probably because of his white hair. Anyway, he ended up as a corsair himself, and the last anyone heard of him was in 1645.

"There were loads of pirates about during the Civil War, easy pickings on both sides. According to what I've read, Roggeveen had attacked a royalist ship and was heading back to

Lundy Island when he got a bunch of Parliamentarian ships on his arse—"

"Lundy Island?" said Cló.

"It was a corsair hideout for a few years, down Cornwall way . . . Anyway, there was a battle, and the Parliamentarians forced Roggeveen into the North Sea. That's all well documented, but after that—poof!" Luna blew on the tips of her bunched fingers. "No one ever heard or saw him again after his ship was spotted not far from here. Most think his ship was wrecked in a storm out to sea." She leaned forward to whisper, "But Gwenn told me his ship was wrecked in Darrow Bay."

"Someone could've told Gwenn about him. Who doesn't love a pirate story?" said Cló, still resistant to the very idea of reincarnation. "She could've read it in a book."

"She knew about the scars on his back, and that's not anything I've read about."

"But you knew he was a galley slave, even I know the slaves were brutally mistreated, and I'm sure whipping was the least of it. It's logical that he would've had scars on his back."

"What about the kiswa? How would my Gwenn, at the age of five, know what the kiswa is? I didn't know what it was until I spoke to my mate Haaniem . . . She's Muslim, so she knew exactly what Gwenn was talking about."

"What *is* a kiswa?" said Cló, who'd never heard the word before the incident in the Hermitage.

"I can only tell you what Haaniem told me, so I may have it wrong. In Mecca, there is a shrine called the Ka'ba, which is covered in a cloth. During hajj, the cloth is changed and people cut off pieces for good luck . . . Now how would my Gwenn know something like that?"

"Perhaps your friend told her about it," said Cló, but her argument sounded weak to her own ears.

Luna pulled a face and didn't bother to argue.

"It's all so . . ." Cló paused, unable to express the sheer enormity of what was going on inside her head.

"Insane? Mad? Impossible? All of the above?" Luna gazed at Cló as though she were the centre of her world. "But *you* know something. Up on the cliff you were damned certain the king's treasure wasn't in the Wash. How could you possibly know that?"

Cló opened her mouth, then shut it again.

"There was something else, wasn't there?" Luna persisted. "You've remembered something from a previous life."

Unsettled by Luna's scrutiny, Cló drank her gin down and held out her empty glass. This strange intense woman was right, she needed rather a lot to drink to get through this.

"When I was in the Hermitage, having that—um—moment of weirdness . . . right at the end, before it all sort of blacked out, I remembered a memory from . . ." Cló sighed with frustration with another wave around the yurt to capture yet another elusive word. "It was like the memory of a memory, or a memory within a memory . . . Yes, a memory within a memory . . . Does this make any sense?"

"Yes. Keep going," said Luna, like an enthusiastic therapist.

"I saw the Wash, but not from above, on the cliffs where we were. I was in it and there were . . ." Cló shivered at the brief flash still imprinted in her mind. "I actually have no idea what was really going on. It was night, and there was this horrible silence, and the place stank of recent death. Not blood, but—" She shook her head, finding it impossible to explain what she was trying to say. "I could hear the buzzing of flies, and I knew there was death nearby without having to see it. I understood death in a way I never have. Like I'd seen death on a huge scale and could recognise it without seeing it . . . It was a sudden, brief image, but it wasn't from the—the woman. It was her memory of someone else." She smiled apologetically. "That sounds even weirder than it did in my head." She rubbed her face, not sure if it was the gin or her gush of words, but she was feeling sleepy and could quite happily have curled up on the chair and slept for a week.

"But now—"

The women whipped around when the door opened.

A white head appeared, then the rest of Gwenn. She smiled sleepily at Cló. "Hello, Effie."

TEN

Cló's footprints crisscrossed the dusty floors of Grimdark Hall to new rooms and new discoveries. The panelled walls pulsed gently around her as she walked aimlessly through the long corridors. With a pang of regret, she realised she would be sorry to leave when Jude finally wound up the estate. More and more she was growing to love Grimdark. Not the village and the few people she'd seen, who walked past her as though she wasn't there. She certainly wouldn't miss the sisters and their hurtful remarks: "Fat Mouse," the "American," said with such disdain, their sly glances, their watchful green eyes when Cló met them during the day, too frequently to be accidental.

But she would miss these nights when Grimdark was hers alone. Hers hands skimmed the walls in apology. She'd been wrong to think its name was a reflection of its nature, misinterpreting the spite and hatred of generations of Honeybornes infecting its very bones. Her thoughts rose through the floors to the Blue Suite and Jude. She sighed. Marriage was an acceptance of another's imperfections. More than love and companionship, it was an understanding of when to persist or retreat, when to speak or remain quiet, when to give space or be seen intimately, to accept that your spouse was shaped by their history before you and could never be totally yours.

Cló had given Jude space since their argument a week ago. They had apologised to each other, though it still felt unresolved. She had not pried when he'd withdrawn so deeply into himself he barely spoke to her. But she understood, too, as she walked Grimdark's halls, imagining her husband as a little boy, wandering from room to room, that Jude was broken, had always been broken, and had been broken here in Grimdark. But without knowing what was broken, she didn't know how to help him.

She slipped into the ballroom. For days she had searched for it, only to stumble across it when she'd stopped looking, as though Grimdark had hidden it from her until it felt she needed a treat. It had quickly become her favourite room after the Hall of Curiosities.

A thick layer of dust smothered the red velvet chairs against the walls and the immense burgundy drapes concealing floor-to-ceiling windows. Her tracks were a secret path across the dusty floor that had been a thoroughfare for mice for decades.

In one of the foster homes where Cló had spent a few years, her foster mother had been an avid reader of Georgette Heyer. Cló had devoured the books, and the ballroom encapsulated all her adolescent dreams of what romance should be.

Here, in the shadow of night, it was too easy for her imagination to fly, crowding the empty, echoing space with brightly dressed ladies and dashing men dancing a cotillion or sweeping across the vast expanse of floor in a waltz. The sheen of sweat beneath the powder of the dancing women shone in the chandeliers' light, their dance cards swinging from their wrists on silk ribbons. The air was scented with lavender and rose. Violins from the minstrel's gallery buzzed over the gentle cacophony of coquettish laughter and the snap of flirting fans. There would be food too—where Cló might've lurked had she been an attendee, or perhaps a wallflower trying to sink into the wall when no one asked her to—

"Effie . . ." The whisper, picked up by the acoustics of the vast room, came from everywhere.

The dancers vanished like smoke in shadows. After a long moment and a good talking to herself, Cló turned slowly, searching the murky corners of the ballroom.

"Gwenn?" she whispered. "Gwenn!" a little more loudly when there was no response. "You know you shouldn't be here. I'm going to phone your mom. You shouldn't worry her like this."

She pulled out her phone, tapped a quick text to Luna and got a quick thumbs-up in return.

Cló's growing friendship with Luna and Gwenn had been a surprising solace during her lonely days. She was rather taken with the odd little girl and the peculiar relationship that had sprung up between them.

More and more often, she would find Gwenn lurking wherever she happened to be. In the village, drawn to the old ruined cottage, or catching a glimpse of white hair streaming behind a small figure running along Grimdark's high walls at night, or, like now, finding each other in the Hall when Gwenn had sneaked in. But Cló was always quick to text Luna and tell her Gwenn was with her.

As a small hand slipped into Cló's, the faintest of sounds crept into the ballroom. A scrabbling . . . claws on brick. A desperate scrabble.

"Can you hear that?" said Cló. She turned her head to listen to the hollow darkness of Grimdark. There was an alertness in the air, as though the old building was listening too.

"No, but you know where it is, Effie," said Gwenn solemnly.

The horrible trickle of unease she got when Gwenn said things that were downright creepy, shivered down Cló's spine.

She squatted down in front of the girl. "I know you and your mom think I'm the reincarnation of Euphemia Figgis, but I'm not. I've had some weird episodes, but I am not her. I am Cló Honeyborne, and no amount of saying I'm someone else or wishing it is going to change that." But the lie curdled on her tongue. It was getting harder to resist the idea of reincarnation when more and more often her own experiences of Grimdark were muddied by Effie's recollections, Effie's emotions, Effie's fears.

She stood. "It's just some poor animal that's got stuck some-where," she said firmly, not giving in to Gwenn's expectant ex-pression. "We'll find it and rescue it."

They wandered from room to room, following the scrabble of claws, though in truth Cló felt Gwenn was leading her.

The scrabbling got louder, then came a plaintive mewl.

"Oh god! It's a cat," said Cló. That was infinitely worse than a stuck rat or mouse. A rat was a job for Jude; those she was happy to rescue from a distance.

"If cats looked all slimy, no one would like them, you know," said Gwenn in a conversational tone. "They aren't very nice. They play with their food when it's alive. I've watched them up at your cottage."

"It's not my cottage," said Cló, resisting the urge to sigh in exasperation at giving the same response yet again.

They entered the Great Hall, adorned in midnight shadows. The desperate mewling led them to the enormous fireplace that had never been lit. The Honeybornes had not wanted to sully their marble with soot and ash.

Frowning, Cló directed her phone's torch to search the stat-ues and columns around the fireplace. She stepped into the hearth where she'd hidden from the sisters once before. It was so large she could stand without hunching. Pale marble tiles lined the interior.

She could hear the cat clearly now, but its mewl was growing weaker.

"The cat is in the wall," said Gwenn. "You'll find it."

"How can you possibly know that?"

"You saved the cats. Before."

Once again, Cló had no response to Gwenn's strange pronouncements. She straightened and frowned at the walls. She looked up. "There's no chimney." Shining the phone's light right up against the ceiling of the hearth, she peered intently at every line and crack. The mewling was so weak now she could barely hear it. "How the hell did a cat get in here? Oh!"

Standing on tiptoe she inspected the scratched marks on a tile in the centre of the ceiling. A small, crudely etched star.

"There's a little star here. I think it might be a pentagram."

"A witch's mark," said Gwenn, nodding with the sageness of someone far older than nine.

Stomach tight with disquiet, Cló frowned at the apotropaic mark with her twenty-first-century disbelief in the face of habitual superstition from previous centuries.

She pushed against the tile with the star. It lifted with a shriek of stone on stone.

Not daring to breathe lest she'd raised the sisters to come on a mission of discovery, Cló waited until the last echo of the grating shriek had been swallowed by the night's silence. Carefully pushing the tile to one side, she pushed her head into the small cavity.

An organic mustiness tickled her nose. Contorting her arm at an awkward angle, she brought her hand up next to her head with the phone.

Desiccated, emaciated and blackened, a mummified cat lay in the cavity in a rictus of horror that brought tears to Cló's eyes.

"But I heard it crying," she whispered, revolted by the non-

chalant cruelty inflicted on an innocent creature because of stupid superstitions. But this cat hadn't cried for centuries. "What
a horrible way to die." Not daring to touch the poor cat, she
could imagine the terror of its last hours too easily. Helpless
and alone. Apart from being burnt alive, this would be Cló's
worst nightmare death.

Withdrawing her head, Cló swallowed her tears, not wanting Gwenn to see what she'd seen. "Maybe there's another cat
trapped somewhere," she said, more to convince herself that
what she'd heard had nothing to do with what was trapped in
the cavity. "Maybe we heard this cat's ghost," she added hopefully; she could tolerate the idea of a ghost cat.

"You remembered the cat," said Gwenn with too much
firmness for Cló's liking.

"I heard the cat, but how did *you* know it was here?"

"You told me about it."

"How could I? *I* didn't know it was here, and I haven't spoken to you about mummified cats. That's a conversation I
would definitely remember . . . And don't dare say it was when
you were Joseph. You know I don't—"

"You do believe, Effie!"

"My name is Cló!" Oddly teary, Cló stared defiantly down
at the girl. She wasn't sure what to do. Should she leave the cat
where she'd found it? She shuddered at the very idea. She had
enough difficulty sleeping without the thought of the little
body trapped so long above the fireplace. She needed Jude. He
would know what to do.

Mind made up, Cló said, "You stay here. I'll be back in a
minute." She took one step, then turned back. "No, actually
it's better if you come with me. I need to take you home in a
minute."

But Gwenn darted off before Cló could take her hand and
disappeared across the Great Hall.

"Your mother is right, you are a bloody menace," Cló muttered, before racing up to the Blue Suite to shake Jude awake.

"You have to come!" she cried, shaking him harder when sleep refused to relinquish its hold.

"What?" Jude mumbled.

"A cat!"

He sat up, wide-eyed and disorientated. "You want me to get up in the middle of the night to look for a cat?"

"A mummified cat!"

He rubbed his eyes and shook his head. "You should have led with that." He got out of bed after a brief argument with the drapes.

"Jude, I heard it! I heard the cat crying. This place really is haunted."

He stopped pulling on the pair of jeans he'd discarded on the floor earlier, a furrow of worry deepening between his eyes. "That's pretty insane, even for you."

Tears gathered in Cló's eyes. "Please, Jude!"

He nodded but kept a wary eye on Cló hovering by the door as he got dressed. When he was semi-decent, she shot down the corridor. She was far more at home in the labyrinth of Grimdark Hall at night than Jude now. They slowed as they neared the Great Hall. Voices drifted on the dusty air towards them. The sisters.

"You woke up Constance and Ruth?" Jude hissed, horrified that he'd have to see his sisters when he'd managed to avoid them almost entirely these past two weeks.

"Of course not! I'm not a sucker for punishment." Taking Jude's hand, Cló smiled at him in the light of the Great Hall streaming through the doorway. "Hi!" she said brightly as they stepped into the vast space together. It seemed the obvious thing to say, but perhaps not in the early hours of the morning, and not to these two women who turned to Jude and Cló with thunderous expressions.

"Phone the police!" Constance directed her command to Jude. "We've had a break-in. Ruth heard the noise and managed to scare them off, but I want the police here."

"Oh!" said Cló, alarmed, with a quick glance at Ruth, who was possibly the most unscary person in the whole of Grimdark. "It wasn't a break-in, it was me. I—er—That is, I—" She faltered under the baleful glares of the sisters.

"Not only do you break our priceless heirlooms, but now you're breaking the house itself!" Constance snarled.

"Oh don't, Con," murmured Ruth, her watery green eyes were glassy in the chandeliers' bright light.

"Shut up, Constance," snapped Jude. He turned to Cló. "Show me your mummified cat."

Cló could've hugged him then, his voice thick with his fondness for her that had recently been absent.

"How the hell did you manage to find this?" said Jude, astonished when Cló pointed out the small opening in the ceiling of the fake fireplace.

Conscious of two pairs of green eyes on them, Cló moved closer to Jude to whisper, "I told you. I heard it crying and followed the cries here." She didn't dare mention Gwenn had been with her in front of the sisters.

He looked at her, rubbed his face, and muttered, "This is nuts," before putting his head up through the square opening. "This should be in a museum," he said, his voice muffled. He withdrew his head. "I've seen one framed in a pub. Years ago, when I was at Cambridge. It was chasing a mummified rat."

"What are you two talking about?" Constance demanded. "What's in there?"

Neither Jude nor Cló missed the look of calculation between the sisters.

"It's a mummified cat," said Jude.

The sisters deflated, interest evaporating in an instant.

"It's horrible," said Cló. "The poor thing needs to be buried. I know the cat won't care, but—"

"Don't be such a soft cock," said Constance.

Jude stepped out of the fireplace, his face contorted with fury. "You will not speak to my wife like that!"

Constance's nose twitched with equal fury. "How dare you? Who are you to tell me what I can and cannot say to whomever I wish in my own home?"

Jude leaned forward until he was nose to nose with his sister. "I dare because I *own* Grimdark Hall. You remain here because *I* allow it. It would pay you well to remember your *place*." He pulled Cló towards him, an arm around her waist; a united front in the face of Constance and her loathing that whiplashed the air between them.

"Father's will stated we had the right to live here for our lifetime," said Constance, who hadn't given an inch.

"No, it was a request. Father's will is quite clear you only live here at my sufferance."

Constance's face hardened. Her eyes flicked to Ruth, who hovered at her sister's elbow anxiously.

Ruth smiled at Jude, then included Cló in the smile.

Not anxious, Cló thought in surprise. She didn't bother to hide her scrutiny of Ruth, whose gaze darted between Constance and Jude, lizard-quick, eyes behind her glasses shining. *She's enjoying this.*

"I'm sure Father knew best," said Ruth, her little girl voice higher than usual. "He always knew what was best for us, didn't he, Con?" She looked at her sister, who snorted at the same time as Jude. "Perhaps it would be best if we all went back to bed," she added.

"Yes," said Jude slowly. He frowned. "Have you been out, at this time of night?" he asked, belatedly taking in his sisters' manner of dress.

It was the first time Cló had seen Ruth without one of her

many weird outfits. Instead, she wore a bright pink dressing gown with a little rabbit on the pocket more suited to a five-year-old girl. Constance was dressed for her nightly trip to the family chapel and covered in a fine layer of dust.

Cló's stomach clenched in anticipation for the lie Constance would come up with. There was no way she'd tell the truth. She doubted even Constance would have the balls to tell Jude she'd been desecrating the family's tombs.

Constance's eyes narrowed and the corner of her lips quirked. "I've been in your favourite place."

Jude's indrawn breath was loud in the following silence. An undercurrent raced between the siblings that Cló didn't understand.

Ruth tittered, her eyes rounder than ever and bright with glee.

Feeling a shudder pass through Jude's body, Cló looked at his face. He was ashen and wide-eyed with terror.

He ripped away from her and stormed out of the Great Hall. Cló hurried after him.

"What did she mean?" she demanded when she caught up to Jude. "What's your favourite place? Jude! Stop walking away from me!"

Jude stopped so abruptly Cló almost cannoned into him. "She didn't mean anything; she was just being cruel."

"I know where she goes. I told you ages ago I'd seen her going into the chapel. She goes there every night."

Jude frowned. "You've been spying on my sister?"

"No! Not spying!" said Cló, stung. "I saw her the first night going into the chapel by chance. It wasn't deliberate, and sometimes I see her when I'm mooching about." When she said it out loud it did sound like she'd been spying, and perhaps she had a bit. Cló opened her mouth to tell Jude about the crypt and the desecrated tombs; that part she hadn't told him.

But Jude was already walking away.

She wanted to run after him, try speaking to him even if he didn't want to, but the frost that had slipped in their relationship stopped her. Instead, she watched him go.

Tears on her cheeks, she returned to the Great Hall. The sisters had disappeared into their quarters, which she'd discovered by chance one night. They lived simply, from the little Cló had seen before leaving quickly to avoid detection: two bedrooms on either side of a shared sitting room. Ruth's room was pink and girlish, with teddies on a counterpane from her childhood, her costumes on a rack against one wall. Constance's room was as stark and severe as a monk's cell.

Stepping into the fireplace in the Great Hall, Cló looked up at the open cavity. She couldn't leave the cat there. Crying openly for herself and the cat, she reached in and took it out carefully. It felt like hard, angular leather and smelt ghastly up close.

Outside in the predawn light, Cló got a shovel from the garden shed she'd seen Constance go into and headed into the walled garden. She thought it might once have been the kitchen garden. Rows of grape arbours had thrived in isolation and reeked of vinegar. Through another arch, Cló found an orchard. The apples trees were gnarled with age, and peaches had dropped everywhere, their putrid stink making her quite lightheaded.

She found an apple tree a cat might like, with crooks and hollows aplenty, the perfect sort of place for a cat to lie in wait on a branch, ready to pounce on someone passing below.

It didn't take long to dig the small grave. Without ceremony Cló buried the cat under the apple tree. She regarded the little plot of upturned soil and sighed, resigning herself to the concept of reincarnation. She couldn't possibly have known about the cat's location if not for a residual memory from Effie Figgis.

She sighed again, cleaned the shovel and put it back where Constance left it.

Cló walked out of the shed and shrieked.

"For god's sake, Gwenn!" she cried. "You have to stop scaring the life out of me."

Gwenn's small hand found Cló's. "Come with me," she said.

"I need to take you back to your mom," said Cló, feeling guilty that she'd utterly forgotten the little girl. But she allowed Gwenn to lead her towards the Hermitage. To her surprise, they didn't enter the crooked old tower, but slipped through a small door in the wall below it.

"Jesus!" said Cló. They were right on the cliffs where they met the perimeter walls of Grimdark Hall. "Not too close," she warned fearfully when Gwenn let go of her hand and stepped right up to the very edge.

Gwenn ignored her. She squinted up at the Hermitage as though she was trying to remember something. She nodded, walked up to the wall and squatted down. She pulled at the grass in a frenzy, then stood up and stepped off the edge of the cliff.

"Gwenn!" Cló shouted.

It was too late. Gwenn had vanished.

"Oh no! Nonononono!" Cló hurried forward, her chest squeezing with a terrible dread, and steeled herself to look over the edge to the little body dashed against the rocks below.

She almost went over herself, tripping over a hole.

"Oh!" Below Cló, stairs had been cut inside the cliff itself. At the bottom, looking up, was Gwenn.

"I'm taking you home," said Cló, her heart racing so hard with relief and alarm she thought she might vomit. "No! Don't go any further, Gwenn! This has got to stop."

Gwenn grinned up at her and disappeared into the darkness beyond the stairs.

Cursing under her breath, Cló climbed down into the cliff and switched on the light on her phone.

A long tunnel with hewn, honey-coloured walls stretched

away before her. Gwenn was just visible at the light's furthest reach. She turned and walked further into the cliff.

"Dammit, Gwenn!" Cló muttered. Her voice was a faint echo that came back to her.

She started after the girl. The sheer darkness swirled around her in chalky dustiness and the trapped summer heat had sweat springing up on her forehead.

Gwenn walked back towards Cló. "Do you remember?" she whispered.

And Cló did.

"My daughter." Cló's eyes widened at the light coming down the tunnel towards them.

1645

"We've been lookin' all over fer you!"

Effie stopped in the middle of the tunnel, the burning torch she carried casting a halo of light around her, her mind still picking over the memory that wasn't hers from a couple of months before. It plagued her dreams and occupied her waking hours, her nostrils still twitching with the stench of remembered death.

She turned to the steward of Honeyborne Hall. "You—" she squeaked. She cleared her throat and continued in her usual gruff voice, "You have?"

"Yar wanted by Lady Honeyborne." The steward peered around the tunnel. "What you doin' down here anyways?" he demanded. "And at this time o' night an' all?"

"Ent got nothin' to do with the likes o' you," Effie snapped, not daring to look back the way she'd come from the Hermitage.

His eyes narrowed to suspicious slits, then looked away from Effie's odd-coloured eyes and spat against the tunnel wall. "No need to take on," he muttered.

"*Lady Honeyborne . . . ?*" *Effie prompted.*

"*She's in a poorly way. His Lordship ent happy about it. Old Bull's been at it fer hours, but my Lady has insisted you be called fer. The babe is breached.*"

"*Then it's as well you found me,*" *said Effie.* "*Well?*" *she demanded when the steward didn't move.* "*What are you waitin' fer, gorpin' like a wet-eyed toad, like you ent never seen me afore?*" *She lifted the bag she carried everywhere with her.* "*I have me bits and bobs so let's be gettin' on with it.*"

The steward shook his head and turned back up the fork in the tunnels he'd come down. "*You've a wicked tongue in yar head, so you have, Effie Figgis,*" *he threw over his shoulder.* "*You'll end up on the cucking stool like yar mum, mark my words. And if it ent the stool it'll be the bridle, or both.*"

"*Scold I may be,*" *Effie retorted, having no time for the opinions others had of her mum or herself, though well aware of them,* "*but only fools git scolded and rightly so.*"

Suitably chastened, the steward said no more as he led the way through the honeycomb of caves below Darrow End, emerging from the entrance that opened out within the grounds of Honeyborne Hall.

Effie's eyes slid to the Hermitage, worried Joseph might be looking down at her now, though she'd warned him time and again not to go near the windows.

Honeyborne Hall was at odds with its name, for it was not honeyed in appearance nor stature, but a huge and forbidding place born of knapped flint that gleamed darkly even on this new moon night. Scaffolding ran up its front façade like a scuttling insect, the only outward evidence of the construction that had been going on for months in the current lord's determination to stamp his own character on the building.

Following the steward around the side of the Hall they entered the kitchens; vast, sweltering rooms that stank of smoke and roasted meat, and always had some activity, even in the middle of the night.

With a nod at the head cook, Effie said, "I'll be needin' water and clean cloth." She turned, then started in horror. "Sophie! What are you doin' here?"

Sophie, sitting at a table with a mug of tea, shrugged. "Lookin' fer you. Whole village turned out when none could find you."

Guilt twinged in her stomach; she had been spending too much time with Joseph in the Hermitage. Truth be told, the ashen-haired man fascinated her. It warmed her heart each time she entered the Hermitage to see him sitting on the bottom step of the curling staircase, his face lighting up with her arrival. She'd never felt so wanted before, so needed, not for her skills as a cunning woman but for herself alone. She couldn't understand much of what he said, but every line on his face told a story she wanted to hear. There was wisdom in his pale blue eyes and kindness in his smile that she rarely saw or received from her neighbours in Darrow End.

"Well, I'm here now, you'd best be off home," she said, more caustically than she'd intended, sharing a quick fearful glance with the cook.

"In a bit," said Sophie, not looking at her mum.

"What you up to?" Effie demanded.

"Nothin'," Sophie said to her mug of tea.

"Listen to yar mum, Sophie," said the cook. "It ent safe fer a mawther such as yarself to be abroad o' a night."

"It's nearly mornin'!" Sophie protested.

"Even so."

But Effie shared the cook's concern. There were worse things to fear within Honeyborne Hall than without for a young woman, especially one as lovely as Sophie. Many young girls from Darrow End worked at the Hall, and rumours abounded of the terrible rites of passage the girls endured when newly employed.

"I'll see she comes to no harm," assured the cook when Effie dithered, reluctant to leave Sophie in the kitchen.

A moment of wordless communication passed between the

two women before Effie nodded, and with a puffed out sigh of harried frustration, she stomped up the servant's staircase tucked into the corner of the kitchen.

Honeyborne Hall was a maze of new construction, the shape of Grimdark Hall changing day by day under a cloud of constant plaster dust. Effie scurried into the Great Hall that was nearing completion, transformed from a dingy series of rooms into a single baroque magnificence inspired by one of Lord Honeyborne's many tours of Italy. Its grandeur was not lost on Effie, though she did not understand the need for such extravagance in a room that was used primarily as a thoroughfare.

"What're you doin'?" she shrieked and hurried across the hall to the two men fighting a black kittling they were trying to squeeze into the ceiling of the newly installed fireplace.

"You would be better suited to your purpose and get on your way, Mistress Figgis. Lord Honeyborne has insisted the kittling be so boarded."

Effie glared at Theophilus Braid. The priest stood on the far side of the fireplace, stiff with disapproval as the men did their lord's bidding.

Helplessly, Effie watched the men push the kittling into the cavity and quickly fitted the tile into position. Her heart clenched at the desperate cries and scrabble of claws as darkness entombed the cat.

Noting the star etched onto the tile, a witch's mark she was seeing more and more often in the cottages down in Darrow End, Effie snarled, "There ent nothin' so evil as those as harm livin' creatures fer no good reason!"

The workmen sped off, not daring to look into Effie's odd-eyed fury.

The priest raised a surprised eyebrow. "For once it would seem we are in agreeance."

"Then stop this gammarattle! You've the power from yar pulpit. Put it to good measure."

Theophilus Braid gazed into Effie's mismatched eyes without wavering. "And so I shall . . . and to all witchcraft and baseless superstition. Our Lord said to Ezekiel, 'Woe to the women who sew magic bands upon all wrists, and make veils for the heads of persons of every stature, in the hunt for souls.'"

"Mayhap he did, mayhap he dint," said Effie, not liking the gleam in the priest's eye, well aware he and his ilk thought cunning folk were magic workers and sorcerers. "But that be yar work to root out evil and you ent doin' a good job o' it."

Intent on releasing the kittling, Effie started towards the fireplace, when the priest reached out a preventative arm. "You may be wayward, Mistress Figgis, but you are not a fool. It would do you well to leave alone what you cannot change. Your services," he added with a sneer, "are needed elsewhere."

Frustrated tears threatened, hearing the truth in the priest's caution that was not said in kindness to Effie or the kittling. There were limits to her power, which was no power at all, for she was a woman and cunning, both wayward in the eyes of man and God alike.

Tightening her heart against the plaintive cries of the kittling, she hurried out of the Great Hall.

This was not Lady Honeyborne's first labour; Effie had attended the first three and knew her way to the bedroom she needed. It was a conflict of dread and relief to see Lord Honeyborne in the corridor; she had no love for the man, but if he were here then he could not be doing harm elsewhere. His expression was long with boredom, without the worry a husband might be expected to exhibit for his wife enduring a difficult labour.

Beside him stood James Bulman, talking rapidly and gesticulating in anger, and his apprentice Benjamin Hobbis, who listened, plucking worriedly at his bottom lip.

Without breaking stride, Effie steeled herself for a confrontation when Old Bull turned puce with fury on spying Effie head-

ing towards him. Hobbis's frown lifted into a relieved smile when he, too, saw Effie. She grimaced internally, for young Hobbis was the most likely reason her stubborn daughter dallied in the kitchens. He had been wooing Sophie these past months. Effie was not against the match; she rather liked the young doctor, even if he was wet behind the ears.

"There's nothing you can do!" James Bulman snarled when Effie reached the men. "The babe is dead in the womb. You've bewitched the babe knowing it to be a boy!"

"That's a load of ole squit!" Effie hissed back, sensing Lord Honeyborne's cold, suspicious gaze on her. She expected no help or quarter given there. "None know fer certain whether it be boy or girl afore the birth."

"I know you for what you are, Mistress Figgis," snapped Old Bull, his tone rancid with contempt. "About all hours of the night with your familiars, sneaking in where they're afeared, casting your hexes on the godly."

Benjamin Hobbis frowned at the older doctor. He caught Effie's raised eyebrow and cleared his throat. "I—er—don't think the babe is dead yet," he said, his tone low and conciliatory. "But I believe it to be breached."

Old Bull's eyes widened to their fullest extent before he turned to his protégé. "You dare to contradict me?"

Benjamin swallowed but stood his ground. "I do," he said quietly.

"I've not the time fer yar pride and nonsense . . . Out o' my way," Effie muttered, and pushed past Old Bull none too gently.

The stench of sweat, blood and fatigue hit Effie as she entered the overheated bedroom.

"Open a window," she said to one of Lady Honeyborne's gossips, for the air was fetid and heavy, ripe for disease and death to set in.

She hurried over to Lady Honeyborne, a thin, frail woman who did not have the best build for numerous pregnancies, yet it would be her lot until she produced an heir and a spare for the incumbent lord of Honeyborne Hall.

"I am so pleased you came, Effie," whispered Lady Honeyborne, when Effie leaned down to wipe the sweat and tears away from the woman's face. "Dr. Bulman said the babe is dead, but I can still feel it moving."

"So he says," Effie muttered gruffly. She felt around Lady Honeyborne's swollen stomach. "He says wrongly, but the young doctor were right. The babe be breached."

"Is it a boy?"

Effie shrugged. "The babe be lying more to the right—it's possible."

"Please save him, Effie. I cannot bear another girl. Edmund will—" Lady Honeyborne screamed as a contraction took her.

"Drink this." Effie handed the woman a concoction of wine and mugwort she always carried in her bag. "It'll help ease the pain." She took out a stone bottle and tipped oil of sweet almonds onto her hands.

Her hands slippery with oil, she slid them into Lady Honeyborne's womb and, through long years of experience, gently handled the baby until he was positioned to come out head first.

She sat beside the labouring woman and wiped her face with a cloth one of the gossips placed into her hand. Much of a woman's labour was waiting for the next bout of pain; the trick for the midwife was to keep their minds off the pain to come.

"That weren't here last time I were in," said Effie, nodding at a glass cabinet on the wall of the bedroom that had captured her attention.

Lady Honeyborne turned her sweat-stained head to the glass birds that prismed and shone in the candlelight, creating rainbows in shadows.

"My lord husband brought them back for me as a gift from Venice . . . It's a collection of islands off the coast of Italy," she added at Effie's blank expression.

"What are they?" said Effie. In her drab and humble life, never had she seen such beauty. The dim light in the room played on the glass birds, giving them life in colours she hadn't known existed in the world.

"Birds."

"Yis," said Effie. "But they ent like nothin' we git about here."

Lady Honeyborne's lips quirked with gentle amusement. "There's all sorts of different ones; I'm afraid I don't know all their names."

Effie stared odd-eyed at her. It was difficult to outstare those eyes and Lady Honeyborne looked away first. "There's a bee-eater, we see them here in summer, and a parrot, those come from the Indies, and the pink one is a flamingo." She smiled at Effie's blank look. "They're from Africa."

"A fine thing be these," said Effie. She longed to take the little birds out of their cage; though they were made of glass, she hated to see anything confined, especially something so beautiful. She looked down at her rough hands; such delicacy did not belong in hands such as these.

But the plight of glass birds dissipated with Lady Honeyborne's agonised howl. A few minutes later the babe's head crowned and slipped into Effie's hands in a slither of blood and mucous.

"It's a boy," said Effie as she cut the navel string and wiped the babe down before swaddling it deftly to place it on the new mother's breast.

Tears ran down Lady Honeyborne's cheeks. "Finally, a boy!" She wept in relief and exhaustion as the newborn mewled like a kittling at the shock of this new, cold world it had entered.

The new mother cried for a few moments, a weak sobbing, before she sighed and sat up against the pillows Effie put behind her back. "You know what they'll say, don't you?"

"Yis. Bewitchment." Effie snorted. "It's been said afore, but nothin' shall come o' it. It rarely does, except as mardle and rumour."

Lady Honeyborne smiled sadly. *"You can't win either way. Save a babe and mother, you've bewitched them; the babe or mother dies, and you've bewitched them."*

Effie shrugged, though her stomach quivered with foreboding at the lady's words.

"It's the lot o' the cunning folk in these times. But talk be talk, and people will talk. Nothin' will come o' it." She looked up at Lady Honeyborne's face, confused by the flicker of guilt.

Lady Honeyborne closed her eyes while Effie set the gossips to tidying up the room and clearing the sheets to be washed. She poured oil of St John's wort onto the new mother's stomach as she waited for the after-burden to come forth. Then she picked up the now quiet baby and opened the door to introduce the new father to his son.

"Where's His Lordship?" Effie said quietly so as not to disturb the sleeping baby.

Benjamin Hobbis pushed off the wall he'd been leaning against and looked down at the sleeping baby in Effie's arms with a smile. *"I knew you could do it."* He smiled again at Effie's surprise at the compliment. *"Sophie said you're the best midwife in the area. That many a babe has survived that wouldn't at the hands of another."*

"Where's Lord Honeyborne?" she asked again, urgent now.

"Dr. Bulman convinced him the babe was dead, so he went off shortly after you arrived."

"Where's Sophie?" Effie demanded, ashen-faced.

"Sophie? I haven't seen her . . . What's wrong? Is Sophie in danger?"

"I hope not." Effie bit her lip; she couldn't leave the new mother when the after-burden had not yet pushed out. Left in the womb it would corrupt and kill the mother. *"She were in the kitchen. Find her and take her home. She only stayed 'cause you were here."*

The fear for her daughter on Effie's face sent Benjamin hurrying down the corridor without needing to be told twice.

It seemed an age before the after-burden oozed out and into the cloth Effie had left ready beneath Lady Honeyborne's legs. All the while Effie fretted about Sophie, hoping against hope that her worst fears, what she had been protecting her daughter from since she'd reached womanhood, had not come to pass.

"My Lady," she whispered when one of the gossips passed her a bowl of broth. "You need to eat, gain yar strength back."

Lady Honeyborne's eyes flickered open. She accepted the mouthfuls of broth, watching Effie under her eyelashes.

"I'll be leaving now," said Effie, edging her way to the door.

"Effie!" whispered Lady Honeyborne, her voice weak, but urgent.

Effie sighed and hurried back to the bed. "Yis?" She leaned down close to the woman's mouth.

"Beware," whispered Lady Honeyborne. "My lord husband has sent for the Witchfinder General, so he styles himself. A Matthew Hopkins."

"I've heard o' him, and the trial down in Manningtree. Eighteen women he hanged fer witchcraft. But Manningtree be miles away. He ent likely to come up our way."

"There are already Watchers in the village, Effie!"

"Who?" Effie shut her eyes. "Dunt tell me, I think I know. Goodwife Kett be one."

"And her cousins she brought in from King's Lynn. I heard Edmund give the order not a week back to watch you and your mother until the Witchfinder arrived . . . I'm so sorry, Effie. But you know Edmund does not listen to me. There was nothing I could do to protect you."

Effie nodded, lips tight. But her hatred for Lord Honeyborne blistering within her chest had little to do with this Witchfinder General, and everything to do with Sophie.

"Rest now," she said, and hurried out the birthing chamber without a backward glance.

Lifting up her heavy skirts, she ran down the corridor, down stairs and through the Great Hall with a crimp of sadness in her heart for the kittling mewling weakly from the fireplace, but had no time to stop and save the poor thing. She darted down the servants' stairwell and into the kitchen.

The head cook, her sleeves rolled up above her meaty arms, kneaded dough on the huge table running the length of the kitchen.

"Where's Sophie?" Effie shouted, startling the cook.

Guilt riddled the fat rolls of the cook's cheeks and darkened her eyes. "There were nothin' I could do to stop him," she whispered, wiping her floury hands on her apron before raising them to ward off Effie's maternal fury.

"Where's Sophie?" Effie yelled, taking a step towards the cook, who took an involuntary step back. "I'll kill him!" she screamed. "I'll do things to his body that he shrieks in pain, so help me I will! And to the Devil he shall go if he's touched a hair on Sophie's head!"

The curse of the cunning woman scorched the air and stopped everyone within hearing in their tracks. It reached the ears of the steward, who had been in his office in the cellars and sent him flying up into the kitchen.

His alarmed eyes twitched to Effie who was screaming bloody curses down on Lord Honeyborne's head.

"Git yarself home if you know what's good fer you, woman!" he said.

"Not without my daughter! Where is she?" Effie shrieked, tears of fury lodged in the back of her throat.

"She's already gone on home," said the cook, when Effie paused to take a breath. Before more curses could be hurled that the cook feared might be directed at her, she added quickly, "That new young doctor, Hobbis, he found her and took her home."

Muttering under her breath, Effie stomped out the kitchen, then took off flying across the Hall's gardens, past the old chapel and through the small gate next to the Hermitage. She didn't spare a glance for the ruined tower and her secret patient within, but slipped into the tunnel, hurtled through the dark, knowing those tunnels beneath the cliffs like she did her own hands.

Through Darrow End she ran as the fishermen, always the earliest risers, hurried through the alleys and byways. She ran until she reached the little cottage perched on the edge of the cliff and ripped open the door.

A single candle lit the gloom and the three faces seated at the table. Germaine turned her blind gaze to the doorway, her old face ravaged with a terrible fury that matched Effie's own. Benjamin Hobbis was white-faced and shaking, while Sophie, her beautiful face blotched from crying, stared sightlessly at the wall.

It was Germaine who broke the heavy silence suffocating the room. "If you dunt kill that bastard, Euphemia," she hissed, "then by the Devil, I shall."

ELEVEN

Cló slunk into the kitchen. Jude stood at the cooker, a delicious aroma of bacon drifting around him. She was surprised to see him here at all. Most mornings he'd been up and away before she'd awoken. She was even more surprised he was here after yet another argument last night. Jude hated the aftermath of an argument. He was terrible at apologising, but hated it when Cló apologised to keep the peace regardless of who was at fault. He'd always said there are two things he would never say unless he truly meant it: tell someone he loved them or apologise.

Jude turned from the cooker. He smiled tentatively. "I'm sorry," he said before Cló could open her mouth. "I've been an utter arse, and I've taken it out on you. It's not just last night; it's been every night, and I am so sorry I brought you here."

Cló gulped down her own apology and pulled him into a tight hug.

"Is something burning?" she said into his shoulder.

"Shit! The pie." Jude let go of her to open the oven, releasing a cloud of vapour.

Cló wrinkled her nose. "That smells ghastly."

Jude frowned in surprise. "It's your favourite, apple pie. To make up for last night."

They stared at the pie he'd pulled out of the oven, its pastry perfectly golden.

"You love my apple pie," he said in a small voice.

Their eyes met, mirroring the other's hope.

"We said not here in Grimdark," said Jude, his caution belying the longing in his eyes.

"Who cares?" cried Cló. "If it's happened, it's happened. I'll get a test." She hared out of the kitchen and dashed along the corridors, puffing by the time she reached the Blue Suite. Grabbing one of the home kits she'd brought with, she sat on the loo with her knickers around her ankles. She ripped open the box and peed on the stick.

She waited the requisite time, her heart rising as the second blue line slowly got stronger and stronger.

Cló hadn't quite got her knickers up properly before she was out of the bathroom and rushing back along the corridors to the kitchen.

Brandishing the test-stick above her head like an Olympic torch, she yelled, "We're pregnant!"

Again scurried around the room like a fearful mouse searching for somewhere to hide.

Jude grabbed Cló in a bear hug and danced around the kitchen table whooping at the top of his voice.

"I want a little girl!" cried Cló, her mind flashing to a certain white-haired ghost of a girl.

"Don't count your chickens," cautioned Jude as he pulled away, unable to wipe the grin off his face. "We've been down this road before . . . and I want a boy, for the record. I hope he's artistic. I always wanted to be artistic."

That took the edge off Cló's euphoria. A boy worried her. Three miscarriages and all were boys. "As long as it's healthy," she said lamely, the wish of every prospective parent.

"What's healthy?"

Cló and Jude pulled a dismayed face at each other, then turned to the Honeyborne sisters. Constance stomped in, glaring, followed closely by Ruth; a faithful shadow in a cerise sequinned flapper dress, which was quite mundane compared to some of her more extravagant costumes.

Cló nudged Jude, communicating silently her desire to be nowhere near the sisters, not after last night. She couldn't bear a snide comment ruining this moment that was hers and Jude's alone.

"Cló was just leaving," said Jude, reading her mind. "And there's some apple pie, if you want some."

Constance's eyebrows rose. "You may eat apple pie for breakfast in America, but we are more civilized here."

Jude's jaw clenched. He was about to snap a retort, but Cló shook her head warningly. "I'm off too," he muttered. He took Cló's hand and pushed past Constance on their way out.

He stopped in the Great Hall. "We need to celebrate, but I can't right now. I have a meeting this morning. Shall we make a date of it tonight? There's a nice pub in Cley next the Sea we could try."

Cló nodded, smiling giddily. "I'd like that."

He kissed her goodbye and strode across the Great Hall, disappearing through the open double-leafed doors. A perfidious thought niggled its way into Cló's brain: Why did Jude need to be so involved in tying up the estate? Surely that was what lawyers and such were for? And what could be more important than their baby?

With a rush of guilt at her treacherous thoughts, Cló pressed a gentle hand to her stomach, and said, "I guess it's just you and me today, kid."

She went up to the Blue Suite, at a loose end, as she was most days. She never thought she'd miss the routine of going to work each day, always looking forward to Friday and the weekends. A few weeks of unrestricted freedom in England had seemed like bliss. It hadn't turned out at all how she'd imagined. She had too much free time, and she was stung by a pang of homesickness for Canada and their little house in Toronto, their little garden, their friends, many of whom were their stand-in family.

The Blue Suite was cold. A misting drizzle pressed against the windows, obscuring the view of the Hall's grounds. Grimdark felt as low-spirited as Cló, the air gloomy and preoccupied. She switched on her laptop, the screen opening on the ancestry site she'd been working through but it hadn't yielded anything new.

She sighed at the passenger list from the *Diligence*, hoping by some miracle she'd glean another little fact of how and why Benjamin and Sophronia Hobbis ended up taking a ship to the New World. What had been so terrible about their lives they would take a dangerous voyage to an unknown, untamed land when Sophronia was pregnant?

Cló pulled up the family tree she'd created. One branch, the Hobbis side, was populated with a few names, of Sophronia she had absolutely nothing before 1645.

She wasn't even sure when they married. "Oh!" she said to the Blue Suite. It was something she hadn't checked. She didn't love the idea of wading through hundreds of marriage certificates, but that loose end of free time was waving at her, and Sophronia was not that common a name, perhaps . . .

After reading a few blogs, Cló discovered marriages had been recorded by the parish churches. Thanking whoever was the genius that invented the internet, she found a couple of sites that did the searching for her. Paying her subscription, she put in all the information she had about Sophronia, which amounted to little more than her first name, her gender and her husband's name.

A few minutes her eyes flicked excitedly across the scanned image of a one-line entry in a parish record from Ipswich.

Benjamin Reginald Hobbis in the parish of St Peter's, &
Sophronia Figgis in this parish was marryed—September
27, 1645

"Sophronia *Figgis* . . . I'm an idiot!" Cló muttered, making a
jumble of connections from Effie's memories and the words on
the screen. Sophie and Sophronia. Same person. "That poor
girl!" The implications of what she'd connected truly sank in. It
hit her stomach hard.

Cló rushed for the bathroom and vomited into the loo.

After a few minutes, she wiped her mouth and scowled at
her stomach. "You really know how to pick your moments,"
she told Foetus . . . or perhaps she or he was still only a blasto-
cyst. She had no idea how far along she was. She was rather terrified of finding out. Her previous pregnancies had terminated
shortly after the third month. Could she be that far along? She
felt her stomach gently, afraid she'd dislodge something important merely by prodding her own skin.

Rinsing her mouth out, Cló went back to her laptop. This
was huge. She needed to share her discovery. She considered
phoning Jude. She went as far as pulling out her phone and opening WhatsApp.

Her finger hesitated over the small screen. Instead, she took
a photo of the parish record.

Shrugging on her coat, Cló walked into the bedroom and
stopped in astonishment. "Ruth?" she said, eying her sister-in-
law warily.

Ruth didn't seem at all abashed Cló had caught her in their
room without invitation. She'd had another costume change,
now a Russian peasant, adorned in a rather beautiful deep red
sarafan. "Are you going out?" she asked.

"Umm . . . yes, I was," said Cló guardedly. "Can I—er—
help you with anything?"

"No."

They stared at each other.

"Sorry, I don't mean to be rude, but what are you doing in our room?" asked Cló finally, hoping she didn't sound too accusatory, but not sure how else to word it.

Ruth smiled faintly. "Oh. Yes. There's no dinner tonight. Cook is off on some family errand, so you'll have to fend for yourself."

"That's fine. Jude and I were planning to go out to dinner tonight anyway."

Ruth nodded, quite obviously disinterested in Jude and Cló's plans. She looked around the room vaguely, as though expecting it to have changed colour overnight, then seemed disappointed it was still the same blue it had always been.

Cló peered worriedly through the open doorway to the corridor, expecting to see Constance lurking there. When she was sure it was only Ruth, she decided to ask the question she'd been dying to ask. "Ruth, why do you dress up like this?" She waved a hand to indicate the sarafan.

Ruth peered down at herself and seemed surprised at what she wore. "It is who I am, who I was and who I will always be." Her gaze returned to Cló. "Such peculiar eyes you have," she said softly.

Cló had asked for it, she supposed, a retaliation for her personal question. "Um ..." she said, her skin crawling under Ruth's scrutiny. Though most people did a double take when they saw her mismatched eyes, not many commented on them. It used to bother Cló, so much she'd worn coloured contacts, unable to bear the stares. It was Jude who persuaded her to put her contacts away. He loved Cló's eyes, saying he got the best of blue and brown eyes, and Cló came wrapped up with both.

"Jude was always such a naughty boy," said Ruth.

Blindsided by the change in topic, it was a moment before Cló collected herself enough to say waspishly, "Well, he's not anymore. He's a good man, a really good man."

Ruth leaned forward conspiratorially. "He used to tease us, you know. Following us around, pretending to find things. Getting Constance all worked up. He really was very naughty to upset Constance so. She had to teach him a lesson; otherwise he wouldn't stop."

"What lesson?" Cló whispered, cold and shivery. "What wouldn't he stop?"

Ruth laughed airily and far too long for comfort, making Cló wonder if the woman was truly unhinged. Jude's parents may have taken the woman to doctors many years ago, but that didn't mean she wasn't mentally unwell now.

"Is there anything else?" Cló asked, wishing the woman would leave, wishing she didn't feel so uncomfortable in her presence.

"Mmmm?" Ruth regarded her thoughtfully for a moment longer, then turned and left the room. No "Goodbye" or "See you later."

"This family is nuts," Cló murmured in bemused astonishment, as Ruth's footsteps receded down the passage.

She walked to the door, stopped, picked up her laptop and shoved it into its bag. She didn't think the sisters would know how to use it, sensing they were the sort to resist technology, but she wasn't taking any chances.

Once outside, Cló zipped up her coat, lifted the hood against the drizzle and set off across the grounds and through the small door in the walls. Darrow Bay was blanketed in a fine mist. It was low tide, the rock-strewn beach elongated oddly out into the bay. Ruddy turnstones strutted about the rocks like self-important butlers in black waistcoats.

Cló paused on the cliff path and gasped in amazement.

Not far from the beach a church tower poked up through the waves. The sea was doing strange things. There was no telltale white-tipped surf surging around the old knapped-flint walls; more a nervous ripple, as though the sea itself was fearful of touching it. Nearby the water ran swiftly, fleeing down hidden alleys of the drowned village, cleaving around what might've been a pitched roof below the surface, or created whirlpools above an open square only visible to the sea.

An old couple had stopped further along the cliff path. The man pointed out the tower with his walking stick.

Relieved she was not imagining the drowned village, Cló's heart still clenched with dread. Through the misty drizzle and above the surge of the sea, a bell tolled. Then again. She counted each peal under her breath.

As the thirteenth toll was swallowed by the drizzle, Cló glanced at the old couple, hoping they, too, had heard the ghostly church bells. But they were gone.

TWELVE

❧

"You're up the duff," said Luna, the moment she opened the vardo's door to Cló's knock.

"Pardon?"

"Pregnant, you dolt."

Cló couldn't prevent the grin spreading across her face. "I found out this morning."

"That's exciting shit. . . . And scary," she said, her eyes narrowing thoughtfully. "You've lost a couple—no, three. Fuck me. This is big, isn't it?"

"Um . . ." said Cló, astonished. "How did you know that?"

Luna shrugged. "Fortune-teller, remember?"

"It was the weirdest thing," said Cló, smiling, holding the memory of that morning tight within her yet wanting to share every detail with the world at the same time, "But I got a sudden aversion to apple pie, and I *love* apple pie!"

Luna's eyebrows rose. "Did that happen with your last pregnancies?"

"No. I didn't have any aversions. Quite the opposite, in fact. I craved pretty much everything."

"Maybe it's not your aversion."

Cló pulled a face. "I know where you're going with this and, while I may be onboard with the reincarnation, I can't see how likes and dislikes can have continued through my lives. And especially apple pie; it's such an innocuous sort of thing."

"Maybe your previous lives hatred of apple pie was severe . . . Come on." She hooked her arm through Cló's and dragged her towards the yurt. "This calls for a celebration. I'll drink for you, of course, as you can't, and I shall do a reading for you."

"Drinking at this time of the day? It's only four!"

"But it's five o'clock somewhere in the world."

Cló couldn't fault Luna's skewed logic. "I don't know that I want a reading," she added halfheartedly, allowing herself to be towed into the yurt, through the beaded black curtains and into the gloom of the inner sanctum.

"Bollocks," said Luna mildly. "Everyone wants to know what's in store for them."

Cló looked around and grinned. It was everything she'd imagined it would be. "This is all very witchy." Skulls leered from pedestals carved into dragons. Crystals gleamed in shadowy corners, and huge black urns filled with spiky, dark-loving plants crouched on either side of the small round table in the middle of the room. Draped with a shimmering black cloth, a crystal ball sat centre stage between two dribbly candles in holders shaped like clawed hands. A stuffed raven hunched on a perch, peering, beady-eyed, down at the table, waiting to whisper arcane secrets into Luna's ear.

"It's what people want, what they expect," she said with a dismissive shrug. "They want the atmosphere, the eerie experience, then they go home and tell everyone about the witch who lives in the fens . . . Sit down," she commanded.

Cló sat.

Luna placed a pack of well-thumbed tarot cards in front of her, and put her head to one side thoughtfully. "Something else has happened. You've discovered something . . . Something that upset you."

Cló showed her the photo of the parish record on her phone. "I'm the reincarnation of my many-greats-grandmother." The words felt strange on her tongue, like she'd burnt it and nothing tasted quite right afterwards.

"Gwenn and I have been telling you this for quite some time."

"Effie wasn't my great-great-something-grandmother then. She was some random woman from a story. It just got a whole lot more personal."

"Why? Plenty of diluting of the bloodline since." Luna frowned. "There's something else."

Cló nodded slowly, used to Luna's perceptiveness. "Benjamin Hobbis wasn't my great-great-whatever grandfather," she said. "Sophronia—Sophie—was pregnant before they got married." She paused to gather her thoughts. "One of the things I feel strongly when I have these . . . visions, is Effie was terrified for her daughter, and she had a real hatred for Lord Honeyborne. I could feel it every time we—she—god this is confusing! She hated him. Really hated him, more than the doctor or the priest." Sifting through memories and emotions that weren't hers, yet weirdly were, Cló felt like she'd developed a split personality. "That's why she was horrified to see Sophie up at the Hall. He used to rape the local girls, taking advantage of his position. It was all there in Effie's thoughts, in her emotions. I knew things I couldn't possibly know, but it's all shadowy . . . secondhand."

"That wasn't so unusual in those times—or now for that matter."

"No, but he took it one step further. If one of them fell pregnant, he'd have them terminated, baby and mom."

"All men are bastards," said Luna, her tone laced with the bitterness of personal experience.

"Not all. Jude's lovely. He would never harm a woman, and certainly not rape them."

"You've kissed and made up then?"

"We weren't fighting. Not exactly." Cló's throat tightened with pent-up emotion. She missed her Jude. The man who came back to the Hall each night was not the same. "It's Grimdark," she muttered. "It's changing him."

Luna patted her hand. "It's a building. It can't hurt you. What's more interesting is you and your husband are actually related."

"No, we're not."

"You are. If Sophronia is your ancestor and she had a child with a Honeyborne, regardless of the rape aspect, you two are related."

"Oh!" Cló sat back, dumbfounded. She hadn't made that connection.

"Are you going to tell him?"

Cló's immediate response was of course she would tell Jude. She told him everything . . . except recently, she hadn't. She hadn't told him about these weird memories she'd been getting from another person. She hadn't told him what Constance was up to in the crypt.

"You haven't told him, have you? Not about Effie," said Luna.

Cló grimaced. Reading her mind was an occupational habit of Luna's.

"I'm not sure I know how. It's all so"—Cló waved a hand around—"so strange. And Jude doesn't believe in anything like reincarnation. He has no religion at all."

"You didn't believe not so long ago either. You can't protect him from this."

Startled by the edge in Luna's tone, Cló hurried to say defensively, "What's that supposed to mean?"

She gave Cló her fortune-telling stare, head cocked slightly, until a blush stole up Cló's face. "What?" she demanded.

"Couples are strange things," she said. "I am endlessly fascinated why some people are together. Take you and Jude; you need to care for someone, and I'll bet any money you like that your Jude needs caring for. And that's what you're doing now. You're not telling him because you're worried it will upset him."

Cló opened her mouth to defend Jude, then shut it. She hadn't thought of Jude and their relationship in those terms, but Luna was not wrong.

"I will tell him," she promised, already envisaging his scepticism. She snorted slightly at a tangential thought. "And it looks like you weren't wrong about something else either. You and I could be related too."

Luna grinned. "I am never wrong. Though I know I haven't any connection to Euphemia Figgis. Wish I did. It would bring in the punters if they thought they would get a reading from the descendant of a famous witch. But every second person in this area is a Figgis, and Euphemia only had one child, who sailed to America, and I'm looking at her descendant right now." She looked down at the pack of cards in front of her, then up at Cló. "I'm not going to go through the usual rigmarole like I do with other readings. Time is money after all, and this is a freebie."

"A freebie I didn't ask for," said Cló dryly. "You don't have to do this. I don't really want to know about the future, I'd much rather it pans out as it should. God knows, I've got enough problems with a past that's not mine to be worrying about the future."

"Humour me. I want to check something."

Cló nodded, alarmed by the worry in Luna's voice; the only person she worried about was Gwenn.

Luna shuffled the deck, saying, "Most people want their futures sanitised. I don't read the future so much as give my clients choices I see in the cards, but the choice is always theirs. It's what people want nowadays. You can put a spin on anything, using your intuition of the person you're reading. I'm not doing that with you because we're friends, and friends should tell each other the truth. Usually, my client will ask a question or have a question in mind when I lay out the cards, but I'm not doing that with you."

"Why not?"

"I want to see what happens if no questions are asked, and simply get an overview of your past, present and future . . . You okay with that?" she asked as an afterthought.

Her alarm deepening, Cló nodded. Tarot cards were a bit of arcane fun to her, but Luna's serious frown tellingly revealed this wasn't fun or funny.

She laid out three cards in front of her, facedown, and flipped them over one by one. Then she did something very un-witchy and took a photo of the cards with her phone.

Cló peered across the table, reading the names on the cards upside-down. *Death, The Tower* and the *High Priestess.*

"What do they mean?" she asked, her stomach tensing with disquiet.

"Past, present, future." Luna tapped each card from left to right. She sighed. "None are good cards; it's a dreadful spread, and they're all from the Major Arcana, which in itself is unusual."

"Death seems fairly obvious," said Cló, eyeing the grim skeletal figure positioned in the past. "My parents died when I was young."

"Doesn't need to be anything so literal; it can be something in your past that ended suddenly. Though I would say you're probably right that it's your parents' death." She tapped the middle card thoughtfully.

Cló couldn't look at the card of the Tower without a slight shiver. A tower against a stormy sky with two people falling out of it made her think of the Hermitage clinging to the sheer edge of the Darrow Cliffs. It couldn't bode anything good. Her present was in for something horrible too.

"The Tower is a crap card to get. It indicates some sort of life-altering disruption." She turned to the third card. "The High Priestess reversed . . . If she'd been upright it would've been good for your future, but reversed she's all about harm and secrets, or harmful secrets perhaps . . . I'm not going to lie to you or sugarcoat this, but you've had big shit, you've got big shit and you've got big shit coming. And when it comes, it's going to hurt like all buggery and you won't see it coming."

She reshuffled and spread out seven cards in a horseshoe. Pursing her lips, she took a photo and reshuffled. She did this four times, each with a different spread, and with each laying of the cards she took a photo, while her expression deepened to acute apprehension.

Luna studied the cards for so long Cló started to fidget, but kept quiet, knowing instinctively she would be told to shut up if she broke Luna's concentration.

After an age, Luna placed her phone beside the last spread and looked up at Cló. "I don't often get freaked out, but this"— she nodded at the cards—"is scaring the almighty shit out of me."

"What?" Cló demanded.

"I've seen these cards before." She held up her phone. "These are the cards I read for someone else."

"And that's unusual?"

"It's never happened to me, and statistically the same reader reading the same cards for two people must be astronomically high." She worried her lower lip with her teeth. "It wouldn't bother me so much if it had been one spread, but I've done every variation I know, and every one of them came up with the same cards in the same positions . . . And they're all dark cards." She sighed. "The strange thing is, I'm not sure this reading is just about you."

"Effie?"

"I think so. She is your past." She focused on Cló for an uncomfortably long time. "I want to read Effie's cards."

"Okay? Although that should be difficult since she's been dead for nearly four hundred years."

Luna grinned. "But you aren't, and she is you and you are her. I've done loads of readings of people's past lives before so yours should be fairly easy, as we know a bit about Effie already. We can connect the dots." She shuffled through the pack, pulling out a card and handed it to Cló. "This is the Fool. It represents you. I need you to concentrate on the card and think of Effie—what you've remembered—and try to get back into her head."

The card depicted a rather angelic man in a floral dress with a white dog at his heels and the sun bearing down on him. Though Cló found it difficult to believe a piece of cardboard could predict the future or reveal the past, she dutifully closed her eyes and concentrated.

"I don't usually let anyone touch my cards," said Luna after a long while, "but the reading will be stronger if you deal the cards yourself."

Following her instructions, Cló placed ten cards, facedown, except the Fool, who lorded it above the others at the top.

"The first three cards will tell us who you were." Luna flipped them over. "Court cards," she murmured, eyebrows rising in surprise. "The first is the King of Swords, which should've shown Effie's gender. But this card is for a man, and he's nothing like you."

"You got all that from a card?" said Cló doubtfully.

"You're the Knight of Cups. I had you pegged from the first moment I met you . . . the third one along. Tell me about Effie, what her personality was like?"

"Um . . ." Cló only had Effie's impression of herself: wild-haired, big-boned, a lined face. But the reaction Effie had got to her eyes was something Cló could relate to, a shared experience. "She didn't suffer fools, but she helped people. She was some sort of healer, and I got the impression she was quite good at it. She wasn't educated; she couldn't read or write, but she was intelligent. She was rather no-nonsense and got on with things. She thought differently too," she said, warming to the topic, "but even though she tried to keep her thoughts to herself, especially things that could be dangerous if spoken by a woman in those times, she often spoke her mind—"

"She's the Queen of Swords," said Luna, tapping the middle of the three revealed cards. "So who is our King of Swords here?" She slapped her forehead. "I'm an idiot . . . There's another life! Before Effie, long before."

"When?" Cló whispered, not wanting to break Luna's concentration.

Luna snorted. "I'm good, but I'm not that bloody good . . ." Her brow furrowed before she took a couple of cards from the deck and placed them beside the King of Swords. "He lived a long time ago, centuries . . . He was a soldier; death was his companion. Intense love for family . . ." Another snort, a tapping of her fingers on the table as she considered the faceup cards before looking at Cló. "When you told me about your memories of Effie, you said she had a memory of a memory. Do you remember anything of that?"

Surprised, Cló said, "Sort of, but it was more . . . impressions. I had this sudden infusion of inner strength, like nothing was impossible because I had set my mind to it. I could conquer the world because that was what I wanted and nothing would stop me."

"And you never feel like that, not even as Effie?"

Cló shook her head, feeling stupid and weak. "I wish I did. It was invigorating, having that incredible belief in myself and my abilities. But it was fleeting, and rather exhausting in a way, having all that self-confidence."

Luna nodded. "Let's move on." She flipped over the two cards in the next row that lay crossed, one over the other. "Fuck," she whispered, drawing out the curse.

"What?" Cló demanded, caught up in the drama of the darkened room with the raven watching the cards like a dark omen.

A heavy sigh, then, "These two cards show important relationships. Someone who had a great impact on your previous life—or lives. But the cards are reversed, which gives them negative traits or connotations." She grimaced at Cló's worried face. "You had an enemy."

"I did?" said Cló, alarmed.

"Reversed Knight of Pentacles." Luna held up a card. "That's your enemy. He or she would've been a rash person, probably not very bright. Tended to act in the heat of the moment, probably dishonest and greedy. Someone who liked their creature comforts but didn't want to work to get them . . . That wouldn't be so bad, but the second card is the Seven of Wands, reversed. That, in conjunction with the Knight of Pentacles, is a person your previous self didn't know was an enemy, was an unknown or hidden threat. Possibly someone you trusted who betrayed you . . . In your memories of Effie do you remember anyone who might have wished her harm? Serious harm, I mean. Someone who perhaps hated her?"

"She didn't like the priest, and he was . . . well, I don't know that he wished Effie harm, but he was wary of her, suspicious. Lord Honeyborne was a pompous ass. And Effie really hated the doctor, and he hated her too, but it felt more like professional rivalry."

"Did she fear anyone?"

Cló thought back for a long while, then shook her head slowly. "No, not for herself, but she feared for those she loved; her mother and her daughter. They were the most important people in her life. And she feared for Joseph. They had become friends."

"So that's bugger all use. Let's move on . . . The next card should tell us what your previous life did as an occupation." Her hand hovered over the first card of four on the lowest row, reluctant to reveal it. Flipping it over, she frowned. "The Knight of Swords? The soldier again. But this is supposed to be a reading of Effie." She wrinkled her nose in consternation and said, "Let's test this. We know how Effie died, so . . ."

As she started to lift the second card, Cló put her hand over Luna's on a whim and said, "What are you expecting to see?"

Surprised, Luna said immediately, "The High Priestess. She's believed to be based on Pope Joan. She wasn't burnt, but she was stoned to death, and it's the sort of punishment meted out to witches."

Cló removed her hand and Luna lifted the card. Her breath shucked out in a gust. "These aren't Effie's cards. They're a man's cards." She held up a dreadful card of a man lying on his stomach with ten swords in his back. "These cards are for the soldier, our King of Swords, and I would say he was murdered, probably stabbed to death, or maybe he died on a battlefield. But something brutal and bloody."

"Then—" began Cló, but Luna shushed her impatiently into silence.

"A man," she continued. "You were a man in a life before Effie, and that life is connected to Effie and you."

"Wouldn't all my previous lives be connected?"

"Not necessarily. Usually people only reincarnate because of unresolved issues in a previous life, but these"—she swept her hand across the spread—"suggest these three particular lives are connected in some way, possibly by a similar unresolved issue. So what we need to do," she continued excitedly, "is find out what that unresolved issue was and try get it resolved in this life." Before Cló could open her mouth to ask a million questions, Luna flipped over the last two cards. She sighed in satisfaction, her intuition proved right. "Two reversed cards . . . The Five of Swords is never a good card, whether reversed or upright. But it must have something to do with the reason for our man getting murdered. It's a card that speaks of hatred and resentment, maybe through some sort of power struggle. And this"—Luna held up the second card—"is Justice, which is generally a good card, but it's reversed, so it is speaking of guilt and punishment."

"But who killed me when I was this man?" said Cló, when Luna took a necessary breath.

"That's fairly obvious—the Knight of Pentacles. He was a threat in your life; it's a logical deduction he was the one who killed you." She placed the cards on the table and scrutinised the whole spread. "This is about vengeance and retribution," she murmured to herself. "I need to do this with Gwenn when she gets back from school."

"It was Gwenn's cards that were the same, wasn't it?" said Cló.

Luna, uncharacteristically, hesitated, then nodded. "I read her daily to see how her day will go, but with your arrival she's got more—" The worried frown crept back onto her face. "She's going more into herself, to a place I'm not sure I can reach."

"But if Gwenn and I are somehow"—Cló pursed her lips at what was about to come out of her mouth—"entwined . . . At least in the past—"

"Yes?" said Luna, watching Cló carefully.

"Well, why? What was so special about us in our previous lives, or this life."

"Maybe nothing about you or your previous incarnations specifically, but what you *did* when you were—"

There was no warning when a small, fluted voice came from the gloom. "We were brothers once."

Luna and Cló squawked in fright and turned to Gwenn. She was in her red, blue and white school uniform and really shouldn't have appeared ethereal in clothing so mundane, yet she exuded an otherworldliness, her long ashen hair framing her small, pale face.

"We loved each other very much," Gwenn added.

"When you were a pirate?" said Cló, thinking perhaps it was not so surprising Gwenn seemed odd; it couldn't be easy having memories of adults from such a young age. It was a wonder it hadn't addled her brain altogether.

"No. Before. When we wanted revenge for Isabella."

"Who's Isabella?" Cló asked, a shiver of horror crawling up her spine.

"My daughter."

"Why are you staring at Gwenn like a tit in a trance?" Luna demanded, when the silence in the darkened space grew oppressive.

Ignoring the interruption, Gwenn took a step towards Cló. "There is another," she whispered, leaning forward.

"Another what?"

"The one who wants to kill you. He is coming for you. You know what he wants."

11 October 1216

The wide skies of the fens had shrunk to a small halo when mist descended with the dawn. The still air was sharp with the looming spite of winter, and an early frost crackled under the horses' hooves, deadening the dank odour of black mud.

The world held its breath, as though it, too, waited with the brothers Walter Hulot and Ralph Honeyborne. Ralph startled at each crackle, each uneasy whinny, peering down the long black bank between two creeks they had ridden up to this dead end in the middle of nowhere.

Not so Walter, who had many times waited for hours before battle, waiting for the signal to attack, the ensuing screams of pain, blood and, inevitably, death. He had a soldier's pent-up patience and could wait until the angel of death summoned the fallen from their unmarked graves to lead them to purgatory.

Walter stiffened and turned his head. A hum . . . no, a murmur: flat, discordant, muffled by the stifling mist.

Closer now, the murmur rose, words forming. "Catch him, Crow! Carry him, Kite! Take him away till the apples are ripe."

Walter put a calming hand on Ralph's arm when his brother

stared wildly into the mist, seeking the whisperer, hearing the
curse, the ill omen.

"When they are ripe and ready to fall, here comes baby, apples and all."

"It's him," whispered Walter, tightening his grip on his brother.
"Keep calm."

Ralph swallowed and nodded. "This fog is wearing heavy on
my nerves," he muttered.

"Let me do the talking," said Walter, his voice barely raised
to a whisper.

Ralph smiled wryly. "Don't I always?"

Walter whistled, low and short. Mist-knotted tendrils an-
swered his call, coiling, swirling, spreading thin to reveal a cowled
figure, its head to one side as it regarded the brothers; one mo-
ment the fens were featureless and devoid of life, the next he ap-
peared like a wraith. If Walter were a more superstitious man,
he would have thought that same angel of death had come call-
ing early for the conspirators who met in this godforsaken spot
in secret.

The illusion of mystery was lost the moment the face ap-
peared from the cowl. It was not a pleasant face: round and baby-
ish, with unnaturally smooth skin for a man in his fifties, and
extraordinary round green eyes that twitched and blinked too
often. Tonsured hair and a head too small for its body. But per-
haps the most noticeable feature was a small birthmark on the
baby-smooth cheek in the shape of a cross.

Walter felt Ralph stiffen beside him when Brother Simon, as
he was now known, scuttled up to peer into their faces in the
predawn light.

"Is all well?" Brother Simon demanded peevishly without
salutation.

Walter nodded. "The king is leaving Lynn tomorrow at first
light. He shall travel separately to his baggage train for he has
business in Wisbech."

"With you as guide across the Wash again?"

"Aye." Walter grinned an evil grin that Brother Simon had seen often in bygone years. It gave Brother Simon hope the Walter Hulot he had once known as a brother in arms was perhaps not as respectable as he now liked the world to believe.

"Then we are well met . . . And you planted the suggestion he ride on to Swinehead to await his train?"

"I didn't have to. It was his intention."

Brother Simon's eyes twitched hard. He licked his lips and glanced between Ralph and Walter. *"His intention, you say?"*

Walter nodded. *"He is raising funds; he's already begged another loan from Ralph. You can guess it's the reason for a visit to the abbey."*

"Taxation!" Brother Simon's bellow blew the surrounding mist into a tickling dance that followed the monk as he paced along the black-earth bank, hands flying, shouting and cursing incoherently.

"Is he sane?" whispered Ralph, staring at the monk with a puzzled frown.

Walter sighed. *"Barely. But he will do for the task in hand. He has . . . talents you could not stomach."*

"Truly, I have never met a man more unsuited to worship God."

"The only person Brother Simon worships is himself," muttered Walter.

"But he saved your life in the Holy Land!"

Walter nodded, for therein lay the rub; theirs was a tangled history of skewed loyalty and indebtedness. He hated being indebted to this man. But indebted he was, for Brother Simon had—for reasons that had never made sense, knowing the man as he did—saved Walter's life, not once, but twice in the capture of Acre. With hindsight, he knew Simon's heroics had not been altruistic, but with a view to the future and his own self-interest with the debt held over Walter. After Acre, and as King Richard's crusading army had moved through the Holy Land, Brother

Simon had used the loyalty he had bought from Walter—his commanding officer—to turn a blind eye to his thieving off the corpses of their fallen brothers, his dalliance with a woman in Jaffa that had ended in violence, and numerous fights with other soldiers when the drink took him.

But thieving off corpses in a distant land was one thing; the murder of a man, a civilian, in London was quite another. And Brother Simon, when he was known by a different name, had called in a final debt from Walter: escape from the noose by changing his name and entering the Cistercian Order at the Abbey of St Mary in Swinehead. But a change of uniform could not change a man's character, and Brother Simon's character was deeply and eternally flawed.

It should've been over. Walter's debt was paid in full to his own satisfaction, yet here he was in the middle of the fens, conspiring with Brother Simon and his brother because of the actions of a tyrannical king. He needed Brother Simon, and that need did not sit well with his already tarnished conscience.

"I think we should abort the plan," said Ralph quietly, who had not taken his eyes off the ranting monk. "Now, before this goes any further. I don't trust this man."

Before Walter could respond, Brother Simon stopped his frothing tirade and turned abruptly to face the brothers, panting gusts of vapour that clashed with the cold mist.

Brother Simon's very round eyes narrowed, then he sneered at Walter. "You said your brother could handle it. Can't be having doubts now, especially as he shan't be doing any of the dirty work. His sort leaves it to the likes of you and I."

"I trust my brother far more than I trust you." Walter hunched so his face was in Brother Simon's.

The monk stared back, but Walter could outstare his own reflection, and Brother Simon glanced away.

"Very well, but as I shall take most of the risk, I want a greater cut."

"We agreed a three-way split," said Ralph.

"I want half of all. I'm taking most of the risk."

The brothers knew each other well enough to read the other's thoughts. There would be no argument. They would worry about the split after the deed was done. The brothers' motives for their conspiracy was not for financial gain but revenge, while Brother Simon's motives would always be mercenary.

Walter nodded. "Very well, we are agreed. But ensure you do not fail; otherwise we will all be for the noose." He turned towards the horses, and threw over his shoulder, "We shall send word when it's safe to come to the Hall."

Brother Simon's eyes narrowed with distrust. Then he nodded, and said, "Go now, for I must catch a toad."

THIRTEEN

The bells tolled thirteen below the thrashing waves. The morning's mist had given way to blue skies, yet Cló shivered, even though the sun was low and warm on her skin as the afternoon edged towards twilight. But in her head, it was still cold and misty. In her head, the world was a different place, a maelstrom of memories not her own. In her head, she saw the old village of Darrow End falling again and again into the bay. The bells tolling wildly as the old church subsided with the cliff, the suction of waves pulling the buildings and their occupants to the seafloor, the surging currents below the surface still swinging the bells, sending out their ghostly toll to warn the living.

Like an itchy scab, Cló picked at Effie's memory, embellishing it with imagination, as she sat on the walls overlooking Darrow Bay, her arms tight around her stomach, protecting the precious blend of Jude and herself growing within.

The waves and cliffs danced together in an intimate relationship. Sometimes the sea was coy, withdrawing to reveal a naked slither of beach. Sometimes the waves were gentle, caressing the striped walls like a lover. Sometimes the waves raged against the cliffs' impassivity. It was a tumultuous relationship, with endless movement, mirroring the quirks and temperament of a marriage of longstanding.

The sun sank and bled slowly into the sea, tracing a sinuous path towards Cló. It had been dark for a long while before she realised she wasn't alone.

Gwenn sat not far from her, swinging her thin, white legs against the wall, leaning forward to look down at Darrow Bay.

"Hello Gwenn," said Cló, warmed by her presence, the one person who could understand her confusion, her disbelief, her anxiety through shared experience both then and now. "Gwenn?" she said, when the girl didn't respond.

Gwenn cocked her head slightly to one side, her long, ghost-white hair blowing around her head like smoke. "Yes?"

"When you—er—get these memories when you were—er—Joseph, and Ralph Honeyborne, what is it like for you?"

"Like?" Gwenn frowned. "It's not like anything. They've always been there. It just is."

Cló's eyebrows rose, then sank again. She was continuously analysing what she'd remembered, searching for logical explanations, but perhaps, like Gwenn, she needed to accept the truth as she remembered it.

Gwenn watched Cló for a long while, before saying, "Did you see us, Effie?"

"See you and who?" said Cló, with the gentle, cautious tone she used when Gwenn was not speaking about the here and now. She'd long since given up trying to stop her from calling her Effie.

"When we sailed away. We could see you burning. Sophie cried."

"You? When you were Joseph? You sailed away with Sophie and Benjamin?"

Gwenn nodded.

Cló's knowledge of Norfolk's geography was vague, but she

was fairly certain Ipswich, where Sophronia and Benjamin Hobbis sailed from to America, was miles from Grimdark.

"Where were you sailing to?" Cló asked.

"Away. We had to leave and never come back." She continued looking at Cló intently. "I owed you my life. I wanted to save you, but I couldn't, so I saved Sophie instead."

"Why did you have to leave?"

"The monk."

"The monk?" said Cló doubtfully.

"Remember the monk. Remember before it's too late." Gwenn looked up sharply.

Cló whipped around to see what had captured her attention, nearly unlodging herself from her perch on the walls.

Familiar hands steadied her, then Jude sat down, smiling as he said, "Talking to yourself again?"

"Sometimes it feels like that," said Cló, gazing at the spot where Gwenn no longer was. She cleared her throat and said, "You're back early."

"Have you forgotten about dinner at Cley next the Sea?"

Cló had. But the excitement from that morning had fizzled into a fear of something she couldn't name. She didn't want to go anywhere. "Do you mind if we don't go?"

Jude frowned. "No. We don't have to do anything you don't want to . . . Are you feeling alright?"

"I'm fine. We're fine."

"Mmmm . . ." he said, doubtful, and eyed Cló's stomach worriedly.

"We're fine, Jude. I promise," she said, and forced a bright smile. "Now tell me how it went today?"

"Good and bad. The accounts are back. Been waiting for them for ages."

"And?"

"And nothing, really. The estate is making ends meet but not earning vast revenues."

Cló heard the hesitancy in his tone. "Tell me," she said.

She listened to Jude pour out his worries without judgement. She didn't fill the silence when he stopped talking. It was a comfortable silence, born from long familiarity. Together, they watched the moon rise; a cold, uncaring eye peering down at the world. The wind whispered through the reeds of the surrounding fens, rivalling the suck and pull of the waves crawling up the exposed beach below. Shooting stars sped across the sky, quick sparkling blinks.

"I used to sit like this when I was small," said Jude after a long while. "I'd forgotten this place has a rare beauty of its own."

"Your view is coloured by hatred."

He nodded. "That hasn't changed. It won't be long now, and we can leave."

The thought of leaving gave Cló an odd, bittersweet pang of fondness for Grimdark Hall. She didn't have Jude's history with the place. She'd been steadily falling in love with its secrets and hidden treasures. She'd be sorry to leave, but it was for the best. This wasn't her world, though she could imagine herself living here, raising their children . . .

"Don't do it," said Jude, breaking into Cló's thoughts.

"Do what?" she said guiltily.

"You're imagining what it would be like to live here. You're already seeing it in your head, picturing our children playing in the garden."

Cló grimaced. "Except your sisters would always be here, watching from the shadows, whispering their snide comments."

"Yes, they would. I'm sorry."

Cló took his hand and squeezed it, then cleared her throat, loath to break the renewal of their pattern of intimacy. It had been ages since they'd sat up all night talking, but now, as time marched towards midnight and beyond, felt like the perfect moment to tell him what she should've told him ages ago. "There's something I need to tell you," she said.

He raised an eyebrow. "I know you're pregnant, so you can't land that bombshell on me . . . Well?" he said when Cló hesitated. "Tell me and I'll be your best friend."

She smiled. "You *are* my best friend . . . And—and it looks like we may be related."

"We are," said Jude, frowning. "We're married."

"No, no. Through blood. There's no good way to put this, but my great-great-whatever-grandmother, Sophronia Figgis, was raped by your great-whatever-grandfather, Edmund Honeyborne in 1645, then Sophronia married Benjamin Hobbis, who I always thought was my ancestor, but he wasn't because Sophronia was already pregnant. Which means you and I are related through blood."

"We're not."

"But—"

"I'm not trying to burst your bubble, but we aren't related. In the 1800s, the line passed to a distant cousin. There's no direct bloodline to Edmund Honeyborne." Jude's lips quirked sardonically. "You realise you could have a claim to the Honeyborne estate?"

Cló frowned. "How?"

"Well, it's only through blood, and it's through the female line, so it probably wouldn't have made a difference then. But if Sophronia really is your ancestor and she really did have a child by Edmund Honeyborne, then you, by rights, should have a claim to Grimdark, as you're directly related to the earlier Honeybornes." He shrugged. "It's all academic now, and it wouldn't stand up in court. You can't go back so long to change anything, and Sophronia's child was a bastard, so wouldn't have had any entitlement."

"And now we're married, so it's irrelevant. But I love that I am related to Euphemia Figgis. It's rather cool having a witch in my past."

"Yes," he said slowly, thoughtfully. "Trust you to be the direct descendant of our local witch. That's one almighty—" He frowned. "Actually, that can't be right."

"What can't be right?"

"Euphemia Figgis can't be your ancestor. It's all part of the legend, the Crone, the Mother and the Maiden. Germaine, Euphemia and Sophronia. Everyone in these parts know their names, and all three of the Figgis women were burnt at the stake."

"They were? Oh. But—no, that can't be right." Cló wracked her brain, speeding through Effie's memories, but there was no memory of her death or what happened to Sophronia.

Reading her mind, Jude said, "How did you make the connection between your Sophronia and Euphemia Figgis?"

The truth hovered on Cló's lips, but Jude jumped in with, "And how did you discover Edmund Honeyborne raped your Sophronia? It's not something that would've gone up before the magistrates or have any sort of documentation that might have survived."

"I—" Cló began, but she couldn't think of a way to broach the subject of reincarnation and, more specifically, her own memories of her previous lives.

"What is it?" said Jude, watching her with concern. "What's wrong?"

"Not wrong, exactly." Cló shut her eyes briefly. "There is something else that's been going on, but I need you to try not to be too sceptical, okay?"

"O-kay?" he said, frowning.

Taking a deep breath, Cló let the words tumble out of her.

The silence that followed was not comfortable. Cló waited, her stomach a roiling bag of nerves.

Finally, Jude said, "How long have these . . . episodes been going on for?"

"Almost since we arrived."

"And you don't think it's just your crazy imagination?"

"No!"

"Cló," he said gently, "you're the only person I know who can make up a whole story out of the shape of a cloud or wonders what yellow tastes like. You can feel empathy for something that's not real in the space of seconds. You cry at sad adverts, for god's sake. I've known you to laugh out loud at something you've imagined in your — "

"This is not the same," she said, hurt that he was doing exactly what she had asked him not to do, but understanding it too, because Jude was a born sceptic.

He rubbed his face hard. "Okay, even if you are getting these . . . memories from previous lives, what does it matter? Who cares what happened in those lives? It's done and dusted — in the past, quite literally. Nothing from a previous life can hurt you or change who you are."

Cló's eyebrows rose. She hadn't thought of it that way. "You're right. Of course, you're right."

"And you can't assume this Sophronia you found in the parish records is Sophronia Figgis the witch because you supposedly remembered a Sophronia being raped by Edmund Honeyborne — I'm sorry, Cló, but that's quite a stretch for me to believe — it doesn't mean it actually happened."

"But why here? Why now?" she said, stung by Jude's disbelief. "I can't tell you how real it all feels when I have these — these memories. I *am* Effie. I *am* Walter. Just for those brief moments. They are me and I am them. I could tell you the layout of Effie's cottage as it was then. I know what the bay looked like and the village that fell into the sea. I could tell you exactly where Effie collected honey in Tangled Wood — "

"That doesn't exist anymore," he said, surprised. "It was cut down when I was maybe three or four."

"See? How could I possibly know it even existed? And I knew my way around the Wash, and it doesn't look anything like it did then. I knew the names of everyone in the village. I delivered the Honeybornes' children for heaven's sake! And how could I possibly have known about the cat in the walls?" she demanded. "There is no way I could have found it if I hadn't had a memory of Effie, who actually saw the poor thing being blocked up into the wall. Oh god!" Her hands to her cheeks, Cló barely noticed Jude's interruptions. "And I've just realised something else; I know where Walter's rooms were in the Hall. I actually stumbled across them a few weeks ago—"

"What rooms?"

"On the far side of the Hall of Curiosities. There's two bare rooms there."

"That's the oldest part of the Hall," he said. "Ten points, Cló."

"Don't be snide! Those rooms felt familiar, but I've only just realised why. It's where I lived as Walter. I was a man in a previous life, a Honeyborne no less . . . And what about Gwenn?" she demanded, now in full vent. "We're sharing the *same* memories! We shared past lives."

Jude sighed, pressing his thumb and forefinger into his eyes. "Now you're sounding like Ruth."

"It's nothing like Ruth! I'm talking about reincarnation, not dressing up because I have some weird fetish, though I'm fairly convinced she's schizophrenic or has DID . . . and speaking of Ruth, do you know who cleans our room?"

Jude blinked in confusion at the abrupt change of topic. "One of the cleaners. There's three, I think, and a cook. Why the sudden interest in the staff, and what does that have to do with Ruth?"

"I thought Ruth might have been cleaning our rooms," Cló muttered. "I caught her in there this morning, and I've smelt her perfume before too."

Jude burst out laughing. "I can assure you my sisters would never do something as kind as clean our rooms. Those two have never cleaned a thing in their lives. Look where they live!" He threw a wild hand around to incorporate Grimdark Hall and its grounds. "And we'd be the last people they'd clean up after."

Cló smiled sheepishly. "Of course, you're right. I'm being silly."

"Yes, you are." But the worried frown didn't leave Jude's face when he said, "It's late. Let's go to bed; we can talk about all of this in the morning."

Cló had never felt less like sleeping, but it was long past midnight, and while she could happily have sat on the wall watching the shooting stars, Jude was not a night owl and would be grumpy as all hell come tomorrow morning.

They walked along the walls and down the narrow corkscrew stairs.

Jude grabbed Cló's hand, forcing her to stop as they crossed the gardens to the main entrance. Stiffly alert, he put a finger to his lips and peered into the dark.

"There's someone going into the chapel," he whispered.

"It's Constance. I've told you already, I've seen her do it every night." A small vindictive spark made Cló add, "I think she's desecrating the tombs in the crypt."

"That stupid bitch!" he hissed, surprising Cló with the venom in his tone. "I cannot believe after all these years she still believes it's buried here."

"What's buried here?"

Jude's lips tightened as he strode across the lawn towards the chapel. "Treasure."

FOURTEEN

Black silence cobwebbed the immense columns and sagged from the vaulted ceiling as the sheer age of the chapel settled around Jude and Cló like a murmur from the past. A sacred hush that insisted on whispers from believers and atheists alike.

"Where is she?" said Jude, switching on his phone's light and sweeping it around the empty chapel.

"She'll be down in the crypt." Cló moved down the central aisle, then stopped when Jude didn't follow. "Come on!"

"I'm not going down there," he whispered, face ashen and shivering.

Cló hurried back to him. "Why not?"

His lips worked, but no words came.

The hair prickling on the back of Cló's neck had nothing to do with the stale chill in the chapel. "What happened, Jude? Did something happen in here?" Her eyes widened with understanding. "Not the chapel, the crypt. What happened in the crypt?" She cradled his face in her hands. "Tell me, Jude," she whispered. "What happened? Was it Constance?"

"I—" Jude shook his head. He swallowed, shook his head again.

"You can tell me. You know you can tell me anything." Cló moved to hug him, but he sidestepped and turned away from her.

"I can't." He was visibly trembling.

"You can't tell me, or you can't go down to the crypt?" said Cló, alarm hitting her stomach until it fluttered as though the baby had kicked for the first time.

"Both."

"She did something to you in the crypt," she said, feeling her way towards the terror that gripped her husband. "When you were small." In her mind's eye a young Jude followed his much older sister down the aisle, a trusting hand in Constance's larger one, excitement of promised adventure lighting his face. Cló followed the image, leaving Jude where he was, and walked behind the old stone altar, stopping at the head of the stairway hidden behind it. "She took you down into the crypt." A terror imagined, the terror of a young boy. Tears for Jude tightened her throat. "Did she lock you in there?"

Jude nodded. He swallowed convulsively, then in a hoarse whisper, said, "For three days."

"How old were you?"

"Five."

"Why?" Cló's question gained wings and soared around the hushed chapel, a faint, dusty echo. "You were so young. Why would anyone do that to their little brother?"

"Because I teased her."

A fury ratchetted through Cló's veins until her face bloomed with the heat of intense loathing. She knew Constance was spiteful, but she'd never imagined the intentional cruelty she was capable of, and for such a pathetic reason. Her jaw locked with hatred. Jude was right: Some families were warped and were no family at all.

Cló walked back to Jude and took his face in her hands again. His skin was cold and clammy, his shiver passing through her fingertips.

Forcing her jaw to unclench, Cló was terrified of giving in to her fury, worried she wouldn't be strong enough for Jude. "And now you're an adult," she said fiercely. "She can't ever harm you again. Remember who you are, who you have become. You are my beautiful husband, my best friend. You have achieved so much with your life, and what has she done? Hidden within these walls, never living as you and I have lived. She has never felt love as you and I love. She has never laughed and felt joy as you and I do. Don't let her take that away from you. Don't let her destroy all that is good in your life."

Jude dropped his head on Cló's shoulder and put his arms around her, hugging tightly, his body shuddering with dry sobs.

In the quiet of the chapel, they stood wrapped around each other, enveloped in the ancient, musty silence.

Jude pulled away. He cleared his throat, but his words still came out as a rasp when he said, "Let's go and find my bitch of a sister." He took Cló's hand and led the way to the altar.

His grip strengthened, crushing her knuckles as he stared down at the old stone stairs disappearing into the yawning darkness.

Cló took the first step. Cló, who had been nonconfrontational all her life, wanted a fight. Fury bubbled within her, curdling in her stomach, fuelling her as she marched down the stairs and pushed the old door ajar.

Jude stepped down behind her, jerky and hesitant. Cló took his hand, anchoring him to her side.

A lamp stood on the crypt floor, a strident intrusion of the modern world in the sepulchral darkness. In its feeble gloriole, the forest of barley-twist pillars strode away into infinite night, its fragile glow brushing around Constance bent over a tomb, engrossed in what lay within. She hadn't noticed she was no longer alone.

Jude's hand tightened painfully around Cló's, his eyes flicking around the groin-vaulted space like a hunted animal.

"What the hell do you think you're doing?" Cló shouted, flooding the crypt with echoes that scraped against the forgotten tombs, before fleeing down the narrow tunnels beyond.

Constance jerked in fright and whipped around into a defensive crouch, a vicious pick in her hand raised to attack. Her eyes widened at the sight of Jude and Cló. She lowered the pick slightly and straightened. "None of your business!" she barked.

Cló opened her mouth to vent her rage, then snapped it shut in astonishment when Jude laughed. A hard, mirthless laugh. "You still believe it's here!" he crowed, an edge of malice in his voice that Cló had never heard before.

Slit-eyed, Constance glared at him. "I know it's here and I will find it. I've always known it's here."

"Because of a dream you had when you were a child?" Jude scoffed. His hand tightened around Cló's, drawing on her strength as he stepped further into the crypt.

Constance's nostrils flared, her glare so fierce it could've set Jude on fire. Then she glanced around the forest of pillars, her lips quirking with spite. "How does it feel, Jude?" she murmured. "How does it feel to be back down here, in the dark?" Her eyes slid to Cló. "But not alone. You always were a snivelling coward, hiding behind Nanny's skirts, now you hide behind your wife's." She took a step towards them. Jude took a step back, dragging Cló with him.

"You know what happens to naughty little boys who tell lies," Constance sneered, her face mottled with shadows like a skull. "What was it like, Jude? Down here in the dark, all by yourself."

Jude released his pent-up breath in a long, slow hiss. "You truly are an evil bitch," he whispered. "But there is no treasure down here." His bark of laughter slashed the air before fleeing into the encroaching darkness. "There never was! I made it all up."

"What treasure?" said Cló, glancing between the siblings. "And what lies?"

"Your precious Jude," said Constance, not taking her eyes off her brother, "was a nasty, deceitful little boy. Always poking his nose into other people's business, snooping and eavesdropping. Always telling stories." Those round, green eyes swivelled to Cló. "Rather like you. I've seen you at night, creeping about the Hall. You two are well suited; a pair of snoops and liars."

Jude's lips whitened with fury. "I was five!" he yelled, flooding the crypt with booming echoes. "And you locked me down here for three days!" He let go of Cló's hand and crossed the distance to his sister. Jude was slightly shorter than Constance, but his anger filled the space around him so he appeared larger, intimidating.

Constance was not a woman easily intimidated. "I was teaching you a lesson!" she snarled in his face. "I had only planned to leave you here for an hour. It was your own fault for wandering off so you couldn't be found."

"Bollocks! You had no intention of letting me out. You wanted to kill me . . . I've spoken to Nanny."

Constance stepped back warily. "Why go troubling her? She's an old woman."

Jude pressed his advantage, stepping towards her, invading her personal space. "She told me the truth! When everyone was searching for me, you claimed you didn't know where I was, you were adamant I was lost in the cliff tunnels. You told Father I always went down to the tunnels, but you knew he had leathered the crap out of me when I did go down there so I never went again. And of course, Ruth backed you up as she always has, telling your lies. And everyone believed you . . . You knew where I was, and you lied to Father and the police. You lied to everyone. You didn't want me found. You wanted me to die down here. And all because you have this ludicrous fantasy that an eight-hundred-year-old treasure is buried down here."

The silence of the crypt beyond the lamp's halo crept into the pause between Jude and Constance, broken only by their ragged breathing as they glared at each other, the air shivering with old bitterness and hatred.

There was no guilt or shame in Constance when she shrugged and turned away from Jude dismissively. "It doesn't matter now. You were found. No harm done."

"Jude," said Cló, watching Constance move casually towards the exit. "I think we should leave." Her thoughts had already leapt forward to Constance making a dash for the door and slamming it shut, the key turning in the lock. Her fingers bunched into fists as Jude and Cló threw themselves against the door that was thick and made from oak that had petrified into something harder than iron over the centuries. Cló's throat closed with imagined terror, the despair as their plight sunk in, their desperate search through the honeycombed tunnels for another way out, haunted by the demons etched onto the walls, dogging their heels, feeding on their terrible anguish until their phone batteries died, plunging Jude and Cló into a darkness peopled by the dead.

It was so real in Cló's head, she leapt towards Jude and took his hand. "Please let's get out of here," she whispered. "Right now."

Some of Cló's fear communicated itself to Jude. He nodded and turned towards the door.

Constance blocked their path.

"Let us out," said Jude. A tremor passed down his arm to Cló's as he glanced back at the crypt, no doubt remembering those dreadful three days wandering around in the sepulchral dark.

Constance ignored him and leaned towards Cló, so close she could smell the older woman's breath, that stale odour between meals, as she whispered, "Jude may have lied, but you know where it is, don't you, Fat Mouse? You know where he hid it."

Cló drew back sharply, her skin pimpling with creeping alarm. "What are you talking about?" she whispered, hypnotised by those round green eyes. She knew those eyes. What Cló said next bypassed rational thought, rising unbidden from her lips, "*Catch him, Crow! Carry him, Kite! Take him away till the apples are ripe. When they are ripe and ready to fall, down comes baby, apples and all.*"

Constance reared back as though Cló had slapped her.

"Cló?"

Jude's voice came from a long way off. All that anchored Cló to reality was his hand clasping hers, as Constance eyed her like a leopard whose prey had unexpectedly bitten it on the paw.

Cló's stomach roiled, Foetus reacting to her remembered horror travelling down through the umbilical cord, sharing everything in that most intimate of bonds. She needed air. She was going to vomit.

Ripping away from Jude, Cló pushed hard past Constance. She stumbled and fell.

"Cló!" Jude shouted, as she rushed up the stairs.

Clutching her stomach, she staggered down the chapel's central aisle in the pitch-black. With trembling fingers, she felt along the far wall until stone merged to wood. She pushed open the heavy door. She nearly didn't make it to a grassy area before vomiting up the contents of her stomach.

Shivering and swaying, Cló wiped her mouth and stood upright. A moan escaped her lips. She took off across the night-shrouded gardens.

Jude called her name.

Cló darted through the small gate in the Hall's walls and ran along the cliff path. The sky was star-speckled, reflected in the sea below, swaying in its eternal dance of suck and pull.

Cló flew through Grimdark village, past shuttered windows

and derelict cottages. Not a single curtain twitched at her pass-ing. Then she was running along the cliff edge, the fens rustling in alarm. The squat ruin was a silhouette ahead, a sanctuary surrounded by murmuring reeds and trickling channels. Black cats scattered from her path. Cló slammed into the ruin and sank to the ground.

Sobs bubbled up her throat, deep and visceral. Her fear was a thing remembered and renewed, leaching from these very walls.

"Cló?"

Jude stepped into the ruin cautiously. He crouched beside Cló, his face a shadow in the faint light cast by his phone that he'd dropped on the floor.

"He knew," Cló whispered, hugging her trembling knees. "He knew."

"Who knew?" he whispered, his voice was gentle as he put a tentative arm around Cló's shoulders. "Who knew what?"

"The Witchfinder. He knew who he had been . . . He knew who I was."

1645

Effie paced round the walls of the Hermitage, her boots clomping, each breath a furious hiss.

Joseph sat on the bottom step of the spiral staircase and watched her silently. His wounds were all but healed, yet he hadn't left the dubious safety of the Hermitage for reasons Effie couldn't fathom, though glad all the same. A bond had formed between them these past months, an unlikely friendship, and Effie found herself drawn to the ashen-haired man, oddly protective of him. She spent more and more time in the Hermitage, teaching him English, bringing him things to read—that had been a surprise request, for she knew few who could, and had taken to pilfering scraps of paper and the odd news pamphlet when she could—and talking all the while of her concerns in her small world, though he understood little of what she said.

And he trusted her enough to allow her to see him praying. That had been a strangeness Effie hadn't been prepared for; the stick in the ground to see where the shadows fell—a crude sundial—the pirate kneeling, head low to the ground, murmuring

nonsensical words but with a lilting charm at odds to the stark-
ness of the Hermitage.

"*Pregnant!*" *she cried as she passed the pirate on another fu-*
rious circuit of the room. "*My Sophie, by that bastard.*"

Joseph cleared his throat. "*Pregnan?*" *he hazarded.*

Effie mimed a stomach large with child and the pirate nod-
ded, then nodded again when she jabbed a hard finger in the di-
rection of Honeyborne Hall.

"*I'll kill him!*" *she muttered.* "*I'll kill the slarvering waarmin!*"

She slumped down beside Joseph and started to cry. "*I must*
kill him afore he kills my Sophie." *She turned her agonised face*
to him. "*That be the truth o' it. None o' our primmicky lord's*
bastards live, fer he kills the women who've taken his fancy."

"*Kill.*" *It was a word the pirate understood. He jerked his*
head towards the Hall. "*I?*"

Eyes wide with horror, Effie cried, "*No, bor! Not you.*" *She*
patted his hand, and sighed. "*No matter how much me mum*
may curse that waarmin to the Devil, I dunt know I have it in
me to kill him." *Her heart broke anew at the anguished face of*
her beautiful daughter, blue eyes dulled, skin blotching with
none of the blush usually seen in mums in their first term. "*I*
must git Sophie away from the village till the babe be born."
She grimaced. "*And that won't be easy neither, fer there be*
Watchers in the village. Goodwife Kett be one. Her and her
slummocking cousins. All as mean-eyed as she."

"*Watchers,*" *said Joseph, his tone guttural and slow as he felt*
the word in his mouth. "*I see they— them,*" *he corrected him-*
self, and jerked his head towards the arrow slits.

Effie's eyebrows rose in surprise, then shrugged. What else
did the man have to do all day but read his bits of paper, pray to
his foreign God and look out the window at the goings on of
Darrow End.

"*And that ent the half o' it, bor.*" *Her voice dropped to a*
whisper. "*The Witchfinder be comin'. It won't be long and he'll*

be among us, maybe today or tomorrow. Our lady warned me . . . All the village knows. They be boarding up black kittlings more than afore." She snorted derisively. *"Even up at the Hall, though our Lord Honeyborne be a pious man, and him bein' a Justice o' the Peace."* She shook her head angrily at the contra- dictory nature of Lord Honeyborne's puritanical and judicial beliefs and his superstitious actions. *"And they ent callin' me out as they did, hurryin' away when they see me. They're scared o' me. And the priest . . ."* Her lips tightened. *"I told you o' that Theophilus Braid. That one has a mean tongue in his head, and fearful o' the cunning folk."* She sighed and closed her eyes. *"Me mum ent helpin' neither. Cursin' all who come near, threatenin' hexes . . . And that's nothin' to Old Bull. He's always had a ha- tred o' me, especially now our Lady's babe survived at my hands, not his. An heir fer His Lordship."* She spat on the floor, the man's name like poison on her tongue.

Whether the pirate understood even half of her rant, Effie didn't care, she was thankful to air her concerns aloud rather than let them fester in silence.

But perhaps he had understood more than she realised, for he shoved a woodcut news pamphlet into her hands with a crude boat on it.

Effie stared at it blankly. *"I told you afore, I dunt know the letters."*

Joseph's face twisted with thought. *"Ship,"* he said and pointed towards the bay.

"What you tryin' to say, bor? Sophie sails away? My Sophie?" She laughed. *"Though we live by and off the sea, my daughter ent got the understandin' o' sailing. She were born to the land not the water."*

Joseph scowled in frustration. He pointed at himself and said again, *"Ship."*

Effie's heart sank. She had been thinking only of her own problems, when Joseph had his own: a pirate hiding in the Her-

mitage, only recently recovered from a terrible shipwreck which should've killed him, who, if discovered, would be for hanging at Marshalsea.

"Yis, a ship," she said, heartsore that Joseph wanted to leave, realising the affinity she felt for the pirate was not reciprocated. "I should've reckoned you'd want to leave as soon as you were able."

A violent shake of his head, then, "Dochter ... ship." He stabbed the bit of paper in Effie's hands. "Ship!"

"There's boats aplenty down in yon bay," said Effie. "Not ships as such, but boats that float and will git you where yar gorn. You'll have to thieve it, mind, fer we ent got a boat, not since my man were alive, and I were that pleased to git rid o' the blasted thing when the storm took his sorry carcass."

Joseph shook his head, frustration in the lines of his thin face. "Dochter," he said again, and he curled Effie's fingers around the pamphlet. "Take ... Dochter."

Effie shrugged, squirreled the paper into one of the pockets of her heavy skirt, and stood up. "I'll be off. I've to see to young Charlie as had a fever somethin' fierce in the night ... that's if his mum ent too afeared to give me entry."

His pale blue eyes lingered on Effie as she took her leave and disappeared into the tunnel leading down into the cliff's warren.

It was gone noon when she emerged into a speckling mist that smothered Darrow End. She hurried through the alleys, intensely aware of unseen eyes watching her from every opening and whispers of "Witch!" as she passed. Goodwife Kett, with none of the caution of the rest of the village, stood in her doorway and watched Effie in silent, narrow-eyed hostility.

"Catch him, crow! Carry him, kite!" Effie murmured as she knocked on the Moores' door. "Take him away till the apples are ripe." It did not surprise her when no one answered, though she heard shuffling within and a whimper from young Charlie. With a fretful shake of her head, she stomped up the steep cliff

towards the Figgis cottage, chanting loudly now to ignore the buzzing of fear in her ears, "When they are ripe and ready to fall, here comes baby, apples and all."

Thankful her great-grandfather had built their home on the outskirts of the village, for she could not have borne the whispers and stares whenever she stepped out her door, she entered the fuggy warmth of the single room that was kitchen, dining room and bedroom.

Sophie, Germaine and Benjamin Hobbis sat at the table.

"What's happened?" *Effie demanded, not bothering to sit.*

"That snivelling shite up at the Hall be what!" *snapped Germaine. She turned her blind glare to Benjamin Hobbis.* "Tell her what you heard," *she snarled.* "Tell her!"

Benjamin Hobbis cleared his throat, looking away from Germaine's wild fierceness. "My Lord Honeyborne," *he began,* "is—er—is aware that Sophie is with child. He—er—I overheard them speaking up at the Hall. His Lordship demanded—er—that Dr. Bulman..." *His expression, which had been tightly held together until this point, crumpled, his dark eyes shining with remembered horror.* "I couldn't believe it when I heard. And so matter-of-fact, as though a life taken was of no account."

"For the love of God and the Devil!" *Germaine snarled.* "Stop drivelling... That shite has only demanded Old Bull do away with our Sophie in a manner seen as natural, just as he has the others."

Effie stepped further into the room and sat down on the vacant chair. Her face creased with worry. "We all together knew that would be the way o' it," *she said into the pall of silence.*

"It dunt make it right," *cried Germaine.* "That shite can do as he pleases, and him a Justice o' the Peace an'all. Where be our justice?"

"Perhaps if we spoke to Mr. Braid," *inserted Benjamin.* "He's a priest, and this goes against God's—"

Germaine spat onto the floor. "What's God got to do with it? He ent of no help to the likes o' us. And that pious bastard has no love fer a Figgis! He'd see us hanged as look at us fer his fear o' the cunning folk."

Effie put a hand on her mother's trembling arm. "Hush, Mum. Shouting fit to wake the dead ent gorn to help us neither."

"What can we do, Mum?" said Sophie, her cornflower-blue eyes, huge and trusting, on her mum, who had always made things right, fixed all Sophie's wrongs, been there steady, strong and true all her young life.

"I dunt know, love, but we'll think o' somethin'."

A hovering silence smothered the four, wrapped in their own terrible thoughts, before Effie reached into her pocket and handed the crumpled pamphlet to Benjamin. "I—er—found this along by the church," she lied, having no intention of sharing her secret with her family; knowledge of it would put them in danger of the noose as conspirators. "You have the knowing o' letters, bein' a doctor's apprentice an'all," she added when Benjamin looked at the news pamphlet in surprise.

"It's a notice, for a ship." He looked up at Effie, then shrugged at her encouraging nod. He cleared his throat and read aloud:

For Jamestown, Virginia in America,

The ship DILLIGENCE, Capt. James Michael Johnson, Burthen 200 Tons, a prime Sailor, being well mann'd and victalled, and properly fitted with every Thing commodious for Passengers of every Degree, and will be ready to sail from Ipswich about the last day of September next.

Whoever has a Mind to go as Passenger, Redemptioner, or Servant, may apply to Samuel Creed Merchant, Robert Wilton Merchant, or to the Captain on board his Ship at Ipswich, where they will know the Terms, and meet with good Encouragement."

Effie's gasp was low and hard, realising what the pirate had been trying to tell her. She paled at the very idea of losing her daughter, only sixteen, to the vagaries of a wild ocean and a wilder land beyond. But was that as sure a death as the one that awaited her here?

"And what o' the war?" said Germaine, her eyebrows raised. "That pissant, Cromwell, be Puritan. Why do them buggers wish to leave, if he be fighting to free them o' the popish king?"

But Benjamin and Effie weren't listening. They looked at each other, then at Sophie sitting with her head in her hands as though unable to bear the mess her life had become through no fault of her own.

Effie noticed something else in the young man's eyes, his posture, the sudden rigidity of his back: excitement. It was a look she had seen in many a young man when talk of the colonies arose; the possibility of riches at the edge of the world, in new lands where traditions meant little and hope everything.

"It's alright fer some," continued Germaine, who poked Effie in the ribs; though she couldn't see, she always knew when someone was not paying her attention. "The Annisons went sailin', dint they, not three year back, and the Astleys, from Thornham way, I heard tell. Whole family up and left. But that ent fer the likes o' us. We Figgises are born o' this land and we'll die in this land."

"And what o' Sophie?" snapped Effie. "Is she to die afore her time because o' the whims o' our Lord who ent able to keep his pecker in his trousers at the sight o' a pretty mawther?"

"Dunt speak o' me as if I ent here, Mum!" said Sophie, lifting her head. "And I ent sailin' to some heathen land neither."

"Just so," said Germaine, looking smug. "Always said the mawther were sensible."

"No, you dint!" said Effie and Sophie together.

Germaine shrugged a bony shoulder. "Well, I thought it on occasion." Her white eyes peered unerringly at Sophie, then turned to Effie. "There be another way," she said, voice low and almost gentle for the old woman.

"No!" cried Effie, knowing the path her mum's mind was wandering down, for she had wandered the same path. "That be a blaspheme against God and everythin' I stand for. I bring life into this world, I dunt take it afore it's had a chance to breathe its first breath."

"That's as may be fer those with mighty scruples, but you and I together know if the babe ent born living, our Sophie ent no longer a threat to that blisterin'—" Germaine froze, one hand raised in the air. Slowly, she turned her blind gaze to the door, and Effie wondered then if her mum didn't truly have the Sight. Unease ratchetted up her spine as Germaine intoned in her fortune-telling gravel, "Without be the end o' all. Evil both grim and dark has come. In the name o' redemption be our damnation . . . Fire shall course, and the sea take to its bosom all it desires."

As Germaine's voice fell away a heavy knock came at the door, startling all in the Figgis cottage.

Effie glanced at Germaine and Sophie, then Benjamin Hobbis, their ashen-faced fear matching her own.

Standing slowly, she walked to the door and opened it.

Before her, hand raised to knock once more, stood a pasty young man with a wispy beard and mousy hair, grown long according to the fashion, and a birthmark on one cheek in the shape of a cross. Already stooped as though aged by the worries of the world, his sombre, black clothes and tall hat hung off him like a scarecrow.

He did not look at Effie but past her into the gloom of the cottage. Round green eyes took in the wild-haired Germaine, Sophie looking beautiful and sad, and Benjamin Hobbis, who was getting to his feet. He peered into the corners of the room, and his thin lips curved into a satisfied smile at the black cats lazing, sleeping or arching in play everywhere.

"Who be you?" Effie demanded, more rudely than she'd intended.

Those round green eyes turned to Effie . . . and widened in astonishment.

She clutched the doorframe as a reciprocal shock of recognition coursed through her, followed swiftly by an overwhelming hatred for this man that made no sense.

There was no time for more. Effie's eyes twitched to the movement behind the scrawny man. Three women, hunched like ravens, stalked up to the cottage. Behind them came the villagers, in ones and twos, as word spread that something was afoot. At their head came Lord Honeyborne, Theophilus Braid and Old Bull, wearing stoic expressions of an unpleasant task ahead of them.

And with the crowd gathering around the cottage came a rustling of "Witchfinder . . . Witchfinder . . . Witchfinder . . ." on the sea breeze curling along the cliff, as though the sea, too, wished to observe the unfolding drama.

The pasty man turned to the crowd gathered on the clifftop. A deathly hush fell, rippled only by the teasing wind. "Witchcraft imperils the lives of the pious," he began.

Effie's eyes whipped around to him. Not so much for the words, but his voice. It was astonishing: deeply velvet, mesmerising, too large for his scrawny frame. Her heart withered with a terrible fear, for which of the cunning folk throughout Norfolk had not heard the dreaded name, Matthew Hopkins, Witchfinder General?

"And in God's name we shall root it out from croft and manor, from farm and fen, until we are rid of these vile creatures that take upon the work of the Devil." He turned slowly to Effie, his silky voice still lingering on the air, his face tight with pious indignation. "Any mole, scar or wen on their skin is the mark of the Devil." He turned to the crowd, gazing at each face until the villagers huddled closer in fear. "A witch shall feel neither pain when pricked nor bleed from the Devil's mark."

One of Effie's black kittlings chose this moment to arch against her skirts as she stood gaping in the doorway of her cottage. It sauntered outside to sit in front of the Witchfinder and lifted a paw to wash its ears, oblivious to the indrawn breaths its presence caused.

The Witchfinder pointed dramatically at the unconcerned cat. "And long has it been fact a witch's familiar be disguised as cat or toad. See here!" he shouted. "The Devil's imp in disguise . . ."

"Yis, and there's more beside within," remarked Goodwife Kett, with a satisfied nod and a dark look for Effie.

Hopkins nodded approvingly at Goodwife Kett. "Witchcraft is treason against our almighty God, and those who defend and harbour a witch be punishable, for they, too, are bewitched." He whipped around and cried, "Strip them!"

Effie slammed the door shut and leaned hard against it. A swelling scream lodged in her throat, her mind scrabbling like a trapped rat.

She leapt towards Sophie, who, with Benjamin and Germaine, had stood up at the commotion. Cupping her daughter's face in her hands, she whispered, fierce and low, "You must leave now. No matter what happens, you must git yarself away." She glanced at Benjamin Hobbis, hovering at Sophie's side, his young face torn by worry. "If you've any o' the love you profess fer her," she hissed at him, "then you'll git her away and gone from here."

"No, Mum!" cried Sophie. "I ent leavin' you! And what of Nan? I ent runnin' because of them duzzy pillocks. It'll pass on."

Effie ignored her and looked steadily at Benjamin.

His face paled with dawning horror, for they could all hear the smooth tones of the Witchfinder outside, the rise and fall of the people being swayed, by his voice if not his words. Benjamin nodded, picked up the news pamphlet on the table and shoved it into his coat pocket.

The door flew open with an almighty crash, and two of the corvine women entered.

"*What are you doing?*" *shouted Benjamin, stepping up to the women, as Germaine yelled,* "*Git me stick so's I can poke yon shite's eyes out!*"

It was the speed of events that shocked Effie most. One of the women gripped Effie's jaw in clawlike fingers and peered into her odd-coloured eyes. "*Eyes of the Devil!*" She whipped around, dragging Effie around by her jaw, and shouted triumphantly through the open door, "*The mark of the Devil be upon this witch!*"

That snapped Effie out of her stocked stupor. "*Witch?*" she gasped. "*I be cunning, no more and no less.*"

The woman smirked at her companion knowingly. "*There be familiars all about the witch's cottage.*" She kicked one of the black cats that had crept out from under the table at the commotion. It shot out the door with a plaintive mewl. "*Say you these kittlings be not yar familiars?*"

"*They're kittlings!*" Effie shouted. "*They ent harmed none and rescued one and all from starvation.*"

"*Euphemia!*" Germaine yelled, struggling against the other woman holding her, who ripped off the old woman's blouse to reveal wrinkled, skin-sagged breasts.

"*Leave me Mum alone, you wretches!*" Effie screamed.

"*Prick them!*" came Hopkins's sleek voice.

Effie turned her head to him as terror crawled through her veins. He stood unmoved and unblinking by the chaos in the close confines of the Figgis cottage.

"*Mum!*"

Effie turned, and her world fell away beneath her. The third black-weeded pricking woman had entered the cottage and cornered Sophie against the bed with Benjamin Hobbis between them, his arms wide to prevent the woman from getting near Sophie.

Straining against the grasping claws holding her, Effie shouted, "*Git my daughter out o' here!*"

Benjamin's expression hardened. He stood taller, dropping his arms though he didn't move away from his protective position of Sophie.

"You will not touch my betrothed!" he snapped, voice loud and firm with a ring of authority Effie had never heard in the young man before. He put his arm around Sophie's shoulders and led her from the cottage unmolested with an apology in his eyes as he passed Effie and murmured, "I'll speak to Lord Honeyborne. He can put a stop to this."

Effie snorted, knowing there would be no help from that quarter, and snarled at the pricking woman who tore her blouse from her torso. She tried to twist away, but the third black-weeded woman was holding her tight. Together they shoved Effie onto the table, face down, beside Germaine.

"The Devil will do his work this day," hissed Germaine. "He has come in our home and nothin' but fire shall cleanse what has begun."

"Mum!" Effie hissed back. "Shut yar gob or we'll be fer the fire ourselves."

"I've seen it, Euphemia. I've seen the flames . . ."

"Hold the crone still," said one of the pricking women.

Germaine fought with what little strength she had in her frail, old body. She writhed and twisted like a landed eel. To no avail.

Effie could do nothing but watch in horror as a long needle was pressed against a dark, horny mole on Germaine's back.

"No blood," whispered the three pricking women in chorus.

"Cors there ent, you harpies!" yelled Effie. "You barely pricked as to break the skin!"

One of the women slapped Effie so hard her head hit the table with a dull crunch.

"No blood!" the women said again.

The words were already drifting through the open door. There they gained momentum and rose to a muttering of "No blood . . . no blood . . ." *as the villagers crowded around Lord Honeyborne and Matthew Hopkins.*

Effie and Germaine were stripped naked, and while held tight to the table, they were pricked again and again. Neither cried out, for there was little pain, the needle tip pressing lightly against their skin so that no blood was drawn. Effie and Germaine endured their humiliation in silence, for there was little either could say or do to the pricking women in their unkind ministrations. Both mother and daughter knew pain would come later, for they had both heard the stories of the Witchfinder, and none had ended well for those poor souls cast as witches.

All too soon, they were heaved to their feet and dragged from the cottage, scattering the last few cats that had remained within.

They stood on the cliff, naked to the stiff sea breeze and the unkind scrutiny of the villagers. A heavy silence smothered the crowd, laced deep with suspicion and fear, for the two went hand in hand.

"What of the daughter," said Lord Honeyborne, his words torn and tattered by a sudden gust. "She is a temptress, led astray by the Devil."

All eyes turned to Sophie and Benjamin. Neither could move, hemmed in by the crowd.

Matthew Hopkins coughed, a wet, hacking cough that shook his sparrow-thin frame. Once the fit passed, he contemplated Germaine, Effie and Sophie. "A crone . . . a mother . . . a maiden." He barely raised his voice though his reedy body shook with emotion, his green eyes luminous with religious fervour. "A coven of witches like a viper's nest amongst the godly."

The villagers' horrified whispering was snatched up by the sea breeze to wrap around those gathered, tearing at what little sense remained until it lay tattered and feathered like torn cobwebs.

One of the pricking women released Effie and stalked towards Sophie at a nod from Hopkins.

"No!" Effie shouted at the same time Benjamin shouted, "There is no coven! Sophie is with child."

Sophie gaped at him with betrayed shock.

Benjamin swallowed hard, tried to smile at her, and said loudly, "Sophronia Figgis carries my child. She is no longer a maiden."

Silence, then a rising murmur of astonishment.

"Ascertain the truth of the claim," said Matthew Hopkins.

The pricking woman pressed her hands against Sophie's stomach and nodded. "She be with child."

No one noticed the tightening of Hopkins's lips but Effie. Relief coursed through her. Her gaze whipped to Lord Honeyborne. She bared her teeth in small triumph as bewildered anger crossed his face before smoothing to careful blankness.

"A word!" Lord Honeyborne snapped at Hopkins.

The Witchfinder raised an eyebrow but stepped towards him. A brief flurry of words and gesticulation between Lord Honeyborne, the priest and Old Bull, but all that could be heard was the rise and fall of Matthew Hopkins's deep voice. It rolled over everyone's head without needing the words understood.

It was Theophilus Braid who unwittingly saved Sophie. "If the maid truly be with child out of wedlock," he said loudly, "That is a matter for the church to save her soul from damnation."

Germaine grunted reluctant approval, for she had little love for the priest, as Effie breathed out the air lodged in her throat.

Another coughing fit shook Matthew Hopkins before he turned to the crowd. Head bowed he waited for the murmuring and rustling to quieten until all that could be heard was the sorrowful sigh of the breeze cresting the cliff to set women's skirts fluttering and men to grab their hats.

"If wrong has been done you through witchcraft by these women," he said, "lay thy claims before the Lord." His voice rose slightly. The crowd swayed, drawing nearer, huddling around Hopkins.

It was Goodwife Kett who spoke first. "That Euphemia Figgis bewitched my daughter so all her babes died afore they could be baptised."

"And what o' our Lady's babes?" said another. "She done bewitched 'em so the babe lived, though the doctor said it were dead in the womb."

Effie's gasp of shock was lost in the babble as she recognised the last voice as the cook from the Hall, whom she had always considered a friend.

"We all know the ole scold to find which none else could find . . ."

"Yis, and she can see the future. That be the Devil's wont . . ."

"Soured my milk, she did . . ."

"And I seen her evil eye upon me so I sickened with fever . . ."

"And what of the sickening of my lambs this spring gone past?" cried a shepherd who hailed from Dunge Marsh. "It weren't long arter that scold cursed me when I wouldn't sell her mutton fer I knew her to be a witch even then," he said darkly. "And not two month later and my lambs did sicken one and all."

"I did see that Euphemia throw out live coals and the same night a fearsome storm blew up and took her man and four others beside . . ."

The complaints came thick and furious, the villagers talking over one another, each dredging up some misdeed from years ago. And all Effie and Germaine could do was stand there in silence, naked to the waist, humiliated that all could see their shame. Denials were futile, for the madness of the mob ruled the sanity of individuals. Matthew Hopkins stood in the centre of it all, nodding his head, his expression sympathetic.

The first stone came from the back of the crowd and glanced off Effie's temple. She staggered against Germaine with a cry. Blood rushed down the side of her face from the gash.

Hopkins raised his hands for silence, though he did nothing to stop the flying stones, and said, "We shall interrogate them until we have a confession, in accordance with the laws of the land."

The second and third stone went wild and tumbled over the cliff. A fourth was being hefted but never flung when a cry rang out from the village.

Up the cliff path came Elijah the blacksmith, and behind him . . .

"Oh, dear God in heaven," whispered Effie, her odd-coloured eyes filling with the tears she couldn't, wouldn't allow herself to shed. "Joseph."

The pirate, hands tied in front of him, stumbled after the blacksmith as he tugged on the rope. "This furrin waarmin were hidin' in the Hermitage, he were," cried Elijah when the two reached the crowd on the clifftop.

A mindless scream swirled around Effie's head, blocking the words. Her eyes slid to Joseph, then Matthew Hopkins . . . and remembered a time when she was Walter Hulot and Joseph was her half-brother Ralph Honeyborne, Lord of Honeyborne Hall. Recognition was in Joseph's eyes too. He and Effie turned in united horror to Matthew Hopkins.

Those dreadful green eyes widened to their fullest, roundest extent, and his deep voice changed to the high-pitched croak of Brother Simon, and crooned, "Catch him, Crow! Carry him, Kite!"

FIFTEEN

"Let me get this straight," said Jude, as he settled Cló on a low crumbling wall of the ruined cottage before crouching down in front of her. A black cat, braver than the rest, had crept back into the ruin and rubbed up against Jude's knees. "You think you're the reincarnation of Euphemia Figgis, who was the reincarnation of Walter Hulot, the steward of Grimdark Hall—"

"It was called Honeyborne Hall then," she whispered, noting the scepticism in Jude's voice but grateful he was trying to hide it.

"Right, and this Walter Hulot was also the bastard brother of the current lord of the Hall, Ralph Honeyborne. And you think this pirate in 1645 was the reincarnation of Ralph and Gwenn Figgis is the reincarnation of the pirate."

"Yeah." Cló rubbed her face hard. It sounded crazy when Jude put it so plainly. "There's someone else—"

"The Witchfinder," said Jude.

Cló nodded. "There was a monk too, further back when Walter and Ralph lived. Not a very good monk. A Brother

Simon. I think the Witchfinder was the monk's reincarnation." She couldn't get those round green eyes out of her head. Eyes she had seen down in the crypt not half an hour ago, that had followed her around Grimdark Hall, uncannily similar to eyes she'd seen in Effie's memories and Walter Hulot's before her. "I—I think Constance may be their reincarnation."

"Yes," said Jude doubtfully.

"She knew who I was," Cló insisted. "There in the crypt. She knew—" She shook her head to dislodge the sensation of familiarity she'd felt . . . except it had only been the eyes; Constance's words made no sense.

Reading her mind, Jude said, "What did she mean about you knowing where it was? Where what was?"

"King John's treasure," said Cló, and smiled weakly at Jude's raised eyebrows. "Luna told me about it. She thinks that's what Constance is searching for."

Jude grimaced. "My sister is unbalanced; her entire life has been consumed by a ludicrous belief of treasure hidden somewhere in the grounds of Grimdark because of a dream she had when she was a child. Your Luna sounds just as bad, barking mad."

"She's not! She's just different. Anyway, I certainly don't know where it is."

"That's something at least," Jude muttered. "Sorry," he added when he saw Cló's hurt expression, "but this is all rather a lot to take in." He sighed and said, "Well, your Brother Simon sounded like a nutter, and god knows, it's no secret Matthew Hopkins was an utter bastard. He put enough innocent people to death on trumped-up charges, and we both know Constance is, frankly, a borderline psychopath." He rose from his crouch to sit beside Cló. "What do you know about Matthew Hopkins?"

Cló frowned. "Not much apart from what you told me. You said he had Effie burnt at the stake, and he had TB."

"And you haven't read anything about him while we've been here, or before? Maybe googled him?"

"No!" Cló snapped, then immediately relented. "Sorry, I know you're struggling with this, but I'd never heard of him before we came to Norfolk."

Jude was quiet for a long time before saying, "I wonder if we can't test this."

Cló eyed him warily. "What are you getting at?"

"I believe you believe what you're . . . remembering is real, you're very convincing, but I could definitely do with some sort of proof."

"Like what?"

"Well, if you're right, and there was a conspiracy against the king, which managed to pull off the heist of the millennium, then I'd be pretty convinced if you discovered John's treasure when no one's managed to find it in eight hundred years."

Cló pulled a face. "I've already told you, I don't know where it is. There *was* a conspiracy, though. Walter and Ralph met the monk, but I can only remember what Walter was thinking. He didn't trust the monk, even though they had history, and Walter really hated King John. I've never felt hatred like that. He didn't just want to kill the king, he wanted to destroy him, wanted his death to be painful. He wanted revenge, but I don't know if it had anything to do with treasure."

"Why?"

"I'm not entirely sure. Something had happened before, something to do with his brother, Ralph. He was very protective of Ralph, but it wasn't Ralph—" Cló's mouth was thick with frustration, the impression, a mere inkling, on the tip of her tongue. "I don't know, I'm missing something. The memories from Walter were flashes through Effie and they were coloured by her impressions too."

"What can you remember of Matthew Hopkins from Effie?"

"Not much"—*except his eyes*, scurried around the privacy of her mind. "Effie was terrified of him." She prodded Effie's memories for something that would make sense, then shook her head. "I think her terror was more for her mother and daughter than herself."

They sat in silence for a long while, listening to the chorus of frogs in the fen that had almost consumed the ruined cottage. More and more cats crept back in, their eyes glowing in the half moon's light peering through the collapsed roof.

"Let's go back to the Hall," said Jude finally. "It's nearly morning."

They walked back to Grimdark Hall, wrapped in their own thoughts. Though the air was dark and still, the fens were never silent, a shiver of constant motion, sometimes soft and sweet, at others, hard and rasping.

Once in bed, Jude fell asleep almost immediately, lying on his stomach with his arm thrown across Cló's waist. She tried to clear her mind, hoping sleep would come. But there was too much swirling in the ether, snippets from Effie and Walter, things Gwenn had said . . .

"Gwenn!" Cló clapped a hand to her mouth when Jude murmured in his sleep.

Checking he hadn't woken, Cló gently lifted his arm and climbed out of bed. Creeping into the dressing room, she switched on the light after she'd closed the door so that she didn't disturb Jude.

Her mind fizzing with possibilities based on nothing more than scraps of memory from a woman who'd been dead for almost four hundred years, Cló waited impatiently for her laptop to whine to life.

A quick scan through her accumulated ancestry before she lit upon the passenger list of the *Diligence*.

With a deep sigh, Cló muttered, "You idiot, Cló! How did I

miss this?" and squinted at the scanned image of smudged spidery writing until she found,

> *Hobis, Benjamin of Kings Lynn*
> *Sophronia, his wyfe*

Right under their names was another:

> *Rogevenne, Josef, Hobis servant, carpenter*

So many times Cló had looked at the name and it had meant nothing to her. Now it was glaringly familiar. Joseph the pirate, aka Jozef Roggeveen, aka Yusef an-Nur, aka Josef Rogevenne. So many names for one man.

How was it possible he had sailed out as Benjamin and Sophronia's servant? Effie's terror for her friend was as vivid as a punch in the gut, knowing what would happen to him if discovered.

Cló quickly typed *Jozef Roggeveen pirate* into Google, then sat back in surprise. She was impressed. Jozef Roggeveen had his own Wikipedia page. She didn't know anyone who had their own page—and while it was Effie who knew Jozef Roggeveen, Cló couldn't suppress a little glimmer of reflected pride.

Reading through the Wiki page, Cló gained a little more knowledge about the white-haired man. His early years in Rotterdam, Holland, were scanty, as was his time as a galley slave. Roggeveen's main claim to fame was his attack on the Royalist ship, *The Unicorn*, in the English Channel, which was believed to be carrying supplies for the beleaguered Charles I. Roggeveen had last been seen fleeing into the North Sea with Parliamentarian ships on his tail. There were a few sketchy accounts of sightings of Roggeveen's ship, the *Algerine*, off the Norfolk coast, some as far away as Norway, and of a storm that reached biblical proportions and theories of shipwreck.

Moving to other sites, Cló found little more except a citation of one Jozef Roggeveen, recorded as a prisoner in Marshalsea Prison in 1645 to be hanged for piracy.

Cló pored over the last site for ages, then shook her head, stumped. How had Gwenn, as Joseph the pirate, seen Effie burning? Cló didn't disbelieve Gwenn. How could she when their memories aligned so often? Gwenn had said Joseph had been with Sophie, when everything Cló had heard, and with the hindsight of living in the future long after the event, suggested Sophie had been burnt at the stake with her mother and grandmother. Maybe Jude was right and there were two different Sophronias.

Frustrated, Cló cleared her browser history and typed in *Matthew Hopkins Witchfinder*. After scanning a few sites that all said the same thing, she gave up. There was nothing about what Hopkins was like, what he had looked like, only accounts of his terrible deeds. There was even less of Euphemia Figgis; a one-line footnote of history and a legend in north Norfolk. Of Effie's mother and daughter, there was nothing at all.

Irritated and tired after a long, rather emotional night, but knowing sleep would be as elusive as ever, Cló shut down her laptop, saw Jude still slept and quietly dressed.

She crept from the room and headed for the kitchen. A murmur of voices floated through the open door.

Barely daring to breathe, Cló paused in the corridor.

The sisters' voices were low, Ruth's high pitch moderating Constance's bass. Snatches drifted out to Cló.

"Are you sure?" murmured Ruth.

An indistinct rumble from Constance, then Ruth saying, "Perhaps asking might be better?"

Constance's snorted in response. "Ask what?"

A muttering, then Ruth again, doubtful, "It seems extreme . . ."

"It worked for you . . ."

A short silence. "You do what you think is best, Con . . ."

"Don't I always?"

Ruth's high-pitched titter flittered out the door.

Startled by her stomach growling loudly, Cló tiptoed away, in case its lack of discipline gave her away. Scampering through the Great Hall, she slipped outside into the beginnings of a glorious day. Early sunlight glinted on dewed leaves like trapped stars.

Cló hurried across the vast gardens, through the walls and onto the cliff path. Darrow Bay lay suspiciously benign below. A couple of bathers were already down on the crescent of beach, towels spread on the pebbled sand, a rainbow-striped umbrella adding a splash of festive colour to the greys and greens.

Breathing in the sun-kissed air, Cló darted through the shuttered gloom of the village and called out good morning to the cats lazing around the ruined cottage with only a twitch of a tail to acknowledge her passing. As she cut through the fens along the raised black bank, the reeds whispered secrets to the trickling channels flowing at their feet. A reed warbler's cheerful *chi-chi-chi* followed Cló's uncertain journey.

Luna's vardo and yurt looked part of the fens, growing organically from the black mud much like the surrounding reeds. Luna was up and about, watering the herbs she grew next to the yurt. She was wearing bright pink from head to toe.

Her head lifted at Cló's approach. She smiled. "You're early this morning," she said and headed into the yurt. Their meeting for morning coffee had become a ritual these past few days.

After Luna poured a couple of mugs of coffee, Cló told her about what had happened in the crypt the night before. She listened, shuffling a pack of tarot cards back and forth in her hands.

"Bloody hell! And I missed all the drama."

"Don't joke. It was horrible. Poor Jude. Can you imagine being locked down there for three days?" Cló's jaw locked with the anger still simmering beneath her skin. Anger and a terrible hatred for Constance. "That woman is a hellish bitch!"

Luna's eyebrows rose at Cló's uncustomary venom. "I think this is the point where I say, 'I told you so.'"

"It's not a joke, Luna!"

She shrugged. "Your Jude sounds like he came out of it alright. He has you, after all . . . Now!" she said, slapping her hands together. "I think we both know who Constance recognised in you. It all makes sense now."

Cló hesitated, then nodded. "It's her eyes. They're horrible, like green lamps that pin you to the spot."

"And she thinks you know where King John's treasure is."

"Oh, there's something else I—"

Luna held up a hand and fanned out the cards in front of Cló. "Think of Constance, then pick a card."

Cló did so and lay the card, facedown, on the counter beside her coffee.

Luna compressed her lips thoughtfully and flipped the card over. "I bloody knew it!" she crowed. "The Knight of Pentacles! Don't you see?" she said when Cló looked at her and the card doubtfully. "Constance is your enemy. She's followed you through your lives—who knows how many—and now she's caught up with you again."

Cló nodded, having drawn similar conclusions without resorting to tarot cards. "There's something else," she said, and told Luna about Jozef Roggeveen.

"We need to speak to Gwenn," said Luna.

"Shouldn't she be at school?"

"Not on a Saturday, you chop."

"Is it Saturday?"

"All day." Luna hurried across the yurt then stopped and said, "Oh, there you are, monkey."

Gwenn stepped into the yurt. She didn't appear surprised to see Cló there, and she couldn't help wonder if the little girl hadn't been listening to their conversation. She walked up to Cló, took her hand and led her out of the yurt, beyond the perimeter of the little camp and into the fens, following tracks in the reeds, with an unusually silent Luna following them.

They came to the edge of the cliff. The Wash shimmered darkly in the sunshine below them.

"What do you see?" said Gwenn, gazing out across the vast estuary. "You know what the plan was. We each had our part to play."

Cló raised her eyebrows at the little girl, then at Luna, who shrugged.

"Um—" said Cló.

The tide was out, the receding water carving a fretwork of channels between black mudflats, exposing slithery lumps of seaweed like dying giant octopi.

"See it as it was before," whispered Gwenn.

And Cló did. Wet rot filled her nostrils, the scream of gulls was shrill to her ears and the sun beat down on her.

12 October 1216

The Wash. Bleak. Dank. Flat. It went on for miles, feature-less and deadly to the unwary. The predawn tide receded into the sea in a hiss and suck of fast-flowing water funnelling into hundreds of creeks between sandbanks, mudflats and scrubby saltmarshes. The geography would change with the tide's return, adding new channels, whirling pots of trapped water and quicksand.

It had been another long, sleepless night for Walter Hulot, and there would be no rest in the coming night either. With the hamlet of Cross Keys behind him, he took note of the changes made to the landscape by the receding water washing over the narrow causeway to Sutton Crosses, on the opposite side of the estuary. Five miles of treacherous mud and running sand.

The sun rose higher into the expansive October sky, and still he waited. He did not harry the baggage train that ran two miles down the road from Lynn. He listened to the cries of those leading the packhorses, the yells of the knights and soldiers trav-elling with the train, the bray of donkeys and neighing of stressed horses. He bided his time, bile rising up his throat at the grim task ahead.

"Catch him, Crow! Carry him, Kite!" *Walter whistled softly to himself, his thoughts on Ralph, who was on his way to London to meet in secret with de Gresley. Walter would that he had made the journey himself, but Ralph did not have his knowledge of the Wash with its insidious tides and ever-shifting creeks, and had not the stomach for this day's work.*

He stopped his absentminded whistling and grimaced. He hated the dandling rhyme Brother Simon had chanted before entering battle. He could feel it all now, the heat baking through his helmet, the tension down the ranks of soldiers around him, the dust . . . and that dreadful rhyme ringing in his ears like a bad omen. Shaking his head clear of dreadful memories, he concentrated on the here and now. So much was at stake, not least their lives. And everything was about the timing.

Seagulls flocked up in screeching alarm when a knight rode up to Hulot. Over his horse's tossing head, he stared across the Wash and shivered in a cold breeze fleeing across the estuary. "No good can come of this crossing," he muttered.

"There is time enough before the next tide," *said Walter soothingly. He squinted at the sun moving past its zenith, and added the ominous, false proviso,* "If we leave now."

The knight nodded. "The king has ventured north. We can begin."

Walter nudged his horse forward, followed by the convoy of carts, wagons and packhorses, servants and armourers, cooks and smiths. A few priests sat at the front of the wagon with King John's treasured relics. Two wagons were surrounded by knights.

Slowly, in single file, the baggage train began its perilous journey along the narrow causeway between creeks and boggy marshes, dependant on Walter's knowledge of the Wash. Tim-

ing was everything. Timing and a slightly longer route, though none would know it but Walter. He eyed the position of the wagons and carts, mentally weighing those that sunk lower into the soft earth.

There was no turning back now; the way forward would devastate a king but not the kingdom.

Hulot's horse answered his every nudge, past a whirling pot of trapped water, skirting the edge of a newly formed saltmarsh that would disappear in a few hours, when the tide returned. It was slow going, the baggage train sluggish, yet faithfully following the path Walter took.

A grim silence descended on the train, broken only by the cries of waders and gulls disturbed by the creak of wheels under strain, the whinnying of a packhorse, an aired curse when a wheel bogged down in a rut, before being freed with a sucking pop.

The sun was dipping in the west when they passed the halfway point across the mouth of the Wash. It was the point of no return.

Not an hour, by Walter's reckoning, had passed before trickles of water flowed back along circuitous channels, filling the creeks. An insidious trickle, secretive and deceptive.

Heart heavy with remorse, Walter pulled forward slightly, allowing the gap to widen between himself and the leading wagon.

A broad patch of black mud that had cracked and dried in the sun like a leper's skin was softening with seeping water as he rode across it. Not so much it would be noticeable to the untrained eye, but . . .

"Hulot!"

Walter kept riding, ignoring the cry. Climbing onto a slender bank of higher, drier ground, he urged his horse forward a little faster, drawing away from the impending doom behind him. Too soon . . . too soon . . .

"Hulot! I bid you wait!"

He slowed his pace and turned in the saddle. The tide was rising noticeably. One of the leading wagons lurched to one side, its fore wheel stuck fast in the mud, forcing the entire train to stop in a jerky sequence. Wheels lost what little traction they'd had from the momentum and sank into the stinking mud, the rising tide swirling through their struts. Horses neighed wildly, desperate to free their hooves from the sinking sand. People stared wide-eyed at the water washing around them, first with confusion, then dawning horror.

The knight pushed his horse through the rising tide, already up to the beast's knees. Terrified eyes stared back at Walter.

There was no need for more. The knight knew his fate and that of all the living in the king's baggage train; it was written in Walter's odd-coloured eyes.

Walter broke their locked gaze and nudged his horse forward along the narrow bank the tide had not yet swallowed. He picked up his cautious speed through the rising water, noting where marshes that had been there moments before were now awash. He hardened his heart to the cries of fear and despair behind him, keeping the hated face of King John in his mind to stiffen his resolve. But it was too late, for only those creatures winged could escape the incoming tide spreading across the channels and creeks of the Wash, hiding the saltmarshes and the sandbanks under a mantle of fast running water.

It was almost dark when he pulled free of the Wash, his horse's flanks wet with sweat and streaked with mud. He paused on the bank to glance back across the Wash. There was no sign of King John's baggage train. The tide hid all from view; the Wash was true to its name, washing all away before it.

He turned his horse and headed through the hamlet of Sutton Crosses, the night hiding him from watchful eyes within the little cottages lining the single track. The day's work weighed *heavily on his heart. His immortal soul was a necessary sacrifice. There would be no place in purgatory for Walter Hulot; there would be no redemption in penance. No penance was great enough for what he had done today. He had this one life and then he would burn in the fires of Hell. It was all he deserved.*

SIXTEEN

Tears of self-loathing poured down Cló's cheeks, the images branded into her brain, the sour breath of the Wash rising up to her.

"I was horrible," she whispered, collapsing to her knees. "I murdered all those people."

Luna crouched down beside her, and said, "What did you remember?"

In fits and starts, Cló told Luna and Gwenn all she remembered. Her nostrils still twitched with the stench of black mud, the sound of water rushing back into the Wash, the desperate cry of someone calling her by another name.

"It's not who you are now," said Luna sympathetically.

"All those people," Cló cried. "All those people died because of me—him—us."

Luna was quiet for a long while, then she put her hands to her cheeks, eyes wide. "Oh, my giddy aunt! The stories are true."

"What?" said Cló, blinking hard as she stepped back into her present reality. "What are you talking about?"

"The king's treasure!"

"It was in the Wash," said Cló, frowning. "Stuck fast . . . all those—" Her stomach heaved as her mind filled the blanks of what the last few hours must've been like for those people stuck in the mud with the tide coming towards them, rising steadily. The shared terror, the frantic cries of the horses and mules, the futile attempts to try make it to safety. All doomed because of Walter Hulot.

She vomited over the cliff edge until all she had left was dry retches.

"What happened to it?" Luna demanded urgently, ignoring the vomit-splatter on her clothes. "What happened to the treasure afterwards?"

"I don't know," said Cló, alarmed by the cramps crawling like maggots in her stomach. "The plan was to make sure the king was ruined in every way possible. It wasn't about the gold."

"But—" Luna looked confused. Her gaze slid to Gwenn. "Do you remember? Gwenn!" she snapped when the girl ignored her.

"I was in London," said Gwenn, her voice faraway and long ago. "I was to meet with de Gresley."

"I know all that," said Luna. "But what about the king's treasure?"

Gwenn knelt beside Cló, took her face in her small hands, and stared deeply into her mismatched eyes. "We didn't care about the gold. It was all for Isabella. We destroyed the king just as he had destroyed our Isabella."

"For fuck's sake!" Luna yelled in frustration, startling a couple of fulmars nesting in the cliff face below into shrieking flight. "Have you any idea what might be locked inside your bloody heads? A king's fortune is what! They can't have left it in the Wash. No one in their right minds would be so bloody stupid."

Cló staggered to her feet, her stomach cramping so badly she had to catch her breath to stop from crying out. "You said the treasure was a load of bollocks," she muttered.

Luna glowered at her. "That was before, when I *did* think it was bollocks. But now ..." She turned away, arms crossed tightly across her chest. She scowled down at the Wash. "Just left there. All that gold and it was just left because you two numpties were all about revenge."

"I have to go," said Cló, staring wild-eyed at Gwenn.

"You need to finish this," said Gwenn, her solemn tone at odds with her high-pitched, little-girl voice. "Break the cycle, or this will happen again and again."

Stumbling away, Cló clutched her stomach, little white spots of pain blurring her vision. Luna called after her but didn't follow as she lurched along the little black-earth tracks through the fen.

Grimdark Hall basked like a cat under the beaming sun, its walls sparkling as though misted with black diamond dust. Cló stepped into the cool of the Great Hall and listened to its heavy silence. Wiping her nose, she felt a little better in Grimdark's gloom, her cramps easing.

Hoping Jude was still in bed, needing to share her worry that she was losing Foetus, she started across the Great Hall.

She was barely halfway across when she stopped. She listened again to Grimdark and the whisper that had echoed not moments before on the dusty air.

"*Come, Fat Mouse.*" It was a spiteful sigh, a breathless murmur.

"Constance?" Cló whispered.

Eyes narrowing, nostrils flaring, her worry thickened to anger at the sustained nastiness of her sister-in-law. "Bitch," she muttered, and changed course, darting into the conservatory to see Constance disappear through the doorway leading to the Hall of Curiosities.

Relieved by the distraction, Cló clung to her anger. Goaded by Constance's spite, she followed without thinking too hard about what would happen when she caught up to her sister-in-law.

The Hall of Curiosities was like a magnifying glass in the sunshine, heating the glass tunnel. She was drenched in sweat by the time she reached the old iron-studded door at the far end.

The door had been left ajar. There was nowhere else Constance could have gone. Cló pushed it open and stepped into the welcome coolness of the rooms beyond.

The familiarity of these stark, poky rooms shrouded in centuries-old gloom settled around Cló once more. To Walter Hulot, a bastard son, these rooms had been an opulence bordering on decadence. Walter's memories painted the bare flint walls with tapestries, the flagstoned floors with rugs, a desk and a couple of chairs in one room, a bed and trunk in another. Walter's guilt at the extravagance of a room just for sleeping, in a time when most shared a single bed or a mattress, was as real to Cló as breathing.

The third door had been locked against her curiosity the last time she'd entered these rooms. Now it stood ajar.

Cló pressed her fingers against it to open it more fully, releasing a dank, putrid stench. A narrow, blackened stairway spiralled down to a faint light at the bottom. There was no creepy creak from the hinges; they'd been oiled recently.

Cló hesitated at the top of the stairs, biting her lip. Grimdark hovered anxiously above her, hot and sultry as a panicked breath.

"*Come, Fat Mouse,*" whispered up the corkscrew staircase.

Knowing she would lose a fight with Constance, Cló's anger dwindled. She turned to leave, stifling her curiosity with common sense that no good would come from stepping down the stairs as Constance obviously wanted her to.

"*You know you want to, Fat Mouse.*"

I do! I do!

"Dammit!" Cló muttered, curiosity overwhelming her loathing of Constance and her common sense. *What would Walter do?* The question sprang to her mind unbidden.

Perhaps it was the immense self-confidence Cló had felt as the man she'd once been, perhaps it was the gamut of mixed emotions she'd experienced that morning, perhaps it was the final straw of Constance's insistent spite since she'd arrived in Grimdark, but Cló was already halfway down the staircase before her brain caught up with her feet.

She squeezed down the tightly coiled staircase, the treads indented by the passage of feet over the centuries. She cringed when her bare arms scraped against the slimy stone walls that seemed to grow tighter, as though Grimdark was narrowing the way forward to prevent Cló from seeing the dreadful monster hidden in its depths. Its putrid odour grew stronger the further she descended, sticking in her throat, her stomach heaving though she had nothing left to vomit.

Pulling her shirt up over her nose, Cló stepped down the last curl in the staircase. Her gasp of horror fluttered around the circular room lit by a single lamp.

Everything in the dungeon was black. Mould and slime coated the flint walls. The solid gloom of an Iron Maiden, like a menacing upright coffin, stood beside a thronelike chair covered in spikes. A large pit shadowed with ash from old fires was sunk into the floor. Medieval torture instruments and scold bridles shaped like pig masks lay scattered on benches, as though discarded only yesterday.

Cló's mind freely supplied torturers moving about the circular room, clothed in black robes and leather hoods. Moans filtered from the dark doorways with each step the torturers took, their victims recognising the heavy treads and jangle of large toothed keys, signalling more pain to come.

Not daring to breathe, Cló turned to run away before the

hulking figure of Constance hunched over a wooden bench detected her presence.

Her shoulders lodged in the tight confines of the spiral staircase. She couldn't move. She couldn't run.

"Stay where you are, Fat Mouse," said Constance without turning around.

Cló licked her dry lips. Excuses to explain her desire to leave stuck in her equally dry throat, all of Walter's self-confidence fleeing before the hard command in her sister-in-law's voice.

Constance turned to face Cló. In her hands was a piece of metal. It wasn't big: two bars, with a screw down the middle.

"Come closer."

Cló obeyed the order without thinking. The narrow staircase released her shoulders with a slight sticky pop.

Constance smiled. A slow, menacing smile. Constance was good at menace. It radiated off her like a visible aura. "I knew you wouldn't be able to resist following me. Such a curious, sneaky fat mouse . . . Do you recognise it?" she asked, her voice dropping to a low, encouraging rumble.

"Why would I?" said Cló, finding her voice, eyes darting around the dungeon, turning slightly so she could get up the stairs if Constance's menace became a physical threat.

Constance stepped away from the bench, stopping when she was not a metre away from Cló. Cló stepped back, hitting the bottom stair with the back of her ankles.

Constance laughed. Cló had never heard the woman laugh before. It was a big, booming laugh that raced up the dank, curved, windowless walls.

"You don't remember?" Her beefy arm shot out and grabbed Cló's bicep in a bruising grip. "You really don't remember, Fat Mouse?"

"What are you doing?" cried Cló, frightened by Constance's strength of a lifetime spent outdoors.

"Forcing you to remember who you were." She dragged Cló across the room to a doorway hidden, as a kindness, from the lamp's light.

"What are you doing?" cried Cló, struggling against Constance.

Constance's lip rose in a sneer, her fingers digging into the soft flesh of Cló's upper arm. "Shut up," she said mildly, and released Cló as suddenly as she had grabbed her. She nodded at the arched inkiness beyond.

Cló's skin crawled with primordial horror. Imagination wasn't needed to envisage the hell that lay in the darkness; its putrid stink of hopeless despair was like the fetid breath of a starved beast.

Light from Constance's lamp washed the narrow corridor with a sickly glow, lined with four wooden doors, each with a small square hatch.

Chest heaving with panic, Cló squinted into the darkness, a darkness not quite remembered, more a residue of emotions felt, tantalising in their nothingness.

Constance's breath tickled her neck as she whispered, "Do you remember, Fat Mouse? Do you remember your screams?" She held up the thumbscrew still clutched in her hand. "In another time, in this place, your screams reverberated where none could hear." She moved to stand square in front of Cló so that she couldn't avoid those round green eyes. "I know it's you, Walter Hulot," she hissed. "I know it's you, Euphemia Figgis. Twice you've been killed, and you shall be killed again if you don't return what was stolen."

Cló was hypnotised by the pinprick of madness she glimpsed in those green depths. "I don't know what you're talking about," she said. Her voice shook, her lie audible to her own ears.

"How can you not?" Constance spat in her face. "The meeting in the fens . . . You as Walter Hulot, your brother, Ralph Honeyborne, and Brother Simon." She stepped closer, so close

Cló saw the cracks on her lips and the deep wrinkles around her eyes in the dim light. "You were Brother Simon's friend, his mentor, and you betrayed him. The agreement—"

"You were to kill the king." The words slipped out before Cló could stop them.

"Hah! I *knew* you remembered. Yes, and you reneged on the agreement. You were to hide the king's gold in the crypt." Constance's wide hands were on Cló's shoulders, shaking her hard. "Where is it? You were supposed to hide it in Isabella's tomb. I've been in there. There's nothing but bones. Where did you hide the gold?"

"You were Brother Simon?" Cló clarified, but her answer lay in Constance's knowing expression.

Slit-eyed with scorn and hatred, Constance was silent for a long while. "So many lives spent searching," she whispered distantly. "But the search is over. And you are not as tough as Walter Hulot, and Euphemia Figgis could not be broken. But you . . ." Her lips curved into an evil sneer. "Fat mice get caught in traps. Only the fast ones escape, but fat mice are not fast."

Any words Cló might have uttered lodged in her throat, unable to escape, except in a scream. She shook her head, horrified by tears of panicked terror slipping down her cheeks.

"Where is it?" Constance shouted, shaking her hard. "Where did you hide it? I know what the plan was. You were to act as guide and lose the king's baggage in the Wash, and Brother Simon was to kill the king in Swinehead Abbey while Ralph was to meet the barons in London. Then you were to bring the king's gold back to the Hall, where it was to be divvied up." She pushed Cló up against the wall of the corridor so hard the rounded flint stones dug into her back.

"I—I can't remember," Cló whispered hoarsely. "I would tell you if I knew, but I don't. I—I can remember some of Effie and Walter's lives, I know there was a plan to kill the king. I wish I could tell you what you want to know, but I don't know!" The last was a wailed plea.

Constance put a heavy arm across Cló's neck, her face so close fine spittle sprayed across her face. "A king was killed," she hissed, "the course of history was changed. The price of the king's life was the gold, and you have a debt to settle, Walter Hulot!'

12 October 1216

The last prayers of Compline had long since passed, yet all was aflutter in the Abbey of St. Mary on the outskirts of the hamlet, Swinehead. Monks hurried back and forth carrying torches, trailing smoke and the stench of burnt tallow.

Not so, Brother Simon. He had avoided the night prayer and hid under the entrance arch of the dark orchard to watch King John and his knights ride into the courtyard of the abbey. He scratched his throat absentmindedly at the hair shirt under his grey robe that Abbot William had decreed he was to wear for the remainder of his life, as penance. Brother Simon hated the reminder of past sins; he felt little need for penance and had every intention of committing future sins. He scowled at the figure of Abbot William obsequiously bowing to the king, so low his nose almost touched the ground.

Shoving his hands into the heavy sleeves of his robe, he fingered the tiny vial hidden within and smiled to himself. It was an unpleasant smile and boded ill will, though whether for the king or the abbot, only Brother Simon knew.

He waited until the king and his retinue entered the refectory with the abbot, while monks led the horses to the stables. Slowly, the night noises replaced the cacophony of the new arrivals.

He was about to head into the refectory himself when he drew back into the shadows of the orchard as another rider entered the courtyard. A messenger, by the look of his attire.

Brother Simon's chest tightened with disquiet. Had they been discovered? His round green eyes watched the messenger dismount and ask a passing monk where the king was.

Leaving the safety of the shadows, Brother Simon hurried into the cloisters, and entered the refectory in time to see the messenger whisper into the king's ear and hand him a scroll.

The Abbey of St. Mary oozed wealth, and this was most evident in the refectory. Four rows of benches ran the length of the rectangular room; pious tapestries were interspersed with stained-glass windows that dappled the floor with rainbows on sunny days—but that beauty was lost at night. At the far end, on raised benches kept for officials and important visitors, sat King John beside Abbot William.

That night there would be meat served in honour of the king's presence in the abbey. Meat and fresh cider. It had been a splendid year for apples. Brother Simon, though he had taken the vows of poverty, chastity and obedience of the Cistercian order, subscribed to none; chastity was not in his nature, nor was obedience, and he detested poverty, having spent most of his life thieving to ensure he was never impoverished. Tonight, with a feast in the offing for the king, he had every intention of dining gluttonously.

Keeping his eyes on the king, Brother Simon scuttled along to his place at a bench. He paused before seating himself, watching the king's lips tighten with fury before turning on the messenger, slapping him so hard across the chest the man flew backwards to smash into a monk holding a serving platter.

In the shocked silence that befell the refectory, Brother Simon's

*round eyes grew rounder with horrible glee at the scene unfold-
ing before him—falling bodies and food and ale thrown up in
the air—before realising the message received by the king might
not bode well for himself.*

*Fearing the worst had come to pass, he turned abruptly and
hurried back the way he had come, passing through a door,
while raining muttered curses down on Walter Hulot and Ralph
Honeyborne. He scurried through the steaming kitchen, along
an arched wooden tunnel and down the stone stairs. Past the
buttery and bakery, he entered the cold cellar, heady with the
sour sweetness of fermented apples.*

*It was the work of seconds to fill a flagon with fresh cider.
No one would question his being in the cellar. He was the cel-
larer; a position he had coveted on arrival at the abbey, and
ensured he gained with the unusual and painful death of his
predecessor. He had learnt many things in the Holy Land;
though few of them were holy, many were useful in pressing
circumstances.*

*Ensuring he was alone in the cellar lit by a single burning
torch, he took out the tiny vial hidden within his deep sleeves
and poured the white, creamy poison he had spent all day col-
lecting from toads in the surrounding fens into the cider, stirring
it well.*

*He left the cellar with the flagon, nodding at a couple of
monks rushing past him. One whispered, "Have you heard?" as
he drew alongside.*

*Brother Simon stopped and grabbed the monk's arm. "Heard
what?"*

*"Dover has fallen to the French king. Even now he rides to
London with the barons. The king got word not moments ago."
Monks had little to alleviate the monotony of their days of work
punctuated by the hours of prayers, and the whispering monk's
eyes were alive with excitement to be at the centre of activity for
once.*

Brother Simon started with surprise. "Dover?" he said blankly, having expected news of a different sort, one that impacted more personally on himself. He didn't give a rat's fart for the troubles of the king and had every intention of making those troubles significantly worse.

"Aye. There was a great to-do in the refectory. The king hit the messenger, who hit Brother Thomas. It was quite a sight," said the monk with open delight. "Abbot William is even now trying to calm the king, who is in a towering rage." He glanced at the flagon in Brother Simon's hand. "You'd best get that to the king. He is calling for wine, but . . ." He shrugged and hurried on towards the cellars.

Bracing himself against the flutter of nervous trepidation congealing in his stomach, Brother Simon accelerated down the arched tunnel. Wine! He should have used wine. Why did he not think to use wine? He had used all the poison he had in this one flagon. Perhaps . . . shaking his head, furious with himself, he passed through the bustling kitchen.

Sidling into the refectory, he looked to the king, trying to judge the man's humour, but it was impossible to tell from this distance. The king was eating and drinking . . . a good sign.

There was nothing for it. Brother Simon scuttled down the length of the refectory and stopped before the king.

"Your Grace," he murmured in his most ingratiating tone, aware Abbot William was frowning ominously at him. "Mayhap you would care to sample our cider? Made fresh with a powerful tang that might suit Your Grace."

King John looked up at the monk through narrowed eyes. His face was flushed, sweat sheening his forehead. He looked ill, to Brother Simon's silent rejoicing. The king wiped his beard with his sleeve and stared at Brother Simon until the monk's left eye twitched with panic.

"An unusual mark," said the king. "Though perhaps a cross prominent on a monk's face is a sign of your calling."

Brother Simon lifted a hand to touch the birthmark on his cheek. He had never thought of it in those terms. Truly, he thought the mark was a curse, for it was an identifiable feature he could well do without.

"I am indeed—er—blessed," said Brother Simon, sounding slightly strangled.

"Come! Pour, pious little monk!" commanded the king, and held out his goblet. "Let us sample the abbey's fabled cider."

The lightness of looming victory filled the false monk until he was quite giddy. He lifted the flagon and was about to pour when King John pulled back his goblet.

"Taste it."

Brother Simon's short-lived victory froze in a rictus of terror on his face, with only his left eye twitching furiously. "Your Grace," he mumbled, unable to conceal the quaver in his voice. "Taste it?"

"Aye. Our taster is with our baggage. You will do for taster."

Brother Simon licked his lips and looked to Abbot William. But there was no help from that quarter. The abbot nodded, his mouth quirking in one corner, though whether he was hiding a smile of displeasure or delight, Brother Simon could not tell.

Closing his very round eyes briefly, he turned to the nearest bench and picked up a wooden cup. Pouring a small measure of cider, he put the cup to his lips, and took the tiniest of sips.

"More!" demanded the king.

Closing his eyes fully, Brother Simon took a large drink, draining the cider in the cup. He thought to hold it in his mouth and make his escape, but the king was watching him carefully. He swallowed.

King John waited a full minute before nodding at his goblet. Brother Simon filled it to the brim and left the flagon on the table. In an instant, Brother Simon was forgotten by the king, who turned to Abbot William to discuss the price of bread.

The monk scuttled down the length of the refectory, keeping to the wall, then turned at the doorway leading to the cloisters in time to see the king drink the cider in one long draught before making his escape into the night.

He made it past the cloisters and into the orchard before his stomach cramped painfully. Leaning against an apple tree with one hand, sobbing and panting, Brother Simon's mind raced. There was no antidote except to purge himself brutally. He knew what would come if he didn't. His end would be excruciating; first cramps and excessive sweating then vomiting. What came after . . . well, he had never been around long enough to see what happened to his previous victims. Though he had heard dreadful tales of bowels bursting, and even one case where a man's heart had flown straight out of his chest to lay beating on the floor beside him.

Gibbering with terror, he staggered through the orchard and out into the fens beyond, as sweat broke out across his entire body, though the night air was cold against his skin.

Where were they? Where had he seen the plants?

Cramps ripped through his stomach with the intensity of a canker. He dropped to his knees and scrabbled about in the mud.

His grabbling hands found a root. He held it up to his face, shook his head, tossed it to the side and scrabbled deeper. Five times his hands did not find what they sought. He wept in pity for the agony he would endure in a few short hours.

There was no triumph, as panting, he pulled out a rhizome of the irises he had seen flowering in this spot in spring. Not bothering to wash off the mud in the small pool of water nearby, he shoved the entire rhizome in his mouth and chewed fast before spitting out the mash.

He leaned back on his haunches and gazed up at the starred sky as he waited for the effects.

They came quickly and hard. He bent over and vomited and vomited, until blood ran down his chin.

SEVENTEEN

❧

"Brother Simon nearly died that night," said Constance. "He nearly died because of you."

Pressed up against the slimed wall of the dungeon, Cló stared at the older woman in horror. It was impossible not to stare with her face so close.

"I've been to Swinehead," she said, as though Cló had asked a question. "Many years ago now. There's nothing left of the abbey, and Swinehead is a grim, grubby town surrounded by commercial farms. Honestly, if it had still existed, I would've knocked the abbey down myself. Ghastly place, all those places are; full of sanctimonious men hiding from the real world."

Cló drew back from those round green eyes. "You were hiding too, when you were Brother Simon. He killed someone, in London. Simon would've hanged if it hadn't been for me—for Walter," she amended. "Simon owed his life to Walter."

Constance shrugged. "Perhaps, but Simon, Ralph and Walter had a deal, and Walter reneged."

"But you and I don't!" Cló snapped, fear getting the better of her, twisting into terrified anger. Constance's restraining arm tightened against her throat. "I am not Walter Hulot, and you are not Brother Simon. That all happened eight hundred years ago! I don't care about the gold. I didn't then, and I don't now. If I knew where it was, I would tell you."

Her eyes narrowed, the pressure on Cló's throat lessened slightly. "You really don't remember?" she asked, uncertain now.

"No!" cried Cló, eyeing the distance between herself and the staircase. If she pushed Constance away hard enough to lose her balance . . . Constance was a formidable unit, but Cló had weight on her side. Never had she been so grateful for her love of food as she was at that moment. "I keep telling you I don't know where it is. Yes, I've had some memories, but not about the king's gold. I think I—Walter—left it in the Wash."

Constance renewed her pressure on Cló's throat. She frowned. "You're telling the truth. You really don't know where it is."

Cló's "No" came out as a strangled croak. She clutched at Constance's arm. "Let me go!"

A shiver of confusion crossed the older woman's face. "But Hulot came back to the Hall. You must remember that. And Euphemia . . . I've seen you snooping about the Hall at night, I was sure you would find the dungeons eventually."

"I did. The door was locked."

Constance grimaced. "An oversight. One I rectified today."

"You—you wanted me to find this place?" said Cló, thinking of the open door, the oiled hinges. It had been so easy too. She was too curious for her own good, following Constance, convinced she was up to no good. Her curiosity had come full circle and bitten Cló where it hurt most.

She felt Constance shrug. "Going back to places where you once lived or spent time can often trigger new memories, in my experience."

"How does me being in the dungeon help? Walter lived in the rooms above, not here."

"Yes." Constance's lips split into a horrible grin. "But Euphemia became well acquainted with this place."

Cló's stomach coiled with panic. She had to get out of here. She pushed hard against Constance's chest, surprising her into releasing Cló's throat. A gap opened between them.

Cló seized the slim chance, shoved Constance out of her way and took off down the corridor towards the main dungeon, lit in all its macabre horror by the forgotten lamp. She leapt towards the spiralled stairs, her foot on the first step . . . Her head snapped back hard as a strong hand grabbed her hair, whipping her about. Constance's arm wrapped around Cló's neck, and in a headlock she dragged her back through the arched doorway into the dark corridor.

Constance paused and muttered, "Now which one was it?"

Cló struggled, yelling incoherently, but Constance was stronger and tightened her grip. "Let me go!" she choked out. "I'm leaving right now! You have no right to do this!"

"Leaving?" said Constance, distracted as she pushed open a cell door with a heavy shoulder and dragged Cló inside. "You're not leaving. You need to remember . . . Euphemia remembered, but she remembered too late. A stretch in her old cell will help jog your memory."

Cló paled. "You're mad," she whispered. "You're utterly mad."

"Not mad," snapped Constance. "Determined. Determined to get what is due." She gripped Cló's upper arms and heaved her against a wall of the cell. Cló struggled, but she was no match for Constance's strength.

The stench of mould and rot was overwhelming. The wall at Cló's back was sticky with a horrible sludge that stuck to her clothes, seeping through the material to touch her skin with slimy clamminess.

The pale light cast by the lamp in the main dungeon revealed little but a tiny room and heavy manacles bolted to the walls. Leaning bodily against Cló to prevent her escape, Constance ripped one of the manacles open. It shrieked with rusted disuse as it was clamped around her ankle. She took the key out of the side and slipped it into her pocket.

"You were kept here with your mother. An old harridan was Germaine Figgis," said Constance, her eyes gleaming in the feeble light.

Cló spat in her face.

Constance wiped away the spittle running down her cheek. Her lips twisted into a rictus of hatred. She drew her arm back and slapped Cló, vicious and hard. "I've wanted to do that since the moment I saw you," she snarled, and took a threatening step forward.

Cló shrank against the wall, a hand to her cheek, as tears of pain pushed into the corners of her eyes. She was so shocked she couldn't retaliate and raised her arms defensively. "I'll call Jude," she whispered.

"On your mobile?" Constance's lips pulled back into a feral grin. "There's no reception down here. I won't even bother to take it away from you. And these"—she slapped the dank wall—"are thick so you can call and cry and scream as much as you like, and no one will hear you."

"So how will you explain my disappearance to him?"

Her eyebrows rose in surprise. "I won't. I don't care what Jude thinks. He will never find you." She walked out of the cell and closed the heavy door.

"Wait!" Cló cried.

The hatch in the door grated open. "What?"

"How will you know if I've remembered? Will you come down and check on me?" Cló hated the pleading note in her voice.

"I'll come down once a day. After all, I don't want you to die before you've told me where the gold is. History repeating itself can be quite tiring."

The hatch grated shut.

Constance's footsteps receded, then a heavier, slower tread as she climbed the coiled staircase. Cló flinched at the faint reverberation when the door to the dungeon slammed shut. She had no doubt it would be locked.

The first thing she did was pull her phone from her pocket. There was no signal, but she tried to phone Jude anyway.

Cló leaned her head back against the wall, then wished she hadn't as slime got caught up in her hair. Tears slipped down her cheeks unchecked. She clutched her phone, pathetically grateful for the pale glow it cast over the tiny cell. Grateful she'd thought to charge it last night and still had eighty percent charge left. She switched it into sleep mode to save the battery.

After she ran a gauntlet of emotions, from fear to anger to self-pity, her tears dried to snail trails on her cheeks, and she stared at the dark. For the first time, it held terror for her, but after a couple of hours, according to a quick look at her phone, drained of emotion and with nothing to stimulate her senses, Cló discovered the dark was boring.

The wall at her back shuddered slightly, as though Grimdark had sighed regretfully. The old building pressed down and around her, and she understood why it had always felt so sorrowful, so fearful, hiding the worst of its history deep in its bones.

In the first hours, she really did try to remember Effie sitting where she sat, tortured, bloody and burnt. But it was only her imagination, not a single memory pushed through from Effie's life to Cló's.

She stared at the dark.

The silence was absolute. No rats scurried about in a place that simply screamed rats' haven. No water dripped down the walls in a steady trickle. No sinister clanging of the ghoul Jude said could sometimes be heard down in the dungeons. The very thought of Jude had Clo's throat tightening with tears.

She felt the need to pee and clenched her pelvis, trying not to think about it.

Cló stared at the dark.

Perhaps she could sleep. She wasn't sure if the dark was the back of her eyelids or the remembered dark of the cell. The light from her phone when she flicked it on quickly to check the time hurt her eyes. Fifty percent and seven hours of darkness.

Cló stared at the dark.

Thirty percent and eleven hours.

"Come on, Effie," she murmured, then shivered when her voice came back in a thousand whispers; Grimdark's response to her, keeping her company as she tried in vain to remember.

Ten percent and fourteen hours.

Her muscles cramped and creaked and ached when she moved, the chains on the manacle clinking eerily.

Cló cried the first time she peed in her pants. The flood of wet warmth between her legs quickly cooled against the cold stone beneath her butt. No one could see her, but she was humiliated all the same.

Cló stared at the dark.

The phone was flat.

Panic set in. The phone was her lifeline. A link to the world above. Tears she didn't know she could still cry came. Cló cried. An ugly cry. Snot slid from her nose. She didn't bother to brush it away. No one could see her. She cried long and loud, the echoes sobbing with her in solidarity.

Cló stared at the dark.

Perhaps Constance had lied. *Of course she had lied.* She had felt Constance's hatred the moment she'd stepped foot into the Hall all those weeks ago. She had had every intention of leaving Cló in the dungeons to rot. How could she have been so stupid, so naïve to think Constance had any intention of releasing her? What if she did remember and told Constance where the treasure was? Would she release her?

"No," Cló whispered. Her trump card, her one chance of survival, was not to tell Constance anything. Which wasn't a problem, as she genuinely couldn't remember anything.

"Have you remembered?"

The voice shocked Cló out of the daze she'd fallen into. "Constance?" she croaked, turning towards the door, though she couldn't see it.

"Have you remembered?"

Cló thought to lie. A lie could get her out of this cell, out of the dungeons. But not a single lie sprang to mind.

"No," she said thickly, thirst sticking her tongue to the roof of her mouth. Before she could ask for water the hatch slammed shut.

Cló was too tired to cry. She didn't think of Jude. She couldn't. She certainly couldn't think of Foetus. If she thought of the life growing inside her, it would be the end of her.

Cló slept. Sleep was a release. And that in itself was strange. All these years, she'd fought sleep; now she actively courted it. But soon she couldn't sleep, a pressing urge from her bowels became the sole focus of her dark existence. "*I will not shit my-self... I will not shit myself...*" became a desperate mantra, flooding the dungeon with gossiping murmurs.

The second time Constance came down to open the hatch and demanded, "Have you remembered?" a couple of bottles of water and a packet of biscuits were tossed at Cló.

The hatch opened again and again. The same demand was made again and again. Water and biscuits were occasionally tossed in.

Cló eked out her scant supplies, not knowing when she might be given more. Time was an eternity in the dark. Her only routine was Constance's daily appearance. And even that she wasn't sure of. Perhaps Constance came more often, perhaps not. Cló grew to long for the grating of the hatch, the question, the hatch to drop, the heavy footsteps receding, all a reminder she was not already dead and existing in some hellish limbo.

The hatch opened.

Cló held her breath, waiting for the dreaded question. It didn't come.

The door opened, and pale light fell across the cell, silhouetting the hulking figure of Constance.

Cló cringed into the wall, eyes squeezed shut against the unaccustomed light. "I don't remember anything," she whispered, her throat sore and dry from lack of use and dehydration.

Constance hunkered down in front of her. "Drink!" she commanded, thrusting a bottle into Cló hands.

Cló drank greedily until her stomach hurt as it distended, full for the first time in days. It pressed painfully against her full bowels, the one indignity she had so far managed to avoid.

"Thanks," said Cló reflexively, then cursed herself and her pathetic gratitude to her captor.

It was a long time before Constance said, "I'm not enjoying this."

"Then let me go," Cló whispered hoarsely, eyeing her sideways, too scared to look at her directly, wanting to avoid those round green eyes.

"I will once you've told me what I need to know. People are searching for you, it's causing complications."

"Jude?" said Cló hopefully, tears pricking her eyes as his name fluttered into the dungeon.

Constance's nostrils twitched. "And the police. Your hippy friend and her daughter have been making a nuisance of themselves too."

Gratitude warmed Cló for two people whom she didn't know all that well but were trying to find her—that she had not been forgotten, as she had feared.

Constance regarded her for a long while, then sighed. "I

don't wish to keep you down here longer than I absolutely have to."

There was an odd hitch in Constance's voice that Cló would've considered apprehension in anyone else. It was at odds with the woman's usual severity and single-mindedness.

"You're going to kill me," said Cló, her tone flat. She knew the truth of her future in her bones. No matter which way she'd looked at her predicament, there was no way Constance would release her without facing jail time for kidnap. Her only solution was to kill Cló and get rid of her body. She'd already imagined countless scenarios of her dead self, slung over Constance's shoulder, slipping through Grimdark in the dead of night, being tossed over the cliffs . . .

"I don't want to." Constance sighed again. "I've lived for this, you know, all my life," her voice softening with what might have passed for kindness. "I've been consumed by the search, and I'm so tired of it."

"Don't you mean lives?" said Cló dully, not wanting to engage with her captor, but unable to stop herself.

A moment of hesitation. "Yes, of course, lives."

Cló looked fully at Constance, her lips tightening with fury. Fury was all she had left. "I hate you!" she whispered, wanting to reach out and scratch the woman's eyes out. She could almost feel the round firmness of her slick eyeballs under her fingertips, the blood running down her arms, the resistance of tendons and muscles as she gouged deep into the eye sockets.

Constance stood up. "You are not alone in that. Sometimes I hate myself."

The pale light left with Constance, and the door shut.

Cló stared at the dark.

She counted aloud for a while, creating her own time. She counted in groups of sixty, making a game out of it, but the sixties piled up and got muddled, and she forgot where she had ended. Grimdark counted with her in a hush of echoes. Grimdark was her only reality, always there, solid against her back, its layers a heavy weight above her.

Counting made her sleepy. She couldn't tell if she was asleep and having some dreadful nightmare that she was trapped in a dungeon; her dreams had always been so vivid. The dark shifted her boundaries of reality and fantasy, certain she was trapped in one of the world's uncertain places, the space between one second and the next, in a twilight that was neither day nor night, neither awake nor asleep, on the cusp of one thing or the other . . .

Cló awoke with a gasp. Her nape prickled, she blinked hard. Turning her head, she strained to hear what had woken her.

She reached out a hand, wanting to touch someone. Something. Anything.

Then she closed her eyes in relief, even as her heart broke at the disembodied mumbling echoing around the cell.

1645

*Despair. It dripped with the slime and damp on the black-
ened walls, it gnawed with the rats in scurrying scritches and
clawed the air, heavy and fetid with disease. And in that darkened hell Germaine's disembodied curses were a mumbling,
half-mad shriek, "May you burst like a rotted sheep's bladder,
you slaverin' snot . . . A pestilence on you and yar hearth and
home . . . I'll make yar blood boil and leak from yar ears . . ."
Germaine drew a breath, "I call on the Devil to make yar head
explode . . . I curse you with nits till yar hair falls out . . ."*

*"Mum," said Effie, her voice low, weary, drained. "Nits?
You and I together know none of them curses will work. We ent
in league with the Devil, no matter what that bastard do say. It
ent real."*

*"It is in me head," snapped Germaine, "And I wish it all on
their heads and worse." But the mumbling shriek didn't continue, and a blunt silence settled over mother and daughter but
for the occasional clink of a chain as one of them moved slightly
within the limits of their fetters.*

There was no way to tell the passing of time; no windows, no light, no clean air or sound filtered down into the dank dungeons beneath Honeyborne Hall. Effie measured time by torture and interrogation in a place where none could hear their screams.

She ached in places unnatural, her body broken and burnt in cruel ways. She bled from her hands and feet, blisters around her ankles that had been held over a brazier in caspie-claws had long since burst and throbbed with the heat of infection. The air, that for a while had smelt of her roasting flesh, now stank of her own rot. She couldn't describe the pain, for she no longer felt quite human, and couldn't stand so much as a drop of water to touch her legs without screaming with the agony. They had been shaved when first brought in, and the growing stubble itched in places she dared not scratch for fear of touching another painful area.

Tears came and went. Tears hurt her burnt cheeks where her face had been pressed to a heated iron bar. Though she tried not to weep at the futility of their situation, tears still came and went.

She and Germaine had had their bodies searched intimately for evidence of teats that their familiars had used to suckle blood. Germaine, especially, was covered in warts and made the pricking women's job simple to find any number resembling teats. They had been dunked in the dungeon's well with thumbs and great toes tied together. Effie still did not know how it was possible they had both floated. That, with the pricking, had been enough to condemn them as witches without need of a confession, yet still they languished in the dungeon after seven other women from the village had been hanged for witchcraft some time before.

"I hopes we dunt have to walk all hours like when we was first here." Germaine's voice was a ghostly rasp in the deep gloom, for the iron collars around their necks choked their

words. "I can take them needles and them pilnie-winks, though my thumbs dunt work no more. But I can't bear the walking, Effie."

"I know, Mum," she said softly, hearing the break in Germaine's voice. She wished she could reach her mum and hug her, take her away from here. Germaine was an old woman, and though a scold to some, she had raised Effie with love; it was more than many in Darrow End could say for themselves. Her mum, though strong, would not last much longer.

"I think we should confess," said Germaine, after a long silence filled only by the occasional plink of water dripping to the filthy floor. "It dunt matter if it be true or not, and if I'm to die, I'd as soon die with the sea's breeze on me face afore the noose slips over me head. That'll be better than a death below the earth. It's the only freedom we have left now, how we die."

It was a long time before Effie said, "I already have, more than once."

A clink of chain as Germaine turned to face Effie. "You what? You've confessed and we ent met the hangman yet?"

"No." Effie had confessed and confessed to anything and everything Matthew Hopkins had claimed as crimes of witchcraft against her, in the vain hope her confession might spare her mum further pain and a swift end. To no avail.

Though she knew herself to be no witch, there was witchcraft about, for Effie was convinced she had been bewitched herself. How else was it possible she remembered herself as a man, a Walter Hulot, when she was also quite certainly a woman, with the necessary bits to prove it? Yet she could remember much of this Walter Hulot, how the world looked through his eyes, how it smelt, his loves and likes, his hate . . . so much hate.

And then there was Joseph. The shock on his face must have mirrored her own when she recognised him for another man . . . a man this Walter Hulot had loved dearly. It had been more than her own fear for the pirate as she had watched him led *away to the cart waiting to take him to Marshalsea Prison to be hanged for piracy; an old fear of a protective brother who would do anything for the other.*

"*What of Sophie?*" *said Germaine minutes later—or perhaps hours: There was no way to tell, and all their conversations, when they were able to speak, were merely picked up where they'd left off last.* "*How will the mawther survive without you and I together to protect her from the likes o' that bastard above?*"

Effie closed her eyes and leaned against the slimed wall of the cell. She had no answer, having not seen a living soul but the Witchfinder and his pricking women from the outside world. She could only hope Benjamin Hobbis had taken Sophie far away; it was the single hope she retained; there was none left for herself and Germaine.

"*He comes,*" *said Germaine after ages of dark silence, with the uncanny hearing of the blind.*

It was a little longer before Effie heard the Witchfinder's cough filter down the narrow spiral stairs leading to the dungeons, then his footsteps on the worn stone steps.

"*That one ent long fer this world,*" *said Germaine with grim relish.*

"*But too late fer us.*"

There was no fortune-telling or wishful thinking in the statement, for Effie, too, knew a consumptive cough when she heard it, and Matthew Hopkins's cough was a deep wet rattle in his thin chest, clearly indicating looming death. Effie hoped, with extreme malice and no mercy, that his end would be excruciatingly painful.

She counted the footsteps down each step—thirty-four—then along the row of cells, with their mean bars and fetid bleakness—twenty-seven. She had no idea how long it had been since his footsteps had stopped at twenty-four or twenty-one, for only Germaine and Effie remained confined in the dungeon.

Blinking in the faint light of the approaching candle, Effie looked at Germaine. Shackled naked to the wall, hairless, and now so thin the old woman was more skeleton than flesh, her one cheekbone completely exposed after being held too long over a fire and her hands and feet a mangled mess of blood and crushed bones.

Matthew Hopkins stopped on the twenty-seventh step, a silhouette behind the brightness of the candle. Beside him stood a couple of his pricking women, hunched like ragged bats.

There was a routine to their arrival. The pricking women would unlock the barred door while Hopkins waited without, with a scented kerchief to his nostrils to avoid the Figgis women's bestial stench. Effie would be unshackled first, and other chains added as though fearful she would fly out of nonexistent windows or vanish in a puff of smoke. Then she was forced to walk on her burnt and mangled feet to a room beyond the cells while Germaine was taken in the opposite direction.

A heavy hand on her shoulder compelled her to sit with a clanking of chains into the wooden chair at the wooden table in the small room. It was bare but for the table and two chairs.

Hopkins stepped into the room, waiting until the pricking woman left and he and Effie were alone.

Effie glared at him with a dull, powerless hatred. It was all she had left of herself: hatred. It scorched the air between them. Effie got some small satisfaction when he flinched and looked away from her hate-filled gaze.

A coughing fit took Hopkins so hard he clutched the table for support. When it passed, he spat a globule of bloody mucous onto the floor, then looked at Effie. "Do you deny sending your familiars in to cause nightmares in the Paston household?"

"I dunt," said Effie, her voice emotionless, dead, simply going through the routine, waiting for the pain that would come after. "I confess to all."

"Do you confess to attending a sabbat in Tangled Wood, as seen by Goodwife Kett on Midsummer's Eve?"

"I do."

Time passed slowly as the same questions were asked again and again, and Effie gave the same answers again and again. She confessed to everything.

"I can make this all go away, Euphemia."

Effie's head snapped up at the change of tone. Gone was the velvet sway of his words heavy with fervour. It dipped low and gentle, making the singed hair rise on her arms. There was power in his voice, its charm hard to resist, when he spoke kindly. For the briefest of moments, a dull flame of hope burnt in her heart that perhaps, against evidence to the contrary, all would be well.

She eyed him warily, not trusting his uncharacteristic benevolence.

"I know you for who you are." The gentleness was gone. The velvet was gone. Replaced by the mad croak of another's voice, from another time. *"Tell me where you buried the gold."*

Effie shut her eyes tightly, the flicker of hope snuffed out in an instant. She had seen it before, when this other . . . being took over the Witchfinder. She had watched his body straighten from its world-weary slouch and shorten with a deeper chest, the birthmark on his cheek in the shape of a cross darkening like a new burn. Two souls twisted together, and both terrified her.

"I dunt know where it be. I cannot tell you what I dunt know."

She didn't hear him move but when she cracked open an eyelid, he was inches away from her face. *"Lie!"* he screeched. *"I know you for Walter Hulot. You and your brother robbed me of my share, and now I shall have it!"*

Effie shook her head in mute denial—voiced ones had never made any difference.

"It was your eyes," he said, velvet again, and saner than the other. *"The eyes of Walter Hulot. Those odd-coloured eyes al-*

ways looking at me with revulsion. I hated you then . . . And I hate you now." The last was a silken murmur.

Effie snapped her eyes shut again to avoid staring into his shining madness.

"Don't deny you cannot remember who you were," hissed the Witchfinder.

"It's witchcraft," whispered Effie, sensing the man move about the small room, not daring to open her eyes, terrified of this aberrant creature that was two men. "You've bewitched me that I know myself as another. It's unnatural. Witchcraft, true and proper."

"You would dare call me witch?" His face was so close, spittle stung her scorched skin. She hadn't heard him move.

Effie swallowed, courage failing. She shook her head.

He moved about the room once more. Effie sat still so as not to clink her chains for fear it would remind him they had not yet progressed to brutal interrogation.

It was an eternity before his voice edged into the room again, enticing with kindness. "Do you care nothing for your mother?"

Effie's eyes snapped open. "O' course. I love her dearly."

"Yet you persist in keeping the truth from me. Insist on denying me what is rightfully mine."

"I would do anythin' . . ." whispered Effie, tone ragged. "Do you not think I would tell you if I knew where this gold be, if it would save me mum from further torture?"

The Witchfinder, his head to one side, turned and walked slowly around the table. He did two laps before he said, "I've always had a fascination with the fabled lost treasure of King John. As a boy, I would go down to the Wash and search for it amidst the mud and marshes. I knew it was there. Not with a boy's belief of legend and tales, but truly believed, in my soul, the gold had been in the Wash."

He stalked around the room again, "It was only as I grew older that it grew stronger, this belief that it was no fable." He turned, his lips curving into a boyish smile. "I followed all the stories, spoke to the old ones, to the ferrymen across the Wash and the mudlarks and the guides. So many stories and legends . . . And then I came to Darrow End. Even as we rode up to the village, I could feel a . . . shift, a change in myself so I wasn't myself, but another . . . And when I saw you and the pirate." He shrugged, a small matter-of-fact shrug. "I knew there was not merely witchcraft in this place, but something else altogether . . . I saw your eyes, and it was all there in my memories. I knew you and I know you recognised me too, when I was someone else, a long time ago."

Two laps around the small room in silence. "For weeks you have resisted me, resisted my every effort . . ." He stopped on the opposite side of the table from Effie, lips curled with frustration. "You have defied me, and you have defied God, and now you will answer to God or the Devil, for there is nothing more I can do in your time left on earth."

A rush of iciness clawed through Effie's veins. The question was on her lips, but no sound came. She had known it had to end eventually, had prayed to both God and the Devil for the day to come swiftly, desperate for deliverance from the hell of these past weeks, knowing her deliverance would be death, not freedom.

"When?" she whispered, as Hopkins prowled around the room, stopping when he was behind her.

"Tomorrow, an hour before the sun sets."

A bloated silence filled the already fetid air, broken only by Effie's gasping breath. She had craved death, begged for it, but now it was upon her, the shock was paralysing.

The decayed odour of Hopkins slid against her neck as he leaned down, and whispered, "'He that overcometh shall inherit all things; and I will be his God, and he shall be my son.'" The velvety voice filled the small chamber, slightly breathless, with the chanting rhythm of a priest. It washed over Effie as she

watched his shadow, hunched over her own, on the wall oppo-
site. "'But the fearful, and unbelieving, and the abominable,
and murderers, and whoremongers, and sorcerers, and idol-
aters, and all liars, shall have their part in the lake which bur-
neth with fire and brimstone: which is the second death . . .'"
So Our Lord said in Revelation, and so it shall be. I carry out
God's work, in His words and His name."

"We are to burn?" *Effie twisted hard, her shackles digging*
deep into her skin, to look into the round green eyes so close to
her own odd-coloured ones. "What o' a hangin'? *There ent*
never been a burnin' at Darrow End and you sent all the others
to the gallows. Why not a hangin' fer us?"

Hopkins held her gaze. Effie looked away first, for the light
of madness lurked within those green depths, though whether
pious fervour or the insanity of true bloodlust made no differ-
ence. She and her mum were to burn.

"A burning to mimic the fires of Hell," he murmured. "Witch
you may be, but you are accused of murdering your husband,
and for that treason you will be burnt according to the laws of
our land. Lord Honeyborne was insistent no expense be spared.
Barrels of pitch and straw are already waiting on Gibbet Hill.
The pamphlets have been distributed all over Norfolk . . . There
is to be a good turnout, no doubt." He stepped away and moved
around the table. He reached into his coat and pulled out a
scroll with a broken seal and spread it flat in front of Effie.

She stared blankly at the crisscross of squiggles with signa-
tures at the bottom.

"Your death warrant," said Hopkins. "Lord Honeyborne
has a particular hatred of witches. And he has an especial ha-
tred of the Figgis women. He has been searching in vain for
your daughter . . ."

Effie's head snapped up, almost gagging on the terrible hope
rearing up her throat. "Sophie?"

Hopkins' slips tightened. "She disappeared along with Dr. Bul-

man's apprentice not long after you were brought here to see the error of your ways."

Effie frowned at the Witchfinder's expression of frustration, the tight lines around his eyes. She laughed, a cackle, for she was feeling quite demented. "They've thwarted you! They've stopped you in yar evil ways and there's nothin' you can do about it."

A ringing slap cut off Effie's cackle. She glared up at him mutinously. "I may burn fer a witch and a murderer, and you and I together know you can torture me all night and all tomorrow, till an hour afore the sun sets, but you only have this night and the morrow, and then you will never find what you search fer. You will go to yar grave not knowin' where the gold be, and it will eat at yar innards like maggots with the bitterness o' havin' what you seek so close and snatched away from you by my death."

Hopkins's hiss was sharp as acid. He leaned across the table and gripped Effie's throat, his thin fingers like bones encased in dry parchment. "You know where it is!"

"Yis, I know," she hissed back, though it was a lie. She remembered herself as Walter Hulot, it was true, she remembered Matthew Hopkins as Brother Simon and the pirate, Joseph, as Ralph Honeyborne. She remembered leading King John's baggage train across the Wash and leaving them to the rising tide. She remembered the screams and the stink of mud, the buzzing of flies . . . And there it ended. She had no memory of where the king's gold might be and hoped it had been sucked out of the Wash and into the sea, that none might find it.

Hopkins released her and stepped back from the table. His eyes twitched with a centuries' old madness. His hands rose, crimped like claws as though he meant to truly throttle Effie this time and save the executioner the trouble of burning her . . . He shook himself, took control.

His pronounced Adam's apple bobbed in his throat. His

hands fell to his sides. He said nothing for a long moment, blinking rapidly, before his velvet tones filled the room once more. "I went to see him," he murmured. "The pirate who was once your brother."

"Why?" she rasped, astonished. Anger rose in her chest. But it was the anger from another time, for though she had grown fond of the pirate in the past few months as she had cared for him, he was a pirate, and he and she had both known the price of piracy, if caught.

Matthew Hopkins shrugged. "Curiosity." The corners of his lips twisted into a grimace. "He was as unforthcoming with what I need to know as you, I am sure you'll be pleased to hear."

Effie's eyebrows rose in astonishment at the admission wrenched from the Witchfinder, and was unable to conceal her glee.

Hopkins saw it and thrust his head across the table. "But he feared me," he murmured in her face. "His fear was a stench most wretched."

"Maybe so. But he ent no witch, and you have no power over him."

The Witchfinder straightened, the skin under one eye twitching furiously. "Yet he shall still die, and I shall be there to watch him hang."

Effie looked down at her bloody, twisted hands, wishing she was indeed a witch and could break her chains and throttle the bastard.

"It is not only you who shall burn," the Witchfinder murmured after a long silence, his green eyes like fevered moons as they bore down on Effie. "I still have the power of clemency."

The word dripped between them. Clemency was a kind word. It held the promise of hope. Effie barely dared to breathe.

"All you need to do," whispered Hopkins, his voice caressing Effie's face with its cruel kindness, "is tell me where the gold is, and I shall ensure your mother is throttled before she burns."

Hope evaporated. She could not tell him what she did not know.

She opened her mouth, then shut it again. A tickle started in the back of her mind that didn't belong in her mind at all. "The crypt," she whispered. "That's where we agreed to hide the king's gold! I remember . . ." She shook her head slowly. "We had planned to hide it in Isabella's tomb. Isabella . . ." The anguish and rage belonging to another swamped her. An anguished rage Effie understood, feeling an affinity for Walter Hulot as she never had before. In a skewed sense, their shared history had repeated itself. Her daughter had been raped by Lord Honeyborne, and she had been as powerless to stop it or get justice for her daughter as Walter Hulot had been for his beloved niece, who'd suffered a similar fate.

"It's not there!" Hopkins snapped. "Do you think I haven't checked? Back then and now?"

Effie blinked at him, confused. "But that is what was agreed."

"And you betrayed me! You and your pathetic brother. You hid the gold elsewhere!" Hopkins lunged across the table, hands outstretched, closing around Effie's neck again. "Tell me where it is! I will have it if I have to hunt through every life, across time and into Hell, if need be! Where is the gold?"

As quickly as he had grabbed her, Hopkins released her. Effie coughed, hoarse and painfully, yet unable to lift her hands to massage her neck.

A vicious, hollow, breathy silence filled the room only to be broken by a coughing fit from Hopkins.

When it passed, he said, "I shall give you the night to consider your answer."

Effie's head sagged against her chest as tears threatened to fall. She did not hear the pricking women enter until she felt their cold hands on her arms, pulling her to her feet, pushing her down the narrow corridor.

Germaine clung to the bars of the hatch in the door of their cell with mangled clawed hands, her face wild and knotted with slime and blood. Her blind eyes glowed in the torchlight, focused unerringly on Hopkins; she looked truly diabolical.

"The one they call the Witchfinder General, Matthew Hopkins," she hissed with a little of her old gravel and spite.

Hopkins raised an eyebrow, while spitting into his handkerchief. In the dim light, Effie saw the stain of blood in his mucous before she was forced back into the cell by rough hands.

"What is it, grey hairs?" he muttered, turning to leave.

"I curse you!"

Hopkins stopped, shoulders hunching, before turning back to Germaine.

Before he could force her silence, she continued, "I curse you in the blood and piss o' the Devil! I call on me creatures, me black kittlings, so's they scratch the marrow from yar bones. I curse you with eternal torment, and may the Devil inflict on you all the pain you inflicted on the unfortunates you've harmed." Her voice changed, strengthened, took on her fortune-telling growl that had scared many a folk in times past. "The rot in yar lungs shall be the death o' you that you won't see the end o' yar seven-and-twentieth year. You shall die in the summer, hated by all who you have met and reviled fer all eternity."

Hopkins recoiled as though the curse were a physical assault, with fear in his eyes. He turned to Effie, nostrils flaring with fury. "There shall be no clemency."

He turned on his heel, followed by his silent pricking women like stalking vultures.

There was little said between mother and daughter on the night before their deaths. Effie populated the fetid darkness with memories. Those perfect moments she treasured of Sophie and Germaine, and their little cottage on the edge of the cliff, each memory rosy-hued with love.

A clink of Germaine's chains broke into Effie's thoughts. "Mum?"

"Someone comes," said Germaine.

"Him?" Fear rose up Effie's gorge; she had hoped the Witch-finder would be true just once and show small mercy by leaving them alone on their last night.

A listening silence. "No . . . A woman comes . . . No, two women." A clatter of chains as Germaine pulled herself upright and hobbled to the door. "Quick!" she cried. "It's Sophie!"

"No!" Effie gasped in horror. She stood with difficulty, her knees almost collapsing with the pain shooting up from her mangled feet. "No! She must be away from here, far away, so that bastard above can't ever find her."

Germaine tsked. "That mawther be as stubborn as you at her age. You and I together know there ent nothin' in the world will stop her from doin' as she pleases if she wills it."

Effie joined her mum at the bars, her heart bursting for a single sight of Sophie, her only light of hope in this place of dark despair.

"Lady Honeyborne?" said Effie, when the capering candle-light drew nearer and she saw the good lady's face.

Lady Honeyborne smiled wanly. She could not be described as beautiful, but she had a certain angular attractiveness soft-ened by kindness in her blue eyes.

"I am so sorry, Effie," she said, "And for you too, Mother Figgis."

Germaine snorted, but managed to curb her tongue, for long had she had a grudging liking for the lady of the manor.

"I would that I could stop this . . ."—Lady Honeyborne's lips tightened—"this farce, for we all know you are cunning folk, not witches, as my lord husband claims." The words came out in a gush, as though she had rehearsed everything in her head and needed to speak quickly, for fear she should forget what she wanted to say.

Effie and Germaine said nothing but watched her with hollow, haunted eyes.

"Though I can do nothing to stop it," she continued, "I thought to make your last night as comfortable as possible"—she smiled and stepped aside—"and bring Sophie to you."

Sophie's golden hair was a flaming beacon in the candlelight, like something unreal and too beautiful for the hell of the dark and putrid dungeons. But her shocked horror at Effie and Germaine's appearance ravaged her youthful face.

"What has he done to you?" she cried. She put a hand through the bars to touch their burnt faces, their bristled heads, their ears that were mere bloody stumps.

"You shouldn't have come," said Effie, though her heart rejoiced at the sight of her daughter, belying the dismay in her words. Then in the same breath, "Where have you been? That bastard said you'd scarpered arter we was taken."

Sophie grimaced with the guilt of one who'd escaped a fate worse than death. "We stayed in King's Lynn, with Ben's uncle. He's a Catholic, Mum, and he's that mad fer the king," she added, her puritan heart scandalised by the popishness, yet her youth relishing the novelty of it too. "He has a secret room fer Jesuits in his house . . . That's where we've been all the while. It were bloody awful—not as awful as this, mind," she added hastily, nodding at the black pit behind Effie and Germaine. "But when Lady Honeyborne heard o' the verdict, she hurried on to tell us . . ."

"Hold up!" snapped Germaine, who had been quiet all the while. "How's it come to pass our Lady knew yar whereabouts when none else could find you?"

"Oh!" Sophie smiled at Lady Honeyborne, and a moment of conspiratorial communication passed between them. "Ben be Lady Honeyborne's nephew . . ."

"Ben's uncle is my brother," said Lady Honeyborne.

Sophie nodded. "It were Lady Honeyborne what organised our escape from Darrow End to Lynn."

Effie's mouth was dry with gratitude laced with a bleak sadness that the one true friend she'd had in the village had been one she had never considered a friend at all, due to their differing stations.

"It's the least I could've done," said Lady Honeyborne. "I would've died, as would my son, if you hadn't saved us both against the wishes of my husband and Dr. Bulman."

A stiff nod from Effie. "I dunt suppose this uncle can git Sophie away?"

Sophie and Lady Honeyborne shared a glance.

Lady Honeyborne shook her head. "I can't ask more of him," she said. "He's already under suspicion after the siege in Lynn a couple of years back. I can't ask him to risk more than he already has."

"And I dunt want to leave," said Sophie firmly.

"And what will be left fer you here come sunset tomorrow?" Effie demanded. "What is left fer you in Darrow End but a bastard child and no prospect. There's nothin' fer you here. Our cottage is already confiscated fer acts o' witchcraft."

"Ben will . . ." Sophie began.

"Ben will what? Provide fer you? Be a father to yar child? Marry you? And if he should do all that what o' the bugger upstairs as put you in the family way . . . Oh!" Effie frowned at Lady Honeyborne's ashen face when she gasped. "You ent knowing the truth o' it, then?" she said, without cruelty, but little kindness either, for she had none left to spare. "You know yar husband and his ways," she added, her tone gentling. "And you and I together know, as do any in the village, what happens to mawthers who've caught his eye and got in the family way."

Lady Honeyborne nodded, her eyes glistening. "Your mother's right, Sophie," she said, voice hoarse with an emotion she dared not release. "It would be best if you didn't stay in the area, and go to the continent as we've discussed. There, you and your babe will be safe."

"Or the New World," said Germaine quietly.

Sophie and Effie stared at the old woman in astonishment.

"You were dead set against the New World," said Sophie.

"And I dunt want to go there neither. Full o' heathens and the like. I ent gettin' scalped or worse by them heathens . . . Anyway," *she added in a more pragmatic tone,* "nearest ship be Ipswich, and I ent gorn along the roads as the place be crawlin' with soldiers . . . and I'd have to go through Royalist-held areas, and lord knows the Parliamentarians ent much better. And there's all them wardens that be out searchin' fer the pirate what escaped yesterday. The roads and lanes are heaving with them, especially after there were a sighting o' the waarmin not far from here."

"Escaped pirate?" *said Effie, her heart rate accelerating with hope.*

"Yis. That one what were caught here. Right under our noses too. Fancy that. And him hidin' in the Hermitage all the while. He up and scarpered. Not sure o' the long and the short o' it, but he done got out o' Marshalsea during the night . . ."

"Joseph," *Effie breathed. She shut her eyes at the relief coursing through her veins until she felt quite giddy with it.*

"Anyway," *Sophie was saying, not having noticed Effie's reaction,* "even if we did make it down to Ipswich, we ent got no money, Mum, and I'd need plenty to buy passage."

"What about Ben?"

"He ent got none neither."

Effie stewed for a few minutes, gnawing at her broken bottom lip, then she brightened. "You'll need to indenture yarself . . . and I've the means to git you to Ipswich. You'll need to sail there."

"What? Me? Are you mad? I could manage a rowing boat

maybe, but I'd never git around the coast o' England. We're talking miles, Mum!"

"You won't need to," said Effie, the idea flourishing in her mind like a lighthouse beacon on a stormy night. "You must find Joseph."

"Who's Joseph? There's none in the village by that name."

"The pirate they took to Marshalsea. He was my friend; I rescued him down in the bay a few months back and hid him in the Hermitage. You needs must git to him. I saved his life. He owes me. He can sail you to Ipswich."

Sophie's eyes grew round with horror. "A pirate? You expect me to first rescue a pirate from the noose, then trust him enough to sail away with him?"

"It sounds like he saved himself from the noose, and if he were sighted in the area, he's coming back here to . . ." Effie's voice petered off, and she shut her eyes. Joseph had escaped to rescue her. She knew it in her heart, knew he, too, had remembered a time when they had been more than friends, when they had been bonded by blood. She gripped the bars and peered out at Sophie. "You listen to me, Sophronia Figgis! You find Joseph, and you take a boat from down in the bay, and you get yarself to Ipswich and on that ship, you hear me?"

Sophie stepped back from Effie's fierceness, her young face cracking. "I dunt want to leave you, Mum," she said plaintively. And all at once she was a little girl again. Effie's little golden-haired girl who laughed and danced and charmed all who met her.

"I—um—" said Lady Honeyborne, as mother and daughter tried to outstare each other with fierce intent. "I could help with a boat that need not be stolen." She bit her lip as though wishing she hadn't spoken, then straightened her shoulders and added, "And I could perhaps help with some money. Not coins, but jewellery. Edmund has given me so much over the years, and

there's much I never wear that would go unnoticed if it should happen to disappear."

"I—thank you, Lady Honeyborne," said Effie, again surprised by the level of trust and kindness this woman was showing her.

Lady Honeyborne's face twisted with shame. "It appears my husband has harmed you and your family more than I'd realised." She glanced at Sophie's stomach only slightly rounded with child. "If I have it in my power to save even one of you, it's the very least I can do. I wish I could save you all." She smiled at Sophie's scowl. "It's for the best, Sophie. Your mother is right. No one will be able to touch you in the New World . . . and I've heard of such wonders there. A place where a young woman like yourself could start afresh."

Sophie gave a half nod, half shake of her head, her scowl deepening. "But only arter I've found an escaped pirate," she muttered.

"Go to the Hermitage," said Effie. "Joseph and I had a code. If it were safe fer me to enter, he'd hang a small rag out o' the bottommost window. If he truly be in the area, he'll have gone back there."

"We haven't much time," said Lady Honeyborne. "We've brought you something to eat. It's not much, but it's all I could take from the kitchen without anyone noticing."

Effie nodded, sad for this woman, who for all her trappings of wealth and privilege, was, in some respects, a prisoner in her own home.

After passing items through the bars, Effie frowned at the apple pie in her hands.

Germaine, whose sensitive nostrils twitched at the fragrance of baked apples, started laughing. "Even God hates you, Euphemia," she cackled.

Effie started laughing too, then Sophie, when she saw the pie. The last thing Effie would eat for her final supper was apple pie.

The gods had not favoured her even now, for she hated apples and, especially, hated apple pie. Their laughter spilled out of the cell and down the dank corridor, to swirl with the dripping slime and brackish water before fleeing up the distant spiral staircase so that it might have one last taste of freedom.

EIGHTEEN

Cló hugged herself tight. It was cold in the dungeon, seeping into her marrow, and she shivered from the inside out. Effie's bittersweet laughter was still a faint echo in the dark corners of the cell, her despair for Germaine still a physical ache, tempered by hope for Sophie. Cló was proud she had once been Euphemia Figgis, a woman of integrity who did some good with her life and had cared deeply for others. Effie made Cló wish she'd done more with this life.

"The crypt." Her whisper slunk against the slimed walls like a thing alive, a shiver in the dark. It wasn't enough. Not for Constance, who knew of the plot hatched eight hundred years ago on a cold, misty morning in the fens, who'd spent her life searching through the crypt.

A terrible, futile rage skewed through Cló. It was the rage of Walter, the rage of Effie, and her own. Cló *hated* Constance. She *hated* Brother Simon. She *hated* Matthew Hopkins. Never had she felt such hatred. She'd always tried to see the good in others, tried to be kind in the hope kindness would be returned. Rage and hatred coiled within her, taut and breathless, an acidic weight in her chest. I *hate* . . . I *hate* . . . I *hate* . . .

When the hatch lifted again, Cló didn't respond to Constance's, "Have you remembered?" She clung to her rage and hatred, and stared at the dark.

She shat herself and didn't care.

She stared at the dark.

She stared at the—

The faintest of sounds broke the absolute silence of the dungeons. A muted, tuneless hum.

Cló's stomach cramped with new dread as the humming grew a little louder. It filled the fetid air with "*Catch him, Crow! Carry him, Kite! Take him away till the apples are*—"

Her breath caught at the last on a sob of terror. She was losing her mind. No one was here but herself. Yet the hum rose from the cloyed floor, it meandered from the slimed walls, it slipped under the cell door, sniffing her hair like a predatory beast, grazing coyly against her skin, delicate and insistent.

Curling herself into a tight ball, Cló rocked to and fro, the manacle clanking in rhythm to the dandling rhythm. Sometimes near, sometimes as faint as the sound between breaths.

Clutching herself, her mind breaking apart, Cló stared at the dark.

She stared at the dark.

She stared at the—

Light blinded her.

Hands to her eyes, Cló cringed from the light she'd craved, half-turned to the slimed wall, the only thing that still felt real and sane.

Slowly, her sight adjusted. She lowered her hands and screamed.

A cowled figure stood over Cló, its face a black hole.

Struggling feebly against the manacle, Cló tried to crawl into her own skin to get away from the apparition.

"I thought Con would try something like this."

Cló's struggles subsided. "Ruth?" she whispered through

chapped lips, not daring to hope when she realised it was not the Grim Reaper come to claim her, recognising the plain woollen monk's habit, the hands that were not claws clamped around a scythe but tucked into its wide sleeves. A habit she'd seen before in the most mundane of places, a kitchen, though her memories from Walter conjured up a different image, different emotions: distaste and suspicion.

The torch shifted to shine on the wall next to Cló's head. The shadowed face came closer, and she caught a glint of glasses hiding watery green eyes.

"Get away from me," Cló whispered, hating the pleading note in her voice.

"I have not harmed you," said Ruth, her sparse eyebrows rising in surprise. She bent down and unlocked the manacle around Cló's ankle.

"But Constance . . ." Cló didn't move, not sure if she could. "Constance will come back and she's mad. She'll—" It all gushed out. Cló clutched at Ruth's robe, sobbing her story, barely noticing Ruth flick her robe away in distaste as she grovelled on the dank floor.

Her story of woe complete, Cló cried softly in relief that she wouldn't die in this terrible place all alone. She'd see Jude again. Jude . . . His name withered on her lips when she saw Ruth's dispassionate expression, her head to one side in an oddly avian movement, quick and bright.

"You've remembered a bit," said Ruth. "But not enough."

Her high-pitched voice sent a trickle of renewed anxiety down Cló's back. It sounded wrong coming from her vague mouth, so wrong in the dank and dark of the dungeons.

"I can see it in your eyes, the fear of what was," continued Ruth. "You cannot fear the past. You must learn from it." She moved towards the door and added, "What are you waiting for? We'd best leave now before Constance comes back."

Cló nodded eagerly, then cried out when she tried to stand,

muscles screaming in protest after their long, enforced inactivity.

Ruth tut-tutted and took Cló's arm reluctantly as though she had an aversion to touching another's bare skin. But perhaps it was Cló's bare skin she had an aversion to, covered in slime, ancient dirt, her own shit and piss. She let go as soon as Cló managed to stand by herself.

"Come with me," she said, and seemed to float towards the door. She stopped and turned her magnified eyes on Cló when she didn't follow. "Come, Fat Mouse."

"Please don't call me that," said Cló, hesitant in her newfound anger, the words bitter with novelty on her tongue. She staggered towards Ruth, pins and needles sharp in her feet, as blood rushed to places it had forgotten about.

"Whyever not?" That avian cock of her head again.

"It's not—never mind," said Cló, so weary it was all she could do to shake her head, her anger fizzling to a short fuse in the pit of her empty stomach.

"Would you rather I called you *witch*?"

"No!"

"But that's what you were once."

"Effie wasn't a witch, she was a healer."

"The cunning folk liked to let people believe that."

Cló frowned as she followed Ruth out the dungeon. "You know?" she said. "You know about Constance and—"

Ruth smiled vaguely. "Constance and I share everything, Fat Mouse. We always have. From the moment I could talk."

Cló's frown deepened as Ruth led the way into the circular room, with a fearful glance at the doorway she'd not noticed when she'd first entered the dungeon. Shivering at Effie's memory of the room beyond, where Effie and Germaine's blood had run down a groove in the slightly sloped floor. Matthew Hopkins hadn't done the torturing himself but had given free rein to his pricking women, who had taken a perverse, unnatural pleasure in the pain of others while he had watched.

Cló followed the robed figure up the spiral staircase and breathed deeply for the first time since she had entered Walter's rooms. The air, though musty with age, was clean and free of ancient rot. Exhausted, relieved tears ran down her cheeks as she followed Ruth through the Hall of Curiosities, her legs still tingling with pins and needles, now very aware of her own stench clinging to her intimately. The glass tunnel was dark, revealing a starred sky above, with not a cloud to hinder their shine. It was late, so late it was morning.

They passed through the conservatory, through long halls, and into the Great Hall. Cló wanted to run up to the Blue Suite and Jude, but her legs were only just obeying her brain to move. She settled for a stumbling stagger. A few short minutes and she'd be safe in his arms, safe from Constance . . .

"Oh no, Fat Mouse. You are coming with me."

"But Jude—" said Cló, not quite ticking on full intelligence yet. "He'll be worried."

"He most certainly has been. Very inconvenient, I might add. Called in the police. We've had them searching all over the Hall and the grounds. He loves you very much," said Ruth, her head cocked to one side again. Cló wondered why she'd never noticed how often she did it. It reminded her once more of a robin discovering a juicy worm, or perhaps a hawk spying a . . . fat mouse.

"Of course," said Ruth, "they never thought to look for you in the dungeons when we told them the key had been lost ages ago, and it would take a battering ram to break down the door." She giggled. "And Jude was most helpful. He insisted you hadn't been down there because he had asked you not to. He seemed to think you would listen to him."

"We *do* listen to each other," said Cló with a flutter of guilt at the lie; she hadn't listened to Jude, and look where that had got her.

She edged across the Great Hall, eyeing the door leading up to the Blue Suite, not sure she had the strength to run if Ruth tried to stop her.

"Well, the police are gone now. They have more important things to attend to, after all. Come on!" she added. "I don't have all night."

That short fuse of anger flamed bright in Cló's stomach. "I am so thankful you found me, Ruth, but I want to see my husband. I'm not going anywhere with you."

"Oh, but you are."

It was a voice that belonged to the dark of the dungeon. The only voice Cló had heard for days.

Whimpering, she turned slowly to face the silhouette of Constance peeling away from the shadows of the Great Hall.

"What the hell have you done, Ruth?" Constance demanded. "I told you I would handle this!"

"Not very well," said Ruth, not at all unhinged by Constance's sudden appearance. "What were you thinking, putting her in the dungeons?"

Constance shrugged. "It worked for you. It was your suggestion if I remember correctly."

Trembling with fear and anger, Cló eyed the sisters. "You should watch out for her," she said to Ruth, ashamed of the terrified quaver in her voice. "If she's anything like Brother Simon in this life, she has no loyalty to anyone but herself."

Ruth tittered. The sound echoed like a startled bird trying to find an open window. "You really don't remember!"

"I've remembered enough to know I don't want to remember any of it." Gathering up the scattered remnants of her courage, aware she only had this moment, Cló started determinedly across the Great Hall.

Ruth moved quickly, one moment a cowled figure in the

shadows, the next, beside Cló, gripping her arm with surprising strength. Something sharp poked against Cló's ribcage.

"This is the dagger I once owned," Ruth murmured in Cló's ear. "Imagine my delight when I found it again in the crypt. It had lain there for eight hundred years, waiting for me to find it." She held the dagger up to Cló's face, the jewels in the hilt gleaming dully in the faint light of the hall. "It is a thing of beauty. I stole it in the Holy Land from a corpse, after the Battle of Acre . . . But you know that, don't you, Hulot. You saw me steal it.'"

Cló's breath came in terrified gasps. "*You?*" she said dumbly.

"I've always known who I was." Her little girl voice was at odds with the ghastly tight smile crinkling her thin face, better suited to a skull. "Oh, I know how you see me. Vague, dithering Ruth, always away with the fairies. No one takes me seriously; most hardly ever notice me when Constance is around." Her voice dropped to a whisper meant only for Cló. "But that is the beauty of Constance and her insularity: She's easy to manipulate." Her voice rose again. "From the moment I could talk, I told Con about my dreams, my memories, and she understood. I sometimes think she knows my past lives better than I do. She researched them all so earnestly. But I didn't need to. I had lived them . . . And I wanted to live those lives again. I was powerful in so many of them. This life, as Ruth Honeyborne, does not suit—"

"Stop wittering, Ruth," said Constance crossly. "It's time to get down to brass tacks."

Ruth ignored her. "I tried to go back to them. To the places where I had lived. To feel . . ." She shook her head, frowning solemnly. "You should never go back to the places you remember. It felt all wrong; they had been damaged by the passing of time. But I remembered you from the first moment I saw you." She leaned into Cló, the point of the dagger breaking through the material of her shirt. Cló flinched at the coldness, and the sudden prick of pain as the tip broke through her skin. "You owe me this. I killed the king as we agreed. I've had to wait eight hundred years for what is owed me. Eight hundred years!"

"Get on with it, Ruth!" snapped Constance.

Cló opened her mouth to scream. Her jaw clamped shut as the tip of the knife pressed just that much deeper.

"Move!" Ruth snapped, with none of her vagueness, the usual wavering voice deepening, strengthening, taking command.

"No!" The short fuse of anger relit, Cló struggled against Ruth, twisting away from the knife point, shouting, "I'm not going anywhere with of you! Jude and I will be leaving. We'll sell this wretched place and never come back, and you'll be out in the cold!"

"Not until you've remembered," said Ruth firmly.

Fear has a way of focusing the mind. Cló opened her mouth again, took a deep breath, ready to scream Grimdark all to rubble. In her terrified mind's eye, she saw Ruth's hesitation and herself wrenching away, Constance making a grab for her as she ducked past, Jude's footsteps thundering through the Hall, alerted by Cló's scream.

Reality reasserted itself with a searing, sharp pain in her side, the warmth of her blood seeping into her shirt. Cló sagged in defeat.

Forced by knifepoint, Cló was marched through the doors and out onto the terrace. Across the gardens, the dew-wet grass slapped against her sneakers. The early morning air was cold and fresh, cleansing the stench of the dungeons still clotting her lungs but did nothing to clear the stench of her own excreta caking her legs, chafing as she walked. A song thrush startled into an early greeting of *see-you-see-you-see-you*.

"Wait!" whispered Constance, a dark presence on Cló's right.

Ruth stopped, pulling Cló to a rough, abrupt halt. "What is it?" she demanded.

"Thought I saw something." Constance squinted into the darkness, then snorted with annoyance. "A bloody rabbit."

The innocent rabbit hopped out of the shadows and onto the grass. Stunned by the torchlight highlighting its progress, it froze, then turned tail and hopped back to the safety of a nearby shrub.

"Stop jumping at shadows," snapped Ruth.

Constance's mouth tightened with embarrassment. "Sorry," she muttered.

Cló felt more than heard the shift in the balance of power between the sisters. But was there a shift? She sighed inwardly at her stupidity. Everything about Ruth had been a disguise of who she really was, the weird costumes, the dithering, the vagueness. This was a different woman since she'd entered the dungeon. This was the real Ruth, the Knight of Pentacles Luna saw weeks ago. Dishonest, greedy, ruthless.

Cló was forced onwards across the grounds once more. She knew where they were heading. She had few options with a knife's sharp point focused on her heart, but she wasn't making it easy for the sisters either. She dragged her feet, stumbling and lurching, hoping against hope that Jude might be up and see the torchlight. Could he even now be pacing the Blue Suite, fretting for her safety? Would he look out of the window? Could he even now be dashing through the Hall to investigate?

Cló's hopes were dashed when there was no cry of discovery by the time Constance opened the heavy oak door of the family chapel and she was pushed inside.

The chapel was as cold and dead as winter. The torchlight highlighted the vast columns in snatches before Cló was pushed down the aisle, behind the altar, down the stairs and through the open door at the bottom. It closed behind them on oiled, silent hinges. The key turned with a slight grate in the ancient lock.

The gloom of the crypt was absolute. Constance went around

the room lighting sconces, forcing the darkness to reveal the slender columns marching away into the secret earth beyond.

"Well?" she demanded when she'd lit the last sconce. "What do you remember?"

Cló shook her head with the plummeting despair that she'd traded one dungeon for another. "Only that we had planned to hide the gold in Isabella's tomb." She gazed at the gentle face, frozen forever in stone, above the pale tomb. "Gwenn was right: it was all for Isabella," she whispered.

But Cló didn't need the crypt to remember Isabella Honeyborne. It was already in her head, the sharp memory of a living, breathing woman, a joy to both Walter Hulot and her father, Ralph Honeyborne.

12–13 October 1216

The moon turned its face from the world, in shame of Walter Hulot, as he pushed deeper across the Wash to complete the grisly task he'd begun hours before. The stench of dank vegetative rot was laced with the sharp tang of salt as he nudged his horse forward, feeling the beast's unease ripple along its withers. An unease communicated to the ten riderless horses trailing behind him, their alarmed nickers breaking the silence of the vast Wash.

The tide was out; all Walter had to guide him was shadows and silhouettes, scattered and numerous, its ever-changing geography remembered and respected from his childhood of mudlarking and fishing in the saltmarshes. For the Wash had been his playground, school and hunting ground.

Walter was thankful for the dark night, cloaking death. Not so the sinister drone of flies disturbed from their feast. The receding tide lay bare the bodies of knights and servants, packhorses and donkeys, trapped in the sucking mud that would wash out to sea in the next tide or sink forever. Some might re-

turn when the tide washed back and forth across the estuary until all the flesh had fallen from the bones and been nibbled by the little fish.

He had chosen the spot well. A slightly raised bank of caking mud held fast the silhouettes of King John's baggage train, mere shadows of half-submerged wagons and carts amidst strewn bodies.

He moved cautiously to the two wagons he'd noted when taking the king's baggage train across the Wash on its last, fateful journey. The horses leading the wagons had fallen awkwardly, still tied to the stays of the wagon. The bodies of two drowned knights lay nearby, one caught in the wheels of the first wagon, sunk deep into the soft, sucking mud.

Walter clamped his jaw against his self-loathing and focused on the intensity of his last memory of Isabella, laid out on cold stone, her stomach still distended from the birth. He had sat vigil with Ralph, his gentle brother, broken by his daughter's death. And as he had sat next to Isabella's cold body with his weeping brother that night, not a tear had he shed for his niece, the stirrings of vengeance already churning in his mind.

Dismounting, he pulled open the mud-encrusted doors of the first wagon and climbed inside. Lighting a taper, he opened the nearest chest. Silver coins glinted in the dim light. He closed the chest and began grabbing all he could, filling the bags he'd brought before loading them onto the horses waiting outside.

It was hard, lonely work. He did not look at what he pulled out except to check they were of value; he cared little for their worth, only what their loss would mean to King John. Gold, crowns and crosses, swords and goblets; they were all one to Walter Hulot.

He emptied one wagon and moved to the next. Hours passed, and the wagons lifted slightly with their new lightness.

Dawn was not far off when Walter picked up a sword that had lost its tip. He knew it by reputation: The Sword of Mercy.

He almost threw it into the Wash, for what mercy had King John shown to the people of his kingdom? What mercy had he shown to the Honeybornes? To lovely, dead Isabella?

Walter climbed out of the wagon and looked around at the dead, half-submerged in mud. And what mercy had he himself shown these poor souls, these sacrifices, consigning them to a mud-filled grave?

Shaking his head free of these thoughts, he shoved the broken-tipped sword into a bag and hoisted it onto the last horse before mounting his own.

Picking his way through the mud, he pushed on across the Wash as the approaching dawn sent out questing fingers, streaking the sky soft grey. Trickles of water felt their way back into the Wash. Slowly at first, creating new channels, filling deeper holes, and smothering marshes.

Dawn had not quite broken when Walter Hulot left the rotting stench of the Wash, and headed towards Darrow End.

NINETEEN

❧

Tears stung Cló's eyes with remembered grief for Isabella, who had been so deeply loved, who had died before her time because of the lust of a man with too much capricious power. They weren't her tears, but those Walter had never shed; his grief turned to anger, to vengeance.

Ruth gripped Cló's arm harder, pressing against her, the dagger jabbing deeper into her flesh. "You've remembered something! What do you mean Gwenn was right? Right about what? What has Gwenn got to do with anything?"

Cló almost told Ruth of Gwenn's reincarnations but stopped herself in time. She cradled the small satisfaction tight to herself that she knew something Ruth didn't.

She didn't struggle away from Ruth but pushed closer, pulled the cowl away from the older woman's head to look hard at her face. She shuddered at the recognition in those round green eyes.

"What do you see, Fat Mouse?" murmured Ruth, staring back at Cló, their faces so close their breath mingled.

Cló's gaze dipped to Ruth's cheek and the birthmark shaped

like a cross, far fainter than those of Brother Simon and Matthew Hopkins, so faint as to be unnoticeable. She looked once more into Ruth's eyes. The coldness had not changed, nor the faint glimmer of madness.

She leaned back, shaking her head, wondering how she'd not made the connection between Ruth Honeyborne and Brother Simon before. "We killed so many people," she whispered, unable to rid herself of remorse for the dead in the Wash. Though it had happened eight hundred years ago, in another life, it sickened her.

"You were there! You are as guilty as I am."

"You're right," said Cló. "But I can't change what I did as Walter. It will haunt me for the rest of this life. But I did not continue to kill in later lives like you have. Why are you doing this, Ruth? Walter was your friend. He saved your life more than once. The only reason you weren't hanged for murder was because he hid you in the abbey."

"I hated him." Ruth's words were a vicious slap. "A bastard, yet he lorded it over me, acting as though he were better. Always watching me. I knew he didn't trust me. In Richard's army, Hulot was always nearby, always suspicious."

"Because you were a murderous thief!" Cló snapped. "And all he did was save your neck."

"As I saved his more than once." Ruth's eyes narrowed with disdain. "And what happened to you? You're a fat, meek mouse now. At least Walter had fire. You're just dull."

"I'd rather be dull than a murderer."

"You've been that too. Now tell me what you've remembered?" Ruth demanded, shaking Cló hard.

"He—Walter—he did bring the gold back here."

"That was the plan," said Ruth, frowning. "To hide it in the crypt."

"Yes. In Isabella's tomb."

"We know all that!" said Constance, arms crossed over her

chest. "This is pointless," she added to Ruth. "She hasn't re-membered anything we don't already know."

"But she will." Ruth leaned in close and whispered in Cló's ear, "I'll make sure of it. Tell me everything you've remem-bered, Fat Mouse."

And Cló did; there was no point holding anything back, for the little she'd remembered wasn't much. "But it was never about the gold," she concluded, not looking away from Ruth's magnified eyes. "Not for Walter. It was vengeance. Walter hated King John, long before that. He had already secretly sided with the Barons, as had Ralph, but when the king raped Isabella and she died in childbirth, that was the final straw . . . It was my—Walter's—idea to strip the king of everything he treasured just as the king had taken what Ralph and Walter treasured." She barked with unamused laughter. "It was noth-ing to do with you!" she cried, some of Walter's rage infusing Cló with a bravery not her own.

Ruth paled with shock. She released Cló's arm and stepped back, eyeing her warily.

Cló's heart fluttered like a wild thing trapped within the cage of her ribs. She eyed the gap between them.

"Carry on," said Ruth, holding up a hand when Constance moved towards Cló.

"You were a means to an end," said Cló, relishing the rage on Ruth's face as she shuffled slightly to the side. "All you were interested in was the gold. Walter knew that about you, and he used it. You were a pawn in his scheme, nothing more."

"And I shall have that gold, pawn or not. I'm a Honeyborne, after all! If that gold is on Honeyborne property, then it's mine!"

"Not unless you have King John's blood running through you!" Cló's laughter was edged with hysteria as she shuffled a few centimetres further away. "The baby!" she cried through her laughter. "Isabella's baby!"

"What is the idiot blithering on about?" snapped Constance.

Ruth cocked her head to one side, alert with suspicion, her hold on the dagger tightening. "You've made a connection," she said.

"You aren't even real Honeybornes!" Cló cried, sobering in an instant. "I am more a Honeyborne than any of you. If anyone has rights or dues, it should be me! King John raped Isabella and she had his child, and my ancestor Sophronia was raped by Edmund Honeyborne, and bore him a child in the New World, in America. She is *my* ancestor. But the Honeyborne line died out after Edmund. You're the descendant of some distant cousin. Connect the dots!"

The sisters frowned in confusion, then Constance shrugged. "Who cares? It was eight hundred years ago. If the gold is here, it's ours."

"Good luck with that," said Cló, covertly eyeing the distance between herself and the stairs leading up to the chapel. That way was futile. The door was locked, she'd seen Constance drop the key into her pocket. The crypt held terrifying options, a honeycombed darkness, and Cló was no Ariadne with a helpful ball of string. A desperate option, but the only one she had.

And words. She had words. Words to change these demonic women's minds. The right lie. The right twist to create a diversion, a distraction. But her usually fertile imagination chose to disoblige. What came instead was rage, fuelled by the rage of Walter and Effie, filling her with reckless bravado.

"What are you going to do?" she taunted. "Keep me down here as you did in the dungeon? Change one prison for another?"

Ruth smiled wickedly. "Perhaps . . . I have watched you creeping that way—" she nodded at the darkness beyond the forest of carved pillars. "You may run, but know the crypt goes deep into the cliff for miles. Even we don't know how deep it goes. But run, Fat Mouse, we will still find you."

Cló stopped her shuffling and grimaced in the shadow of Isabella's tomb. Shutting her eyes briefly, she stepped away from the tomb, putting all her hope and trust in words. "And what will you do then? You forget that without me you have nothing, but I am everything to you. Leave me to die here, or kill me, and you have nothing. You'll have to wait until the next life when we meet again. And what then? We go through this macabre dance over and over through eternity? So what will you do?" she jeered. "Leave me to die of starvation? Or go back to what you know best and burn me again? It didn't work the last time."

Ruth's left eye twitched. She half turned, but not before Cló saw a calculating expression cross her face.

"You're insane," Cló whispered, with horrified comprehension, her bravado evaporating into gut-churning fear.

Ruth flicked her cowl forward, hiding her face that had revealed too much. "Perfectly rational actually, and as you said, I've done it before."

"It didn't work," said Cló, a note of pleading creeping into her voice. "If it had, we wouldn't be here having this conversation. Effie would've told you."

"She was a stubborn bitch!" snarled Ruth. "And she remembered. As the flames consumed her, right at the end, she remembered. The vile witch taunted me with her knowledge, then took it with her to hell." Her magnified eyes glowed from the cowl. "That knowledge is buried within you, and I will have it," she said softly, "in this life, in this time. I will strangle it from you, or drown it from you, or burn it from you . . ."

"Ruth," said Constance, her tone wary, uneasy. "We never said anything about killing her. The dungeon was one thing, but not murder."

Sensing a possible unlikely ally, Cló caught Constance's attention, imploring her silently for help.

"You'd never get away with it." Her voice cracked, feeble in her denial. "We live in a different age. You can't go around burning people alive."

"Can't I?" said Ruth. "And who will stop us? Who will find us? In the middle of the night, in a crypt none enter except Constance and myself? I could burn a thousand women down here, and no one would ever find their remains."

"Ruth!" Constance cautioned again. "This is going too far. Listen to yourself; we can't kill—"

"Shut up!" Ruth howled.

Constance stiffened, her face creasing with unease as she regarded her sister like she was a stranger. Then her expression emptied of all emotion, and she focused on the floor.

"You have wanted this as much as I have!" cried Ruth. "We've lived for this moment. I am not about to stop now. Now take her to the Stuarts."

"Jude will find me! He'll find me and you'll—you'll—" The words died on Cló's lips when Ruth smiled with awful glee.

"Jude would never come down here." Her glee surged to triumph. "We taught him a valuable lesson when he was young, to fear the crypt . . . And even if he did, we will deal with him as we deal with you." She frowned at Constance. "I said take her to the Stuarts!"

Constance hesitated.

Cló's heart beat too fast as she watched them, holding herself stiff, hoping Constance was not as much in Ruth's thrall as she feared.

"Why the Stuarts?" asked Constance.

Ruth smiled grimly. "I've prepared for every eventuality. Even this. You'll find the stake ready in the Stuarts' crypt. Tie her to it."

Confusion darkened Constance's face. "Ruth," she whispered, darting a quick, startled look at Cló. "This really is going too far."

"Do it!"

Constance flinched at her sister's screech of fury.

Heavy silence crowded into the crypt. Cló held her breath. Constance licked her lips, uncertainty deepening her frown.

"Do it now!" Ruth screamed.

As Constance recoiled with hurt astonishment and started to obey like an automaton, Cló ran.

She wove between the slender pillars, into the darkness beyond, before Constance and Ruth had a chance to react. Then Constance was after her, her breathing loud in the dark.

Cló ran blind. What little light there was behind her was no use for what was ahead. She hit a pillar with a deafening crunch. She cried out, warm blood gushing from her nose.

She used a sleeve to staunch the blood and listened to the darkness. She couldn't hear Constance, not her breathing, not her quietly approaching footsteps.

"*Catch him, Crow! Carry him, Kite!...*" Ruth's girlish voice was a coiling high note winding between the pillars, seeking Cló.

"*Take him away till the apples are ripe...*"

A panicky sob caught in Cló's throat. She pressed her back against the pillar, moving around, desperate for a sound of Constance's position. This was a stupid, stupid idea. What had she been thinking running into the unknown dark? And yet she didn't dare move towards the faint glow of light beside Isabella's tomb.

"*When they are ripe and ready to fall...*"

Arms snaked out of the darkness, brushing blindly against the pillar, then they were around Cló. She shrieked, twisting against Constance's grip, scratching at her face.

She grunted in pain, squeezed Cló tight in retaliation, lifting her bodily.

"I've got her!" she yelled, panting. Her sweaty face slicked against Cló's, as she hissed in her ear, "I told you: fat mice always get caught."

The pale pillars glowed, spectral sentinels, as swinging light came towards them. Ruth stopped in front of them, head cocked to one side, lantern loose in one hand. "*And here comes baby, apples and all,*" she breathed.

"Take her to the Stuarts," she said, and turned to walk between the pillars without waiting to see if she was followed, disappearing into one of the entrances leading off the first crypt.

Constance half carried, half dragged Cló after her, down the tunnel, and into a longer one.

Ruth went ahead lighting sconces, their smoke wafting behind her like a scattered vapour trail. And with each lit torch the crypt opened up, revealing carved doorways to more rooms filled with tombs, marching back into the cliff with the bones of centuries of Honeybornes buried within the chalk and flint labyrinth.

"Don't do this, Constance," Cló whispered.

"Keep quiet!" Constance muttered. She was panting as they turned down another tunnel lined with arched niches.

Cló was as tall as Constance, not stronger but much heavier. She stopped struggling and slumped into a deadweight, dragging the tips of her feet along the floor.

Constance's breathing grew laboured, her arms trembled with the strain.

"Get a move on, Con!" snapped Ruth, as she entered a large room and lit the torches. They flared in the breathless, musty air, their smoke lost in the vaulted ceiling. The space was peopled with statues that had not seen the light of day since hewn from marble.

"No!" cried Cló, shrinking from the stake in the centre of the room, a square of firewood at its base. "I can't tell you where it is if I'm dead!" she shrieked, as Constance dragged her to the stake.

Ruth raised a hand. Constance stopped, panting hard. Her grip loosened slightly, but not enough for Cló to rip away, though she tried.

"Have you remembered anything?"

"Give me time," she pleaded. "If I remember, I will tell you, I promise! Why is it so urgent I must remember now?"

Ruth stepped forward, her cowl falling away. "I have waited centuries, and I have grown tired of waiting. As you pointed out, you and Jude will leave Grimdark, and I shall have to wait until the next life when our paths cross again." She smirked at the stake. "If anything will jog your memory, it will be fire."

Cló struggled as she had never struggled before, already feeling the imagined flames licking at her feet, her legs, boiling her blood, melting her skin, the odour of singeing hair deep in her throat. She knew she would scream liked the damned of hell, and no one would hear her, not here in this tomb of dead marble and bones.

"You don't have to do this," she whispered desperately to Constance as she leaned near to tie the ropes around Cló.

She felt Constance's hesitation. "Please!" she begged. "You are not a murderer, and this is murder. Please don't do this! You can stop this. You're the only one who can."

Cló caught the sidelong glance Constance gave Ruth, her features softened with a trusting adoration Cló would never have imagined on her sister-in-law's hard face. Her lips tightened. "Ruth has always said I am constant in name and nature," she muttered.

"And you would murder for her?"

Constance ignored Cló's desperate appeal. She finished tying her to the stake and stepped off the pyre. She stood beside Ruth, her expression inscrutable, arms crossed against her chest.

Cló's flash of hope withered to nothing. She wilted against the stake, hampered by the ropes tied tight around her waist and chest. It was her nightmare all over, her past life merging with her current one, as Constance took down a burning torch from the wall. She waited for a confirming nod from Ruth before stepping towards the pyre. There was no hesitation now as she shoved the torch into the edge of the kindling. The wood was dry, it took quickly and started to burn.

Ruth's glee lit her face, then her expression emptied with

shock. She stepped towards the stake as a thick wisp of smoke rose up before her.

"The witch's curse," she whispered, staring up at Cló. "*You're* the blood of kings."

Cló didn't respond. She shut her eyes tight as tears of terror of what was to come in the next few minutes trickled down her face. She wanted to beg, to rail, to scream; instead, here, at her very end, she was silent, her words formless and unuttered.

The smoke got Cló first. She coughed, spluttered, and lifted her head to the vaulted ceiling to avoid it.

"Look at me!" shouted Ruth. "I shall watch you die again and again, Fat Mouse! Understand that as you go into your next life. I will find you again."

Cracking open her watering eyes Cló found Ruth's, the light of thwarted fury in those green depths as a flame leapt up between them.

Cló pulled against the ropes, leaning forward as far they would allow, and hissed above the building crackle, "*None shall a king's ransom claim until that same king's blood returns to these lands both grim and dark.*"

1645

Effie shut her eyes tight as she and Germaine were forced up the narrow stairwell and out into the daylight they hadn't seen for weeks. Though the day was overcast, it took a full minute before Effie was able to crack open a crusted eyelid and glare at the world. Even Germaine, blind as she was, shambled within the limits of her shackles with her eyes shut, whimpering as she walked, for each step was a thousand needles lanced into their bare soles.

The cold hit them next. When they had entered the dungeon, it had been summer; now the world was transformed into the fiery wonderland of autumn. A peevish breeze launched the bright leaves into a final skittering dance before their death in winter. With the cold came renewed pain, chafing fretfully at their blistered skin, grating their infected wounds.

From the sea came a sullen wind, bringing with it the salty scent of fish, bird shit and the threat of a storm. It capered and cavorted, cajoling skirts to lift, and sent men's hats bowling across the swaying grass. Gibbet Hill, on the edge of Darrow

End, was little more than a meadow rising a few feet above the flatness of the land. It still had some advantage of height over the fens rolling away to the horizon in all directions but the east; there it was cauterised abruptly by the cliff edge and the sheer drop to the sea.

On Gibbet Hill, beside its single dead tree, stood a pile of kindling, with straw packed around barrels of pitch and two stakes. A lonely magpie sat on the dead tree. One for sorrow *ran through Effie's mind, and she looked around for another magpie, hoping for* two for joy. *Without success. Sorrowful would be her final hours.*

The whole of Darrow End and many from the surrounding villages had turned out to watch the burning of the witches. An atmosphere of carnival rustled through the crowd. Fathers held sons on their shoulders so that they might see and, one day, tell the next generation they had been there at the burning, they had smelt the roasting flesh and heard the screams of the witches, then gone home with the heavy odour of smoke in their clothes.

A small wooden platform had been built to one side, upon which sat a few chairs for officials. The seats were already filled: Lord Honeyborne, as Justice of the Peace, sat front and centre alongside Lady Honeyborne. Beside them were a couple of men Effie didn't recognise but assumed they were officials from King's Lynn come to see justice was done to their satisfaction. A little further away, stood Matthew Hopkins, hunched and coughing into a handkerchief.

Hope was a funny thing. Even now, as Effie regarded what would be her pyre, she had hope. Something would stop this madness, surely someone would shout out against this travesty of justice; the officials on the platform would conclude she and Germaine were merely cunning folk, as the Figgis family had been for generations, not witches to be burnt on trumped-up charges, with confessions coerced through torture. Mostly she hoped for a miracle, but miracles were a sort of magic and in short supply.

Effie and Germaine shuffled up the hill, with the rising wind pushing them along with the pricking women at their backs. Louring clouds were moving in quickly from the sea, balling and rumbling, darkening the skies ahead of the wind that pressed the grass flat.

By the time they reached the pyre, Effie's hopeless hope had tattered to cobwebs in the wind. There wasn't a single cry of pity for the state she and Germaine were in; bloodied, torn and charred, with a prickly stubble above their blistered faces. Surely, she and her mum would be creatures of pity? But she had misjudged human kindness. There was none for the Figgis women, as the crowd parted and they shuffled to their death with "witch . . . witch . . . witch . . ." a hideous murmuration competing with the wind. There would be no aid from the crowd, from people she had known all her life, people she had cared for, those she had brought into this world, and those whose parents and grandparents she had sat with as they left it. It all counted for naught.

The first stone cast hit Germaine in the chest. She staggered against Effie, sending the two tumbling to the ground in a tangle of mangled limbs and chains.

Effie helped her mum to her painful feet, and whispered, "Dunt give them the satisfaction, Mum. We're Figgises, and we'll show these pillocks how to burn with dignity." Her tone fierce and hateful.

She looked up at the platform of officials, searching for a shred of kindness in those austere faces, finding it only in Lady Honeyborne's. A single tear slid down her cheek. The one person who would stop this farce was the one with no power to do so. Even so, Effie hoped Lady Honeyborne would try with an imploring hand on her husband's arm to stop the mob madness, or with a word to the officials, to sow doubt in their minds. But all she did was sit there and cry. Effie turned away; she had no use for tears.

The executioner stood to the side of the pyre with a tinderbox in one hand. He looked perfectly normal, though no one Effie knew. He was not unkind as he took Effie by the shoulder and lifted her up onto a pitch barrel and tied her securely to the stake. He did the same to Germaine, who was little more than a skeleton draped in wrinkled skin, making his job easier, though the old woman fought feebly as he tied her to the stake beside Effie.

Once they were secure, the executioner stepped down and looked up at the platform, as obedient as a trained dog.

Effie's stomach curdled with rage. It coursed through her veins like acid, hardening her heart, wishing malice and pain on everyone here who bore witness to her death and her mum's.

Matthew Hopkins walked to the edge of the platform. With the wind in his face, his cloak swelling around him, he appeared taller against the darkening sky.

Even with her hardened heart, Effie feared the power of his silver tongue. She had felt its caress, its pull, on occasion doubting herself: that she was indeed a witch and not cunning, that she had cavorted with the Devil, as the silken voice had implied, that she had bewitched and hexed and done all manner of dreadful deeds in the name of Lucifer and his demons.

"Do you confess your sin of witchcraft before the legal powers of this land?" he began.

"NO!" screamed Germaine, her blind white eyes flashing hither and thither. "I curse you all fer fools! Vile creatures one an'all. I curse you all that yar eyes melt and maggots eat yar liver! I curse you ... I curse you ..." But that was all the venom Germaine had left within her. She slumped against the stake and whimpered pitifully.

Effie said nothing, the sour futility of fury and hate eating her stomach.

Hopkins gave a small shrug and faced the crowd. "Punishment, as you can all see," he said, with a careless hand waved at the Figgis women, "has little bearing on witches. It is little more than a preparation for the eternal fires of Hell ... yet Our Lord God does preach clemency ..." He raised an eyebrow at Effie. "Clemency of a swift death in this life before the everlasting agonies you will endure in the next when you return to your master, Lucifer."

Effie heard the message meant for her. A clement death. A quick throttling before the flames licked their skin. She turned to her mum, who was muttering and whimpering to herself, spittle clinging to the corners of her mouth and dribbling down her chin. Never had her mother looked more demented, more like a witch, more like a frail, terribly afraid, old woman.

If she had known where the gold was, she would have spoken there and then, to give her mum a swift death. But she didn't know where it was. She remembered Walter's midnight journey from the Wash, laden with a king's ransom in the packhorses behind him. She could still feel Walter's terrible guilt at the deaths by his hand. She could still taste the bitterness of his need for vengeance.

And yet ... Her odd-coloured eyes flicked up to Lord Honeyborne, to his wife, to their baby, not yet a few months old, held by his wet nurse seated in the chair behind Lady Honeyborne.

She turned her head slowly to Matthew Hopkins, who had grown silent and stood watching Effie with narrowed, suspicious eyes. If she'd had a glimmer of joy left within her, she would have laughed long and loud that none on the platform had an inkling that the baby, the Honeyborne heir, was the direct descendant of a king.

But as the knowledge sank into her mind, her eyes whipped

to the Darrow Cliffs and the Hermitage stuck up like a finger to God on its very edge—for there was another who carried that long dead king's lineage. And flapping from a window of the Hermitage was a small scrap of red cloth.

Finally, a small sign of hope. Not for herself or Germaine, but for Sophie and Benjamin and Joseph.

Her attention was wrenched back to the crowd, hissing like angry geese. A pent-up feverish hiss, as the clouds, black as a raven's wing, seethed over the sea, rushing inland with the speed of the wind that set the waves to rage against the cliffs below the village.

The air tasted of tin, the wind howled, and the earth trembled. The crowd's hisses rose to shrieks of fear.

Matthew Hopkins pointed a dramatic finger at Effie. "Even now the witch summons the Devil and His imps to her! Who else but the Devil could move the earth so?" He whipped around to the officials. "The witches must burn and return to their master in Hell, for who knows what the Devil might do to the righteous if we do not act now? BURN THE WITCHES!" he yelled.

"Burn . . . burn . . . burn . . ." rippled through the crowd. The officials looked uneasily at the approaching black storm and the cliffs trembling before it.

"Mum?" said Effie, glancing at Germaine, who had straightened and was staring blindly at the storm. "Mum!" she called again when Germaine didn't respond.

Slowly, Germaine turned her head to Effie. "God or the Devil, Euphemia?" she snarled. "Whose work be it this day? Who do we serve?"

"Neither, Mum, fer they have both forsaken us."

Germaine's lips pulled back in a gummy snarl. "Then curse the bastards, and let the old sea-gods have them all as sacrifice."

"How? I am a cunning woman, not a witch in truth."

"It dunt matter. The earth be ripped asunder. I can feel it beneath me, fer the sea be all powerful and callin' the land to it. You make sure the world never forgets this day, Euphemia. Curse all these bastards fer what they have done to us, so all fear to ever forget the name Figgis."

A terrible sadness gripped Effie's heart. Her mum's mind, always so sharp, had snapped at the end. But perhaps it was a blessing she was mad, for soon the flames would be consuming their flesh, and madness could be an escape from the cruel pain to come.

The last thing she could do for her mum was get her a clement death. She wouldn't get it from Matthew Hopkins. Instead she turned to one of the people she hated most in the world. Lord Honeyborne. The man who had raped and impregnated her daughter, who would kill her daughter for his own crime. But also, the only man who had the power to give Germaine a clement death.

"Lord Honeyborne," she cried. She had no pride left. Pride was a luxury granted only to men and the free. "I saved yar baby and yar wife . . . I beg you to give my mother a clement death. Throttle her afore the flames take her, I beg you. A small mercy in payment fer the lives o' yar wife and son."

Lord Honeyborne was cold and careless in his disdain. "Burn them alive," he said, his voice loud and carrying so all could hear.

Effie roared her terrible fury at the same time the storm hit the Darrow Cliffs and the world darkened to night. A shudder ran through the earth, up from the village before racing to Gibbet Hill, setting the officials' platform shaking with a natural uproar that all there took to be Effie's witchcraft.

"You bastard!" she shrieked. "You godless bastard. I saved yar heir and wife whiles you raped my daughter, you sack o' pus and snot!" Effie turned, wild-eyed, to the crowd who still stood

watching, though Gibbet Hill shook like a living thing. "Keep yar daughters away from the Hall!" she screeched. "Keep them safe and locked away from the hands o' yar lord, fer he will rape them, and should his seed take, he will kill yar daughters! You have all heard the tales, and they are all true."

"Burn. Her. Now!" snapped Lord Honeyborne, through gritted teeth. He glared at Matthew Hopkins, who had opened his mouth to argue. "Now!" he shouted. "Burn the witches, or as the Lord God is my witness, I shall burn them myself!"

The Witchfinder hurried down the steps and nodded to the executioner.

It took a few tries before the tarred torch lit, though the wind tried its damndest to blow out the spark. The torch was shoved into the pyre of straw and kindling.

A wisp of smoke, then the flames took, the wind driving them up, fierce and roaring.

Through the rising blaze, Effie glared down at Matthew Hopkins, the Witchfinder General, who had once been Brother Simon. Those round green eyes glowed with a terrible, thwarted hatred. Throwing caution to the howling wind, he yelled, "Where is it, you vile strumpet, where is the gold?"

But Effie's attention was diverted to a movement in the bay. Her heart sang with joy at the sight of a boat sailing out into the raging storm. From her vantage point on Gibbet Hill, she could see it and its three passengers quite clearly, one of whom had golden hair and stood at the helm staring up at the cliffs and the bonfire consuming Effie and Germaine.

Effie laughed, a maniacal, wicked cackle, for her daughter was safer in the embrace of a black storm than if she'd remained in Darrow End. She laughed as the heat blistered her skin anew, and the earth cracked and shuddered around them.

"God damn you to Hell!" Matthew Hopkins shrieked, stepping closer to the pyre. "Tell me where it is!"

And there, moments before her death, Effie remembered the last moments of Walter Hulot's life, merging into her own. She squinted down at Matthew Hopkins with watering eyes.

"*I remember!*" *Her voice was merely a crackle in the flames. Her eyes lifted, blazing with hatred for Lord Honeyborne, who still sat on the platform, though the wind howled around him and the earth shook.*

"*Call me witch, so witch I shall be!*" *Effie screamed, her voice hoarse from the smoke. "I curse you that none born o' the Honeyborne name shall live with honey, but grim and dark be their futures and their children's futures, that no heir shall suffer to live beyond a score o' years.*"

Throat burning with the need to cough, Effie strained against the burning ropes binding her to the stake and turned her furious attention to the Witchfinder, "And none shall a king's ransom claim until that same king's blood returns to these lands both grim and dark. You, who be called Matthew Hopkins, Witchfinder General . . . my mother spoke true. You shall die in yar seven-and-twentieth year, yar lungs wasted, and choke on yar blood as the sun shines on you. History shall treat you unkindly and show you fer the vicious monster you be."

The earth trembled and shook.

Vision blurring, flames licked up her dirty shift, devouring it in a second before blistering onto her skin and filling the air with her own roasting flesh. In the light of the pyre, the crowd ran towards the village, holding steadfast against the storm that cracked and frazzled around the flint cottages. The wind roared down the twisted alleys, driving away the odour of herring and cat piss.

Effie's fury had a hollow shape within her, filled with a righteous inferno, even as the pyre consumed her. A vast, seething fury, her last words born of hatred for these people she had cared for and now scorned her, turned their backs on her and her family. "Yis, flee!" she screamed. "Flee to the village and yar doom!" The flames creeping up the tarred stake burnt through the ropes binding her. She cackled and choked on the smoke, barely aware now, her eyes so blurred all she could see were her own burning arms as she lifted them to the roiling heavens and cried, "I call on the old gods o' thunder and storm, o' wind and sea. I call on you all to claim back what be rightfully yours!"

As though the old gods had heard Effie's plea and her curse, the earth was rent with an almighty crack that cleaved the land in two and shook the world that was quickly shrinking around Effie and Germaine. Effie's voice rose to a shriek of burning torment, a gasping screech, then cut off abruptly by the violent crackle of flames.

Effie never saw the disappearance of Darrow End as part of the cliff broke away and subsided with an earth-shattering groan into the horseshoe bay. She didn't hear the startled, terrified screams of those sucked beneath the heaving waves. She didn't hear the church's bells ringing violently as it, too, succumbed to gravity, or see the boat fighting against the storm, far out to sea as the aftershock sent a freak wave towards them, washing over the boat and its crew of three escapees: the witch's daughter, the man who loved her and the pirate who had been saved by the witch.

The flames of the pyre burnt bright and furious as the banshee wind tore through it, consuming Effie and Germaine, their flesh charred and shrivelled, their bones baked to ash. The thundering rain erupting not moments later was too late for the Figgis women.

Nothing was found the next morning on Gibbet Hill, for the flames had leapt before the storm and burnt the platform, the gibbet, and the old tree to little more than a gnarled, blackened stump that still smoked wet ash into the air. Nothing was found on the parched earth, not a scorched bone or scrap of singed *flesh. Euphemia and Germaine Figgis had sunk into the earth with the night's rain, a sacrifice to the old gods to ensure the witch's curse be fulfilled in due course.*

Afterwards, much that Effie had screamed to the four winds came to pass. Most of Darrow End was consumed by the sea, and it wasn't long before her curse was enshrined in Honeyborne Hall and the remnants of the village's new name: Grimdark. For nowhere in England was a place so grim and so dark, so tainted with suspicion and fear.

It took not a generation for Effie's curse to feed into myth and legend. It was said that on stormy days the curse of Euphemia Figgis could still be heard on the screeching wind, sharp with malice, anchoring her hatred to the land through the centuries. And on stormy nights the denizens of Grimdark crossed themselves and hurried indoors when the bells of the old church tower tolled thirteen beneath the waves.

The odour of witchcraft clung to the remaining flint cottages, and the ghosts of Effie and Germaine roamed the alleys and remaining tunnels in the cliffs with many a story of clomping footsteps in the tunnel leading to the Hermitage, and the tap-tap-tap of an old lady's walking stick, an old lady who'd had the misfortune to be blind and a wayward tongue.

The Hermitage was not immune to ghost stories, with flickering lights seen from its narrow windows and sounds of a foreign tongue chanting in prayer within. As time passed, few entered the gnarled and twisted building, until it became little more than a forbidding ruin, an unsightly gargoyle above the striped cliffs.

The curse held true for the Honeyborne family, for not a single heir lived beyond twenty until the line passed on to a nephew some centuries later, and even they were tainted by the curse; their fortunes dwindled, and the Hall grew as grim and dark as its name, disappearing into obscurity, wreathed in the mists of its own misfortunes.

Perhaps the least surprising of the curses cast by Effie before her fiery death was that for Matthew Hopkins, the self-proclaimed Witchfinder General. He died not two years later, at the age of twenty-seven, from the consumption that had wracked his body and destroyed his lungs. As legend would have it, he died with the sun on his face as Effie had predicted, choking on his blood. And history had, rightly, not been kind to him and his persecution of women and cunning folk in his three-year reign of terror. For truly, if anyone had been bewitched by the Devil to deal cruel misdeeds on others, it was the Witchfinder himself.

TWENTY

Flames licked the edges of the pyre hungrily, their crackle amplified by the acoustics of the crypt, their light throwing cavorting shadows against the walls.

Cló's mind was wild with Effie's memory and her own terror of being burnt alive. The heat blistered her skin before it had even reached her, she struggled to draw breath in the smoke. She couldn't think what came after, though the memory was there in her head.

"It wasn't hidden here!" she shrieked, twisting desperately against the ropes. "It's not here!"

"Where then?" Ruth called over the hiss and pop of the flames.

Frantically Cló tried to remember specifics. "It wasn't the crypt." Her words came out in a tumbled gush. "Walter meant to hide it here, but then—then he didn't. Please Ruth! Let me go!"

Ruth came closer to the flames. "Where did he hide it?"

"Please let me go!" Cló screamed. But knowing she would get little mercy from Ruth, she appealed to Constance. "Don't do this! Don't let this happen."

"If you don't remember, you shall burn, Fat Mouse!" Ruth's face lit with dark glee as she watched the flames take a firm hold, filling the crypt with heat and smoke. "And when you are dead, I shall send Jude after you. I shall leave him here, as I did when he was a child, and let him wander the dark with only the dead for company."

"No!" Cló howled. Her howl turned into a screech when a flame leapt up in front of her, twisting like a dervish as it ate through the wood, racing towards her.

"Enough!" snapped Constance, and she leapt through the flames, ignoring Ruth's furious shriek of "What are you doing?"

She cut through the ropes binding Cló's arms, pressed something skin-warmed and metal into her hand, and hissed, "Run!"

Throat clogged with smoke, not daring to waste a second of her reprieve, Cló scrambled off the pyre, sobbing and coughing, and lurched out of the crypt before Ruth had a chance to move.

Cló didn't need a mythic ball of twine to find her way as she ran through the tunnels, following the lit torches beckoning her urgently away from the stake and the horror of Ruth and her mania.

Bursting into the first crypt, her fingers brushed briefly against Isabella's tomb. A moan of terror escaped Cló's lips at the echo of running footsteps behind her. The key Constance had pressed into her hand was hot and slippery with sweat. She fumbled it into the lock of the door. Her heartfelt cry of relief caught in her throat at the loud, grating click.

Wrenching the door open, Cló could already taste the musty air of the chapel above. She slammed the door shut, scrambled up the stairs, and sprinted blindly through the dark chapel, bumping off pews, with the muffled sounds of pursuit behind her.

Cló hit a wall. Her feverish sobs reverberated around the chapel like bygone whispers, as she felt along it until stone became wood under her questing fingers.

"Cló!"

She froze. The voice was familiar but far away.

She scanned the chapel, but it remained dark and secretive. There was no sign of the sisters.

"Cló!"

"Jude," she whispered. The old iron handle was a nudge of coldness in the dark. She grasped it, yanked hard, and launched herself into the pearl-grey of predawn.

Three beams of light dipped and nodded about the grounds in different directions, highlighting a tree here, a wall there, a fountain, a statue.

"CLÓ!"

She turned to the walled garden; her lips didn't work properly as shock set in. "Jude," she whispered, her throat sore from smoke and terror, her voice a low rasp.

Jude strode across the lawn towards her, following the wildly bobbing beam of a powerful torch.

"Jude!" Cló scarcely dared to believe her eyes, unable to bear the desperate hope she'd cherished for days to be dashed by a figment of her imagination. "Jude!" she cried more strongly, stumbling down the stairs.

He stopped at the sight of her, eyes wide as they ranged up and down her shirt smeared with dungeon slime, her jeans black with excreta, her face streaked with dirt, smoke and old tears. Then he was running and Cló was in his arms.

"Where have you been?" he muttered into her hair. "We've been searching for you for days. I called the police—" His voice hitched, conveying a small portion of the horror he had endured during the search, fearing the worst. He pulled back slightly. He looked ravaged; unshaven, dark rings under his eyes and a pallid sheen to his skin. "I had almost given up, thought you might have got lost in the fens or—" He shook his head, eyes closing briefly, unable to relive his worst imagined nightmares. "Then Gwenn said she saw you in the grounds with Ruth and Constance. Why would my sisters pretend not to know where you were?" His nose wrinkled. "Not to be rude, but you stink." He looked Cló over again. "Where the hell have you been?"

In a torrent of incoherency, Cló told Jude everything. His eyes widened with horror as his lips tightened with fury.

"I will kill them! I will fucking kill them! Where are they?" The last was a shout.

"No!" cried Cló. "Don't even say that!"

Jude gaped at her in astonishment. "Constance kept you prisoner in the dungeon, Ruth tried to burn you alive—"

"I know, I know," she said soothingly, amazed at her own calmness, though she was as furious as Jude.

Hands grabbed Cló from behind, spinning her around.

Luna peered deep into her eyes. "You've remembered," she said. "Where is the Knight of Pentacles?"

It took a moment before Cló understood. "It's Ruth," she said, her jaw clenched and hurting.

"Ruth?" Caught off guard, Luna frowned in bemusement. "That can't be right. I could've sworn Constance was the one—"

"*Ruth* was Brother Simon."

"What are you talking about?" demanded Jude, glancing in confusion between them. "Who the hell is Brother Simon? What gold? Oh god! Is this all about that ridiculous reincarnation nonsense? Is this why my sisters tried to kill you?" He shut his eyes briefly, pursing his lips against the words battling to come out. "Let's get you inside and we can phone the police. They can deal with those two bitches." He pushed Luna aside and put an arm around Cló's shoulders.

"No!" said Cló firmly, glancing at the chapel door, expecting to see Ruth and Constance emerge at any moment. "We're leaving. We're going back to Canada, and we are never coming back here." She wanted to run away and never come back to this wretched place. She wished she'd never heard of Grimdark Hall.

"You can't leave." Gwenn appeared out of nowhere, little

more than a small shadow in the predawn light. "You found the monk, but now you must finish it or he will find us in the next life and the next. It will never end until he gets what he wants."

Cló's heart was clamouring to be away from this terrible place, but as she looked down at the little girl, she knew she couldn't leave. Her life was entwined with Grimdark, just as her previous lives had been. She might free herself in this life, but what of the next? And would Ruth wait until the next life, or would Cló forever be looking over her shoulder, fearful of seeing round green eyes searching for her?

Her head was still cloudy with Effie's final moments. Walter's memories were there too, pushing through the burning agony right at Effie's end. Their memories knotted together with Cló's like a snarled ball of twine. She put her hands on her knees to give herself a moment to think, plucking at a thread of Walter's memory, following it through Effie to herself.

Her shuddering gasp of understanding nipped the air. She knew where the gold was.

Straightening, she looked down at Gwenn. "You're right. I do need to finish this," she said. She cared little for the gold herself, but some stubborn sentiment, twisted by loathing and fury—perhaps a delayed retaliation from lives past—insisted she didn't give it to Ruth freely.

"Finish what?" said Jude, confusion crumpling his face.

"Something that started eight hundred years ago."

"Cló, we've discussed this. You aren't reincarnated from anyone. You are who you are right now, right here."

"Where is it?" Luna demanded again. "Where's the gold?"

Cló hadn't a chance to respond. The chapel door burst open and Ruth stormed out, her robes billowing around her, the dagger still clutched tightly in one hand. She eyed them all, huddled in front of the chapel, with slit-eyed fury.

She pointed the dagger at Cló. "Where is it?" she snarled.

Cló put a hand on Jude's chest when he moved towards his

sister, his face contorted with fury. "Don't," she murmured, not taking her eyes off Ruth.

Ignoring the question, and feeling a lot braver with Jude and Luna beside her, Cló glanced at the chapel door. "Where is Constance?"

"Dealt with," snapped Ruth. "I will not tolerate betrayal."

"What have you done to her?" said Jude. "Burnt her alive like you tried to do to Cló?"

"Why do you care?" demanded Luna, staring at him in astonishment. "Constance is a bitch, and she hasn't done either of you any favours."

But Constance had done Cló a favour. She had saved her life, and she was the only person who might still be able to talk Ruth down from the knife-edge she strode between sanity and madness.

"I will have it!" Ruth howled. She leapt forward, the dagger at Cló's throat. "Where have you hidden the gold?" With whiplash speed, she swung round, the point of the dagger at Jude's throat. "I will kill him, Fat Mouse. You know well I shan't hesitate. I shall kill you all."

Cló's breath snagged as her world swayed, watching the sharp point pressed against her husband's throat, spotting his skin with pearls of blood.

Luna snorted. "There's only one of you and four of us. You don't scare me!"

"Don't, Luna," said Cló quietly. "Let her have it. She can have it all." Her chest was tight, burning with panic for Jude. "Let go of Jude, and I'll take you to it."

Ruth hesitated, sensing trickery. Slowly, she removed the dagger from Jude's throat and pressed it close to his side instead. "I'm not about to lose my bargaining chip," she snapped.

Jude frowned at Cló. A moment of wordless communication passed between them. His face cleared, and he nodded slightly, ready to go along with whatever Cló was planning.

"Show her," he said. "Let her have the lot. I hope she chokes on it."

Cló looked up at the Hermitage soaring above them in silhouette, then sighed. She wanted to run there, to get this over with, but she forced herself to walk at a measured pace, her heart pounding in fear for Jude. Her beautiful, traumatised Jude.

Luna walked close to Cló and whispered, "What are you planning?"

"Exactly what I said: letting her have it."

The first flush of dawn washed the old ruin, the knapped-flint walls gleamed mulberry dark, as Cló climbed up the spiral staircase, onto the walls of Grimdark and into the Hermitage.

It hadn't changed much in four hundred years, still the same as Effie had known it. The twisted spine of a staircase still ran up the centre to a bricked-in door; the arrow slit windows still revealed only a slither of the world outside. Only the walls were slightly more pitted—not even the hardness of flint could survive the abuse of the coastal weather eternally.

"Walter hid it in here," said Cló.

"Liar!" Ruth spat and put the dagger to Jude's throat once more. "This place has been a ruin for centuries. There's nowhere to hide a king's treasure. Do you take me for a fool? I am warning you, Fat Mouse, I will have no qualms killing my snivelling little brother."

"But this is where it is." Oddly Cló hadn't expected not to be believed. "It's here. I can remember where Walter hid it."

Ruth's roar was a savage thing that came up from her belly as she thrust Jude aside and launched herself at Cló.

Cló staggered under the sudden onslaught, pushed hard against the outer wall facing onto Darrow Bay. The ancient flint stones gave way under their combined weight. A sudden openness yawned behind and below Cló as the wall tumbled away in a shatter of stone and crumbling mortar.

Cló teetered on the edge, arms windmilling. Terror drew her

eyes down the striped cliffs of Darrow Bay and the deadly rocks at their base. Church bells were tolling their warning of her imminent death, thirteen ghostly chimes, as the waves surged above the drowned village, each toll an echo of her panicking gasps.

Ruth stood victorious in front of Cló. "It seems I must wait until the next life, after all," she said and raised her hands for one final push to help Cló on her way down, down, down to the rocks below.

It all happened in the space of seconds. Cló could see herself—fat, clumsy Cló—teetering, Ruth's hands raised, her mad green eyes widening with surprise.

A hand grabbed Cló's shirt, another grabbed her arm.

Ruth, eyes still wide, flew past Cló, her mouth opening into a scream as she fell into the open space and disappeared into the dawn.

13 October 1216

A shushing sea fog rolled in with the dawn. Bruise-yellow and heavy, it smothered the faint jingle of the horses' bridles and suppressed the crisp crunch of hooves on the frost-shrouded turf. The walls of Honeyborne Hall rose up before Walter Hulot and his caravan, carrying a king's fortune.

Walter ignored the call of hearth and home, and skirted the outer wall, stopping at the door behind the Honeyborne chapel, its roof just visible. Deep within it lay the crypt, with tombs aplenty to hide a king's fortune as planned.

Walter's odd-coloured eyes crinkled with uncharacteristic hesitation. Plots hatched and acted on between conspirators needed implicit trust. Walter's trust of Brother Simon was hampered by his knowledge of the man, and his scalp prickled a warning. Trust and loyalty were commodities to the false monk, bartered and sold to the highest bidder, and only kept if not outbid at the last minute.

His gaze wandered along the walls where they melted seamlessly into the sandstone cliffs. On the corner, the lighthouse

Hermitage stood like a crooked finger. No longer did a lantern glimmer from its upper window to warn passing seafarers of the snaggle-toothed bay below, with its deceptive currents flowing into the warren of caves with a relentless shuck and booming thud, now muffled eerily in the clotted mist. The Hermitage had stood vacant for near on fifty years since the last anchorite hermit had died: a redundant sentinel that had lost its purpose.

Decision made, Walter led his caravan a little further along the walls. He dismounted and went to the small door of the Hermitage. There was no lock, for none had been needed. Entering, he looked around the barren chamber. A stone stairwell rose up the middle of the building against the walls like an elongated snail's shell. It would suffice.

With urgent, quick steps, he slipped into the Hall's grounds unseen and gathered all the tools he needed. He deposited them in the Hermitage, then dragged the bags from the patiently waiting horses. It was sweaty work beneath the blanketing mist that looked settled for the remainder of the day. A perfect day to hide a fortune. And one by one King John's treasures disappeared into the Hermitage.

It was nightfall when Walter entered through the main gates of Honeyborne Hall, a mere shadow in the mist still hugging the land in a tight embrace, smothering the normal chatter and busyness as servants hurried about their work, appearing and disappearing like wraiths. The clip-clop of the horses rang hollow on the cobblestones of the vast courtyard.

The exhaustion he'd held at bay over these past days and sleepless nights was a pleasant heaviness in his limbs as Walter led the horses to the stables. No one would question the odd hours he kept. No one questioned the steward of Honeyborne Hall.

Horses in their stalls, each with a well-earned bundle of oats, Walter stepped out of the stables and breathed deeply of the moist air.

A whistle came to him on the dense mist. Muted, muffled. An echo captured in ether.

Tired nerves twitching, Walter peered into the darkness, tendrils of vapour swirling about him like questing sepulchral fingers.

The whistling drew closer. Flat. Discordant.

Walter whipped around. "Show yourself!" *he cried. The steady, comfortable sounds of the Hall were silent, the mist a smothering veil around the manor and its occupants, leaving Walter out in the cold.*

"Catch him, Crow! . . ." *A slithering murmur threaded with the mist in a tangle of menace.*

Walter twisted again. "Simon?"

"Carry him, Kite! . . ."

Breath sharp and cold, Walter stepped back towards the fuggy warmth of the stables. "Childish games now, Simon?" *he said, keeping his voice loud and confident.*

"Take him away till the apples are ripe . . ."

Walter reached out in front of him, grasping at wisps of feared phantoms.

"When they are ripe and ready to fall . . ." *Hot breath on Walter's neck. He turned to the round face inches from his own.* "Here comes baby, apples and all," *whispered Brother Simon, a foulness leaking from his lungs so awful Walter stepped back from it.*

A dull shlick of a blade unsheathed, and a dagger pressed to his throat.

"Where is it?" *Brother Simon hissed, his breath repellent.*

"Where we'd agreed it would be hidden."

Brother Simon's round green eyes ticked madly. Twitch . . . twitch . . . twitch . . .

"Lies!" *The blade depressed against Walter's throat, slicing into his skin.* "I've been down to the crypt. Dead men keep their secrets, but those had none to reveal."

Walter noted the dried blood on the false monk's chin, the stench of stale vomit, the blotchy bloatedness of his skin, and the sweat trickling into eyes gleaming with an unearthly madness.

"You don't trust me, your brother-in-arms?" whispered Walter, his throat jerking against the blade with each uttered word. "You have taken ill, perhaps your eyesight has been affected. Come with me into the Hall. I will send for the cunning woman to tend to you."

Brother Simon's face twitched with confusion, the blade moving slightly away from Walter's throat. "You lie! You've betrayed me. You would steal my share!"

Walter's lips pulled back into a grimace that passed for a grin on his scarred face. "We are brothers-in-arms. I would not steal from you." His voice was gentle, like that he would use on a startled horse, but wary of the blade wavering in front of his face.

A relaxing of the monk's shoulders. He swayed as though he had an ague, unsteady on his feet.

Walter stepped back, out of reach of the dagger.

"Where is it? I will take my cut now. I've fulfilled my part. The king even now rides to Lincoln with a bellyful of poison. He shall not last more than a day at most."

"But he is not yet dead," said Walter, his voice soft and dangerous as he took another step back. "He was to die at your hand. Your end is not fulfilled until we receive word he is truly dead."

A flare in Brother Simon's twitching round eyes.

Walter stepped back again, the short distance between himself and the monk quickly filling with mist.

Pointing the blade at Walter, Brother Simon snarled, "I will take my cut now!"

"No!" Walter snapped. "We shall send word once it's safe." He turned on his heel and strode towards the Hall.

"There is no trust, Hulot!" shouted Brother Simon to Walter's retreating back.

Walter stopped at the underlying menace, the desperation in the monk's voice. Heard the staggering footsteps following him. He fingered the dagger at his waist, needing only a second for it to be in his hand.

He turned quickly. His odd-coloured eyes widened with shock at the hilt of the dagger buried deep in his stomach. He scrabbled for his own, found it gone. Looking up, his whole world was filled by the green madness of Brother Simon who held his dagger, lips pulled back in a rictus of triumph.

"Where is it? Where have you hidden it . . . brother?" The monk spat the last word, rancid with hatred. He pressed Walter's own dagger to Walter's heart. Pushing until the tip broke through fabric and touched bare skin.

There was no pain, though the heat of his blood flooded down Walter's stomach, saturating the top of his breeches.

"There shall be no secrets between you and I." Brother Simon's fetid breath blasted into Walter's face. "I shall take what is owed to me. Where is it? Where is the king's gold?"

A jangle, followed by a horse's hooves striking the cobbled stones of the courtyard broke the smothered silence.

Walter closed his eyes as the tip of the blade at his heart pierced the skin. Ralph was home. His beloved brother's voice was soft in the mist as he called to the stable boy to take his horse.

His knees collapsing beneath him, Walter grabbed Brother Simon's robe, pulling him down. He peered into the monk's green eyes and saw all he needed to see.

"Ralph!" he shouted as blood bubbled out of his mouth.

His brother's strides towards the Hall faltered, then stopped. "Walter?"

"Get indoors!" shouted Walter. "The monk is here!"

Running footsteps, whether they ran towards him or away Walter would never know.

"I shall have what is due to me," Brother Simon hissed as he *pushed the knife deep into Walter's chest.*

As he crumpled to the ground, the last thing Walter heard was "Catch him, Crow! Carry him, Kite!" *muttered under the monk's breath as he staggered towards Honeyborne Hall.*

TWENTY-ONE

Constance stood on the lip of the broken wall, her arms still outstretched after pushing Ruth out of the Hermitage. Her breathing was ragged, tears streaming unchecked as she gazed down at Darrow Bay.

Bile surged up Cló's throat. Not moments before she had been standing on that broken edge, flailing wildly. Jude still clutched her arm so tightly it would leave bruises after pulling her out of harm's way. He seemed unable to relinquish his hold, his face ashen with shock.

Gwenn and Luna were frozen, mouths agape, eyes wide with shock. Luna had one arm raised, whether in supplication or to push Constance over the wall, Cló couldn't tell; both options were flitting across her face.

Luna blinked, and looked at Gwenn. "Get away from there!" she cried, and swept her daughter from the edge, hugging her tight against what no child should witness.

Gwenn wriggled out of her grasp, forcing Luna to crouch down and take the girl's face in her hands, peering hard into her pale blue eyes. "Are you alright?"

"I'm fine, Mum," said Gwenn. "I've seen death before."

"Not in this life," said Luna grimly, and hugged her again.

Constance stood frozen on the wall, her arms still out-stretched, her gaze steadfast on the bay below them. "I loved her," she said, her voice hoarse, ravaged by grief and guilt. "I loved her more than anything in the world, but I couldn't let her murder anyone, not again, not like she has before."

It was an age before Cló's heart rate slowed from a gallop of sheer terror and she was steady enough to clear her throat, and say comfortingly to Constance, "I know you did."

Constance stiffened and dropped her arms. She turned to Cló slowly, her round green eyes alive with loathing. "No, you don't!" she snapped. "I didn't do this for you. I did it for Ruth."

She staggered, reaching out a hand to steady herself. Blood seeped across her shirt like a crimson blossom.

"You're hurt!" cried Cló.

Constance looked down at her stomach. Conflicting emotions rushed across her face before she lifted her head to glare at Cló, daring her to air the unspoken accusations that Ruth had stabbed the one person who had loved her above all things. That Constance, the one person who loved Ruth, had killed her to save her from herself. A final, brutal act of love.

"Jude," said Cló quietly, "Constance is hurt. She needs to go to the hospital."

Jude's mouth worked, but no words came.

So Cló did what she'd always done, and wrapped herself around him, comforting him with deep pressure. His thin body shuddered as some of the tension dissipated into Cló. She absorbed it as she always had, holding him tight until his shock and horror receded to manageable levels. Pulling back, she took his face in her hands. "I need you to help Constance. After everything, she is your sister and she needs you now."

Jude nodded, though Cló didn't miss the downturn of his

lips, revealing his distaste for doing anything with or for either of his despised sisters.

"I'll stay here," Cló added. "We'll call the police and make sure nothing is touched."

Jude nodded again and turned to his sister, who glared at him with familial venom.

Jaw tightening, Jude gingerly took Constance's arm. She shrugged him off, then swayed and held her side. Blood seeped through her fingers; she didn't resist when Jude took her arm more firmly and slung it over his shoulders to best support her.

"Nicely done," said Luna, coming to stand beside Cló. "Though I doubt this will make for a future happy families scenario. Hatred runs too deep with the Honeybornes."

Cló shrugged. "I owe Constance. She saved my life. What goodness was left in her was stronger than her loyalty to Ruth and her hatred of me . . . What were you two doing here, anyway?"

Gwenn smiled her eerie serene smile that creeped the hell out of Cló. She didn't seem at all fazed that she'd just watched a woman plummet to her death. "I knew you would need me," she said.

"Get away from the edge!" said Luna, dragging her daughter to a safer position. "For the love of all things unholy, will you listen to me for once?"

Gwenn ignored her and looked at Cló solemnly.

"You were in the garden," said Cló, remembering the flash of movement she had seen earlier, when she'd been taken at knifepoint to the crypt. There had been more than rabbits creeping around Grimdark Hall.

Luna grinned fondly. "Told you she's a bloody menace. Gwenn got out of bed without me realising. When I did, I came looking for her. I knew she would be up here, and I found Jude and this little minx running around the grounds looking for you."

"He killed me too," said Gwenn, coming to stand beside Luna and Cló as they looked down at the bay and the splattered remains of Ruth. "Afterwards."

"Brother Simon?" Cló clarified.

Gwenn nodded. "You warned me." She smiled sadly. "You always tried to protect me, even as you were dying. But it didn't stop the monk."

"What happened?" asked Cló.

Ignoring Luna's muttered, "Don't encourage her," she hunkered down in front of the ashen-haired girl, noting it was the exact shade of white of both Ralph Honeyborne and Jozef Roggeveen.

"He took me to the crypt and demanded to know where it was. The monk thought I knew where the gold was, but I didn't. He stabbed me . . . there was blood." Gwenn shivered. "I don't like blood. I don't like red . . . The monk was mad, but he was dying too. He was shaking and frothing, and kept moving about, trying to open Isabella's tomb, but he had no strength left. I had no strength left either, but the monk died first. He collapsed in front of me and lay shaking on the ground, then he lay still. And I was tied up. I couldn't get free, so I died next to the monk."

With Walter's grief clogging Cló's throat, she bent to hug Gwenn with the strength of their eight-hundred-year-old bond that had not been severed by death or time. But Gwenn wriggled away and watched her solemnly from a short distance away.

With a sigh, Cló straightened and stood beside Luna, who seemed unable to tear her eyes away from the small figure of Ruth Honeyborne lying dashed against the rocks of Darrow Bay.

"Do you think we've broken the cycle?" said Cló. She was trying to feel some sympathy for Ruth, mad Ruth, who had spent her life searching for something she wouldn't ever attain. She felt nothing except guilt for feeling nothing.

"I don't know," said Luna. "Ruth was killed, which makes a nice change. Even if you didn't do the killing, it's more than Walter and Effie managed to do."

"She never found the gold."

"No, she didn't. Guess you'll have to wait until your next life to find out."

Gwenn slipped her hand into Cló's, her little face turned to her. "No, we won't meet again."

Luna and Cló shared a glance at the girl's unsettling certainty. Then Luna shrugged and said, "Speaking of gold, where the hell is it? After all this, I'd like to think you know where it is."

Cló grinned and lifted her gaze. "Above us."

Luna's jaw dropped. "Are you telling me King John's treasure has been in this mouldy old Hermitage for eight hundred years and no one found it?"

"Why would they? This place is unstable, and no one would dare go up those stairs. Even if they did, they'd have hit a wall. That's what Walter did when he came back. He stashed all the gold in the room above and bricked it up."

Luna gave a sharp bark of laughter. "So what are you going to do with it?"

Cló frowned. What was she going to do with it? It wasn't hers, it never had been. She bit her lip, and glanced at Gwenn.

She nodded, reading Cló's mind, and said, "There's only one thing you can do. Keep it in a place where Brother Simon cannot touch it."

EPILOGUE

Grimdark Hall had been a flurry of excitement these past few months. The discovery of Bad King John's lost treasure made world headlines, fuelled by twittering speculation of a suspicious death and the looming trial of Constance Honeyborne. But the world today had a short attention span and, as summer bled into autumn, the feverish interest in found treasure and dramatic death finally dwindled to ripples felt only in academia. One day that, too, would shrink to little more than a footnote in Grimdark's history.

After Ruth's body was released by the police, Jude and Cló buried her in the Honeyborne crypt without ceremony and only one mourner, Constance, who was remanded on bail, awaiting trial. She lurked about the Hall, a shadow of herself, lost without her sister. Cló hoped the judge treated her kindly, though it was more than she deserved, but with kidnap and imprisonment charges, and murder, she was unlikely to return to Grimdark Hall after the trial.

It was Jude and Cló's last day at Grimdark. This place held too many terrible memories for them both. Jude gifted the estate in its entirety to the National Trust, and after a brief legal tussle—all found treasure belonged to the crown according to English law—they reached an agreement for Bad King John's treasure to remain on display at Grimdark Hall. Cló hoped the old building would rest easily now, without Honeybornes to stalk its halls.

Every day since Ruth's death, Cló had sat on the perimeter walls of Grimdark Hall overlooking Darrow Bay that had seen so much, hid so much and would see much more. Sometimes Gwenn came to sit quietly beside Cló, sometimes she didn't. Cló thought today she would come.

Endings were a bitch, Cló decided, her eyes drawn to the spot where Ruth had met the jagged rocks, hidden now beneath the surging waves. The shadows of lives from the past coming to an end in a single fraught moment. Walter Hulot and Ralph Honeyborne's terrible vengeance had ended after eight long centuries. And Effie . . . Cló's heart withered for the woman she'd once been. A woman who had loved fiercely and dared to walk her own path as best she could in a time that had not been kind to women. Cló hoped Effie rested easily now that the cycle of vengeance and death that destroyed her life had been broken. The Figgis women's ashes were part of this land so flat and majestic. And Ruth was dead. Her story had ended in this life, taking with her the spite and greed and evil of Brother Simon and Matthew Hopkins.

Cló smiled as Gwenn sat down beside her, her thin legs clad in jeans kicking against the wall. Every day she looked more and more like a girl, rather than the ghost Cló had once thought she was.

"We won't meet again," Gwenn said after a long while.

Cló nodded, knowing the truth of it, for this, too, was an ending. She would miss Gwenn and Luna, but Gwenn most of all. The bond they shared had spanned centuries, but Cló could already feel it loosening its grip. Gwenn would remember Cló with fondness as Cló would Ralph Honeyborne and Jozef van Roggeveen.

"I don't think we'll meet Brother Simon again either."

Cló hoped she was right. In another life, that twisted soul might come back to Grimdark Hall, but what he sought so desperately for eight hundred years belonged to the world now. The treasure had not moved far, but it would be out of his reach.

So much had ended, but it was also a beginning, as so much of life tended to be. Jude and Cló would go back to their lives in Toronto. It wouldn't be long now, and they would welcome their daughter into the world. They were going to name her Euphemia Walter Honeyborne. One day Cló would tell her daughter how she came by her unusual name. But that was all it would be: a story.

Author's Note

I am often asked if my characters are based on real people and events, and occasionally, they are. The alleged loss of King John's baggage train in the Wash is a case for reality being stranger than fiction. Though mostly legend, there are numerous theories about the location of Bad King John's treasure, which is still being searched for to this day (*The Lost Treasure of King John*, by Richard Waters, is a fascinating read about the various conspiracy theories). Amongst these various theories is the elusive figure of a Brother Simon, who was a possible Knight Templar sent to Swinehead Abbey to assassinate King John, and on whom I very loosely based my Brother Simon in *Grimdark*.

Matthew Hopkins, self-styled as the Witchfinder General, is another character from history. For a man who caused more than two hundred men and women to be put to death for witchcraft over a three-year period, there is surprisingly little information about him. He did, however, write a short pamphlet, *The Discovery of Witches*, outlining his methods for investigating witchcraft. Most of his victims were hanged for witchcraft, so I took a little creative licence and had Effie and Germaine burnt at the stake, using the historical legality that a woman who was believed to have killed her husband (considered high treason) was burnt at the stake as punishment.

Finally, I would like to apologise to the inhabitants of North Norfolk for changing your geography to suit my story. Additionally, the Norfolk dialect is glorious (I had great fun delving into the delightful little guide *Larn Yarself Norfolk* by Keith Skipper), and I've tried to do it justice while also allowing readers to understand what is being said. Any errors are my own.

Acknowledgments

My thanks always to my husband, Anthony, and our boys, Rory, Owen, Nate and Luke, for the constant chaos, noise and laughter that somehow keeps me sane. And thanks to my mum, Zoë Fourie, for her steadfast enthusiasm for everything I write— even those dreadful second drafts.

Thanks always to Melanie Michael, Sumi Watters, Catherine Stainer, Haaniem Smith, Barbara Toich and Nicole Clark for your friendship. And especial thanks to Karen (K.K.) Edwards, my Michigan Goose, who has been there with me right from the start of my writing journey.

A special thank-you to Haaniem Smith. I've yet to meet a kinder, purer soul, who's always up for marathon midnight calls though we're hemispheres apart. I so appreciate your help in making up a suitable name for my Dutch sailor turned Barbary corsair, as well as aspects of Salaah times in the seventeenth century. Any errors are my own.

And an especial thank-you to Catherine Stainer, who hared around North Norfolk at my breakneck speed when *Grimdark* was just an ink stain in my head, and for a delightful night spent watching shooting stars explode above the fens. And further thanks for allowing me to listen to your tarot readings.

I'm ever thankful for my agent, Kaitlyn Katsoupis, my go-to for all things publishing—lots of confusion on my part and soothing wisdom on hers! I can't believe we're on to book 3!

Behind the scenes is a village of people who rarely get the recognition they deserve for the hours of work they put in to get a book into readers' hands. Thanks to my editor, Elizabeth Trout, at Kensington, whose enthusiasm, commitment and sharp editorial eye makes the editing process so much easier. And my heartfelt thanks to the Kensington team, who beaver away in the background and have created something extraordinary in *Grimdark*: Carly Sommerstein, Michelle Addo, Lauren Jernigan, Andi Paris and Alex Nicolajsen.

GRIMDARK

Shannon Morgan

ABOUT THIS GUIDE

The suggested questions are included to enhance
your group's reading of Shannon Morgan's *Grimdark*.

DISCUSSION QUESTIONS

1. Much of *Grimdark* revolves around how women were perceived and treated in the past. Did reading Effie and Germaine's story give you a greater insight into the difficult lives women led?

2. What are your thoughts on reincarnation? Do you believe in it? Who would you like to have been in a past life?

3. *Grimdark* is told in three timelines. Do you feel the structure worked well overall? Were you able to follow the story easily? Did the various timelines end in a satisfying manner? Did you enjoy one timeline more than the others?

4. Do you believe in tarot? Have you ever been for a reading? Has anything in the cards come true?

5. Curses are a theme throughout the book. Do you believe in curses, or do you believe they are self-fulfilling?

6. There are a number of themes in the book revolving around familial relationships: mothers and daughters, husbands and wives, and sibling loyalty. Do you think blind loyalty to family is a good quality or damaging?

7. Have you ever been treasure hunting? What would you do if you discovered a fabulous hoard?

8. Grimdark Hall is a fictitious building. Did you enjoy Cló's perceptions of the building? Have you ever walked into an old building and felt its history dripping from the walls?

9. Most gothic or mystery stories have a villain. Did you guess who the villain was early on or did it come as a surprising twist at the end?

10. Did the setting in the fens and the fictitious area of Grim-dark contribute to the characters and the plot?

11. *Grimdark* has a blend of historical facts and fiction. While reading, did you feel the portrayal of the past timelines were authentic? Did you research historical elements to see if they were real?